Jesus
CLONED

Jesus
CLONED

WILLIAM HAGENBUCH

ARCHWAY
PUBLISHING

All scripture within Jesus Cloned is from the New Living Translation Bible.

Archway Publishing books may be ordered through booksellers or by contacting:

Archway Publishing
1663 Liberty Drive
Bloomington, IN 47403
www.archwaypublishing.com
1 (888) 242-5904

Scripture quotations taken from the Holy Bible, New Living Translation, Copyright © 1996, 2004. Used by permission of Tyndale House Publishers, Inc., Wheaton, Illinois 60189. All rights reserved.

ISBN: 978-1-4808-3075-2 (sc)
ISBN: 978-1-4808-3076-9 (hc)
ISBN: 978-1-4808-3077-6 (e)

Library of Congress Control Number: 2016909438

Print information available on the last page.

Archway Publishing rev. date: 11/14/2016

WHAT THIS NOVEL IS AND ISN'T.

Fiction is a series of "what ifs." For example, what if a multimillionaire holds an affinity for ancient religious artifacts and shares this love with her grandson, an odd kid who knows *a lot* about the Battle of Hastings? What if a college sophomore introduces his best friends and the setup flops at first? What if a new deacon's stomach flutters around the committee chairperson, a single dad nicknamed Hunk? What if a well-intentioned neighbor stumbles upon a national security level surveillance device pointed at his neighbor's house?

In chronological order, *Jesus Cloned* includes these and other "what ifs" within this question: what if burial shrouds from a mountainside tomb in Jerusalem have been miraculously preserved for two-thousand-years and the DNA from these wisps actually produces a human being?

Let this novel be what it is—fiction.

JC is not a Christological resource. No intentional stances on the nature and/or the being of the Son of God are here. Instead, *JC* invites reflection on our sinful natures and our need for what Jesus did on the cross.

Let me be clear. I mean no disrespect to anyone's theology, belief system, religious views or traditions. I did not write *JC* for anyone to argue over, though it's your prerogative to do so if you wish. Instead, the intent of this novel is to understand in a new way that we have a Savior who understands our sins and forgives us for them when we turn to Him.

Study guide questions are at the end of this novel, and I hope they bring depth and personal applications to your journey with the Author of your lives. Engage them as you like, or use only a few as springboards into small group conversations.

Daily I prayed for this novel to be published. Now I pray for those who read it. May God bless you with peace and a connectedness to Christ.

Will

"I am the LORD; that is my name!
I will not give my glory to anyone else,
nor share my praise with carved idols."
— Isaiah 42:8

PART I
THE FATHER

PROLOGUE

"Now Roland," she announced with an emotion I did not understand, "we do not know for *certain* whose grave cloths these are."

I didn't have to look at Grand directly; we had established this years earlier.

"What we do know is that these ancient dressings are the spoils of wars fought through the Middle Ages."

The towering grandfather clock clicked to 12:28 PM, and at that precise moment I knew I was exactly nine-and-a-half-years old. In readying myself for what I would have to do over lunch—engage in dreadful conversation—I considered the obvious: I knew three-hundred-thirty-two facts about the Middle Ages, eighty on The Battle of Hastings itself.

"The burial linens I'm about to show you date back over two-thousand-years." Slowly Grand's memories traveled down the dining table that in her golden era could seat at least twenty, but now hosted only two.

Emotions meant nothing to me; they were unpredictable; but Grand's silence forced me to consider her feelings for fourteen unproductive seconds.

She turned to me. "Roland?" Her expression told me our first course would not be served until I spoke. "What would you like to say about these linens?"

"Interesting."

She waited for more.

"Very interesting."

Grand knew her only heir was little more than a machine, a human computer. My lack of enthusiasm neither dissuaded nor dulled her interest. Instead, her eyes swirled from their placid brown to an enveloping black as she peered into the box. I had seen them change only one other time, which was at my father's funeral one year ago. A gauche yet well-intentioned employee offered in a receiving line what was untrue. He said Grand loved her son loved so very much.

She inched closer to the safe's contents. "We do not know their precise origin, dear child. That alone keeps this so intriguing."

The once religious New Englander measured her next words carefully, as if she'd inhaled incense from a dark, dank, depressed church whose stern pews sagged with a rudimentary theology that drove more parishioners to hell than to some so-called heaven. "How intricate the tension between fact and faith, especially to the disenfranchised."

She wasn't telling me anything I hadn't already considered.

"Just the thought that these tattered, ancient wrappings *could be* the very articles left in Jesus' tomb—fascinating."

"The whereabouts of that tomb are unknown."

I suddenly realized Grand was interested in what things were whereas I was interested in what things could do. Though the matriarch had made her own millions, I would quadruple my inheritance in the next thirty years by living out her overuse of the commoner's saying, "Never say never."

My attention returned to the box so that we could dine and I could return to my studies. "You don't know that these were, in fact, Jesus'."

"Roland, listen. These wisps of fabric are over two-thousand-years-old. The Gospel of John states Jesus was not buried in a single shroud, such as the one venerated in Turin, Italy. Whether or not these are Christ's remains unknown. Regardless of who was buried with these linens, this is certain: these contents came from a stone tomb in Jerusalem at the time of Pontius Pilate."

I stopped paying attention at that point because the Morse code she was sending through her shaky hands, though erratic, became my greater interest. *Tomorrow. Blue Bonnets. Stop. Cocoa. Chocolate. Cocoa. Stop. Bonnets. Blue. Bonnets. Stop.* Meaningless.

Seven-and-a-half years before fellow scientist Ian Wilmut and his famous cloned sheep Dolly launched headlines across the globe on July 5, 1996, I did succeed at the challenge indirectly instilled within me. I cloned the human who had been buried in these remains. Advancements unavailable to my grandmother at the time she presented her treasure did prove that these two-thousand-year-old remnants originated from a mountainside stone tomb in Jerusalem. What has yet to be determined is whether the clone has a divine nature, or a human one. Either way, I remain intrigued. Grand had ancient cloth; I have what could be a living Jesus.

At eight pounds, twenty-one inches, the clone was born on December 19, 1989 at 9:19 PM. The surrogate mother, who was virginal, will receive only a nod in the future. The young woman from Nazareth, whose linage there dated back at least three-hundred years, would have been induced at 9:15 on the evening of December 24, but "God" or nature had its own timetable.

The birth night was unexceptional. The starry array sang no song. The breeze didn't twirl in any dance. As forecasted, the wind flowed at an even pace out of the southwest at six miles per hour. No guiding, blazing star filled the darkness. No shepherds found their way to the lab. This newborn was no miracle. In fact, the clone immediately performed in the most normal ways. At both a glance and under intense scrutiny, Joseph was just that, Joseph.

I named the subject after his earthly, carpenter father. I do not regret not calling him Jesus because the ancient words within the scrolls of Isaiah may be right in what they assert: there was only one pure, spotless, sinless lamb. To date, no contemporary Simeon or Anna recognized the child's divinity when he was taken by mock parents to be presented at the temple in accordance with the traditions of Moses.

Another sign that cast doubt on the theory of the clone being divine was no modern magi brought gifts. No one with great affluence met and then averted a present-day Herod by going home another way after having been in the company of this god on earth. Of course, travelers from the East, or anywhere for that matter, would never think to present my little king with their valuables because my Joseph, as the trite saying goes, never went without the proverbial silver spoon in his mouth—at least at first. Just as calculated however, that changed.

Lab tech Larry Dunkin O'Dell thought he had rescued eighteen-month-old Joseph from my lab. Under a false agenda, Larry, who tested best in how I wished the toddler to be raised, had been strategically placed under my employment on January 14, 1990—exactly three weeks after the birth. A series of planned events beginning on January 3, 1991 compelled Larry to take little Joseph, whom he stupidly nicknamed Joey. On schedule, the chosen caregiver actually believed he was kidnapping the clone, or delivering the clone, from a center of science to a home of love.

All this time, Larry has believed in his success. The now forty-one-year-old high school science teacher has had Joseph for seventeen-and-a-half years, but I have been the one who has had the ever watchful eye and ear—the omnipresence?—on the distinctively Middle-Eastern looking dark-haired, dark-eyed nineteen-year-old. Indeed, I have known *exactly* where my subject has been since he left. Physicians, geneticists, psychologists, sociologists—even a developmental behaviorist doubling as a soccer coach—have reported directly to me. For the past six years, two employees have posed as next-door neighbors to spy on the subject in what has appeared to be a typical, suburban life.

While Christianity wearies me in its inability to solidify its facts, some theologians over the centuries have suggested Jesus never became fully divine until his baptism in the Jordan River. If this was indeed true, then it may be the clone must reach the age of at least thirty before godly powers manifest. A few incredible events have been documented through the years, including the boy knowing lyrics to a song he had never heard. He also revived a Golden Retriever from death. While these isolated incidents do not prove divinity, they do make this the most *fascinating* experiment of my career.

The subject will meet the one who could be the love of his life, and that, according to careful planning, will be tomorrow morning. I will make myself known shortly thereafter. He will need medical treatment only I can provide. In a very short while, I will close the distance between us. Until this fast-approaching time arrives, I will do what I have always done: wait to see if Joseph is—or will be—the Son of God cloned.

CHAPTER ONE

The water wanted to laugh. The rushing cascades certainly appeared to be excited, and Mike reflected all of this in his smile. With open arms, he turned to help his best friend Betsy down to the angled boulder that jutted into the fast-paced creek. From here, the two could see his new Bible College roommate a short distance downstream. In front of this picturesque view, Mike was surprised to see Betsy holding storm clouds in her eyes while light danced within his. He looked out again. Joe dropped down to the clear water's edge. His short, soft brown hair shined in the sun. He had just rolled up the long sleeves of his shirt and set his chest on a rounded rock so he could peer into the tiny waves that had slowed down in front of him. His expression held joy. When Mike glanced back to Betsy, it was clear she was looking in the same direction he was but took in something entirely different. Mike thought on this. What surprised him even more than the fact that she wasn't seeing the same scene was that she wasn't seeing the same person.

Betsy knew from Mike's expression that he was going to ask her what was wrong. Before he could open his mouth, she said, "Oh nothing."

'Oh nothing' always meant something. While Betsy knew Mike was in some happy place, she wondered how they wound up here because she had thought the day would include just the two of them. In fact, that was what they had agreed upon when they planned this outing weeks ago. She did not know she'd meet this new guy at the Bible College until she arrived at Mike's dorm an hour ago.

"Oh," Mike had said casually as the three stood near student parking where she had just left her car. "This is Joe. He's coming with us, okay?"

It was not okay. For her, this day had been filled with unwelcomed surprises and sudden turns, both of which she did not like. This park was not her idea. Having this third wheel along was *definitely* not her idea.

Here, on this stupid, insanely big rock, she bit down on her lower molars and her bad mood because she'd been duped, tricked. It should have been obvious that her real-life Cupid would plot to get her out of her current relationship rut. Captain Mike was, after all, the self-proclaimed champion of her happiness.

Though clearly not dressed for an outdoor adventure, Betsy wanted to get back on the nearby trail, or, even better, get out of this mess altogether and return to her car which they had left near the park's entrance a quarter mile back. This obvious set-up with the Water Boy Wonder was *not* the answer. The straight-A mechanical engineering major with a full social calendar, which included two dates with two different guys next weekend, was far from needing to be fixed up with anyone. And this truth would set her free: this river rock loving religious dork was well below her level. If Mike's new Bible College buddy were a fish, and the imagery seemed appropriate given where they were, she'd toss this deep-thinking, non-materialistic, artist-type back into the water. Done. Move on. Next?

Mike, who only saw love and delight in the one he bunked with at the school they both cherished, caught on to her body language. The best buds didn't always agree on everything, but it was rare when they didn't align at all. "Tell me what is wrong."

"You honestly don't get this."

"I honestly don't get this."

"Mr. Splish-Splash, your frog prince who has moved to be ankle deep in the silt? Yeah, he's all yours. I'm good. Trust me, I can find my own dates."

Sure, you can find guys to go out with, Mike wondered, but are any of them close to being right for you?

Betsy returned to their original idea, which was not a trip to a park with a guy she did not care to meet. The two were going to shop for her parents' wedding anniversary gift and then have lunch at a high-end restaurant to celebrate her first summer internship. Mike loved her parents, was the shopper between the two of them, and he was deeply glad her long-lived dream of being a mechanical engineer was taking another step. When Joe laughed freely from the perch of a smaller rock further from them, she had had enough. "Mike, really. This is so stupid."

"This is so stupid, or I'm so stupid?"

He has done this before. Playing the victim was not new. What annoyed her this time was that he was sounding soft and philosophical like his new roommate. Yes, Mike was taking on the airs of Joe who was too confident, too content. Stretched out in the back seat with the sun across his shoulders on their ride to the park, the inward guy, this complete stranger, didn't seem bothered by anything or anyone. This unnerved her.

Mike tried again. "Is this stupid, or am I stupid?"

She did not like Joe, and she certainly did not like this. "Save your inner turmoil, Michael. Carrying around my therapist's couch for you every day gets a little heavy."

He could not believe what he had just heard. Suddenly shut down, Mike found himself staring at a fern growing across the narrow ravine. The level-headed girl he had been inseparable with since first grade has not been herself for more than a year. Yes, he knew her upcoming weekend included meeting two upperclassmen with great resumes and even greater social credibility, but he sensed this was all wrong.

Mike focused on the sound of the current and realized Joe was exploring the water like a nine-year-old so that the two could have needed space. Yes, Joe loved nature, particularly the water when it rushed past him, but he was choosing to remain apart from them so that they could come together.

Betsy shook her head. "Honestly? I just don't get this."

Mike hoped that Joe would see Betsy as a fellow adventurer who needed to explore her inner terrain on her own terms. He shrugged one of his mile-wide shoulders. If the Bible College actually had a football team, which it didn't, he could be two linebackers, not one. "You mean, you don't get him."

She stepped up to his chest. "I know you see me and my dating life as an ongoing train wreck, but it's my wreck."

Betsy attended Indiana State University, about three hours northwest of where they were now. For months, she'd been pulling away from Mike, the boy next door to her parents' stately All-American Colonial. She had casually dated guys she knew he wouldn't approve of, especially now that they were at different schools. Her personal choices were hurting her—she herself would admit that—but she could not see why he ruined this day by including a fellow sophomore who was a little too esoteric, a little too easygoing.

She gathered her long, light-colored hair which had recently folded over her shoulder and returned it to her back. "And don't give me sympathy. I don't want those looks of yours."

Mike sank his hands into the front pockets of his shorts. He glanced back to Joe, and then to his hiking shoes. Part one of his plan was failing. He may not get to part two of why he brought these two together today.

"Yes. Keep the 'boohoo' to yourself."

Together Betsy and Joe did make sense, at least to Mike, yet he began to give in to his own doubts. Still, he knew he wasn't entirely wrong. Joe had character and charm. This new person in his life could soothe a heartbreak with a few wise words, welcome the stranger, and see the person no one else noticed.

Betsy couldn't take Mike's silence. "I need some space." She turned to leave the water's edge. "I'll be at the car."

Mike had always been the one to hold onto an argument until it was settled, but this time he said something neither expected. "Go." He looked in the general direction of where her car was parked. "Yeah. Go."

"Oh, I am out of here."

When she reached land, Mike called back to her. "You were right. Today was about you meeting Joe. I didn't play this right in introducing you, I get that. I should have told you about Joe, and about how I wanted him to come with us." The often soft-spoken one was good with other people's messes, not his own. Nevertheless, he had to say it. "But today is also about me."

"What?"

"There was a reason I wanted the two of you to get together. Yes, I did want you two to meet. But this isn't just about you. Could it be that I want both of you to hear something? For me?"

She couldn't take another twist, another turn—at least not now. Uncertain if Joe could hear her over the sound of the rushing water, she said loudly, "Enjoy the view."

He'd just been cut inside.

"And take your time."

<hr />

As the two guys sat quietly, Joe prayed. It was obvious his roommate needed time and space. The newcomer sensed some hard words had scraped against this longstanding friendship. Joe remained still beside Mike and realized he was—and then again was not—a part of their spat. Even before he met Betsy, Joe had guessed Mike was setting up what could be a romantic connection. Joe knew Mike wanted two of the most important people in his life to say hello and spend time together, but it was more than that. After a few minutes had passed, Joe figured it was time for his buddy to open up. "Okay man, you have to spill."

Mike stretched out his long, athletic legs. Staring just ahead, he waited a moment. "She's a good soul, Joe."

"You've said that since you first started telling me about her."

"I don't know how to help her."

"Yes, you do."

Mike knew Joe had a way of talking like this. "What do you mean?"

"You love her. You care for her." Joe pulled on the sleeve of his shirt. "And this is my hunch since we got here. There's a good reason why you planned this day, this meeting."

"Yeah," Mike offered sarcastically. "And it's going so well."

Joe laughed. "This is going well."

"Maybe you didn't hear everything between Betsy and me."

"I didn't hear anything between you two. But I sense how this afternoon has been a battle for the two of you."

Even though they were born on the same day in the same year, Mike could be like a student to this teacher. "So then, how is this going well?"

"You're helping her see what she doesn't want to, and that's herself."

"How'd you get so smart?"

Joe looked at his feet. Trying to be funny, he answered, "I go barefoot a lot."

Mike waited for Joe to say more, but Joe just wiggled his toes.

"That's your answer? You're smart because your feet are often naked?"

Staring ahead, Joe stayed quiet. In the comfortable quiet between them, Mike returned to how neither he nor Betsy saw Joe in the same way. He remembered a remark his New Testament professor had made just yesterday. Not everyone saw Jesus the same way.

As if he had just read Mike's thoughts, Joe turned to his friend with a look that showed great care. "You just keep doing what you're doing."

"Which includes giving her time."

Joe nodded. "Which includes giving her time."

⊷────────⊶

On the winding path to the car, Betsy suddenly stopped. Mike was right. This was not just a setup with some skinny dude with a warm voice and a buzz hair cut who seemed to know both her and Mike a little too well. She and Joe had been invited here because her super-sized Prince Charming had something he needed to share.

She swallowed. How cruel she had been, how stupid. She knew what Mike had wanted to tell them. In fact, she had known about this for a long, long time. As she quickly pivoted to get back to the water, she realized how wrong she had been.

After hurrying along the path, she stopped a few feet from the creek because she was puzzled. Mike was standing alone. Curious, she took a step closer. She jumped back when Joe shot out of the water.

His heavy shorts tugged at his trim waist, but he either didn't notice or care. Instead, he focused on how the rushing cascade danced over his chest and arms. It was a delight on his bare skin. The whirling water exhilarated and refreshed. It revived and relieved. Joe loved this.

Mike caught Betsy out of the corner of his eye. When she stood beside him, he said what was obvious. "He's crazy, you know."

Betsy knew the water temperature was chilled in the mid-fifties range, if that. "I'm beginning to see this."

Despite what had happened earlier, Mike still wanted her to see even more. "He is a good guy, Bets. I know this didn't start out so well, but you two do share a lot in common."

Betsy realized she'd rather go along with this hopeless romantic and be bumped a bit from where she was standing, which was in a place where she was not interested in being smitten by this new guy. Despite her reluctance earlier, she could at least *try* to go with this not-so-subtle setup. To honor Mike, she looked not into the white-tipped water but into her own heart and found she still wanted to keep it locked, boarded up, and closed for a season or two.

"He's your type. Brainy. Sensitive. Attentive. Politically ignorant. He has a blank canvas for you in that he thinks the White Soxs are white socks."

"Uh, white socks are just white socks."

Mike barely shook his head and she knew, of course, what he was thinking. His silence forced her to reveal what happened last night with her team, the Chicago White Soxs. "The Royals took them at home in a doubleheader."

"And Wilson was on the mound to start, or was it —"
She didn't answer.

Mike rocked back and forth on his feet. He glanced left and right. "Bets?"

"It was Wilson."

"Ah, yes. Wilson."

Before he could ask, she added, "No, I don't want to know something else."

"You sure 'bout that?"

She was never as good at this banter as he was. Into the quiet, she caved. "Alright. What? What don't I know?"

"It's just a something."

"What?"

"Joe doesn't leave toothpaste smudges in the sink either."

Head down, Betsy muttered about a sports article she never should have mentioned.

Mike continued. "Me? I'm glad you shared Wilson's bathroom sink hygiene with me. I'm a better guy because of it. Wilson? He's a role model, a gem. When he's done, he probably dries the sink too, or at least wipes the countertop with a ..." He let her finish.

"...with a towel he refolds."

"A hand towel, right? Isn't that what you said? Not one of those unnecessary big ones."

She raised one hand as she thought of that fact-filled sports article one more time. "Just so you know, there will be no more over-sharing with you."

Mike decided he'd won, which, if Betsy were to keep score, was something he often did. He lifted his square jaw. "So, this is a go?"

"This is a no."

"Oh?"

"No."

"Whoa."

Before she could shoot another word, rhyme or not, and on a good day the two could compete with a kindergarten teacher's Dr. Seuss read aloud, a thundering rumble like an eighteen-wheeler sounded from above. There may have been a voice, too. Then again, the creek was loud. The two along the shoreline watched Joe's toes bob in the water. The five-foot-eleven, one-hundred-seventy-one pounder stretched out on his back. He spun counter-clockwise against the current.

Betsy felt it was time to share what she needed to say. "Mike, listen. Enough silliness." She held his hand, which was something she rarely did because Mike could be weird about touch. "You were right. I made this about me, and that was wrong."

"Bets."

"I am really sorry."

Betsy spotted a nearby clearing with two fallen trees that could be seats. Still hand in hand, Mike followed. She chose to sit on the trunk where she faced the woods, not the stream. "You are right," she said. "I am not dating the best guys."

"You are this whole, wonderful person—fun, complicated, assertive, even insecure. You become someone else when you date." He leaned closer to her. "Do not box away who you are."

She tried to hear him. He had spoken most of these words with her before, but then, like now, it was hard for her to hear.

———————

Neither Mike nor Betsy knew exactly when the moment happened, but the plan B part of this day had begun. Betsy ignored the fact that Joe was shirtless and wet when she called for him. He found a nearby rock where he could join them. Joe and Betsy looked at each other, and then to Mike. The time had come.

Mike felt himself starting to lock up, but he prayed for strength. This day had been hard on him, even before Betsy had walked away. This life had been hard on him, too. With good parents, good schools, and good friends, he realized this difficulty was his own masterpiece. He swallowed a truth he'd rather avoid: unlike Joe who could find such joy in splashing around in bone-chilling water, he couldn't walk into being happy with himself for any length of time.

The two people who meant the most to him waited for him as the walls that had been securely around him for so long began to slide from their familiar places. Moving closer, Joe set his hand on Mike's shoulder, then the top of his arm. His warm brown eyes spoke volumes of care, more so than Betsy ever would have imagined. Silent, she just watched.

"We love you, Michael. We do. We'll wait. Take your time."

CHAPTER TWO

On his twin bed, wearing just a pair of soft, striped boxer shorts under the tattered sheet that has been with him for two consecutive summers at a nearby Christian camp for kids, Joe rolled onto his back. As he did this, he could smell a trace of the afternoon near the creek. He could have showered when he and Mike returned, but didn't. Scents from nature were always good to him. The other reason he didn't shower was the library book about Saint Augustine had pulled him into its pages.

Wiggling his toes over his mattress, which was something he did without thinking about it, Joe set the book down on the floor under his bed and reflected on the day. After leaving the park, the three stopped at a quaint country store for something to drink. Mike had stayed in the car alone while Joe bought two Spark Sharks, an almost dangerous blue soda. He saved the tabs because the glance Betsy gave him when they were at the cashier's counter was one he never wanted to forget.

Here, in the quiet of this early summer evening, where the circle of his lit desk lamp overlapped Mike's, he considered how Betsy had changed in the hours he had spent with her. After Mike had shared what he did, Betsy moved from being guarded and argumentative to open, kind, and trusting. Her spirit and spunk kept him guessing, and he liked that. He knew she was one who would not deviate from the plan, which was actually Her Plan. In fact, each chapter in her story better have a happy ending, or she'd push or pull until it did. Joe saw that she fought for balance, not just for herself but for those closest to her. Betsy wrestled with fate like no one he had met before, and Joe knew that if she did lose, she would not stay down long.

Her angry mood told him that she was one who was devoutly faithful to those closest to her. When she did commit to someone, the commitment meant forever. In the little things she would say and do for Mike, like to make sure he not only heard but also accepted a compliment, Joe knew of her ability to love. He could taste her care, and it was sweet. As he continued wiggling his toes, he laced his fingers behind his head and wondered what it would be like to see her again.

"Am I a friend or foe?" he would ask if they met a second time.

He imagined her answer.

"Both."

In drawstring PJ bottoms and a sleeveless tee shirt that read DOGS RULE, Mike hopped out of his bed to shut their single window after the cool night rain began to tap on their sill. Once back under the covers with his book in his hands, he looked over at his friend who wore a familiar, far away expression.

Joe did have a lot on his mind. He considered again what Mike had shared while the three were seated by the creek.

"You're thinking, aren't you?"

"Yeah."

Mike had told Joe and Betsy his most painful secret.

"I love you, man."

Mike set his book down without looking at a page. "I know."

Staring at the ceiling, Joe knew the often quoted verses in Leviticus spoke to sexual misconduct or perversion. He also knew the verses spoke to violence and darkness, not to loving relationships. His mind kept wandering. What about the others here at the Bible College? How did they read the text? What about what was taught of the city of Sodom? And what did Paul say in Romans? And in Corinthians? The Apostle made it clear: homosexuality was a sin.

Joe silently recited 1 Corinthians 6:9-10 from memory. "Don't you know that those who do wrong will have no share in the Kingdom of God? Don't fool yourselves. Those who indulge in sexual sin, who are idol worshipers, adulterers, male prostitutes, homosexuals, thieves, greedy people, drunkards, abusers, and swindlers—none of these will have a share in the Kingdom of God."

He considered some of the courses he has had on this campus. He knew his professors, their voices, their social positions, and their attitudes which could brighten or burn a soul. Joe also knew his prof's outdated ties and longstanding systems of belief were not going to change any time soon. In fact, one of the most revered professors on campus, a self-proclaimed dogmatist claiming to be as "old as dirt" had addressed the college through one of the weekly worship services toward the close of their spring semester less than a month ago. Behind the campus pulpit, which was the very voice of the school, this professor had just allowed one of his well-known pauses to seep into the souls of his listeners. Joe remembered it had been Mother's Day, and the sermon had been about mothers and family. After that quiet moment, the professor's voice shook the floor of the chapel. Pews trembled. "God's order," he nearly yelled after a second pause, "was for the family to be that of a man and woman, husband and wife. Even though our culture seems to be doing all in its power to mock, denigrate, attack, and deny the veracity of that basic relationship, God's truth stands."

No one in that congregation moved. Silence was consent as he continued. "We who honor our mothers and our fathers must respect the institution of marriage and give it the honor it deserves."

The school's other professors and administrators, whom Joe did respect, held similar stances. Their unshakeable biblical tenants reached right into Joe's chest, which suddenly hollowed. *What will Mike be in for here? What will happen?*

Maybe they could leave. Maybe they should leave. Another school. A different theology. They could shoot up to Boston, the second largest city in the world behind Rome to house seminarians. There they could find a school that opened rather than closed, that remained accountable to the undeniable Word of God yet brought down the law of love that Jesus lived on this earth, even to death on a cross.

Yes, the two could just move. They could head off in some small moving van with their baseball caps down low on their heads and open Spark Shark soda cans raised high. Bad junk food on the bench seat between them would show cellophane wrappers waving 'high-fives' by way of the wind from wide open windows. Barefoot in the cab, they could jam their air guitars and dashboard drums to the sounds of all the new Christian artists. The long, winding interstate at every bend would open something new, something promising. Yes, they could go. Just go. Maybe they could leave as early as the end of this summer.

Mike could sense his roommate's struggle, a struggle he wished he'd kept to himself because he couldn't stand to see someone conflicted in his own mess. He propped himself up on his elbows. "I can hear you getting all worried from here."

"Mike."

"Oh, ye of little faith. It will be fine."

Joe wasn't sure. He had heard homosexuality was not a choice. According to many here, however, its practice was. Joe certainly understood that everyone sinned. On that front, even today, if he was honest, he knew there was a little bit of lust for the senior religious education major who served him breakfast this morning, a meal neither he nor Mike ever missed. That was a *heterosexual* sin though, which churned up a question. Do his heterosexual preachers single out homosexuality as some sin bigger than others?

Conflicted, Joe sat up quickly and swung his legs off his twin mattress. He suddenly thought of his dad, Dunk O' Dell, a deacon at his home church. If Joe had this right, this was the night his dad met with newly installed deacons to talk, among other things, about an upcoming retreat this October. He knew what his dad would do at a time like this.

"Let's pray about this."

Mike also knew what to do. He sat up, too. "Yeah."

A quiet moment filled their space. The two have done prayers like this many times since sharing a room. Each one sat in the middle of his own bed, bare feet on the floor. Each waited, breathed, and found the still small voice within.

Under an umbrella, a passerby on the sidewalk below would see the ideal picture of life in a Bible college: two students facing each other on their beds gathered in Christ's name to pray. Through the rain-splattered window, they'd see just the tops of two heads bowed. If someone outside were to really peep or pause a moment longer, they'd also see Joe's bare shoulders. Except for Joe's smile and some truly thoughtful expressions, there was no physical interest Mike held for Joe. Nothing romanticly turned, either. Fortunately for Mike, they were what they had been from the moment they started—brothers. Oh, Mike could love Joe, in fact, Mike did love Joe, but it was simply, always in friendship.

Mike started praying out loud. The two volleyed words back and forth as their prayer pressed into the dark corners of their long, narrow room. Each man had time to talk this over with God. When they finished, Joe was the first to speak after an extended silence. "I love you, man. Truth on. I do."

"Love?" Mike asked. "What do you know of love?" He waited the right amount of time to do what he always did, move any conversation about himself away. "Betsy would likely say you don't have a clue about that."

As Joe set his head back down on his truly lumpy pillow, he twisted and turned as he was prone to do before he fell asleep. "Betsy, huh?" He clearly recalled her smile, her eyelashes, her long hair and the sparkle of her soul. "Now, who is she again?"

"You're asking me?"

Joe stared out the window after Mike turned both desk lights out. "Uh, you were the one to introduce us. Cupid, bow, arrows."

"Uh, you're the one who owns red heart boxers."

It was true. Joe did receive goofy underwear as a gift from home this past Valentine's Day. "Red? Nah. They're maroon."

"Red."

Never one to appreciate or understand the complexity of color—for example, what exactly was the difference between pink and dusty rose, or gray and charcoal—Joe considered the gift he should have given away immediately. After a moment, he conceded somewhat. "Deep red."

"The road from deep red to red is very short."

Joe sighed. It felt good to be tired. It was also good to goof around with his friend.

Minutes passed. Mike said from the quiet, "Those hearts? They are red, Joe."

Joe was about to add more, then realized he was almost ready to let Mike be right. The bells from the campus chapel's tower rang on the hour. In the lengthening silence between them, Joe tried again. "Deep red."

Mike had drifted into half asleep. "You know it is okay to let some arguments go, right?"

Joe drew his old sheet up to his chest. "Of course I do."

CHAPTER THREE

Vanessa looked into her rearview mirror again. Her eyes told her what her heart felt. She could do this. As one hardwired for romance and love, she could get out of this car, walk into that courtyard, meet deacon chairperson Dunk O'Dell and wait to hear if fate would play a duet for them both.

She was more than nervous though, she was terrified. It was one thing to daydream; it was another to go through with it.

The pre-owned car she bought last summer came with dark-tinted windows—mafia windows—as she liked to call them. She never would have chosen this option in a new car but was glad to have them in the moment because Dunk, who had been standing alone with a clipboard in one hand while twirling the cord of a whistle with the other, didn't know he was being watched.

At thirty-eight, Vanessa knew she should be content on her own. Talk show therapy and self-help magazine articles have told her she should make it a point to build her own happiness. She should be independent and self-reliant, a champion of both her self-worth and her destiny. It did not help that Dunk, also known as Hunk to a good number of the female faculty and staff at the nearby high school where he taught science and chemistry, usually wore thoughtful, engaging expressions, and he looked kindly into people's eyes when they spoke to him. While she had hope, he had optimism. As she took pride in being level-headed, he had a natural, easy way about him. Knowing all of this, Vanessa had every intention of getting out of her car as soon as she arrived for her first deacon's meeting tonight. Why not just walk into the church like any other time? He wasn't the first handsome guy she'd seen, and he wouldn't be the last. She couldn't get her hand to open her car door though. Something caught in her chest.

She proceeded to stare straight in front of her. Dunk represented something she did not have, and might never have. She knew about appearances, in fact, her ex was all about the façade, but the Dunk she had known since she started coming to the Presswater United Church of Christ church just over two years ago was a man of God. From afar, she admired how he was so present to so many people in the church. He was the get-it-done guy when it came to organizing events. While Pastor Smith was the idealist, Dunk was the one who built—and sometimes rebuilt—plans to get God's love out where it could be seen, heard, and felt. Firsthand, Vanessa had seen a great plan wobble from fear within the church, and before the heartfelt idea fell apart, Dunk would rally the congregation's courage and regain their conviction. Somehow he would find the words, speak them with passion, and singlehandedly tip the scales, so that good ideas that started to get blurry would stay clear. From the start-up free meal program to new soccer nets in a needy part of town, Dunk made things happen. Never had Vanessa met someone as hard-driving as this often soft-spoken one, and never before had she been so scared to get to know him better.

By profession, Vanessa was a committed, outgoing, and devoted social worker. For fourteen years, she put in the long hours at home or in the office without additional pay, which, in these parts, didn't do much more than cover the rent on her two bedroom townhouse that, like the interior of her car, never received direct sunlight. While she was a well-known and a deeply respected public care provider, she knew she didn't have Dunk's deep connection to Christ. She had known church people in her past to be all talk with very little action. Dunk was talk and action.

Because her parents were very sporadic in attending church when she was growing up, her faith was new. Sometimes, and she was hesitant to admit this to even herself, she wasn't sure if submitting to God's will was something she could pull off. For starters, when not near her church family, this faith business was becoming inconvenient. This walk with God had been mostly okay—she could appreciate some of its benefits—but she could see down the road. Her life would have to be rearranged at some point. Did she really want to do that? Since nothing was obviously broken now, why go through the hassle of fixing it for something that might not be that much better?

She figured her walk with God was like repainting a bedroom that really didn't need it. Oh sure, an update would be nice, but if she were really going to go to all that trouble—cleaning out the whole room, laying down drop cloths from the basement, and setting out the cost of good paint and quality brushes—she might as well change the color, even if it were just a shade or two lighter or darker. Why do all of that? She knew some of her old, treasured accent pieces just wouldn't go in the newly refurbished space. She was okay now. Things were alright. Sure, there could be improvement, but would it be worth all the work?

When she thought like this, she knew she was far from Dunk. More importantly, she knew she was far from God, and as uneasy as she was on the thought of change, the thought of this distance from the divine was far more painful. She knew it was time for drop cloths, whether she liked it or not. With her hands holding the steering wheel, she prayed.

In the following quiet time, she realized something unexpected. The reason she didn't rush out her car as soon as she pulled into the church parking lot was because she didn't want to do the dating game anymore. In front of this single parent, she didn't want to be someone she wasn't. While she'd become good at it, she didn't want to flirt with Dunk, or with any other man for that matter.

She stared at herself in the rearview mirror. The deeper reason she didn't want to get out of the car was because she didn't want to fail again. Dunk represented something good and real. What if she tried and this didn't work out either?

Vanessa reminded herself that she was one of those married-for-lifers, or at least she thought she was, until her ex opted out of their marriage by leaving his ring and a note on their kitchen island. When she married, the thought of divorce for her was not an option. She believed 'for better or worse' meant for better *and* worse. By no means was she perfect in her marriage, but the divorce stripped her of her dignity and her identity. Much to her surprise however, she was able to date several professional men once she had the divorce papers, but each date made her realize she was somehow giving in, or losing pieces of herself in the silly things she'd say or find herself doing. As a result, she barely knew who she was now. The Vanessa she was would live in a house with sunlight, and she would drive a car that by no means looked like it was owned by a big city drug dealer.

<hr>

A sudden tap on the driver's side window startled her. It was Viola Munson, the church queen bee. How she even knew Vanessa was in the car was a mystery, but maybe that was why she was the queen.

Viola said through the closed window, "Well hello there, pretty young lady."

Vanessa smiled, even though the last person she wanted to see now was a senior who made it clear that no woman needed a man, but the best women had one.

"We should be getting along to the meeting, honey. We don't want to be late."

Vanessa froze when she realized Viola was also a deacon.

Before she opened her car door, Vanessa quickly opened her glove compartment, pulled out a soft napkin and wiped away a lipstick shade she should not have bought. She decided in this moment that she would be herself tonight. She could do this. She could make the right conversations not only with Martha Washington's grade school classmate, but also with Dunk. Certainly she would offer the right expressions during this meeting. Self-assured, she would completely be herself.

Viola had turned back to lock her underpowered tin can car that, like her three-piece floral living room furniture, seemed to never show signs of age. Rejoining Vanessa with a cackle and a remark about how forgetful she could be about locking her vehicle, she dropped her keys into a purse the size of carry-on luggage that would make an onboard flight attendant cringe. Having known Dunk since he moved into the area and joined the church—who could forget meeting a single dad with such a young son?—Viola patted her full head of perfectly coiffed silver curls at the man in the courtyard who was filling out a plain tee shirt a little too well.

Vanessa's eyes widened. Viola Munson was like, what? Three-hundred-years-old?

Viola glided across the parking lot, never quite lifting either foot off the ground. "What? I can look!"

Wisely, Vanessa did not respond.

"Now deary, I hope I'm not being too forward, or speaking out of turn, but I want to say that Dunk is the guy you know him to be. I've not met anyone like him. And look at you. You are beautiful."

Viola's hand on Vanessa's forearm looked and felt like what an actor would wear when dressed as an alien in a *Star Trek* episode. "Get to know him. He may be all defensive at first, but that's because he gets scared."

Vanessa had never thought about this.

"Yes, he can be seen as a church hero. He is an incredible, godly man. He listens and he loves. But he has doubts and insecurities. He's not always as confident as he appears."

"I'm not either."

Viola smiled inwardly. "I know. I say these things to you because I love that man, and even an old church biddy like me—some old broad who taps on car windows—can sense what you're feeling now. You're uneasy, and understandably a bit nervous. Dunk has those same feelings, too. When you get to know him, you'll see what I mean."

⊗⎯⎯⎯⎯⎯⊗

"Hi, ladies." Dunk turned when he saw them walking toward him. "It's good to see you both here tonight."

"It's good to see you, too," Viola replied matter-of-factly. After what had only been thirty seconds of polite welcome, Viola dropped a bomb. "Miss Marl wants to talk with you for a moment." She glanced at her watch but never really looked at it because she knew the time. She would be late if she was less than as twenty five minutes early to any gathering. "We have *plenty* of time before the meeting starts. You two go on. I'll be inside when you're finished."

Thinking ahead to tonight's agenda, Dunk did his best to remain businesslike after Viola entered the building. "Vanessa, what is it? How can I help you?"

Vanessa tried to speak but could only stare at his hand. She knew there was no wedding ring. Without fail, she looked every Sunday before a church service, during a hymn, or in the coffee hour following worship. No ring, no girlfriend. No one sat with him except a new batch of youth group kids and his neighbor, a friendly old man you might hire to fix a leaky sink or mow your little lawn.

"So," she swallowed nervously and proceeded to jumble her words. "Just what are you whistling with that doing?"

Dunk wasn't quite sure what he had just heard.

"I mean, what are you doing with that whistle?"

As he answered, Vanessa could not believe she had just used what could easily sound like a pick-up line. Her heart sank. So much for being her true self. She was just a flirt, and not a very good one.

Realizing her thoughts were somewhere else because she wasn't listening to him, Dunk tried a second time. "I said it's for the little ones. We are working on setting up a game."

"Soccer?"

"No, that's when I'm in school. That's a fall sport. Here I'm helping out with Vacation Bible School again this summer."

This is just small talk, Vanessa. You can do this. "How's that going?"

"It hasn't started yet."

"Right." Vanessa tried to keep her composure which drooped like the neglected tomato plants on her neighbor's deck. "I mean, that's right. The sign, the big one, on the church's front lawn. The one that reads VBS and the date…"

"Which is in two weeks."

"Which is in two weeks."

Despite her uneasiness, Dunk knew there was something special about Vanessa. She was wise enough not to hide or get herself lost in church talk or current Christian buzzwords, which always sounded so fake to Dunk. Instead, the qualities she had were genuine and refreshing. From a distance, Dunk could see how she deeply cared for others. Having become a full member here at Presswater United Church of Christ a year ago this month, she didn't have a longstanding history with this church. This interested him. She had signed on to be a deacon on her own; no one approached or recruited her—which to him was a good sign. When she headed up the Thanksgiving take home meal for area shut-ins, found the live sheep for the Christmas pageant, and was the one behind several Sunday school classes making and then giving away four dozen Easter baskets, he knew she was one with a heart for serving.

He was glad for this quiet time with her. "And you're a social worker, right?"

"Yes, I work with the local hospitals."

"That has to be something." Dunk nodded.

Vanessa realized that she hadn't sounded like herself in such a long time. When she spoke about her job, her true self resonated. "I love what I do."

What she had said startled him. He always wanted to be with someone who had such passion for what they did. It didn't matter what the passion was—making jelly, organizing a community garden, or being a Canadian bobsled fan—he just wanted to meet someone *invested*. Sadly, he had not yet met that person. As a single parent, he'd tried dating and would just as soon leave nearly all of those experiences behind. Vanessa was somehow different. Suddenly nervous, he fumbled with his words. "W-we really d-don't know each other all that well."

Vanessa knew Dunk had a son, Joe O'Dell. She had heard that

Joe was an intense young man who went off to college somewhere. Other than the fact that the head deacon was also a teacher, a youth group advisor, and the junior high school boys' soccer coach, she knew nothing else about Dunk except for what Viola had shared. "It's true. We don't."

Moving his whistle to his front pocket without realizing it, Dunk spoke of how his interest in soccer began when he started coaching Joe's young age group because the team needed someone to head up the young boys and girls. The conversation flowed from there. Warm and funny, Vanessa made him laugh—deeply laugh—like only Joe could do.

In the middle of her story about her own soccer days where she was the team captain at Michigan State University, Dunk stopped with this sudden thought: he really liked what he was hearing. This instantly put him on guard because even though Joe was an out-of-the-house college sophomore, he was still a father to his 'special' son.

Dunk knew who Joe *really* was, and the word 'special' couldn't cover even half of it. Firsthand, he had seen the boy do miracles like fix a butterfly's wing, and catch an enormous amount of fish in record time. Once he brought his neighbor Earl's dog back to life. This was no canine CPR; Joe only held his hand over the Golden Retriever's side. Maybe unseen angels revived the pet, maybe the butterfly wasn't all *that* wounded, and boys can catch dozens of fish using nets in less than ten minutes, but there was still the whole issue with the cloning, and technically he did steal the then eighteen-month-old from billionaire Roland Rolls' lab.

Then there was the big problem. He never knew how he would introduce Joe to a woman he could be serious about. He looked at Vanessa and could not picture himself ever asking her, or someone like her, this question: "So, what do you think, is this nineteen-year-old philosophy major at the Bible College *really* Jesus walking on earth again by way of test tubes and science?"

It appeared to Dunk that Joe was Jesus' clone. On his daily hikes around the nearby lake, he had a lot of time to think about what he has read and seen. When Joe was a high school freshmen, Dunk had read about the Infancy Gospel of Thomas. This ancient writing was never canonized, and Dunk remembered learning that if a book was never canonized it meant it was never put into the Bible. The Gospel of Thomas told of Jesus' human nature as a youngster. Dunk figured the Infancy Gospel of Thomas was never placed in the Bible for a reason, and that God's will was in the reason. While other scripture said clearly that Jesus was sinless, this text opened this window: it was at least *possible* that, as a boy, Jesus was *sometimes* just a normal, playful, inquisitive, not always so perfect child.

Of course, Dunk has also considered Luke 2:41-52 many, many times because this was the only time the Bible mentioned Jesus' youth. He remembered the story. Twelve-year-old Jesus had such love, passion, investment and clarity for the ancient scrolls. When he should have left the Temple to head home with his parents, he stayed back and sat with the religious teachers for three days, much to the chagrin of his mom and dad.

Through ongoing Bible studies, Dunk also knew the Word he loved so much was clear about when the Holy Spirit came upon Jesus: at his baptism in the Jordan River with John, not before. Dunk's studies, while by no means exhaustive, did suggest that Jesus was not some nineteen-year-old Bible College philosophy major, but a thirty-year-old man when this happened.

Dunk needed to stop this with Vanessa, at least for now. Pastor Smith would be along soon, or maybe he was already here if he had made his way to the conference room through another door. There were a few incidentals Dunk wanted to talk with the pastor about privately before the meeting started.

Vanessa read his mind. "We need to get going."

He held the door for her, looked down at his shoes as she passed and, for the life of him, could not think of a thing he wanted to talk with Pastor Smith about.

The perfect night surrounded him. As he passed two lawn sprinklers hissing at each other, and then a half dozen kittens tangling by a large flower pot of geraniums on a front porch, he replayed the last few hours. Joe had called just before dinner. He had asked if his new roommate Mike could join them for breakfast this coming Sunday before church. Joe's summer semester continued to go as well as the spring semester did. Joe had managed work at the day camp while continuing the two compressed courses on his schedule now. There had been some talk about him being transferred to another camp, one for special needs children, but Joe had said that was still in the works.

Dunk wondered. What would happen if he headed off to this new camp? What would he see? What would he feel? What would he do? As he rounded a corner in this sprawling, suburban town, he remembered a time, years ago, when the two of them were sitting face-to-face in a fast food restaurant. They'd stopped for an early lunch over his son's mid-winter break. Joey was nine-years-old then, and a boy his age sat with the help of many straps and buckles in a wheelchair not far from where the two were eating.

Joey, who loved fast food and could be all animated when he ate it, sat solemnly. His shoulder was propped against the fake wood edge of the booth where they were seated. Sensing his son had been working through how a boy his age could have such profound challenges, Dunk left his young tablemate to his thoughts for a few moments. After praying for the little angel in the chair, Dunk said quietly, "I wonder what God had in mind the day that boy over there was born."

"What do you mean, DOD?"

Dunk smiled at his new name. Since the start of that school year, Joey had started calling Dunkin O'Dell by his three initials, DOD. It was a joke they shared together when the third grader learned what monograms were through a worksheet he brought home from school. After that, "dad" was always DOD, even in public.

"What do I mean? Well, that boy is different than most."

Without adding another word on the subject, Joey said matter-of-factly, "That boy is wonderful, you mean, just like me."

Dunk nodded when their eyes met. *Just like you.*

Walking past a third lawn sprinkler set too close to the sidewalk so that it sprayed his shins and shoes with cool water, Dunk couldn't easily let go of the memory of Joey nibbling away at a burger that, at any other time, he would have downed in seconds.

"Yes, God," Dunk said out loud as he idly crossed a quiet street, "Yes, those boys—both of them, my son and the one whose name I don't know—are wonderful."

Passing a push lawn mower in front of a storage shed made him think of his next door neighbor, Earl. He should visit him soon. They could share grilled fish and a couple of cold ones on his back deck next week.

Two houses down from the sprinkler that made his shoes squeak, he read a bumper sticker with his school logo on it. He thought of his no-nonsense friend and colleague Jolie who taught health in the classroom across the hall from his science lab. When Dunk thought of cold ones being shared, his mind often turned to Jolie. Back in the day, she taught the brand new dad the fine art of cooking one of the staples in a kid's life, macaroni and cheese. After several cooking disasters with even simple meals, Jolie agreed with his kitchen philosophy: a microwave is a man's best friend. Dunk repeated those very same words as he stepped over a pile of Frisbees left in the middle of the neighborhood sidewalk. While he was still smiling at memories of mac making with a woman who was like an older sister, a strange feeling turned in his stomach.

A car that cost as much as two houses on this block coasted by, almost without a sound. Dunk froze. The softly lit rear license plate carried only two initials—RR.

Roland Rolls.

CHAPTER FOUR

He did not return Pastor Smith's calls about a hanging issue from last night's meeting. His over-priced hiking shoes stayed hidden under the well-worn wooden bench by the back door because his deeply loved early morning hike around the lake never happened. The morning paper, which rarely landed so close to the front door, remained in its neat bundle. Around 9 AM, Jolie wondered why he never showed up for their standing midweek breakfast date at the Dairy Barn. Dunk never missed this time together during their summers off together.

The only call Dunk made following the car sighting—and even then he didn't use his own phone because he thought it could somehow be traced by that mad scientist—was to the bank. To be safe, he used neighbor Earl's landline to dial People's Savings and Loan. Cowering in the old man's only bathroom that needed a thorough cleaning, he squeezed the receiver tightly. One ring. Two.

"Hello, and welcome to People's Savings and Loan. My name is Melissa and I want to know how I can help you today?"

"Yes. Melissa." He sighed almost silently because Melissa was the best teller at the bank, and he knew she was the mother of a fourth grader who just couldn't wait to play soccer with him in a few years on the junior high team. He offered a pleasantry after giving his name, or at least he thought he did.

"How much money do I have?" Dunk knew he sounded abrupt. "Total. The bonds. The two money market accounts. And my savings."

He shouldn't have to call. Everything he needed had been right in a plain envelope taped to the back of the hall medicine cabinet that really did look built-in to the wall. Diligently, he had kept all bank info up to date and handy in a single envelope if, at any moment, he might have to fly off and hide with his stolen son.

Now he had become too casual, too lazy. Roland Rolls was one powerful man. The anxiety under his sternum pressed down again, just as it had after the long, near silent car passed hours ago.

"No, Melissa. I don't mind waiting." *Actually, I do mind waiting. I'm hiding in my neighbor's bathroom.* He counted each racing heartbeat in his chest. He slumped to the floor. His back pressed against the tiled wall under the little window facing his own backyard. *Melissa, hurry.*

His greatest fears were actualized. Of course Roland Rolls could have swept in at *any* moment, taken the boy, and left not so much as a fiber bent on the carpet. Dunk's only hope was that with each day passing the scientist would either lose interest, or become involved in another consuming project. Sure, last night's car sighting may have been happenstance. Roland probably enjoyed taking a spin around middle class neighborhoods six hours from his lab just for fun.

Dunk swallowed. This was not happenstance and his former boss knew nothing of fun. Roland had planned every move down to the finest detail. The car was meant to be seen exactly where it was.

Years ago, the runaway employee did have the wild idea of a grand escape that included torching a small boat in the Pacific Ocean. Father and young son would return to shore in a tiny lifeboat, whereupon the duo would slip off to Europe with new, hidden lives. Deep down though, Dunk knew this truth: he could never outrun or outsmart the billionaire. Given this obvious fact, it stood to reason that he could be monitored somehow. He tried to think. Even Roland wouldn't bug Earl's bathroom, would he? His fingers shook. He had never been this frightened before, but he kept his goal clear. At all costs, he would protect his son.

At all costs. He smacked his forehead. Why was he calling the bank? What did it matter how much money he did—or didn't—have? He thought of Joe. *Sorry son, I couldn't hatch an escape plan because I was $4.93* *short.* Trembling, he ran his hands through his already tousled hair. His stomach knotted, his pores sweat, his heart hurt, yet he knew he needed money—whatever money he had—in hand. "Come on, Melissa."

He stared at Earl's closed bathroom door and realized how perfect he appeared to so many. If his congregation could see him now, they'd see this truth: his proverbial pants were down around his ankles here near a toilet. He pictured his close-knit teacher colleagues. Their faces. Their support. In thinking of his people, he forced his racing mind to stop. Focusing first on relaxing his shoulders, he straightened his back, breathed, and looked to heaven. *Jesus* was the one-word prayer he sent.

With his eyes still closed, Dunk thought of his Savior's name again and again. Words he remembered from Ephesians 1:11 began to comfort him. *Because we are united with Christ, we have received an inheritance from God, for he chose us in advance, and he makes everything work according to his plan.*

He could hear Melissa on the other end of the phone. Her voice was distant as she was not near her window. She laughed a bit before giving depositing instructions to another teller. Dunk stretched out his legs and held one of his knees. He knew this situation—this glorious mess—would all fold into God's plan. He just needed to be united with Christ again, and again, and again—even in a neighbor's bathroom, or especially in a neighbor's bathroom.

Dunk forced his heartbeats to slow down. He stood, took two steps, and sat again, this time with just one shoulder to the wall. From this angle, he stared at the little linen closet exactly the same size as his. He thought this was too weird, too wild. This whole concocted event with ancient, burial wrappings and test tubes? It was far too crazy, far too insane.

As a brand new lab tech, Dunk didn't know how the recently born Joseph had come to the science center. Of course he'd heard of the sheep Dolly through the daily buzz from his co-workers and, as a scientist, he knew genetic advances continued to appear on the horizon, advances the Christian world would challenge. Still, he never imagined cloning a human—not even by his very distant and very demanding boss. Dunk knew Roland was eccentric, unorthodox, and driven to make a high mark in the scientific community ethically or otherwise, but all he had seen was a bright, engaging toddler who looked up at him with the best brown eyes ever. Though Dunk was scared and lost in the moment, he knew he would do it all again, including this part of calling the bank on his neighbor's bathroom floor that did need serious scrubbing.

Joey. He could still feel the weight of the little one he carried away all those years ago. He loved that boy. Oh, how he loved that boy. The memories, the laughter, the goofiness, the joy, and the endless fun lifted away all the stresses of the last few hours. Tears rolled off his cheek and splattered on his jeans. *Love. This is love.*

"Ride?" Joey had asked as they came close to his well-worn Toyota Corolla in Roland's employee parking lot.

With a free hand fishing for his keys, Dunk answered, "Ride."

"Good ride."

Dunk stared ahead at the door in front of him. "Yes, Joe, it has been a good ride."

"Yes, Mr. O'Dell? I have that information for you. Would you like to come to the bank and get it, or should I—"

"Tell me over the phone."

"Tell you over the phone." Melissa giggled after she repeated what he just said, and then her voice sounded strange. "I guess you're kinda in a hurry, huh? Vacation?"

"No...just...curious."

"Well, your total, and this is everything now, including early withdrawal fees on your bonds and CDs, is $67,043.07."

"67,043.07. Got it."

"Will there be anything else, Mr. O'Dell?"

Can you think of a way to help me outrun a billionaire?

"No. Nothing. Thank you."

❦

Rather than fire up his push mower which he believed would take his mind off what has happened since Dunk came home last night, Earl decided he had had enough. He needed to know why Dunk needed his phone, and he needed to know now. Sitting across from his neighbor at a kitchen table the same size as his own, Earl ran his calloused hands over the chewed up straw hat he only wore when mowing his incredibly well-cared for lawn. In the quiet, he waited for Dunk to take the initiative. The younger man didn't. Not one to waste time, especially his own, Earl repositioned his hat on his knee. "You called the bank. They called back about ten minutes after you left my bathroom."

"Oh."

"I know Melissa. Her grandmother and me went to Christian camp back in the day. Margaret was her name. Now I know a bank is a private place and I didn't do anything too wrong, but I know you asked about money. I also know you haven't left your house since you left mine."

"Earl, I—"

Having two daughters of his own, the seventy-six-year-old could smell excuses and tangents faster than an approaching rainstorm through the joints of his well-worn body. "Now you wait, son, and listen here. Yes, you are like a son to me. I'm not asking any questions. I'm just sayin' things. In the thirteen years you've been my next door neighbor, I've seen truly good things in you. You're a church guy. But more than that, you're a God guy. I know this."

"Earl."

He stared at his straw hat. "And I also know about that boy, that boy of yours. Now, he may look just like his momma because he certainly don't look a whole lot like you, but there's something there. Something you're not telling me. And it's something you're not telling me because you can't tell me. I know this."

"Earl, I—"

The old man continued. "He's a special boy, that Joey. I've seen it with my own eyes when no one was lookin'. No, we don't need to talk about this. Not now, and maybe not ever. But I know things." He paused. "And I see you haven't slept good. And I feel the knot in your stomach. And I know that knot isn't there 'cause you spent time last night with the lovely Viola Munson."

Dunk tried to hear what his neighbor was saying, but in ways it was like water spilling over an already full jar. He did crack a smile when we realized what Earl had said of Viola, a woman who could literally be Earl's opposite.

Earl became quiet because he knew Dunk was not completely following all he had said. Earl was fine with silence—too much talking was nonsense—but he never liked feeling powerless. A born provider, Earl ached in a way that was unfamiliar to him. During a time in his life when all he had was a bad reputation, he knew what it was like to be scared and alone. The day he met Dunk as the new guy next door, he felt in his gut that this young science teacher with the wee sprout had a past somewhat like his own, one that needed to remain untouched.

Memories rolled through Earl's mind. The years the two neighbors helped each other hang outdoor Christmas lights, how they talked in depth about any and everything related to cars, shared garden mulch, and enjoyed cold beer together on hot summer nights came to him. This tender, honest, and soulful gift from God meant the world to Earl, so he did not question what he was about to do. He pulled a wide envelope out of his back pocket. "Here's $204,000 and change. You take it."

<hr/>

"Talk."

"I can't."

It was Jolie. She set her motorcycle helmet on a secure garden stake Earl must have set in Dunk's vegetable garden because even though the two of them were on Dunk's property, and Earl clearly had his own garden a hundred feet away, this was indeed all Earl's handiwork. With her signature drink in hand, iced tea with lemon that she had made herself, which was something she'd never done before in his house, she watched as Dunk sat on the ground. Thirty minutes after Earl had left Dunk's kitchen table, she forced her way inside by pretending to be the cop she had once wanted to be. Oddly, Dunk suggested they see his parsley. A man who could still screw up a macaroni and cheese meal would not grow parsley.

"My dear brother," she said, eyeing a man she barely recognized, "talk."

Her friend barely shook his head. He wondered if any recording device would be this far from the house.

Like any seasoned teacher could do, Jolie shot him one single cannonball-through-the-chest look, and Dunk, who hadn't cried this hard since his mother died when he was eleven, burst into tears. He cried everything—the fear of being found by Rolls, of messing up as a single parent, and of letting God down if indeed the DNA cloned was, in fact, Jesus'. After literally coming up for air, he wailed on the frustration of raising a boy who knew too much, felt too deeply, and thought too profoundly. Jolie, the only woman who truly understood him, listened through all the loneliness, the stress, the walls, and the worry. After the sobs passed, he considered Earl's money. With Jolie here, they could create a distraction. He could take her bike and find Joe.

Jolie knew her scientist was a methodical, careful thinker. This enabled her to be the impulsive one. She liked this role because, while she was fine with being single, she could get tired of making all the serious decisions on her own. Sure, she could help spruce up a bachelor's bland and dated living room—and the space did look bad before she made him buy a new carpet, couch and twin chairs from a discount furniture store last year—but where was she going to house her aging mother? Where would she invest her fun money? Given how school policies kept changing, when should she retire? All of these big questions have become challenges.

Raising his hand to his forehead to shield his red eyes from the sun, he shrugged. "What?"

"I'm reading your mind honey, and it won't work."

"Why won't it work? I haven't even shared what I've been thinking!" He lowered his face. "And you have never called me honey."

He could be adorable, especially because he didn't know he was. She kept his tired mind focused. "It won't work."

"Why?"

"You don't know how to ride a motorcycle."

"But your helmet would fit. It's a start."

"My helmet would mostly fit your big head."

"So, that's a yes?"

She bit into ice cubes. "That's a no."

"Remember when we went windsurfing on Lake Ontario?"

Jolie didn't know where he was going with this, which, in itself, didn't happen often.

"We took little Joey to the lake for a Fourth of July weekend the year they moved you to middle school. Remember?"

"Ye-yes."

"Remember the rental shop and the guy with the alligator hat? I suggested you could meet up with him later. Yes?"

"You said I *should* meet up with him later."

Dunk came to his feet. "Okay, here's my point. Windsurfing. Choppy little waves. I didn't fall."

"Where are you going with this?"

"I'm a quick study."

Jolie had always admired Dunk for adopting a child when she herself, a single woman nine years his senior, had not. Unlike Dunk who had been looking to marry, she never worried about it. Someday a man, with or without an alligator baseball cap, might intrigue and hold her attention, or not. There was no sense spending time on something she couldn't control. But she did love Joe. Firsthand, this blunt, stocky, terse and outspoken friend had always seen how odd—how different— Joe was. This independent spirit with a tattoo she would never regret had been a sounding board since the day the new employees met at their first orientation day for high school faculty.

This was still a challenge to process. She had heard of Roland Rolls. She knew he had made several scientific breakthroughs, but cloning? Beyond all the ethical, moral and religious barriers he crossed, how on earth could he successfully secure and manipulate two-thousand-year-old DNA from what had to be only wisps of fabric? She rolled her fingertips over her left hand ring finger that would likely never hold a rock. "Rolls. And he did this cloning long before that sheep? What was her name?"

Ignoring Jolie, Dunk continued to stare at her helmet. He could handle a mountain bike and a ten-speed with no problem, and he did master windsurfing, at least for a while. She could give him a quick motorcycle riding tutorial using cucumbers, green beans and corn.

Jolie took another hit from her iced tea. "What was that sheep's name?"

Dunk shot her a look that made it clear she wasn't helping. "Dolly."

"Right. Dolly." She ran her hand through short, gray and brown hair that had never been styled beyond the look of a thirteen-year-old boy. "And Joe, he doesn't know any of this, right?"

"I've never told him." As he sat back down, Dunk wondered just how tight that helmet would be, and then stared at an area in front of him that needed to be weeded. "I mean, I haven't told him everything. He knows he's not mine biologically. I've told him about Rolls' lab, at least in part."

"Did you ever tell him Rolls' name?"

"We just need to go. I need to get to Joe."

"Hold on. Let's figure stuff out first. Did you ever share Rolls' name with Joe?"

"No, never. I just said I worked for a lab company before I began classroom teaching."

"And nothing about the cloning?"

Dunk looked at his friend. "How would—how could—I even begin to tell him that?"

"Old pal, if this boy is the Son of God, then God Himself will take care of this. He'll guide you." Knowing he was still thinking about her motorcycle, Jolie took both of his hands. "Now I'm going to do what you always have done for me when my wings have been clipped, like the year I went to middle school. I'm going to pray with you."

The prayer, like Jolie herself, was straightforward. Nothing soft-focused, eloquent, or poetic spilled from her lips. Just the facts. The only thing Dunk felt when she let go of his hands was that he should sit up straighter, and he did.

●———————●

The two came up with a decoy plan they shared out loud once they returned to the house, but the real plan was that Jolie would go get Joe right from school. She would get that boy on a bus to Detroit, which was two hours west of the Bible College. At the bus terminal, Joe would meet Dunk in a car that Dunk would borrow from Jolie's aunt who lived near Detroit. No planes. No big or known destination. Father and son will just sneak away under the radar.

There was not a minute to waste.

As Jolie left his narrow drive, which was caked with dried grass clippings so unlike Earl's immaculately clean drive, Dunk knew this wasn't the best plan, but it was the only plan, and he had to do something.

CHAPTER FIVE

Roland Rolls himself rang the doorbell, and then stood exactly four feet from Dunk's front door. Wearing a silver suit that showcased his motionless silver hair, he pressed his right hand against his stark white dress shirt that cost twice as much as Dunk's average monthly grocery store bill. The mastermind waited silently for forty seconds, his mind keeping track of the time as precisely as the diamond-framed watch on his wrist. Having successfully spied on this surrogate father since the day Larry left the lab, Roland knew this former employee wouldn't run now. He couldn't. The game was over.

Dunk's front door whined open. Defeated, the lab-tech-turned-teacher stepped out onto his cracked concrete stoop. There would be no decoy plan, no Detroit, no living life under the radar.

Roland's crisp voice cut the midday humidity into pieces. "We should talk, Larry."

Dunk's mind stayed still. Only his lips moved. "Alright."

"Not here. My car will be behind me in nine seconds. Let's walk to the curb now."

Dunk, whose eyes were still red and sore, nodded.

Once inside the back of the car Dunk could not identify because he had never seen anything like it—was this a Rolls Royce? A Bentley?—he leaned against the fine upholstery, even though his back muscles remained locked. He sensed he was going to die. He would actually be surprised if Mr. Rolls did not kill him. Dunk shut his eyes and, like his time in Earl's bathroom, arrived only at the word Jesus, which he silently said over and over again. Strangely, he was alright now. His plan had been to get to Joe first. Here in the quiet, he realized in the presence of this much power that none of his plans would have worked.

"I want to begin here," Roland broke the silence in a tone as crisp as his starched dress shirt. "For the sake of curiosity, that is. I'm 93% certain you left your neighbor Earl's $204,093.00 in the house before you came outside to meet me. Is that correct? Did you leave the money behind?"

"You know Earl gave me $204, 093.00?"

"Larry, I successfully cloned two-thousand-year-old DNA. There isn't a lot I don't know."

Dunk set his hands on his lap and confirmed what he expected. "My house is bugged."

"Yes."

"Surveillance cameras?"

Roland reached for sunglasses in the handsome wooden compartment between them. "Everywhere."

"Did you see and hear Jolie and me in my garden?"

"Yes."

"Did you get Earl's house too?"

"I didn't go that far. There are just two recording devices in his backyard aimed at your property. To a great extent, you're predictable. For example, it was Ephesians 1:11, wasn't it?"

Dunk squinted. "What?"

"Ephesians 1:11. That is the scripture I predicted came to your anguished mind to comfort you."

How much does this man know?

Turning, Dunk glanced out the window onto Main Street. It was odd to think he would never see Holman's Market or Jerry's barbershop on the corner of Vine and Cherry again. The Dairy Barn Ice Cream Shop Restaurant came up on the left. A new kid had just started as a server there. He was one of the few students Dunk did not have in class and therefore did not really know. If he had not seen his name tag while out to lunch with Earl about a week ago, he would never been able to call him by his name, which was Ben.

Dunk set his fingers under his eyes. His mind was wandering. Fatigue settled in again.

Ben had a scar on his neck that seemed so painful. That was just an outward pain. In all his years of teaching, Dunk knew this teen had a soul that needed attention.

"Tired Larry?"

Dunk tried to focus. "My neighbors, those to the left of Earl's house and mine, they're spies, aren't they?"

"The couple known as Mr. and Mrs. Jenson are my employees, yes."

"I like their dog."

"I know."

Dunk relaxed his back now. If he was going to go, why worry about it? "Nice touch."

"Don't get too comfortable, Larry."

A long pause seeped between them. Dunk couldn't determine any of the driver's features, except that she was Caucasian with long, straight dark hair pulled tightly at the base of her neck. In all the years he had thought about being caught and having the situation unfold just as it has so far, he never imagined Mr. Rolls would have a female driver. How progressive.

On the interstate, eleven minutes and seven seconds after their ride began, Dunk took the lead after recalling Zephaniah 3:17, which he knew by heart. *With his love, he will calm all fears.* Peaceful, Dunk wanted to understand Roland's plan. "Mr. Rolls, can I ask a question?"

Roland didn't respond, though he knew what Larry had been praying. Most likely he was using scripture in that prayer, probably something from the Old Testament. The exact scripture did not matter to Roland, of course.

"Before I ask the question, I'll tell you I was praying with Zephaniah 3:17."

"I don't care."

"I do."

"You're being uncharacteristically bold."

"And you're being as calculating as ever." The only way Dunk could play this would be to stay fresh, innovative, and unpredictable. If he were to win Roland's curiosity and leverage the best outcome for Joe, who he assumed Roland had already tucked away at the lab, he had to use the one thing Roland didn't have or understand, and that was faith. Dunk had God; Roland didn't. The younger of the two crossed his leg over his knee. "It's kind of nice one of us is changin' it up a bit, eh?"

"Your question?"

Dunk spoke with a candor he never thought he could have in front of this genius. "Why now? Why now, when he's between his sophomore and junior year of college?"

"The risks for his wellbeing have increased. I've detected from his last physical that his ulmintin levels are dropping."

Dunk was no medical doctor, but he'd never heard of ulmintin levels. Realizing he had nothing to lose, he decided to joke. "Oh no, dropping ulmintin levels? Maybe more starch in his diet?" His voice took on an air similar to Roland's. "Perhaps more potatoes this Thanksgiving."

"You are not funny."

"Oh, and that was just what I was going for, chief."

Roland wished this imbecile would be respectful. This cavalier attitude could only go so far, but he knew this boldness came as a result of Larry's frequent prayers. They freed him somehow. There was a five percent chance of this happening. Most calculations indicated this average man with what could be gaged as an average faith should be pleading for the life of the one he claims as his son. Could faith truly being enabling this assertiveness?

There were several conversation paths Roland had planned. Given Dunk's relaxed demeanor, this was the most unlikely one. "You weren't so confident in Earl's bathroom."

"I thought you said there were no recording devices there."

"This is what I said. 'You are predictable.'"

Dunk realized Roland was trying to take control back through fear. "Confidence? Yeah, that's one thing you really don't have when sitting on Earl's bathroom floor." He wiggled his foot. "You know, germs."

"You're not that clever."

"It was not that clean."

"Does this banter stop, Larry?"

"Does this car stop, Mr. Rolls? I think we'd have a fun time— just the two of us—at a waterslide park two exits from here. Did you know I was remembering the time out on Lake Ontario when I went windsurfing?"

"I did hear you." Roland lied. "You are predictable."

"Hmm, you've said that twice now. Did you predict that?"

Roland didn't answer.

"Me mentioning a waterslide park for the two of us. What was the chance of me mentioning *that?*" Dunk rubbed his chin to mock contemplation. "And we'd need sunscreen, of course. You do look pale."

Roland remained impressed with Dunk's assertiveness. The likelihood of this happening was .0003 percent. "You are trying to free your son by trying to trip me up. Even for you, this is an overly simplistic ploy."

"Oh drat, I've been foiled." Dunk smirked. "That's a line from a Batman comic book, I think." He faced Roland. "Do you know all about comic books too?"

Fascinated by this idiotic faith practice and its misguided power, Roland stared straight ahead. He would regain control. "The ulmintin treatment will take six consecutive days to complete. It's both delicate and precise. They are in response to the intense screenings, biopsies, and testing that has and will continue to happen on the clone. You're somewhat of a scientist, Larry."

"Always a charmer."

"Certain temperatures and a specific environment are required to obtain the medicine's peek proficiency. Yes, I could have crafted an alternative way for this treatment to happen; I've successfully done this before when testing through the years; but it's time he knows he is not Joseph O'Dell."

"You're going to tell him."

"Yes."

"And I'm still alive because I'm going to substantiate this."

"Larry, let me say what is obvious. If I wanted you dead, you would die. It's that simple. But I set this up from nearly the start. I didn't want Joseph to be raised anywhere near me or the lab. In your coarse vernacular, I'm a freak. Socially odd at best. And for this to work optimally, Joseph needed to be in a home environment."

"So, you let me have him?"

"Precisely."

"Why me?"

"You were the best candidate at the time. Young. Passionate. Wholesome. Others possess these same qualities, but my search team found you and determined that you tested well in raising the clone religiously. And I wanted that."

Dunk wanted this to go further. "Search team? And I tested well?"

"I want you to remember the Bible Study called *God's Indispensable Plan for Me.*"

There have been dozens of Bible Studies in his past, some with very similar titles. He tried to bring this particular one to mind.

"It was held at the then newly constructed Calvary Baptist Church with—"

"With Pastor Smith. I met my current minister there."

"He was an expected part of that, yes. But it was mine. All of it. See, everything is calculated here, Larry. You were in my sights even before you found out about my company and were interviewed for a position I did not need. It's that simple, really. I knew you would take the clone. That was the plan, and that is why I brought you in when I did. A real employee of mine? Hardly. You're really not that bright, particularly as a scientist. You didn't know you were even being tested."

"And Joe? He's been tested too, not just physically?"

"Of course. I've set up obstacles and experiments for him. Remember, I didn't know for certain if those two-thousand-year-old garments were Jesus', or someone else's."

"And are they? Is Jesus cloned?"

Roland did not answer the question. This much conversation at one time was beginning to wear on him, plus he knew that, within a few minutes of quiet, Larry would realize on his own that he was not yet 100% certain that Joseph was Jesus' clone. They sat silently for five minutes and six seconds.

Roland turned to Larry, though it was a strain to do so. "You've been thinking two thoughts in this time."

"Have I?"

"Yes. One, you cannot reach the driver from here. You cannot overtake this car with the intent of killing everyone in it in order to save or spare Joseph. There's a force field in place between the front and back of the car." Mr. Rolls tossed his sunglasses forward. They electrified in mid-air and melted before reaching the floor of the car.

"Burnt plastic," Dunk whiffed the air. "What a welcome fragrance."

"Your sarcasm exhausts me, Larry."

Dunk hadn't met his demise yet. Maybe what he was doing was working. He could tell that Roland had been redirected several times during this car ride. Everything Dunk had said was probably on the charts, including the bit about a waterpark, but he was on the edge. Knowing that faith was the subject most foreign and likely most interesting to Roland, he continued playfully knowing this: God was in charge here, not this brilliant, detached and lonely scientist for whom he suddenly felt compassion. "Oh, hurry Mr. Rolls, what's the other thought? I really want to know this one."

"You do know this one, Larry, only now it's confirmed. There are some strikingly obvious resemblances, of course, even though we have no known artist depicting Jesus at the age of twenty. But—"

"You don't know if Joe is divine."

Roland's stomach tightened. He was never interrupted.

Dunk continued. "It may be that you just cloned all the human aspects of Jesus, not those that are holy. And I do think it is Jesus we have here."

"Do you think that, or feel that?"

Dunk considered his answer. "Both." He stared at the puddle the sunglasses made. "Why did you ask me a direct question?"

"Because you've lived with him. You've touched him. You've smelled him. You've held him."

"And I love him."

"That too."

The two returned to silence. Mr. Rolls rested his head against his headrest as he folded his arms onto his lap. He released air almost silently.

"Do you, Mr. Rolls, do you love him?"

Roland closed his eyes. "What a strange question to ask."

"Answer."

"I don't know."

Everything began to turn for Dunk when it came to the subject of love. Whatever solid ground he had been on began to slip away because the thought of Joe going through these treatments frightened him. Even with prayer, he could not play this confidence card any longer, especially as thoughts of Joe being scared and alone began to play in his mind. Within seconds, Dunk reverted to being what Roland anticipated, the scared and pleading parent. The thought of Joe being in any kind of pain was too much to bear. His neck tightened. His voice pinched. "Please don't tell him this. Please. Don't. Let him go. Do your... whatever treatments. Ulmintin. Is that what it's called? I'll help him through this. And then let him go. Let him live. Please. Let him live as normal a life as possible."

"I can't do that. The world needs to know."

"No, for some reason that is either wrong or unhealthy—or both—you need to know. The second coming of Christ is not now. It's not like this."

Dunk touched Roland Rolls' trigger point. The seasoned scientist could not take any more. From seemingly nowhere, he quickly fit a plastic mask over his nose and mouth as a spray covered Dunk's face.

"Enough for now, Larry," Mr. Rolls said through the protective mask. "It's been an exhausting few hours for you, and yes, really, you'll need your rest."

When the mist sprayed from the ceiling of the car directly into Dunk's face, the tired, defenseless man immediately slipped into unconsciousness, precisely as planned.

CHAPTER SIX

As soon as Joe left his classroom building, the feeling that he was being watched sounded like an alarm. The feeling wasn't new; he has experienced this for over ten years, but it was so much stronger now, so much clearer. It told him he wasn't safe. He jumped into an instinct mode and ran. Down flights of stairs, across two campus quads, and through a grove of manicured trees around the administration building's pristine parking area, he never stopped racing. He was not surprised when he looked over his shoulder and saw not one but two athletic-looking men pursuing him. Somehow Joe knew these two weren't plain clothes police officers or federal agents. These were top notch bad guys.

Faster Joe. Run faster.

There was no time to think about why this was happening; he just had to outsmart the duo who weren't gaining on him.

Thank you, God, for all those soccer practice sprints up and down the field that my DOD made us do. He rounded a corner and dodged headfirst into dense bushes as old as he was.

Safety. At least for now.

He heard their dress shoes slapping the sidewalk a minute later. Complete silence followed. It was too early to tell if he was safe, but he let his breath out rapidly. His tight stomach expanded and contracted. Sweat rolled down his face. It stung his eyes. Below twisted limbs of protection, he tried to piece together what he knew.

The face of one of the two thugs, where I have seen him? Was it back in high school? The parade with the youth group this past fall? An old soccer game?

It was hard to think clearly but he didn't have a choice. Holding one of his shins with both hands, he knew he couldn't stay here in these dense bushes forever. He leaned his face into his raised knee and began to pray simply with the two words, "God, help."

The prayer reoriented Joe. He had to move, but where would he go? Back to his dorm?

A few people passed along the sidewalk in front of him as he tried to figure out what to do. Joe guessed that maybe ten minutes had passed. He was never good at time, though. If he didn't wear a watch, and today he had left his back in his room, he was lost. From the direction he had come, he could hear two voices getting louder. One belonged to Professor MacElvoy's, the other to a student. They couldn't be more than a few feet away.

As he was called by some upperclassman, 'ProMac' was a great guy, a wonderful professor. He taught Joe's first ethics class this past spring semester. Though ProMac was new to the campus this school year, he had a casual way about him that reminded Joe of DOD. Joe sensed he could trust him with just about anything, including this. The sweat had dried and most of the dirt could be brushed off his knees. From behind, Joe quickly caught up to the thoughtful professor who was now alone.

"Oh, Joe," ProMac said, turning. His smile came across as measured and somewhat distant, which seemed unusual. "I didn't see you behind me."

"Like I came from nowhere." The alarm sound he heard outside the doors to his classroom building went off inside his head again, but this was a professor. Here was the friendly face of someone he obviously knew.

ProMac shifted his heavy shoulder bag higher onto his thin shoulder. "How's it going? If I remember right, you're taking two accelerated courses this summer, aren't you?"

This was a small college, which Joe liked. That a professor knew a bit about his schedule was reassuring.

"Yes," Joe answered. "My classes are great."

"Well, I'm heading to my car. Unfortunately, it's in Outer Mongolia today. Would you like to tag along? I'm curious to hear what you're learning now."

'Outer Mongolia' was the nickname for the parking lot furthest from campus. Maybe if he could catch a ride with the professor, he could get away from the school fast.

"Sure, professor."

Joe took a long, sideways glance at his walking partner. He appreciated a professional who cared to know a lot about his students. When together in class, ProMac knew Joe's high school by name and once mentioned the area of town where he lived with his DOD. That kind of investment really impressed Joe.

The two easily talked about Joe's courses—*The World According to Paul*, and *The Pentateuch Through the Eyes of the Hebrew People*. They easily brought Mike into the conversation, though Joe wasn't quite sure how that happened. He was surprised ProMac knew Mike was his new roommate, especially since Mike had not yet had a course with the professor, and faculty never hung around the dorms.

As the two walked on, Joe thought more of Mike. Betsy's best friend had not outted himself to anyone here, but if Mike wanted to do so, he could start with the man beside him. As the sidewalk began to curve through a grove of oaks and elms, Joe continued to think about his roommate who had always made time for Joe. Since their day with Betsy though, he had quieted down. Deep in his own thoughts, Mike had become more difficult to read since he had opened himself up to his friends. Then again, Mike was working hard on a challenging paper. This could explain his distance.

Tonight the two had plans to eat supper in the West Cafeteria. Mike's paper would be done. They could sit alone at a quiet table in the back of the long hall. Face-to-face, Joe thought they could really talk. To the guy he truly loved, he could ask good questions, listen, and say what they both needed to hear.

It dawned on Joe that his roommate would be coming out of *Pastoral Presence* soon. With ProMac, he was near the building where Mike had the class.

What should I do? Bail on the professor and get Mike? And do what?

Joe's heart spun. Should he involve his friend in this? The two guys—the chasers—meant business. It would be great to have Mike's size and strength at hand, but this was dangerous. Just as Joe was trying to figure out a way to ask the professor how to get off campus, ProMac readjusted his eyeglasses and simply offered exactly what the runner needed. "Hey, Joe, would you like a ride someplace?"

Joe didn't hesitate. "I sure would."

ProMac pulled his car keys out of his front pocket. "I'm heading down into town. Is that alright?"

Joe ignored the funny feeling in his stomach. "Oh, yeah. I'm totally on my way to town. You will save me from hoofing it. Thanks."

⊶————————⊷

The ride off campus was uneventful. Occasionally, Joe did look over his shoulder or into the nearby side mirror to see if they were being followed, but this wasn't a Hollywood movie. No vehicle consistently stayed behind them.

Just as he wondered why it had been so easy to get a ride off campus with ProMac, the professor jerked the car to the left. He whipped the agile red sports car into a two-car garage, just off of a quiet residential street. As the garage door began to close behind them, Joe scrambled to open the car door but it was locked. He felt a sharp sting in his left leg and saw he'd been stabbed through his jeans with a large syringe. He looked up at the professor's expressionless face. As the tingles started to race and the numbing began, Joe glanced back out of the passenger side window. The two men from campus, standing side by side, wore similar grins. The door unlocked and one of them reached in to lift him out of the car.

Not exactly how this was supposed to go down," the employee posing as ProMac said, "but this will work."

CHAPTER SEVEN

The dreamlike place where Joe found himself was unending, but somehow he found a way back to that pristine ravine. If he concentrated, he could hear the rushing water as it hurried between his fingers and danced over his chest. The angled boulder that jutted into the creek was there, and on it Mike and Betsy were talking about the Chicago White Soxs, clean bathroom sinks, and a player named Wilson.

His thoughts jumbled. Maybe he was under a sedative of some sort because he had a vision of two men in the backseat of a long car being driven by a woman with a dark pony tail. Joe didn't focus on this because he had other mysteries on his mind. He trusted a professor who literally stabbed him. He couldn't explain why he fled from two hired hands yet trusted a Bible College prof he obviously did not know.

He was still in danger, but his eyes would not open. When he tried to move his torso, he realized he was completely naked. Not even a single sheet covered him. When he stirred again, he discovered his arms and legs were secured with soft yet incredibly strong bands. This should freak him out, but the medicine given to him still ran through his veins and kept him calm.

Forcing his eyes open for the first time, he tried to focus on what could be a space-age lab on a movie set. Gleaming metal machines beeped and buzzed around him. New-age lights moved above his bed. They twirled. The ceiling shifted. This could be a dream except his head hurt. His jaw ached. His mouth felt full of cotton. When he turned his head, he noticed a man with a silver suit and silver hair. Manicured,

Joe thought, and very expensive. His icy eyes were clinical, calculating, and cold. Instantly Joe realized no one loved this man. Something else became clear: this was his captor, the one behind the actions of the professor and the two men chasing him.

From the distance where he had been standing near a clear glass wall, the inquisitor came forward. "You're awake, my son."

Joe took a deep breath. This space smelled like a hospital, or the high school lab adjacent to DOD's classroom when, as an early teen in late summer, Joe would help unpack every Bunsen burner, vial and petri dish before the beginning of the school year.

"Welcome. Or maybe I should say welcome back." The Silver Man frowned. "Maybe I should say welcome home."

It was warm here. A space-age looking thermometer that Joe could easily read on a nearby blue glass wall to his left indicated the temperature was perfectly controlled at seventy-seven degrees Fahrenheit. Other numbers on that screen interested him. While plugged into no monitor, he could read his blood pressure, pulse, and body temperature.

"Yes, you can wake up now. It's alright."

Suddenly, Joe felt a wide bandage on his right forearm. It itched.

The Silver Man's hand skimmed along his thigh.

Joe jerked his head up. "DON'T touch."

The Silver Man made his lips pucker as if to say, "Sssh," but there was no sound.

"DON'T touch."

The Silver Man tilted his head. "Hmmm, someone woke up on the wrong side of the bed this morning."

"You're the one behind all of this."

With an expression of pain and shock, the Silver Man seemed taken aback, until Joe realized it was an act.

"And your hand, Daddy-o? Aren't you just a little too close to my privates?"

Based on new information gleaned from his recent car ride, Roland was not surprised by this flippant, aggressive manner. In fact, he interpreted this to be a product of Joe's environment, proving 'nature' versus 'nurture' studies continued to hold validity. With no surprise, this brazen personality trait annoyed Roland. Larry, who was also outspoken when scared, truly had left quite an impression on his clone. Skillfully however, this could be undone.

"I thought it would be Michael, your new roommate, who would make you move further into your suppressed homophobia and antiquated fundamentalist anti-homosexual theology. But quite literally I hear you're still lagging there, a disappointing sign of your narrow studies."

Joe didn't comprehend everything he just heard.

Roland understood the anesthesia was still having predictable effects. Still, this conversation engaged him, particularly since it was not thoroughly planned. "You're not quite settled on the issue of homosexuality, despite what you say and, interestingly, despite what you do." His eyes took a full sweep of Joseph. "You know what I mean here, dream boy. Sleeping in your boxers all the time, what's a poor boy like Michael to do?"

Joe knew exactly where he was on the issue of homosexuality. "It's your hand here, buddy, that's the concern. Michael is my friend."

Roland laughed. It was forced and fake, like a bit actor would deliver in a community play when the script called for a chuckle. "Friend? This terminology is a product of your environment at that Bible College. Friend." He mulled over the word. "Friend? Interesting. You didn't choose to enlist your friend's help when you could have when on your walk to the parking lot. He was, after all, just a minute or two from you. In fact, what's that course he's taking? *Pastoral Presence?*"

Joe's eyes widened.

"You could have ditched the professor I planted, and, in some heroic feat of escape, both you and Michael could have tried to outmaneuver my other two employees. You certainly considered Michael's size and his strength for a moment, but you didn't let him help you."

It was the medicine. This man was talking too fast.

"And what? You decided to leave poor Mikey behind? What was your noble justification there? You were concerned for his safety?"

"Stop."

"Here's the truth. You doubted his ability to help you. Had you trusted him, maybe your internal radar would have picked up on something with ProMac."

Joe knew this line of thinking was wrong. He forced himself to speak up which was a challenge. "You don't know me. And you don't know Mikey. Michael."

The Silver Man bit into his own words. "You don't know yourself like I do. But I can tell you this: that boy is in far more trouble than you are. Trust me. I'm literally a calculator. His life? His orientation? His inability to see past the very confines he puts around himself? Yes, the one to be saved in the moment you thought of him there in his class was him, not you."

This continued to be unscripted, which thrilled Roland. He never planned to be here now, let alone engage an initial conversation. His time with Larry in the car had changed that. The unpredictable spirit of his former employee intrigued him. He had never had a conversation like the one he engaged in with an average high school teacher. There was no need. Certainly there was no gain. Yet, to an extent, Larry had worn Roland out. That anyone could do this fascinated the scientist.

Roland restructured the initial schedule with the clone as a result. Three technicians were to be present when Joseph woke after his first ulmintin treatment, but that plan altered not only as a result of Roland's time with Larry, but also when Roland felt something. Yes, Roland Rolls actually *felt* something when Joseph was, as the saying goes, under his roof. Maybe it was God. Maybe it was a Holy direction. Maybe it was the faith of a single man, or the faith of both of these men so near to him for the first time. Rather than watch behind glass or through the lenses of cameras, he wanted to be close. How primal he felt. How exciting this was. And here, now, to touch the absolute perfect copy of what could be God's body was *amazing*.

Joe somehow knew who this man was for a split second, then his knowledge blurred with the medicine he was trying to fight. "You cannot have me. Not like this. Not ever."

The scientist calculated six possible responses in three seconds after hearing this soap opera gibberish from the clone. He decided to proceed with his top choice. "But I do have you. I have you exactly where I want you."

"Not quite. I see you want more."

In being challenged for the second time in such a short period, Roland's tiny pupils moved a sixteenth of an inch. This was a reflex he'd always been able to control, until now. "My dear boy, even drugged you are perceptive—or gifted."

"You will not get what you want."

Even the well-paid gatekeepers who watched him pass occasionally knew the man in the backseat of those expensive cars never, ever played. Interestingly, however, Roland wanted to play into this. *Yes*, Roland thought, *maybe my being here now is Holy direction.* He moved his hand three inches back toward Joseph's middle.

Joe set his head back down and repeated what he just said. "You will not get what you want."

Roland's decision making capabilities suddenly blinked. They came back for an instant and then disappeared again, as if he had been abruptly unplugged somewhere. He knew that adding this new sensory component of touch jammed his abilities to gain and process new and needed information. His thoughts began to reboot in an unlikely place, his stomach. He noticed the whirling sensation in his midsection.

Nothing like this has every happened before. He swallowed. He was certain he tasted metal. *What is this?*

His answer came from a place within he'd never accessed. He realized he felt his own sinfulness because of where his fingers rested. Suddenly, his hand jumped from the clone's body. Weak and foolish— two emotions too new to him—he asked in a voice he'd never heard himself use, "What do I want, Joseph?"

Joe simply muddied his already dark eyes. His anger drained from him as his concentration increased. He swallowed some of the dryness out of his mouth and met the gaze of Silver Man with an expression of pity. "Me. You want me. You want my body, my soul. You can touch the first, obviously, but you cannot have what you really want, and what you really want is the me that's inside. Your machines? Your calculations? They are not enough. You are not enough."

Roland's voice held a breathy quality, which, like everything else happening to him, felt brand new. "How...how do you know this? How do you know who you are?"

"Let me go."

"How do you know who you are? Tell me."

"Let me go."

"And me, how do you know who I am? Did you know I've been watching you for years and years?"

Joe's anger reheated. He has been watched. The mechanical shadow—that odd, cool feeling he has tried to ignore for years—has its origin with this man. His voice boomed louder, stronger. "Let me go!"

"I cannot do that. I will never do that. I am your father."

A new persona welled up within Joe. His voice sliced with frustration. "No, what you are is lost. You have tried to collect every piece of data except the passion of my soul. You cannot measure all of me by the devices you have. You are limited."

Unless it pertained to a social situation, Roland had never heard or considered the words "you are limited."

Joe growled. "Yes, this is weird. This is just so weird."

Roland stood speechless.

"And this bondage thing?" Joe squirmed under the straps. "Buddy, just get some help."

Proceeding in any direction would not be to Roland's advantage now, and that was just what he needed. An advantage. He would retreat.

Noticing the Silver Man backing away, Joe asked, "Where are you going to hide?"

Six feet from Joseph, Roland said from a fearful place he tried yet failed to conceal, "For someone with limited options, you have a lot to say."

"Ah, can I at least get my boxers back? It's a little drafty in here."

All this data, Roland said to himself. *Riveting.*

With that, he walked out of the lab.

———————

I touched him. I touched him inappropriately. Or almost inappropriately. No, it was inappropriate. Wrong. Sinful.

Roland had never had an internal conversation like this before. He had also never been this overloaded or confused, and, not surprisingly, he had never applied religious language to himself. Even though he felt he was racing down the long, straight corridor, he was actually moving at 3.3 miles an hour, which fell in his normal range of 3.2 and 3.5 miles an hour. To this, his Grand would say, *fascinating.*

How interesting to think of her at a time like this. A second thought quickly followed. She had died forty days after showing him those burial linens. Forty days and forty nights of rain were significant to the story of Noah and the Arc, and for forty days and forty nights, Jesus was tempted by Satan in the desert. Those were just two examples of one of the Bible's most significant numbers. He wanted to laugh at this religious foolishness.

As he rounded a corner, his staff averted their eyes. Per his longstanding instructions, no one was to make direct eye contact with him. After he turned another corner, he reconsidered one of his choices. The subject didn't need to be nude. The clone could have easily been in a hospital gown for the successful implementation of the first ulmintin injection. Anyone would know that, even Larry.

So, he asked, *why naked? And why did I touch him? And why did I touch him there?*

Suddenly he stopped and Roland Rolls never stopped. The wryest smirk played over his lips. He just asked himself questions and, for the first time in at least a decade, he didn't know the answers.

CHAPTER EIGHT

Mike stood in the parking space vacated by ProMac's sporty little car. The paper was done but he wasn't. It seemed as if he was just beginning. With his face set and his arms crossed, he considered something Joe had mentioned only last night. Maybe this college wasn't the right fit for him. Maybe he needed a fresh start in a different place. In a different university. With a different theology.

He stared at the two-lane road on the far side of the parking lot that, when taken east, would put him on the interstate within a few miles. Maybe he should go. Maybe he should travel to Chicago, or even California. As Mike weighed out what the West Coast could mean, he realized his jaw had remained locked since he left his class ten minutes ago. That paper. That professor. He began to heat up with an anger he should not hold onto. Unlike Joe, he was the student who didn't argue. The teacher was right. Rules were rules, and this was always clear: expectations were to be met, not challenged.

Mike appreciated being guided by the professors here. He didn't always align with them, but he was unlike Joe in that he simply took what the scholars offered without question or debate. Later, it was his choice if he held onto the methodology of a professor, or let it go. He would forget this professor because he took Mike in one direction and then another. He did this not to see if Mike was malleable, but compliant. It was a power game between a tiny prof and a big student.

No other student in the class had a similar experience, and here in this open space Mike realized this man wanted to beat him up internally so that, once down, Mike would follow the rules not only in the class, but also within the brand of religion this controller represented.

Again Mike stared at that road leading away from campus. His own compliance had been used against him. Back in that classroom, he wasn't allowed to question or expand, only absorb and repeat.

He thought of his best friend and tried to picture what she was doing now. Looking within himself, he missed what she had: spunk, grit, and determination. Like Joe, Betsy had passion. On the high school debate team, no one would mess with their captain. It took a great deal of knowledge and skill to chisel away a point she had made.

As he watched a green leaf skip in front of a few nearby cars, he wondered if he'd ever have that layer of invincibility. He knew the answer. Unlike the leaf, he couldn't be that free, that flexible.

He buried his hands in his front pockets. He wouldn't go. He couldn't leave. The Bible College was the only school he had applied to as a high school senior. There were no other options.

He turned back to the school. After having had enough turmoil for what he hoped was a good, long while—he was *not* a drama guy—Mike faced the college. Joe waited there, somewhere.

Passing the school library on his way back to the dorm, he thought the single leaf in the parking lot was like his roommate. The two found the breeze, slid over hard surfaces, and flew in the freedom of God.

⸻

He tried not worry when he saw their room empty. It was not that the two left notes for each other, but they usually had a general sense of where the other was. Mike knew Joe loved his books, and Joe's reading load was heavy this summer. Mike also knew that Joe had made it off to class just fine. In fact, Joe had left a few minutes early. So, Mike reasoned that maybe he was under one of his twenty-pound books in a quiet spot, was having fun with a new friend, or was likely kicking back a bit. After all, the joy of summer often asked for Joe's attention.

Mike opened their window. Even though the afternoon sun cooked the building's bricks, the breeze he felt in Outer Mongolia followed him here. Straddling his desk chair before sitting down squarely, Mike opened a new chapter from a book on his desk. Several pages into it, he stopped and studied his roommate's empty chair. He found himself smiling as he remembered their second day of freshmen orientation, which was the day they met. The theme that day was "fun and games at the beach."

A letter went out before school started inviting all incoming freshmen to bring beach clothes for the special afternoon which would begin with a Hawaiian luau in the center courtyard. Using most of the upscale set from the nearby high school theater company's production of *South Pacific,* the college went all out for this. Sprawling ocean banners, two dozen fake palm trees and king-sized tan sheets that, when draped over the patio, did look like sand made the whole scene complete. The games started after lunch, including one called Surf Board.

"God must be good," one of the upperclassman orientation board staffers said as she stood in front of a theater flat with a crashing ocean wave, "because here in the state of Indiana, which is *just* a little less than a billion miles from either the Atlantic or the Pacific Ocean, we have a real, authentic, genuine surfboard."

One guy off to the side clapped and cheered at her words. His clothes alone told the story of who he was. A thin, well-worn tee shirt with cutoff sleeves sported a faded Vacation Bible School slogan Mike couldn't make out in the distance. A straw-colored, rope-like belt kept up his shorts that were frayed along the bottom hem. His medium-brown hair was long then; it fell to the base of his neck and scruff lined his strong, sharp chin. His clunky, open sandals somehow stayed on his feet.

"From the sounds of it," the upperclassman said as she eyed Joe, "we have our first contestant."

Those near Joe pushed him on up to the front.

"And you are—"

"Joe."

"Did you know you were a surfer?"

Thinking of his DOD and Jolie one summer on Lake Ontario, Joe grinned. "I do now."

Mattresses surrounded the board. Joe didn't quite wait for directions before he climbed on the board that wobbled from the start. He would be the first contestant of five who was to dance on the board to a *Beach Boys* song.

He kicked off his sandals as it was explained to him that he'd be judged in four categories: style, playfulness, ability, and what was called "ultimate surf factor." The judges were three faculty members and Joe completely *rocked it*. One guy his size could have been competition. One girl showed a lot of personality, but, unlike Joe, all four fell off the board.

"Encore," Mike said. That was the first word he said to his soon-to-be friend when Joe was named champion.

Joe laughed from the crowd. "No."

Mike's word caught on though, and the chanting crowd brought Joe back. "I'll only dance again," he said from the board, "if you all do it with me from where you are." He pointed to the faculty judges. "You too." Joe offered so much light and fun, even then.

As Mike returned from the memory and stared at his roommate's empty desk chair, he wondered if Joe ever hopped onto that seat and danced up there like a crazy man. He wouldn't doubt it.

Through the window, he heard the sound of the chapel bells floating into their room. They informed him it was 4 PM. The rich, familiar bell tones made it clear what he had decided earlier. He did not need to hit the road by the Outer Mongolia parking lot, turn west, and slide out of here toward California's beaches. This was only a day of growing pains. God worked here. He'd find the right professors and work harder on his next paper. He stared at the book on Joe's desk, then to Joe's open closet door. He breathed in deeply. The road west was for another guy at another time.

Without quite knowing how he did it, Mike found himself flat on his bed, some four feet from his desk. Maybe he'd just shut his eyes for a few minutes before Joe showed up for dinner. The two had talked earlier today about grabbing food together. He'd be ready to go when surfin' Joe returned.

———————

The sound of distant thunder jarred Mike awake. Immediately he searched for and found his alarm clock which read 8:04 PM. Had he slept this long? Impossible! He scratched the side of his head.

Joe? He sat up quickly.

Yes, it was just after eight. The curtains rising and twisting warned that a summer storm was on its way. Mike scanned the room. It was exactly how it had been when he fell asleep. Joe had not returned.

Something was wrong.

His phone rang. It had to be Joe calling. Surprisingly, Betsy's voice came through clearly. She distracted him for a few minutes with a story about a friend of theirs from home who had met her for dinner. Mike listened well but, after closing the window, kept his eyes on his watch or the alarm clock. As his best friend was saying goodnight, Mike grabbed his shoes and headed for the first place he should look, the infirmary.

At the main door to the dorm, the big-shouldered boy bumped into an upperclassman he recognized from a class last spring. Just after they passed, Mike turned and blurted, "You, you haven't seen Joe around lately, have you?"

He answered, "No, I haven't."

Mike suddenly remembered the guy's name. It was Holden. Just before the door clicked closed between them, Holden added quietly, "Precious, I hope you find your boyfriend soon."

Mike's heart rushed to the top of his throat at what he just heard. He made it nine steps onto the terrace outside. Without air, he found he could not move. Rain began its assault. Angry drops bit into his skin. After Mike had made his way to the campuses' small medical center where Joe had not been, he started walking without knowing where to go. The rain was a deluge. No one was outdoors.

Fifteen minutes later, he did stop. He found himself in the dead center of the road that could take him west on the interstate, so far from here. Two headlights from a car heading out of town announced themselves in the distance.

He said, "I don't hear the chapel bells now, God."

Sopping wet, he started to cry. The dam walls just burst. It was not what Holden could say or even do. The prestigious senior could talk. What made Mike break open was this truth: he hated who he was. He hated that he was all these pieces, the quietest being his sexuality which just didn't fit where he was, or what he really wanted. He hated that he could only be what people saw, but he had no real idea of who he was or what he could be.

From a wrenching place where the very bones around his heart could shatter, he snarled into heaven. "Oh, and God? I don't hear you, either."

CHAPTER NINE

Exactly four hours and three minutes have passed since his first meeting with the clone. As a heavy rain continued to fall outside, Roland Rolls constructed a new plan based on the information he had gleaned from his experience with Larry in the car. Perhaps his dimwitted former employee could do more for this experiment than substantiate to the clone that he had been taken from the lab at eighteen-months of age. The likelihood of this outspoken public school teacher adding any new information to the experiment remained at one percent, but another interview may be worth Roland's precious time.

The one behind all of this set his wrists on the arms of the finely crafted upholstered Egyptian chair. Here, in a quiet, nearly non-descript room, he asked the subject in front of him, "How do you know when you've sinned?"

Dunk knew the only reason Roland would ask that question was because he had been with Joe recently. He nodded. "You've met him."

Having calculated this response, Roland refused to deviate from his new, memorized script. "How do you know you've sinned?"

Dunk still felt groggy from the drug that put him out in the car. "You just know, Mr. Rolls. It's something that wells up inside. It festers. It needs to be released, removed."

"Sin is a thought or action away from God."

"Yes."

Roland looked off into the distance, a move he had planned.

Dunk fidgeted with the straps that kept his arms locked. The soft, restricting bands of fabric did not bother him, but he moved enough to indicate that they did. "I know that look you have, Mr. Rolls. It is your invitation for me to say more. I also know it is something you've planned."

"You want me to stop calculating."

"Yes."

"I can't."

"You can."

Both men fell silent.

Three seconds passed. Four. Five. Six.

"You want me to tell you what it's like to be with him," Dunk said. "You want me to tell you what it's like when I hug him." He slowed this down. "You want me to tell you what it's like for me when I touch him."

Roland moved right to the end of his internal option cards. "Yes."

"He brought something out in you, didn't he?"

"You are not to play psychologist, Larry."

"He did."

Three more seconds ticked by.

Dunk continued in the warm way he met everyone. "Joe did bring something out in you. Something real. Something human. And with your illness, you don't know how to process this." Dunk barely shook his head. "Excuse me, that isn't completely correct, Mr. Rolls. You have processed this, you just haven't done it successfully."

"My illness."

"Would you like me to address your issues using different terminology?"

This response from Larry was one of Roland's predictions. Interesting. Larry had a three percent chance of saying this.

Dunk made sure to keep eye contact with the one sitting directly across from him. "I assume you've met with the best psychologists—and maybe even psychiatrists—through the years. The brightest educations accrued. The clearest, most accurate diagnoses of your social ineptitude, and, while I'm sure she meant well—I'm sure of it—your Grand must have really messed you up."

No employee knew much about his grandmother—or even himself, for that matter. He was puzzled, which was an incredibly rare event in and of itself. How could this Neanderthal possibly know how he addressed his grandmother? Roland realized Larry was reaching for something he could not grasp. He lied. "You do not interest me, Larry."

During his time alone here, Dunk had given thought to what he was going to say. "Yet you interest me. I don't think I would have said that before, honestly. But now that we're together again, I have to say what is true. What you do—and how you do it—has my curiosity."

"Why don't you do your amateur therapy session at another time with another person?"

Suddenly thoughts—words—filtered through. Dunk followed them out loud. "Mr. Rolls, I sense you think you are better than everybody else. Okay, *that* may be obvious. But maybe this isn't: perhaps you inherited this elitist quality from your grandmother. As a gifted scientist you surpass her intellectually, of course, but probably you both hated and respected this elevation."

While he may have held a mild interest a moment ago, Roland had become truly bored. This forty-one-year-old boy was an amateur at best. "Stop."

Dunk could not. He realized what he shared was a direct result of prayer. In a caring voice, he continued. "Excuse the pun, but she birthed something. She valued those ancient linens from a stone tomb in Jerusalem; you merely implemented them into a plan, your plan. The idea of you wanting to create a pop culture Jesus clone must appeal to your sense of superiority over ignorant people of faith. It's intellectual snobbery."

"Stop."

"But none of these doctors have actually held what you still call your clone. None of these highly professional people have been with Joe day in and day out. None of your team can help you like I can."

"You are a peasant offering meager gifts to the king."

"What an apt metaphor. But I am in a position to help you."

"I do not need your help. I simply need your information."

Dunk sat back. "You mentioned sin. You need my help."

As he has done before, Roland Rolls drew the parallel between Joe's assertiveness and Dunk's. Both demonstrated dominance by running with their assumptions. They used their feelings to control and perhaps overpower.

Dunk met Mr. Rolls squarely in the eye. "You saw God in there, didn't you?"

"What do you mean?"

"You saw God in Joe. You experienced the divine in some way. And you, who can barely touch the seat you are in without noting at least five characteristics about it, felt him. You touched his skin. You felt his warmth. You are not all scientist, Roland. You are human, too."

"What makes you think you know this?"

"You are different now. Sure, all of your airs and defenses are intact. You held a spark of interest in me and now you don't. As expected, your pristine, analytical mind is functioning within what I imagine you call your normal perimeters, but there's a new crack. And no, Roland, to answer your next question, I don't see this crack, this bump, or this fester. I feel it."

"Calling me Roland does not bring you closer to me."

"What did you do?" Dunk paused. He pictured what might have happened and then almost laughed. "Oh my, you almost groped him!"

Roland set his hand at his temple. "Grope?"

"It's colloquial."

Roland had no response. Dunk, however, did. Looking down to the carpet he could never afford, he stashed a smirk. By no means was this funny; *this was not funny;* but he knew Roland, at least in part. His former boss was a pure scientist, not a sexual predator.

Remaining distant which was a defense he was certain would maintain his maximum proficiency, Roland reconsidered what he had already analyzed: Larry has been the only unpredictable person he has encountered in eleven years. Larry was also the only religious person he has experienced firsthand, save for the clone's birth mother, who had some sort of moral or religious guidepost until it came to money, then she could be manipulated.

"And grabbing Jesus like that? Um, yes, that would be sin."

"Have you?"

"Grabbed him there?" Now Dunk openly laughed. "I'm his father, Roland." His face suddenly blanked. "Wait, you probably want to reserve that father language for yourself and 'the clone.'"

Roland did not respond.

"You've called him your son, haven't you?"

"You are guessing."

"You can't process whether I'm guessing or not. You can speculate, yes, but the processing will take time."

"You're not displaying care for Joseph now, Larry."

Dunk wished he could move more. "No—surprise!—I'm presenting care for you, Roland."

"Aiding me will not release Joseph. Your strategy is flawed."

"Aiding you will help you, Roland. That is why, ultimately, you began this project. You need help. You need answers. You need connections."

As with Joe earlier, Roland needed to retreat, this time out of boredom. He planned this exam would take exactly twelve minutes. Without a need to check his watch, he knew that when he finished this thought, this interview would be at eleven minutes, forty-three seconds. While he didn't have all the information he wanted now, he would again gain leverage and control by retreating. Without provocation, he surprised himself by going off script. "As we are both painfully aware, this conversation is now futile."

"This conversation is the byproduct of what you created. This is all about you, once godless, and now experiencing God for the first time. Are you surprised to discover that your sin is what connects you to the rest of us, Roland?"

"Roland Rolls is never surprised."

"The real Father is controlling all of this, even you."

Roland rose to his feet. "That is enough."

Dunk shook his head. "No, this is only the beginning."

Roland turned to leave.

"So," Dunk bit into his words, "you don't know if you cloned the divine components of God. Yes, 1 Peter 3:18a says *Christ suffered for our sins once for all time. He never sinned, but he died for sinners to bring you safely home to God.* This all said, it's probable that you did indeed clone Jesus from the burial shrouds—not some poor soul who was buried in a stone tomb anonymously. But did you actually get the divine element?"

Roland did not speak.

"That's not the real question, however. That's not why God has let you do this. This—" Dunk glanced around him to indicate the scientist's whole world—"this may be the way to bring you safely home to God, Roland." If there had been an actual wall between the two of them, it was much thinner now. Dunk tilted his head. "A sinless Jesus, a sinful Joe, and you." He waited a moment, and frowned. "What? I'm overtime, aren't I?"

"This is more than enough, Larry."

Dunk jumped right back in. "But that's the question here, isn't it? If you've watched Joe as closely as you claim you have, you see the human component so clearly. And in and of itself, that remains incredible. Like any newborn, he came into this world like Christ did, and that's sinless. But Joe inherited sin from Adam and Eve. He stepped into the fallen world created by the first couple." Dunk paused just enough, and added, "I supposed Adam, Eve, and the Garden of Eden is only a myth to you."

"Stop."

Dunk couldn't. "You probably stood under the stars the night of the birth, didn't you? You gazed into the night sky to see if there was anything even remotely close to a bright star. Forty days later you went to a temple, as was the Jewish custom and the time of Jesus' birth, and I imagine there was no modern day Simeon or Anna who experienced a Son of God in the baby they held."

"Your words are a waste."

"Here's a thought for you. God is in all of us, Roland. And God manifested God's self in Simeon and Anna, those two devout souls who knew what you've yet to discover, or, more actually, uncover."

Roland suddenly listened.

"Here it is, Mr. Rolls. Each of us can experience divinity."

"Stop."

"Each of us is made in His image."

"Stop."

"Joe may or may not be Jesus cloned, but, like all of us, he has a part of God within him."

Quietly, Roland shut the door behind him. He would delete all the remarks this theological imbecile spilled haphazardly. Larry was wrong. Worse, the fool had extended the interview time. Wrecking the schedule, the clod had subsequently wasted time that at this point he could not lose.

Roland could erase these idiotic remarks from his mind, of course he could.

CHAPTER TEN

Joe's first smile in this overly hygienic place came when he thought of one person, Ms. Viola Munson. The super senior served as one of the deacons with his DOD and Pastor Smith. His smile brightened. Of all people to wander into Joe's mind in this pristine yet strange place, it was Viola.

Joe had heard rumors that Viola was in her mid-nineties, but how could that be true? She couldn't be a day past eighty, if that. Joe suspected she had just jumped to her age one day after playing a round of hopscotch with the kids on the playground at church. While she might be off-putting to some, and Joe had seen she could be a gossip machine with petty motives every now and then, Joe also saw the best in this woman. She often came across as ceremonial and self-righteous, but after just minutes with her, Joe knew Viola never pulled any polite, phony business with her Heavenly Father. She didn't just come to Him when she was all smooth and polished because she wanted something. No, as a sinner with a sharp, critical nature, she knew she needed a Savior, not now and then, but always. Her son's longstanding illness and eventual death, her failed business, and her outspokenness which usually bit more than brightened someone's day, made it obvious to her that she needed her Jesus.

Candid as only she could be, she uncharacteristically shared her faith one evening last summer while she sat with Joe who, though just a wayward teen, reminded her of Jesus somehow. The two sat side by side before their pie selling church booth closed on the last night of the annual street carnival. The frank and controlling way about her had softened in the late afternoon heat enabling Joe to see her—and bring out in her—the child of God she was, one that was daring, fun, and bold. The two laughed because it was clear to her that God did have a sense of humor.

Just three pies remained on the vinyl tablecloth covered counter. Viola, who had lost her prim and proper ways to the humidity earlier that day, began to tell the story about a decision she had made about twenty years ago. For her business, The Pretty Pampered Pooch Boutique, she opted to get a very high tech hose for the tub she used to bathe the dogs.

As she had expected, Joe was an easy, engaging audience. He questioned her. "A high tech hose? Is there such a thing?"

"According to its directions, this hose could do almost anything, including deep muscle massage."

Before Joe could question this feature, she set her hand on her knee. "Don't ask."

Joe tilted his chin and frowned.

"Don't."

Viola moved on quickly. "It included inner magnets that worked against each other to keep it from ever tangling, but that wasn't the best feature. The hose also had the ability to stay in place where it was left. An arsenal of buttons made the magic happen, until a telephone company truck parked outside the Boutique. Somehow the truck's electronic equipment jammed the new gizmo's circuitry. All at once, the seemingly harmless hose became a very angry six-foot rattlesnake with one clear, obvious goal: to get me very, very wet."

Joe laughed.

"Snowball, the white standard poodle I had been working on, wisely jumped for his life and left me, a practically defenseless damsel in distress, to fend for myself."

"Damsel?"

"Damsel."

"Distress?"

"Oh, very much so."

Though Viola's sales pitch was flawless, a couple passed by the pies without a sale, and Viola continued. "Only after becoming sopping wet did I think to turn off the water at its source. And when Snowball's owner came for her dog, she took one look at my tightly-curled hair where there had been perfect waves and said, 'Now Snowy's cute and all, and so are you, but let's just say no right now to you two being identical twins.'"

Joe studied her hair. Even in the evening's humidity, there was no sign the perfectly wavy mound would ever spring free with tight, power-charged curls.

Not to disappoint her approving audience, even if her audience was a well-intentioned yet cultureless male who didn't know how to bring frizz to fabulous, Viola patted the back of her head. "A moment after Snowy and her owner left the Boutique, a man walked in who could never decide on the look for Russell, his red labradoodle. He took in the mop over my ears and said, "Yep, that look.""

Joe laughed again, looked to his right, quickly hopped out of his seat and leaned over the counter. "Yes, it's that red labradoodle coming this way! Quick! Let's get a pitcher of water!"

Joe could almost feel where she pinched him—hard! All these months later, here in this darkened room, he remembered that pain. Viola. Viola Munson.

He remembered a time when, as a sixth grader, he had tagged along with his DOD. Their pastor had asked the newest deacon if he wouldn't mind returning Viola's large plant stand that the church had borrowed to hold poinsettias that Advent. His DOD was noticeably nervous on the ride.

'I got this," Joe said from the front passenger's seat as they passed a father and son taking down Christmas lights from a front porch.

"You know who she is, right?"

"She's the queen."

"Joe."

"She is." They stopped at one of the few traffic lights in town. When the car started moving again, Joe added, "I think the word is elitism."

"How old are you?"

"It's not how old I am. It's how smart I am."

"And humble."

"That too."

Keeping his hands on the steering wheel, Dunk avoided his son's smirk. "Joe, it's just…"

"It's just that Viola has her 'Violaisms.' All of her airs are defense mechanisms, DOD. She plays the snob well—"

"Joseph!"

"Let me finish. She plays the snob well, DOD. But that Queen has met Jesus and she knows she needs him."

Here in the quiet room, Joe thought back on the father and son taking down their Christmas lights. More images followed. He had a vision of a red-haired woman in her late thirties standing in their church parking lot. Joe picked up random details, like dark-tinted car windows, lipstick on a napkin, and a whistle. This woman was not entirely comfortable with the evening. Something about an alien arm startled her.

A machine clicked on and hummed behind him. Something odd began to happen. A medicine of some kind was taking him beyond the church ramp and the alien arm. He was falling further into sleep, deep sleep.

———•———

He felt Betsy beside him, warm and curled on her side. She was sleeping. Joe remained still and then imagined being able to slide closer to her and kiss her forehead. He kissed her a second time, and then a third. His lips were tender, gentle, and slow. Kissing her was a gift to do, and he made the moment matter between them. Through this, she remained asleep. Her milky eyelids told him so. To bring Joe comfort, all he needed to know was that she was comfortable and secure. And that he could be near her, of course. He kissed her again and again.

"What?" Betsy said when she finally looked at him.

Joe frowned. "What what?"

This moment, this very conversation, couldn't really be happening right now—it actually wasn't happening right now. It must be something to do with the machine behind him, but this did not stop Joe. She was here, at least in his heart.

She looked at him matter-of-factly. "Joe."

He slowly shook his chin. Playing innocent, he frowned.

"You just woke me up!"

Joe shrugged one shoulder. "I was just hanging out over here minding my own business."

"You kissed my forehead. A lot."

"Wasn't me."

"Joe."

"Alright, truth. It was me."

She looked around. "Where are we?"

His voice was deep, warm, and soft. "I don't know."

She opened her mouth and seemed to taste the air around them. It wasn't unpleasant. She considered her next words before she shared them. "Doesn't it sort of bother you that you don't know where we are?"

He wouldn't tell her of the machine, or of the Silver Man and this place. The stories of Snowball, Russell, and the final three pies that eventually sold would wait for the long ride home where it would just be the two of them in Joe's car. Joe's warm hand rested over Betsy's forearm. "We are together. That's all that matters."

Betsy frowned. "That sounds like a line from some cheesy movie."

Still keeping his eyes on her, Joe moved to his side. "We are together. That is all that matters."

"You brought me here."

"Somehow. Yes. Or we just found each other." She turned to face him. "Should I go back?"

"No."

"Should I be worried?"

"No."

Betsy's eyes slid down to Joe's chest and then slowly returned to his face. She tried to get a sense of where they were. "This isn't your dorm room, is it?"

Joe looked around. There was not much to see. "No, this isn't."

"We aren't dating, are we?"

"No, we don't even know each other really."

She sat up. "It's true. We don't know each other. But this doesn't feel weird, does it?"

"Not to me."

"Not to me, either." She closed her eyes as she curled up beside him again. "Will we remember this, Joe?"

Joe's fingers actually clutched a wad of the sheet at his side. He found himself on his back, exactly where he'd been for the last three hours. The second ulmintin injection slid up and down his arm, running warm and fast through his veins. He might forget everything about super hoses, wet hair, darkened car windows and alien arms, but said out loud to no one, "We'll remember this."

CHAPTER ELEVEN

With his old straw hat on his head, Earl fired up his push mower. He loved the feeling of having his shoulder taut and then free after he released the chord to his little red Toro. Happy for any reason to be outside, the go-getter sought exercise however he could get it. He started to the right of Dunk's narrow sidewalk just like he has done a thousand times with his own lawn. There were exactly ten passes between Dunk's concrete walk and gravel driveway, the same as his front yard. Even while mowing, which typically put his mind at ease, he couldn't ignore the fact that four days had passed since he'd seen his neighbor. Of course, he didn't expect a goodbye of any sort. He imagined Dunk might have to leave in a hurry. Still, he wished he knew something, anything.

Finishing the first section of Dunk's front lawn, Earl recalled recent posters made by the Sunday school children near the church's wide entrance. Clearly each read, "Worry or pray, don't do both." Despite what he knew he should do, he worried. He figured it was the father in him, and that it must be the Father nature in God to ache when His children chose not to be under His care. Both Dunk and Pastor Smith would call this an epiphany, even though Earl still wasn't sure what that five dollar word meant. Whenever it was mentioned in worship or in the Bible studies, he'd rather stay right on track, moving from Point A to Point B. He'd allow for a few sidetracks or illuminations, but simple and direct worked best for him.

With his eyes open and his mower humming along, he gave his

worried thoughts to God in prayer. For the first time in his life however, the prayer did not end with the single word "amen." Sure, the formal part closed up, but the prayer continued to weave through his thoughts. Before today he would have said that he was completely wasting God's time with this rambling; after all, the Creator of the cosmos probably could stand far less jabber all around, especially from a guy who never did get too fancy. Now though, Earl wasn't so sure. Before today, he had considered himself to be just one small factory worker, whereas God was the mega boss of an infinity of businesses. In the heartache of missing a neighbor who was like a son, Earl came to understand that God did hear every word from an old guy pushing a little red mower. It was a Father/Son thing. God cared that much, and listened that closely.

As Dunk was like a son to him, Joey was a grandson. When Earl considered that boy, his heart literally locked up. As Earl swung around his neighbor's mailbox, he didn't know what to pray when it came to the college kid. Then he remembered what the Apostle Paul said in Romans 8. He knew Paul had said that the Holy Spirit pleads on our behalf when we ourselves have no words. Not one for recalling scripture, Earl suddenly remembered Romans 8:26. *In the same way, the Spirit helps us in our weakness. We do not know what we ought to pray for, but the Spirit himself intercedes for us with groans that words cannot express.*

Dunk, of course, would love all of this. The church's head deacon would just flip with Earl's ebb and flow prayer. Add the Apostle Paul's verse squeaking in there, and Dunk would think of asking Earl to lead a Bible study. That was Dunk though, a guy so deeply missed; and this was Earl, a man never frivolous about anything.

The word frivolous caught in his throat. His own dad had spent money freely, especially when it was loaned to him. He believed in a way of life where, if you were smart enough, you didn't have to work. That philosophy broke up Earl's childhood home, and even though Earl tried to locate his two much older brothers over the years, he has never had luck finding them. Thinking of his lost brothers always brought him down, so he did what he did best: work harder than anyone he knew.

Finishing up the front yard, Earl tried to imagine a way he could cancel the subscription to the newspapers he'd fetch off Dunk's front lawn very early each morning. As he moved toward the back yard, Earl knew twelve-year-old paperboy Bobby Elliott belonged to Brenda and Kyle down at 311 Hemlock. He also knew that if he said too much to Brenda then the whole neighborhood—heck, the whole town—would hear about it.

"It's best to just lay low," he told himself as he wrestled around an overgrown lilac off the side of the house, a bush he'd level with his chainsaw in fifteen minutes if the monster was in his yard. After brushing lilac leaves off his sleeve that he'll mulch with the mower on the next pass, his mind returned to those newspapers, and then to Dunk's refrigerator. Had he left milk in there? Any leftovers that would spoil? Was the house itself set for Dunk to be away for an extended period of time? What about the mortgage? Earl was pretty sure it couldn't be paid off yet, not on a teacher's salary. He could cover a few months, but his own funding had taken a recent hit.

As he mowed away, the senior caught a clear view of the kitchen window and thought of the many times he'd been in that kitchen, opened that refrigerator and, when asked, pulled out two cold ones for Dunk and himself. The two would head out to the simple back deck and sit down with their feet in the grass. Without much family of his own, Dunk would sometimes need a sounding board. Having two daughters, Earl had both a good ear and good advice—even though his girls usually fell under his late wife's domain. Growing up, both kids were into what was then considered girly things—art, dance, crafts— and Earl, always close by, learned long ago that he would just have to sit back and watch, otherwise he'd mess something else up or say something that would make one of his girls roll her eyes.

Oh, Earl loved his girls. Neither lived too far away—one an hour north, and the other two-and-a-half hours west. He knew both women, now young moms, had lovingly filled in some of the gaps when their mother died. With neither fuss nor complaint, they stepped up when Janet first got sick. As his wife's health slowly worsened, he never asked them to do anything. During the last year of Janet's life, he could cook a four-course meal that involved basting or broiling, sew loose buttons or hem his pants, which he always bought too long. He could even hold meaningful conversations with the two about competitive ice dancing on the international level. When he tried to shoo them away so they could get on with their own busy lives, the girls were always nearby. His kids were two gifts that, in sure ways, kept some of Janet right here with him.

Earl mowed over an area where Joey's swingset once was. There were two identical swings on the set, and Earl knew Joey used them as his office. He'd idly swing just a bit, never taking his feet off the ground while his friend for the day talked through the problems he or she had, usually in great detail. Still shaking his head, Earl could not understand how a boy his age could be so mature. Sometimes it was like Joey could see right through you, that he knew you better than you knew yourself.

Once, while Dunk had to spend two days at a statewide science training for high school chemistry teachers, Joey bunked with Earl. The boy was in second grade at the time. Janet had been gone for about ten months and there, with spaghetti on his dinner plate, little Joey asked, "You talk to her in heaven, don't you, Earl?"

You could never circumvent little Joey. It was always best to be straight and honest, or he'd call you on it.

"Why, yes, Joey, I do."

The eight-year-old twirled spaghetti on his fork and said, "If you could hear her talk back to you, she'd say she loves you. And that spaghetti is nice for a little kid, but next time you might want to cut it up some before you pass it to him. Oh, and make sure it's not too hot."

Earl ripped off a chunk of fresh Italian bread from the white paper bag between them. He couldn't believe what he was hearing. That was Janet, alright, always good with specific directions. He knew his wife would want the Italian bread served in a wicker basket with a cloth napkin underneath. He could tell that Joey also knew this, but didn't say anything. Instead, he looked Earl in the eye. "And she has that song for you there."

"I'm sorry? What did you say?"

"That song."

Earl, whose throat had almost closed, tried to downplay this. "What song?"

"The one they played at your wedding. Your wedding dance song."

Neither Joey nor Dunk knew anything about Earl and Janet's wedding. Even the girls, who at the time were sixteen and eighteen, didn't know about the song because, as Janet would say to her husband, "That memory is between the two of us, dear."

Earl set down his fork and stared at his overnight house guest.

"You know the song, Earl. It's the one that goes fast with the words sha-na-na, lollipop, sha-na-na."

"How, buster? How do you know this song?"

After not so neatly scooping some spaghetti into his mouth, he said, "I've heard Janet sing it to you. It's a song from Eddie Shafaun and the Satellites."

It was like this with his Golden Retriever who died in the back yard, only to be 'revived' by this little boy. There was no making sense of this one either.

After they finished their meal and Earl cleared the table alone, he stood at the kitchen sink with the dishes. In the quiet, he guessed that Janet must have sung their silly wedding song to Joey when just the two of them were alone together.

But how could that be?

Janet was awfully sick when Dunk and Joey moved in, and, at that time, she didn't have much—if any—of a voice for singing. And the only record they had had of that song had long, long been worn out.

"That kid," Earl said as he finished Dunk's lawn. "That crazy little kid."

⚬————————⚬

He figured it was a camera, one of those little high-tech ones. And it had a transmitter. Earl faithfully worked for forty-seven-and-a-half years at Deft Manufacturing, where, among other gadgets, the little company produced camera parts until they were outsourced by a company in Japan.

"Yes," he said to himself as he lifted his specialized magnifying glass from the pencil-sized two-inch object he spotted in a tree over Dunk's roof as he was walking his mower home about two hours ago. "It's a camera." He turned it over and over and knew from all his years at Deft that this little gadget cost a boat load of money.

He walked into his bathroom. Here he had a good view into Dunk's backyard. He swallowed when he realized from all his experiences at work that that single little recording device cost upwards of a million dollars. While he still held great questions, he knew one thing was definitely clear: none of this was adding up in a good way.

CHAPTER TWELVE

"So," Dunk said, his hands bound behind him in soft yet secure straps, "it's a catch and release."

Roland hesitated. Dunk's phrasing appeared awkward to him. "Yes."

"You're going to let him go."

"I'm going to let you both go."

Side by side, they'd been walking along a long, glass corridor. Towering ficus trees guarded the way every thirty-six feet. It seemed as though this was a very private area, but Dunk knew this was not true. Knowing Roland, he guessed at least three unseen guards had them in sight at all times. "What day is this on the ulmintin treatments?"

"Day six."

"And you'll let me see him, when?"

"Tomorrow."

"Why then?"

"You will need to substantiate what I'm going to tell him. It will be quite a shock when he finds out who he is, and where he came from exactly." Roland delivered the next words carefully. "You will also need to support him."

"So," Dunk turned so that they stood face-to-face. "You are going to let me go, too."

"This experiment, especially this phase of it, cannot stay in a Petri dish."

"Experiment."

"You are reticent to see the larger picture here, Larry. I cannot successfully contain the Son of God, if indeed that is who the clone is. Keeping the clone would be an error. The results of the testing would be skewed. No, the clone has to see the world; he has to live in it."

"Just as the original was designed."

The scientist tried not to literally calculate the distance of every step he was taking. "Now you're beginning to understand. If God is to intervene, then it should be in a place far more 'every day' then this complex."

Dunk considered what he had just heard.

Roland stepped into the quiet between them and decided to experiment with the man so far beneath him. "You had a line there, Larry."

"I did?"

"You were supposed to say, 'Wait, I thought you were God. Oh, I'm sorry, Mr. Rolls. You just play God with all your cameras and controlled experiments and buying people to manipulate Joe.'"

Dunk was actually confused. "I had a line? There's a script?"

Roland looked into the distance. "Your sweet, tender dad bit is predictable, and I dare say boring."

Dunk remained warm. "And your relationship with God—distant as it is—is also somewhat predictable, Roland."

"That's Mr. Rolls to you."

"You said, 'if God is to intervene...' and I say this: God, Creator of the earth and stars, is intervening."

"That's a theory."

"That's a fact, Roland."

"We'll see about that."

In the distance, two French doors stood before them. Dunk stopped as they reached them. He waited for Roland to look at him. "You haven't seen him again, have you?"

Roland remained silent.

"I was right. You decided to have the next conversation with me, not Joe. What is it that you need from me in order to proceed?"

"Your understanding."

Dunk gave an honest answer. "I don't understand any of this."

"Larry, this isn't a place where we'll dissect some fictional superhero. I need you to reorient any thinking you have that this is some evil lair and we're dealing with Spider-man, the Green Lantern, or Superman."

Reorient any thinking? Who talks like this? Dunk stayed with the conversation. "But Joe is a superman, of sorts."

"Don't complicate matters. There is a focus here, a purpose. Have I, in fact, cloned Jesus of Nazareth? If so, is this clone fully divine like Jesus *and* fully human, or is this clone just fully human? If the clone is just fully human, then what is his nature? We will not find that out in some lab, and even I can't control all experiments."

"But you'll monitor them."

Roland did not immediately respond.

"What?" Dunk chuckled. "You're calling off your guard dogs?"

"Perhaps some of them."

"Why?"

Roland sighed. "You keep missing the point, Larry. This whole project is to understand the true disposition of this Christ Jesus, whether He's divine, human, or both. There's so much we can learn. See the good here."

"You are playing God."

"Am I playing God, or did 'God' give me the abilities to see Him in this unique, particular way?"

Dunk considered this, and was impressed. "Good point. What have you learned so far?"

Roland came closer to Larry. They stood face-to-face, which was something Roland would have never even considered doing six days ago. "What have I learned so far? That I don't know enough yet."

It began to rain. The glass roof overhead made a wonderful sound. "What, Larry, have you learned?"

"The same. I don't know enough yet."

Roland turned toward the door.

"But I'll never know enough, Mr. Rolls. Not in this life. And maybe

God's crying right now because He knows I don't need to hold any answer save this: there is a Father of love, and He sent His one and only Son so that I might know Him."

Roland didn't respond. Dunk's pious Christian speak had consumed too much of his time. As they walked through the doors the rain increased, sweeping and pelting the glass.

———————

Dunk's hands were freed as he was presented a telephone and a list of five numbers to call. One call was to Earl, the second was to Joe's roommate, Mike. The third was to his teacher friend, Jolie. The fourth was to Pastor Smith at his church who was immediately to put poor Joe on the prayer chain, and the fifth was to an administrator at the Bible College. Without much detail, Dunk was to tell everyone most of the truth: that Joe was fine, that he had been hospitalized, and would quickly make a full recovery. When finished, he looked back to Roland.

"Very good, Larry. Perhaps now you understand why you are here. You're to make this transition easier for the clone."

"If I am to call you Mr. Rolls, you are to call Joe by his name."

Roland hesitated.

"Mr. Rolls?"

"Yes, fine. That has been how I planned to address him tomorrow, by the way."

"You'll be leaving me again shortly, won't you?"

"Yes."

Dunk glanced back at the phone. Perhaps he agreed to making those calls too easily. Maybe he should have refused. "Mr. Rolls, before you go, answer this for me, please. Why did you drive by the night of my deacons' meeting? You didn't stop me there in the street as I was walking home from that church meeting. Why did you do that?"

"I wanted to scare you."

CHAPTER THIRTEEN

"I didn't buy it," Mike said as he folded his long legs into the front of Earl's twelve-year-old Buick that still looked like a brand new ride. "That wasn't Joe's DOD on the phone. I mean, it just didn't sound like him."

Earl started his car, slipped his baby into reverse and turned out of his driveway. "Listen son, I know Dunk far, far better than you. And no, that wasn't Dunk on the phone with me, either. Not completely, anyway."

Mike wasn't quite sure how he ended up in this old guy's car. He didn't really need ice cream, even though it was hot day. He had arrived at Joe's dad's house about twenty minutes ago looking for more answers than he had received on the phone. The moment he stood in front of the door to Dunk's house, a man with a severe buzz cut, who might have been a Marine in a not so distant life, poked his head out of his own house next door.

With at least one camera sighted, Earl didn't trust a conversation out in the open. Then too, he also suspected his own house might be bugged. The idea of going out for ice cream dropped into Earl's head, but it took a few minutes to sell the college kid on heading over to the Dairy Barn downtown.

Mike, who really did not fit well into Earl's car even with the seat pushed all the way back, was still worried. Pretending to be an investigative cop, Mike tried to find clues through the windshield that would explain what really happened to this father and son team. None of the following told him anything—a bent mailbox with its faded red flag pointing toward the curb like an arrow, fresh tire marks across a front lawn, a new jump rope wound around a tree.

Having met Joe's DOD twice—once the day before the summer semester began, and then again weeks later for dinner—he could not let go of the thought that Dunk would have called sooner to report on Joe. Mike kept trying to figure this out. Maybe Dunk didn't know how close the roommates were. Or maybe he didn't like Mike. Or maybe Dunk knew more about Mike than Mike wanted him to know. But still, that phone call. How strange. The old guy sensed Mike's uneasiness as they came to their first stop light. Turning onto a busier street, a car passed that reminded Mike of the one from that rainy, fateful night. The driver who stopped in the middle of the road for Mike was a young, athletic man. He wore a wedding band. His wife was in the passenger seat and two small children were silent in their car seats behind them. The driver asked first if Mike was okay, and then, not as politely, asked him to step out of the middle of the road. It was dark, yet Mike could see how handsome he was, how strong. He was confident and safety-minded. Mike's heart tightened and then knotted when he realized this stranger was living a life Mike would never have.

"Buddy," he had said. "You're still in the middle of the road."

Buddy was a nickname Betsy used for him years ago.

"You understand me, right? You're in the middle of the road."

Soaking wet, Mike was lost and scared, but more than that he was angry at himself for being himself.

"I don't have a boyfriend."

The driver, having wiped his now wet forehead, didn't hear him. "What?"

"Nothing." Mike looked down at his feet. He literally stood on both yellow lines. If he looked into the guy's eyes again, he'd feel what he shouldn't feel.

A conversation started between the young couple in the front seat. The rain was so loud that Mike couldn't hear. The two were probably debating on what to do with a crazy guy in the middle of a road on a night where you couldn't see forty feet in front of you.

"I'm a college guy here," Mike said loudly. "I'll just get back to my dorm." With that, Mike moved to safety. He had not known he was in harm's way, at least fully. A serious injury could have happened to him, but he didn't care. The car stayed still in the middle of the road until Mike was well into the school's outer parking lot.

"I don't have a boyfriend," he said to the same spot that was still empty from where ProMac's little car had been. He dropped his chin. "But I do love him."

Mike dropped his chin in the passenger's seat of Earl's car just as he did that night because pretending to be an investigative police officer turned into him feeling like he was an unwanted, unwelcomed, and unemployable spy. Standing on two yellow lines on a road where teens in souped up cars could buzz by on a dark night in the middle of a powerful deluge of rain made him one word: crazy. He looked down again. He couldn't see any more of Joe's hometown slide past him. He couldn't see anymore of Joe's world.

It was hard to breathe, but he swallowed. He did love Joe.

Was that wrong? Weird?

Earl, who was so familiar with the route to the Dairy Barn that he could, in fact, drive blindfolded, noticed Mike's expression move from sorrow to confusion. "That Joey," he said as if testing the water with a young man he was certain he would like, "I bet he's a kicker of a roommate."

Mike pulled a thread at the knee of his shorts as he remembered the surfboard contest at the Hawaiian luau. He was so fun that night, so full of light and life.

"Yeah," Earl added. "I bet he must be something at school."

Mike missed his friend so much it hurt. As he had done many times, he pictured Joe sitting beside him by that creek minutes after Betsy had marched off toward her car. Wearing an expression of peace that afternoon, Joe had been so patient and understanding. What guy would sit beside him so quietly? Who would give him the time?

Yes, Mike thought, Joe was a kicker of a roommate. He was the best. And Joe wasn't just fun at school; he made school what it was.

Stopping at their second traffic light, Earl sensed his companion was troubled and far away. He tried bringing him around again. "You two must be good friends, I imagine."

A careful driver, perhaps too careful a driver, Earl stopped fifteen feet before a stop sign at the end of the next street, and then crept up to the sign. "You did the right thing in coming here. I want more answers, too. You're one I can trust."

Mike didn't know what to make of the last comment.

Earl kept his foot on the brake even though no cross traffic was in sight. "It's your tee shirt, kid. Who wouldn't trust a guy wearing the Bible College insignia on a chest that size? A guy that could, in all likelihood, crush a small car?"

Warming to the old guy's words—what was not to like about this trusting nut who wanted to buy a stranger ice cream—he turned and looked Earl in the eye. "Well, I'm not that strong. Yet."

⊷⸺⸺⸺⸺⊶

Earl knew any college kid could eat. With the jumbo-sized burger and fries that had been set before him now gone, ice cream was ordered. The young waitress who thought Mike was really, really cute said their desserts would be out in a minute or two. More relaxed now, Mike sank back further into the booth of the family restaurant known for its sundaes. Lacing his thick fingers, he thought about what Earl had just asked him. When it came to his roommate, he was not quite sure what his companion was looking for here. "Special, Earl? What do you mean?"

Earl rolled the paper wrapper from his plastic straw into a ball. "Well, I've known your college roommate since he and his dad moved in right next door. Joey was just about four-years-old then. I asked you what I just did because, even at a young age, Joey just always struck me as, well, I don't quite know how to say this…different."

"Different?"

"Yeah." Earl paused. "Different."

Waiting for more from Mike and then not hearing anything, Earl thought maybe this conversation had not been such a good idea. The big kid who had seemed so perceptive now studied the wall behind Earl's head.

"Well," Mike answered into the quiet, "I'll say he's special, very special. He cares for kids. I mean, he *really* cares. You should see him with the ones he works with. And they respond so well. He just...I don't know...he just brings out what's special with each young person. It's like magic, or something. Or no, he's magic. He always sees something unexpected. But he's pretty intense, too. There aren't many philosophy majors out there like Joe."

"What do you mean?"

Mike shrugged. "The questions he asks. That's one thing, sure. But then, on the other side, wow, the answers he gives. He has this authority, this wisdom. Have you ever heard of someone having an old soul?"

"Young man," Earl leaned forward, "especially after a night of league bowling, there are mornings I feel like I'm about a hundred-and-ten-years-old."

"Well, Joe is like that. It's as if he's already been around for a long, long time."

Earl began to realize his companion saw Joe the way he did.

Mike continued. "Another way to say it is like this. You know how it's good sometimes to be with your best friend on a wide, warm, sunny porch where you can just rock and rock in well-worn, comfortable chairs, side by side?"

Earl thought of Dunk, the back deck, and their feet on the lawn. "Yeah."

"When you're with Joe, and he's talking to you, especially one-on-one, well, it's like you're on that porch...only there's no porch, and there no chairs. He's just—I don't know—he's just *with you.*"

The memory of Joe's backyard boyhood swingset came to Earl's mind. "Like he knows what's on your mind, or something."

"Yeah," Mike paused as their ice cream arrived. The dessert was delivered by a server named Ben who moved nervously as he set their sundaes down on the table. Earl remembered him from the last time he was here dining with Dunk. It would be hard to forget the burn mark on the side of his neck. Earl couldn't quite explain how, but this time the boy seemed invisible. Ben was so much smaller than Mike in many ways more than size, and moved like he didn't want to be seen.

"Yeah," Mike said,. "It's just like that." He skimmed past an uncomfortable feeling about their server and watched Ben walk away without speaking.

Alone again, Earl wondered if he should share the story of Joey bringing his dog back to life. Enjoying a spoonful of his ice cream, he also wondered if he should tell him about how, as a second grader, Joey heard his dead wife sing the song played on their wedding day.

All of a sudden, Mike stopped eating. "I'd like to tell you something else, Earl. But this just between us."

"Alright."

"He wakes up really early some mornings. Really early. And college kids? Ah, we just don't do that."

Earl never went to college. When he heard things like this, he understood why.

Mike made sure their eyes met. "Now I know Joe and I are going to a Bible College and all—but to some students, that doesn't always mean a whole lot—and in the middle of his being incredibly busy with the kids and his classwork, and in getting hammered with a lot of reading and long papers—he goes off and prays. With the hood of his sweatshirt pulled up over his head, Joe slips off to the lower quad and sits under the early morning stars. Now that makes me think of somebody I study in the Gospels. And do you know who that is?"

Earl answered, "Yeah, I do know. Jesus."

CHAPTER FOURTEEN

Just as Earl waved Mike off in one direction, he heard that familiar motorcycle sound coming up from behind. He didn't need to turn to see that it was Jolie. Her obnoxiously loud bike became even louder, and Earl didn't realize he was grinding his teeth until he forced himself to stop. He didn't call to meet her. She was here on her own.

Earl never understood Dunk's friend, at least fully. Like Dunk, she never married, and at this point it didn't look like she ever would. Outside of her classroom, he questioned what brought her joy or contentment beside that motorcycle of hers. He knew Dunk's pure joy, and that was Joey. Oh, he loved that boy. Outside a few rumors about Dunk's friend that he purposely chose to ignore, Earl never understood the one on her way. Maybe today that would change.

In the Dairy Barn, Earl had decided not to tell Mike about the camera he had spotted. He also didn't share all his own special Joey stories. From what he'd sensed in their time together, he just didn't think the big kid could handle—or keep a lid on—all of this. Jolie, on the other hand, probably could. A bit rough around the edges, Jolie was so unlike his own daughters. Earl worried he might find her hard to understand, but there was no time like the present.

He waited for the bike's sounds to get louder. When the two were at a distance of twenty feet, both Earl and Jolie knew they had to meet. Before Jolie dismounted, Earl looked right at her. "So, you've heard from him."

"Yes. You?"

Thinking about the cameras again, he said quietly, "Hey, why don't the two of us take a walk?"

This is strange, Jolie thought. *But not as strange as that call from Dunk.*

"Why, Earl," she replied in a voice completely foreign to her in that it was filled with gooey sweetness, "I think it's a lovely day for a walk."

⁕

Five blocks from Earl's and Dunk's houses, in the middle of a more affluent part of town, Jolie considered all she'd just heard. "A camera. A minuscule, super-tech camera was right there? Right in front of you? Concealed on a tree branch?"

Earl knew she was mulling this over.

Remembering what Dunk had said of that Rolls guy, Jolie kept her voice low. "Yes, I agree. There would have to be more. You found just the one?"

"Yes."

"Aimed at their house."

"Yes."

Jolie suddenly stopped and thought of her friend and colleague. All Dunk had been through in all the time they'd known each other sent chills down her spine. He was a little brother to her, and there were times when he needed protection. "And there could easily be sound equipment. Bugs, as you say."

"Yes."

"Oh, my gosh." Jolie's jaw dropped.

"What?"

"There was a teacher. He left the year Joe graduated. I never thought too much of it then, but one afternoon, there on his laptop, I found these odd notes."

"What do you mean?"

"I just went into his classroom to drop off a file from another teacher in his department. I was just a Jane Messenger girl. And there, on his desk, his laptop sprang to life when I set the file down. Now I did snoop, it's true, and I did it because I thought when I read the word 'subject' that it had to deal with an online course we were to take together. In fact, we had talked about this enrichment course in the faculty room at lunch that very day."

"Yes?"

"So, I checked it out. It had all these entries marked, 'subject, subject, subject.' These entries included dates and times. In way too much detail, they were responses to what the subject said, particularly in regard to ethics."

"You know what this means, Jolie."

"Yeah, our guys are in a whole lot of mess."

CHAPTER FIFTEEN

This space was unlike the first one Joe had experienced when he woke and met the Silver Man. At first Joe thought this new room was in a hospital, but couldn't imagine any floor being this quiet, unless of course he was in a remote corner of an ICU. Even there he would overhear something, or someone.

The drugs he has continually received through a drip into his forearm messed with his mind. This annoyed him because he kept thinking about unlikely scenarios. For example, he pictured Earl and Mike together in Earl's car. The two didn't know each other, but there was Mike in the passenger seat looking at a bent mailbox with its faded red flag pointing toward the curb like an arrow, fresh tire marks across a front lawn, and a new jump rope wound around a tree on his street. That was a far easier sight than seeing Mike in the middle of a road during a powerful rainstorm.

Joe realized he had to get to his roommate. There was trouble. He had to help him, but was still restrained in this bed.

As Joe tried to piece more together, he guessed there may have been an accident of some kind, something he did not remember, or truly could not remember. For many hours, he did his best to hold the possibility that he'd been seriously injured. This would explain a great deal, but he wasn't hurt, at least not in a way that he could tell. Whatever was happening through his forearm was changing him. He was still himself, but something was off, wrong, and different.

Joe had been able to put together that days had passed. What made this a challenge was that there was no one he could talk to about all of this, even if it were someone he didn't know. He wished he could ask even a complete stranger a question, but what question or questions would he ask? Where would he begin? Sometimes there were near silent people around—nurses maybe—but, as if planned, he'd always been in a deeper sleep when they came into his room.

He wanted to move. This was too much. This had been too long. He ached. Worse than all of this, he missed DOD. If there actually had been an accident he could not remember, his DOD would have to have been involved in it. Otherwise, he'd be here.

Was his DOD okay? Where was he? The father/son combo may go a day or two without connecting, but Dunk O'Dell liked to check in with his grown son regularly. Despite the fact Dunk felt he was hovering at times, and Jolie would tease him on that, he was always a good parent. It was true that the two were becoming friends now that Joe was out of the house and busy with life in college. While they did live independent lives, they'd never go this far in silence. Something was wrong.

Suddenly the thought of his DOD and the Silver Man talking together popped into his mind. There were ficus trees and a long, glass ceiling. This flipped him out. Joe did not want to picture this. To keep his mind busy, he found another vision, a dream. He saw two bored Bible College students standing in the corner of an L-shaped staircase. A minister who didn't know what she was doing read poorly out of a little black book. Betsy, wearing black, was standing by a back door. DOD was there, Earl too. In fact, the three of them were talking after the service. DOD had tears in his eyes.

He tried to focus on what was real, not a dream. What was clear was that he wanted to spend more time with Betsy once he got out of here. Maybe he'd buy her another *Spark Shark,* the blue drink that fizzed and would, as the message on the side of the can read, 'bite you back.' Maybe they could go back to that State Park, find a real, old time movie theater playing classic films from the thirties and forties, or just enjoy an afternoon on her campus or his. Joe wanted to see her. He wanted to be close to her face again, take in her bright and expressive eyes. Get her to smile. Make her laugh. They could rent bicycles and find a winding country road, or spend an entire day in the pulse and the drive of a big city. They could enjoy street music, a sidewalk cafe, and a museum or two. To be near her. To study her expressions, hold her hand, wrap his arm around hers. Because he didn't know her—he had met her only once—he knew this was crazy. He should stop thinking about her. He should just stop.

Joe raised his chest. He rocked his hips. He wasn't naked anymore, and this was good. He had to think clearly though—much clearer than this—and it was just impossible.

Opening his eyes for the first time only to see a flat white ceiling, Joe realized this wasn't a hospital; this was a lab, his lab. The Silver Man came back into Joe's mind a third time. He knew these injections in his forearm weren't just pumping him up with something, they were taking something, too.

His heart pounded. Panic shot through his soul. Whatever this was, whatever that man wanted, whatever that human computer planned to reveal or expose, Joe would not go there.

"Help!" He cried. "Help. Get me out of here! Get me out of here!" He cried again. "Help!"

No one came. No sound came from the other side of the doors.

He closed his eyes. *Dear God, please listen. Oh listen. Help me. Please, please help me.*

CHAPTER SIXTEEN

Joe's legs buckled and wobbled as if they were brand new and jelly-filled. Walking for the first time in so many days was so weird, it almost hurt. A woman who introduced herself with a name he immediately forgot stood beside him ready to help should he stumble. With her hand holding Joe's elbow, she kept his pace steady as they made their way down a long corridor.

I'm going to see him again, Joe thought. *This is where we're headed.*

Joe noticed her long white lab coat. "Are you a doctor? A nurse?"

She did not answer.

He swallowed. Maybe this wasn't a trillion dollar lab. "Is this...is this some kind of a hospital? And is my dad okay?"

She didn't respond.

"His name is Dunk O' Dell. He lives at 14 Poplar Street. I have his phone number. Can I call him?"

Again, she gave no response.

Joe's voice gained volume. "Is my dad okay? I need to know!"

"Joseph," the woman said, "you'll have all your answers in just a few minutes. Just continue to walk with me. You're doing a good job here. Nice and slow and steady."

"How do you know my name? What happened to me?" Joe wanted to stop and face her, but his legs quaked as she propelled him forward. "And is my dad okay? Is he?"

"Just ahead, Joseph. Just ahead."

Joe and his walking partner rounded a corner. A large, sunny room opened up to them with floor-to-ceiling windows at the far end. An immense lawn with perfectly rounded trees in the distance greeted them. Having not seen sunlight in many days, it took Joe's eyes time to adjust. When they did, he noticed two men seated beside an empty chair. He centered his attention on only one of the two men.

"DOD?" *Yes! DOD! And he's okay! He's okay!*

As best as he could, Joe rushed to meet Dunk who stood and hurried toward his son. Joe fell into his dad's arms since his steps remained clumsy. Immediately he started to cry. It had been too long. He had been too scared. "DOD, DOD! I was so worried about you!"

The hug between them was good and strong. Into Joe's ear Dunk whispered, "I'm okay, Joe. And you're okay. You will be okay." That last sentence sounded funny to Joe, foreign. *What did he mean "will be" okay?*

From the direction of the three chairs, someone moved to stand near them. Joe didn't need to look. He knew who it was. With his eyes closed, he kept his arms locked around DOD.

Roland did his best to sound animated. "A family reunion! How welcome the sight."

Dunk's embrace loosened and he slowly pulled away. "It's going to be okay, Joe. It's going to fine."

"Yes," the man echoed, "It is going to be fine, just fine."

Joe kept looking at his DOD, who turned his attention to the one who was speaking. "So," Roland said, "why don't we sit down and talk, shall we?"

"No." Joe remembered too much too well. He replied abruptly, "I'd rather stand."

The senior of the three shook his head. "This is not a good idea, Joseph."

Joe's voice was as chilled as the man playing host. "First of all, you should call me Joe, and second, honestly, I don't want to be very close to you."

Dunk was stunned. He had never heard his son talk like this. Sure, as a teenager, the occasionally moody boy shot some attitude now and then, but it was directed at a situation, never a single person.

"I remember where your hand was, sir, and, even with my DOD nearby, you creep me out. You were weird then, and you're weird now."

Roland intertwined his fingers. "Your mild hostility is interesting, Joe." He nodded once to his employee who brought Joe into this area and had since been absorbing far more than Roland found necessary. "That is all."

She pivoted and began to leave.

"Oh wait," Joe said to the woman's back. "Would you show us the way out? My DOD and I are ready to leave."

Roland turned to the chairs. "This technician now leaving us alone reminds me so much of your surrogate mother." He slid his fingers over the back of the nearest chair. It was an action he will never do again because trying to move casually to enhance points in his conversation consumed too much energy. He lied. "They have the same height, the same hair color. And your birth mom, oh, what would Jennifer say of your manners now, Joseph?"

Whatever momentous anger Joe directed at this creep suddenly fell to the carpet and seeped into subflooring. It was gone, all gone.

"Yes," Roland asked again, "What would she say?"

Lost, Joe glanced over to Dunk who watched all of this through half closed eyes.

If Joe's legs were shaky before, now they trembled. He pointed his question to his DOD. "Jennifer? That is my Mom?"

Aware of how to play this for the best results, Roland stopped near his prefered chair. "Why don't you take a seat now, young man? You look like you could use one. There's a lot we have to talk about."

After sitting himself, Dunk motioned for his son to join them.

Joe dropped down reluctantly. While he looked in his DOD's direction, he could not quite face him. "You never told me her name, DOD."

"I never knew it, Joe. I never knew her name."

Joe looked to the Silver Man. He locked into something he had never experienced before, something powerful beyond his measure. "He's lying. DOD, her name isn't Jennifer."

Dunk looked at Joe. He had never seen that expression on his son's face. If they were at home, he'd share everything—everything—including the fact that he had never known the name of Joe's mother. With regret, Dunk realized he should have opened more of his son's history long ago. Had he told Joe the whole story when his son was old enough to understand, Mr. Rolls would have no influence now.

Intrigued, Roland wanted to know more. "Joseph, how do you know her name isn't Jennifer?"

Joe shrugged.

The immature attitude Roland received from the clone was interesting, but not entirely surprising. He took a slightly different angle. "Joseph, do you know my name?"

"No."

"Why?"

Though he came close to making eye contact, Joe kept his focus precious inches from a connection. "Because I don't need to. I don't want to."

Roland sat back and crossed one of his legs at his knee. "Here we go with those manners again." He threw a theatrically disappointed look toward Dunk—one he'd never made before—and then produced a level-headed one toward the clone who still would not meet him in the eye. "And this flippant attitude? This is not how were you raised, son."

Joe mimicked Mr. Rolls' last action of crossing his leg, only he did it effeminately. "Oh, manners. Yes. Let's talk about manners. You, darling, are the most intelligent man I've ever met. Yet you must have somehow forgotten that I told you to call me Joe."

"Joe," Dunk said with a bite in his voice. "Stop this. You need to listen to this man."

"The slimeball wants me to produce manners, DOD? Why, of course, let's talk about manners. Let's talk about kindness and consideration, too." With contempt, Joe looked to the Silver Man, and then to his DOD. "Now, let's see. My whole stay here has been...what do I say? A top vacation destination? Yes. Everyone here is so bright and sunny, and mannerly, like our friend here. I've really enjoyed my time."

Roland unbuttoned his suit jacket. "Friend? You need to know that I called you son because that's what you are to me."

"And you need to know I know her name isn't Jennifer."

Roland tapped his fingertips together. "That again?"

Dunk interjected. "What is her name?"

"He's right," Roland answered. "It isn't Jennifer."

The foot Joe kept in the air bounced now, and then he rolled it at the ankle. "And you need to know, from what I can guess is your highly scientific background, this simple junior high school DNA/RNA replication fact: you, Silver Man, are not my father. My father could not possibly have the heart of a statue. I can smell that you are stone."

"Joe!" Dunk leaned forward in his chair. "Stop! Listen to Mr. Rolls."

"Oh," Roland said, "this is most entertaining."

"Only to you, Mr. Rolls." Joe continued to twirl his foot. "DOD, that is his name, Mr. Rolls?"

"Yes," Dunk answered.

With both feet now on the floor and his elbows resting on his thighs, Joe leaned forward and looked very studious. "Rolls, by any chance, is your first name Tootsie?"

Studying his manicured nails, Roland took four seconds to respond. "How charming." He looked to Dunk. "Charming for a boy of ten, I should say."

"'Cause if the answer is yes," Joe beamed, "I just love Tootsie Rolls."

Roland had had enough. He stood. "I am your father, in a manner of speaking, and you are a clone. Twenty-nine years ago, my grandmother showed me garments from a two-thousand-year-old tomb in Jerusalem. There was blood on them. She said the blood belonged to Jesus Christ of Nazareth."

"Did you get all this money from inventing Tootsie Rolls?"

Roland continued. "Speaking of DNA, Joe, I had what I needed from those garments to clone you."

"Clone me, yes. Of course."

"Joe," Dunk said. "Listen."

Knowing the nonsense and defiance must stop, and that the control will once again be his own, Roland pressed. "Now, there's speculation that the garments, which have been proven to be two-thousand-years-old, weren't from Jesus' tomb. They could be someone else's. That 'someone else' happens to be male, obviously, and, as you've seen in a mirror in recent years, very strongly resembles the figure artists over the centuries have depicted as the Son of God. Or, if you want to address yourself as the Gospel writer Matthew did, the Son of Man."

Joe looked to his DOD who kept quiet. "I prefer the Matthew version. It's just a little more humble, you know?"

Roland did not appreciate the interruptions. "Your jokes are crude. Stop them."

"Your words aren't meaning what you thought they would to me. So Toots, you too, can stop."

"You are trying my patience."

"And my being cooped up for how long has done what to my patience?"

Roland quickly considered his calculations. Based on his initial, one-on-one interview with the clone, the subject was scared and defensive.

Joe stood. He looked Roland in the eye. "Is that lab rat who escorted me here coming back, or are we on our own? DOD, it really is time to go."

Dunk didn't know what to do.

"Larry," Roland said, "stay seated."

Joe took a step closer to the Silver Man, and leaned down so that they were face-to-face. "How much do you think you control?"

Roland knew Jesus asked questions to those who challenged him. "Why do you ask?"

"What sorrow awaits you who are rich, for you have your only happiness now."

Without a pause, Roland said, "That's Luke 6:24. And that's the New Living Translation, I believe."

While Joe knew Roland was right about the translation, he laughed. He turned, stood behind DOD, and then awkwardly moved toward the wall of windows. He wondered if he and DOD could get out of here. A property this well-kept would probably have a gate and boundary walls.

He turned back to Silver Man. "You do not believe."

"Of course not."

"Blessed are your eyes, because they see; and your ears, because they hear. I tell you the truth, many prophets and righteous people longed to see what you see, but they didn't see it. And they longed to hear what you hear, but they didn't hear it. Matthew 13:16-17."

Roland processed not himself, but the one before him. Even without his computers at hand, he was able to scan all the conversation and movements the clone had made so far and arrive at the conclusion he had alluded to three minutes and twenty-one seconds ago: the clone was not divine. Joe was "just human." Even though the subject correctly guessed that the surrogate was not named Jennifer, it was just a guess, a hunch. Yes, the one before him was not God's Son.

This did not disappoint Roland in the least. While indeed it would have been the scientific success of all time to replicate the divine to both study and record it with the technology available, this experiment was just as interesting, just as meaningful. After all, what was it like for humanity itself to engage with a strictly human Jesus? Quickly and continuously, he studied the young man through his own eyes, not familiar cameras. Joe was human. While the boy pulled off a few interesting feats in the past and may do more in the future, his thoughts and actions were not always pure. He was no spotless lamb.

With one nod, Roland looked into a nearby long-leafed plant housing one of fourteen cameras in the room. Instantly, a large white, blank wall opposite Joe became a movie screen. A projector silently dropped from the ceiling and began showing film footage with clear audio.

"What?" Dunk said to Joe, "That's us."

The first scene was innocent and sweet. The toddler and his young, handsome dad were playing in the living room. A tower of building blocks toppled and Dunk's recorded voice laughed and cheered. Joe shot an angry look toward the Silver Man who merely returned his attention to the movie being played.

A few years passed before the next scene lit the wall. There, in front of a bright, sunny window was a large glass bowl of goldfish. Joe was seven. A camera shot revealed the boy holding a kitchen knife as he beheaded one of the fish.

Joe didn't have to look over to know how surprised and then disappointed Dunk was.

A scene in Joe's elementary school followed. Like an ice hockey player, Joe checked a student with learning disabilities. Slammed into the wall, the boy cried out before bending over a nearby garbage can. A closeup shot of Joe showed the faintest, slyest smile.

Joe swallowed all his emotions. "Will there be popcorn with this movie?"

"How about those orange-like goldfish crackers?" Roland offered, "Would you like some of those, son?"

On the wall, the famous after Sunday school temper tantrum came next. Here Joe took a baseball bat and broke both side windows on the house because he had to help his Sunday school class after church deliver soup to shut-ins rather than go to the swim park to celebrate Tommy Morr's twelfth birthday party. Next, Joe ripped up a photo of DOD and, with a cigarette he stole from Earl's youngest daughter, burned it in the kitchen sink while cursing God using words DOD never knew the boy had heard before.

Roland looked at Joe. "I know you brought Earl's dog miraculously back to life. Unlike Larry here, I also know you cheated on three eighth grade English tests. That scene is next, I believe. Yes, you cheated not on one test, but all three. And you said you'd pay Sandy Loe for helping you, and you never did."

Dunk's stomach turned as Roland continued. "And you really did start masturbating very early. Would you like to see those shots? No pun intended."

"Enough!" Joe burst. "I HATE you!" The power he found when he knew the surrogate's name wasn't Jennifer wheeled back around. He used it now. "It was the Battle of Hastings. That's what you thought about when you were with her."

Roland *could not* believe he was hearing this.

"She was old, Her hand shook. Something about Morse code. And there was a tall clock and a long, long dining table and a metal box."

"You do not know these things."

"I'm not divine?"

Roland was in shock. "How?"

"The wrappings were inside."

"No! You cannot know this."

"You CANNOT know me!" The temper tantrum with the baseball bat was similar to what hit now, only Joe punched the wall where the movie was being shown with his bare hands. He turned to his captor and screamed, "You are a freak! How dare you do this!" Joe lowered his voice to a low growl. "How dare you do this not to me, you viper, but to Dunk O'Dell. Trapping him like that, an employee. He is the *best* thing that has happened to me. You are not."

"Despite your misguided rage, I still know you. I still control you. Yes Pinocchio, with or without strings, you are mine. You are an experiment, a clone."

From nowhere, Dunk's anger exploded. The prize deacon at the Presswater UCC Church squarely landed a fist into Rolls' stomach. "Joseph O'Dell is NOT puppet, a plaything. He is NOT an experiment! He is *my son*."

Guards immediately appeared.

Roland sank to the carpet. Dunk dropped on one knee. "You will not hurt him. You will not hurt him anymore. Is that clear?"

When Dunk stood, he met Joe's bewildered expression with a sure one. "First these guards. They're like middle school parking lot cops at an eighth grade graduation. Then, we'll break through these windows. This is not Fort Knox."

Joe couldn't believe what he heard, but Dunk leveled all three guards who even whipped out billy clubs on him. With a bloody lip and one side of his face turning bright pink, he said clearly, "Joe, use one of those chairs to break a window. Sorry, unlike in the flick, this time I don't have a baseball bat with a pro player's name etched on it for you."

Joe stood still. "His name was Wilson."

"What?"

"A pro ball player. Wilson is someone Betsy really admires. But he's a pitcher. I don't know if he's much at bat."

"Joe, who is Betsy?"

"She's this awesome girl, DOD. I mean, she is really awesome."

"Are we doing this now, having this conversation?"

"Right. Focus."

With weak legs and arms, Joe actually could not break the window, though he tried four times. It was Dunk who, from a distance, hurled a chair hard enough that it shattered glass in a hundred directions.

Joe shook his head.

"So, you said her name is Betsy, huh?"

Remaining glass from the top of the tall, long frame fell and crashed loudly. Joe stared at their way out, and then to his DOD.

"What? This isn't the first time I've broken out of here. Let's go."

CHAPTER SEVENTEEN

It helped that the pristine driveway gently sloped downhill because Joe was currently not built for speed. In fact, he thought Earl's ninety-seven-year-old father, who was very much alive and well, would actually beat him to the gate if he were here.

"You could say this is kind of anticlimactic," Joe said to DOD, whose face was swollen on one side and now ached.

"What do you mean?"

Joe's legs were rubber. "The science rats Mr. Creepy invariably has should have circled us by now."

DOD put his arm on his son's back. "Here's something about Mr. Rolls, buddy, something I've learned. If Mr. Creepy wanted to stop us, he could. He's letting us go."

Joe stepped away from his dad, bent down to a small, pampered bush with mulch and a light pole behind it and said loudly and slowly, "YOU ARE A FREAK, MR. ROLLS." He pretended to knock on some of the shiny green leaves. "HELLO? DID YOU HEAR ME? YOU'RE A FREAK."

"Joe."

Joe stepped away from the bush. "OH, AND I'M GLAD MY DOD WHALED ON YOU!"

"Joe!"

"It's okay, DOD. I'm touching my cleansing, honest emotions."

Dunk frowned. There was a lot he was going to have to talk about with his son.

"YES, TOOTSIE," Joe shouted to the sky, thinking he may also be recorded by some global satellite tracking system. "I WISH I'D CLOCKED YOU IN THE STOMACH MYSELF."

When the two came upon a long, low fence, Dunk said, "You can stop talking that way now."

"But DOD, big brother is watching."

Dunk considered this. "After today, I don't think so. He has what he needs. I think this is all going to change."

"What, no more cameras? No more recordings? And our neighbors, you know the robot ones, Laura and Lane, they'll be moving?"

Laughter spilled from Dunk's lips, even though it hurt. They both suspected these next door neighbors were spies. The couple was too stilted, too perfect, and too odd for Poplar Street. Laura hovered at home writing her 'romance' novel from her home office that faced the side of their house where the windows were once broken, and Lane had an unspecified communications job in a strip mall with no other employees.

Dunk remembered what Roland had said to him in the car on their way here. "All those years, buddy, we were right about those two. Only Laura and Lane weren't spying on foreign governments, which, if you remember, was your idea."

"That was me, wasn't it?"

"Yeah." Dunk was happy to have his son back. He had no idea what the next ten minutes could bring, but he felt such joy the two of them were together.

Joe looked worried. "And Earl? He's a spy, too?"

Both said, "Nah!" at the same time.

As they came upon a closed gate and wondered how to scale it so that they could put this weird week behind them, they heard a quiet click. A second later, one of the tall, ornate, heavy iron gates automatically opened. While they could see a quiet street that could take them far from here, neither moved. Just as the gate fully extended, DOD's car appeared. A man wearing the same uniform jacket that the driver of Roland's car wore when Dunk was taken from his house, stepped out from behind the wheel.

The driver, who appeared as machine-like as Laura and Lane, left the car idling in park with the driver's door opened. When father and son were close he said, "A thousand dollars in cash is an envelope on the front seat. You have six-hundred-sixty-three miles to travel from here to your home. Your oil has been changed, your gas tank is full, and the engine has been serviced. Your timing belts were replaced."

The driver took a step closer to Dunk. "Directions for continued care following the clone's ulmintin injections are in the envelope as well. They are very simple. Keep the injection site covered for the next seven days with the gauze and tape provided in a small, brown paper bag on the floor of the passenger's seat. You will find a mild prescription antibiotic cream in that bag as well. Use the cream on the subject for the next seven days, even if the injection site shows no signs of redness or irritation."

The driver now faced Joe. "This is unlikely, but you may experience times of slight nausea or dizziness over the next twenty-four to forty-eight hours. Do not medicate yourself in any way with an over-the-counter remedy. This will interfere with your treatment which was necessary for your wellbeing. Your symptoms, should they appear, will easily pass."

Glancing back to the car, the driver said, "Your neighbor Earl has discovered one surveillance camera. He has shared this with Jolie, but not Michael. All three are highly suspicious, however. For some semblance of authenticity, we recommend you explain the past seven days in your own way. We expect that you'll agree that the less you two say, the better."

The driver looked to the car and then back to them. "Also, for your information, the team known as Laura and Lane Madoo will be moving by the end of the month. Both will be repositioned elsewhere. We will have no control over who buys that house once it is on the market."

Joe shrugged. "There goes the neighborhood."

"And clone, any new professors you experience will not be our employees. No one you encounter in the future will be associated with us. Any suspicions you have will be unwarranted. In addition, all recording devices have been removed from your home, your vehicles, your dorm room, your classrooms, your day camp, and all other areas including your neighborhood."

Dunk held the side of his face. "He's probably right, Joe."

"Finally, Mr. Rolls predicts you will be contacting him next." The driver presented a card to the two of them. "Here is his contact information."

"He's...he's leaving us alone?" Joe asked. "I don't believe it."

The driver said to Dunk, "There are a lot of things the clone will not believe. With you and your support, he'll come to understand that his doubts and suspicions all fall within the normal range of human emotion. As you have predicted over the past seven days you've been here, this integration will take time."

Joe stepped between them. "You could talk to me, not about me."

Without a trace of emotion, the driver stepped back. He began a slow yet measured walk up the drive. Having followed his directions flawlessly, he was about to add his employer's final touch. Precisely fourteen feet from the both the clone and his surrogate dad, he stopped and turned. "You've both been through a great deal. Try to enjoy the rest of your day."

CHAPTER EIGHTEEN

The last time he made this trip an eighteen-month-old toddler filled a car seat behind him. Dunk should have known then that Roland had that first escape planned. The mastermind probably even made sure Dunk's car was running just fine on that day also.

With great love, Dunk looked over to the passenger seat. Joe had been in a deep sleep there for over an hour. For the last twenty miles on the quiet interstate, Dunk thought about one of the last remarks the driver said. "Integration will take time."

Dunk whispered. "But how much time?"

He kept thinking. Now that Joe knows what has been kept secret from him, how will he be? Will he change, reject, rebel, or...what? Who can his son talk to about these totally unfamiliar, if not downright weird, ulmintin injections? Since Joe was at least fully human, has anyone else received ulmintin shots, or was this just a clone thing? Dunk remembered he had placed Roland's contact info into the front pocket of his jeans.

No, I am not calling him.

After he passed the only car he'd seen in half a mile, he glanced over at his son again. Partially on his side, Joe faced the center of the car, his studious face soft and calm. His right eyebrow twitched now and again. This told Dunk what he had known for years when checking in on his sleeping son, that the boy's dreams were good, simple, and happy. The bandage on Joe's right forearm rested in plain sight. Trying not to look at—or even think about—what happened under that bandage, Dunk faced the road and swallowed hard. What selfish needs had he been fulfilling by not giving Joe more information? The last seven days didn't have to be hell. Had he shared more with Joe, perhaps a little at a time, then this seismic interruption in their lives may not have happened. He couldn't do it though. He couldn't imagine Joe's reaction as a thirteen-year-old saying, "Oh, okay. I'm a clone. Got it!" and then, after a simple shrug of his shoulders, grabbing his helmet to go skateboarding with his friends.

As more miles passed, Dunk wished Roland had never come around because a dream came true in the one beside him: he wanted to be a dad. From the very, very start, being a father brought him such joy.

There was more. As he zoomed around three tractor trailers in a caravan, Dunk realized Joe provided a way of moving beyond the messy dating phase into a more permanent love, the love of a parent for their child. He thought of his own dad on one coast of the United States and his mom on the other. Their marriage was a mess from the start, which technically was his start. The young couple did try, and they did hang on until Dunk graduated middle school, but it was worse that way.

The thought of dating turned Dunk's thoughts toward Vanessa, the fellow deacon he met before her first meeting eight days ago. Dunk shook his head. Eight days was a lifetime ago, yet he remembered the two had talked about Vacation Bible School and soccer. She had made him laugh, think, and interact like he hadn't done in a long time. He was an optimist who could move quickly with an idea that excited him, so he knew to slow down. Adults were complicated. With the exception of Jolie, his partner in crime, and Earl, who was the dad his own father was not, he had learned the hard way that adults could be tricky. Kids, on the other hand, were fun and love.

He breathed deeply. He had done enough thinking, at least for now. He had his son with him, and that was all that mattered. God had tomorrow. He didn't need to wonder or worry. When he started feeling anxious about the trouble Joe could have as Roland's experiment, he quietly and reverently sang the hymn he learned by heart the month he went off to a Christian camp so that his parents could divorce without him anywhere near them. The hymn was *Only Believe*. When he finished with the chorus, *"Only believe, only believe; all things are possible, only believe…"* his grip loosened on the steering wheel.

He smiled. As the interstate rolled to the right, he looked far down the road because a view had opened before him. Joe would finish the summer session with no problems. After all, he'd only missed a little more than a week. The good student could make up the class time with visits to his professors and notes from his classmates. Joe could complete the projects or papers in no time. It would be a given that Joe would step right back into the life he had before this harrowing ordeal ever happened.

Dunk thought about the future. He could drop in on Joe more than he had before. He had given Joe space as a freshman, but now that the theology lover was in his sophomore year, he could easily pop in for more dinners out with his grown kid. They could plan a father-son getaway, maybe even a real vacation, not the "quickies" he'd budgeted with Joe in the past. They could really travel and bond in significant ways. And Joe, who had never seriously dated as a junior or senior in high school, would find a girl probably sooner than later, and this, of course, would be a good thing. Dunk would love to meet and spend time with the young lady his son would someday bring around. The three of them might enjoy special outings and good times together.

Dunk smiled at the thought of Joe dating. The "old man" really was ready for this next healthy phase in Joe's completely, totally normal life.

Those last two words caught in his throat. *Normal life.* For the hundredth time since he began driving away from the lab, Dunk prayed hard. *Dear God, guide us. Protect us. Keep us safe. Give me the words to say to the questions he'll have. Grant us peace through this so that your will be done.*

And thank you. Thank you for getting us out of there alive.

"Let me drive."

Dunk didn't take his eyes off the road. It started to rain and traffic had increased a great deal. "Why? I'm good."

Joe had been awake for the last twenty miles. "DOD, pull off. Let's get some ice for your face. Maybe it will help the swelling."

Dunk checked what he could see in the rearview mirror. What he saw looked bad. This would have to be something else they'd have to explain when they pulled into the driveway.

"And yeah," Joe added, "maybe we should stop somewhere for the night. Find a motel off the road like you suggested earlier. Otherwise, it's just going to be really late when we get home."

This wasn't the young man Dunk knew. While it was true they'd never travelled that much, just short car trips here and there on a teacher's salary, Joe would always insist upon putting in longer hours on the road so that he could be home in his own bed whenever possible.

From the quiet, Dunk knew something was up by what his son just suggested. And it was true. They were going to need a little more time to get it together before they pulled into their own driveway.

Both of their phones sat side by side in cup holders in the center console. Both men usually kept their devices in their front pockets. Without either of them saying a word about it, they realized someone put their phones in plain sight because Dunk left the house with his charging by the coffee maker in the kitchen, and Joe had his in his pocket when he'd been given that short ride by the professor.

Joe slid his hand down his thigh. He wore brand new clothes he'd been offered by someone who wouldn't give Joe her name. She was on hand when he awoke in a room he'd like now to forget.

Joe reached for his phone. "I should call Mike. Tell him I'm okay."

"Okay." Dunk frowned. He waited a second before asking his next question. "What are you going to say when he asks about where you've been?"

Joe shrugged. "I don't know. Keep it simple, I guess."

"Maybe you're right, son. Maybe we should find a place to stay the night. Get some rest. We've got people who are going to want to know a lot."

"And our story has to be the same."

"Right."

"DOD?"

"Yeah?"

"I don't want to do this."

Dunk's fingers barely touched his swollen face. "I don't either."

———•———

Dunk never wanted to use the cash left for them. But he also wanted to get rid of it. The clean, fresh bills that were in his hand felt funny. When he could, he usually paid by credit card to earn dollar points for the next car he'd buy, which, with college tuition, would be a long, long way off.

"Your room is number 441, sir." The clerk behind the desk was peppy—maybe a little too peppy—as she returned change from a sleek drawer tucked under a shiny marble counter. "Now, to get to your room, take these elevators to your left to the fourth floor, and then head to your left, okay?"

"Okay."

"Have a good night, sir. And I hope your face feels better."

As he began checking in a few minutes earlier, Dunk tried his lie out on her. It was a test to see if first, he could do it, and second, if it actually would hold up and make sense. Fortunately for Dunk, she easily bought that he'd fallen end-over-end down concrete stairs at a hospital where his son had been staying.

"And I hope your son feels better, too."

The clerk had been subtly eyeing Joe all the while he stood somewhat still in front of the gas fireplace in the lobby. For years, Joe has been invisible to the opposite sex, but now, with a little more age, broader shoulders, and some movie star expressions he could give without realizing it, more girls were noticing his son. Simple flirting from the opposite sex became more obvious since the boy had started college.

"Oh, he'll be fine," Dunk responded. *He's going to have to be.*

In the elevator with him alone, Dunk thought about sharing with his son that a certain young lady had an interest in more than the fireplace, but saw that that the color in Joe's face left him looking very, very pale.

"I'm nauseas, DOD. Bad. Stop this ride."

By the time Dunk hit the button, they were already on the fourth floor. Fortunately, there was a thin, stylish waste paper basket situated just inside one of the four legs of a sofa table holding a box of tissues, a plant, and a lamp. The basket caught all Joe threw up, which, since he hadn't really eaten, wasn't much.

"DOD!"

If there's one thing Joe did not like, it was throwing up.

Dunk took the little waste paper basket, found and unlocked their room, and waited a second for Joe who was just behind him. "How do you feel now?"

Joe's one shoulder was the first to hit the hallway wall. Just as his knee touched down, Dunk was there to scoop him up in his arms.

In two minutes time, Joe was almost unresponsive. Watching his son stretched out across one of the two beds, Dunk reached for the nearby phone, stopped, and slid his hand into his pocket for his cell phone. Mr. Rolls would recognize that number faster. Holding that little white RR card, he had no choice. His back locked just as it did when he was first with Mr. Rolls in the backseat of that expensive car. He had no other option. Nervously, he dialed.

One ring. Two. "Yes, Larry?"

"What are these ulmintin injections? Tell me what I need to know."

"What happened?"

"He nearly passed out. He's just thrown up."

"Is he feverish? Can you get his temperature?"

"WHAT ARE THESE ULMINTIN INJECTIONS?"

"Okay. Relax. Joe is a human, a completely, normal human. I ran the risk of giving him some extensive cell exams when he was seven-years-old. The procedure wasn't dangerous, per se, but it did come at some cost."

Dunk ran his fingers through his hair. "What are you saying?"

"You thought he was having his tonsils taken out, remember?"

Oh my God. You creep.

"That's when the extractions took place. You thought he was in surgery."

"At the Children's Hospital? Your reach goes that far?"

"Larry, yes. The cell extractions were highly successful, but to get what I needed, the clone had to have been given some interesting drugs."

"What did you do to my son?"

"Nothing that I can't fix. Now tell me, is he experiencing a fever?"

Dunk stared at his son who was quietly looking up at him. "Tell me exactly what these ulmintin injections are."

"In simplest terms, they are hormone stabilizing shots. Now that may sound scary to you, I know. But it's not. The shots were designed here to balance a deficit created when I administered that test. The likelihood of the deficit is under two percent, but we did detect it here. The injections were successful."

Dunk's eyes scanned Joe's. "No, they weren't."

"Relax. We will work together on this. Tell me the symptoms."

Oh God, Dunk prayed. *Do I trust this weirdo freak?*

Joe turned. "I can hear him, DOD. Through the phone. Tell him my symptoms."

"He's pale. Clammy. Cold. There's no fever. He threw up about thirteen ounces of mostly liquid."

"What has he eaten since he left?"

"Nothing. Just a soda."

"What's his pulse?"

Dunk grabbed Joe's wrist with one hand. Joe's eyelids have never looked heavier. Scared, he couldn't find his son's pulse. "I—"

"Take your time, Larry. You don't need to hurry."

With the secondhand on his wrist watch, Dunk shared what he learned thirty second later. "It's forty-six."

"Okay." Roland's voice stayed calm for Larry, though he had great concern. "Now tell me about him nearly passing out."

"We were just up in the hallway."

"You're at a hotel."

"You didn't know that?"

"No."

"Yeah, he threw up after stepping off the elevator. We're on the fourth floor. The nausea came on really fast. And as we...we were walking to the room..."

"Okay, this is what needs to happen."

"What?"

"He's lying down and you have blankets available, yes?"

"Yes. Yes. To both. Roland—"

"Keep him warm. Keep monitoring that pulse every fifteen minutes. You will have to give me the location of this hotel. We have no choice here. I'm on my way."

Dunk didn't make a sound.

"Trust me, I will not stay, unless you invite me to do so. There's one dose of medicine I will have with me. It's in liquid form. I'd like to see him get this as quickly as possible."

Dunk glanced out the hotel room window. It was dusk. Stopping only once, they'd been on the road for nearly five hours.

"The address, Larry. You have to give it to me. You have no option. You have to trust me."

CHAPTER NINETEEN

He prayed and paced and prayed and paced by the hotel room window until he heard the helicopter. It had been an hour and three minutes since he called Roland. Dunk folded the fingers of both hands over his chest and stared into the darkness. "Right on time."

Roland used his helicopter, the fastest mode of transportation available under these specific circumstances, to get close to the hotel. The pilot was to land the craft on a baseball field nine tenths of a mile from the hotel. One of Roland's employees would meet the helicopter and take his boss to the hotel. The only factor they didn't know at the time of the conversation was whether or not there would be a game on the field during the time of the landing. A schedule of possible games could not be accessed at the lab. The employee would take care of that, however. The field would be clear for a landing.

Dunk sighed. The digital alarm clock in the room read 9:43. In less than eight minutes, Mr. Rolls would be here.

"Stay with him," were Dunk's directions before they ended their one and only call. "Ring me if something changes, Larry. Otherwise, keep him comfortable."

Joe actually bounced back somewhat. His pulse rose to fifty-six the last time Dunk checked twelve minutes ago.

"He'll be here in a few minutes, Joe. I'm going to meet him in the lobby. He says he has specific medicine for you. Except for the cream on your forearm, that should be the last medicine you'll have to take. And he'll be gone. Gone."

Ashen, Joe met his DOD's eyes with his own. "I'm not sure of this."

"I know."

The color in Joe's eyes reflected a dark cyclone within. "DOD, I don't trust any of what has happened, or could happen."

"I'll be right here, right beside you, buddy."

Joe sat up slowly and with difficulty. "I don't trust him."

"You have to."

"No, I don't."

Dunk moved to the door. Unfortunately, the time for this conversation was not now. "It's going to be okay. Remember, he didn't even know we were in a hotel. So, I'll be right back, okay? Give me five minutes max."

Just before he closed the door on his son, Dunk heard, "DOD?"

"Yeah?"

"I love you."

⸻⸻⸻

Over a dress shirt, Roland wore a plain dark sweatshirt Dunk could tell was not his. Costuming. Maybe it was not to draw attention to any of this. Then again, someone was going to report a helicopter had landed on a baseball field in a matter of minutes.

Based on the square footage of the lobby, the amount of furniture and the ceiling height, Roland stopped eight feet, three inches from Dunk. It was the furthest distance he could stand and not raise his voice. "You could have stayed upstairs. I can find the fourth floor and room 441."

Dunk turned and held the elevator button. "Oh, this is the welcome wagon."

"You and your colloquialisms."

"You and that sweatshirt. Nice look."

As they waited for the elevator, Roland asked if there had been any change.

"He's better." His pulse is up to fifty-six."

"That's still too low. And how's his skin temp? Is he still cold to the touch?"

"Yes."

"That's not normal."

"No."

The elevator arrived. The doors opened. Dunk motioned for Roland to go first.

When the doors closed, both men realized in this tight, quiet space how much the dynamic had changed since this afternoon. Dunk spread his feet and looked down. "You can bill me for the window I broke earlier today."

Roland did something he hadn't done since he was a child. He tried to be funny. "I did. You only received a thousand dollars, didn't you? It was going to be twenty-five hundred."

"A fifteen-hundred dollar window? Really?"

"Well, medical bills, too. You did hit me. Hard. You know what an ER doctor's visit cost nowadays?"

Dunk glanced sideways at Roland. "What? Tell me you don't have good insurance."

Roland watched the numbers change from three to four. He hadn't had a friend in forty-six years. He wasn't sure he wanted one.

Dunk stopped in front of the hotel room door. "Listen. Thank you for coming, and so fast. I never thought I'd have to use your number. Least of all today."

"And I never thought you'd take down three guards, soft-bellied though they were. I know you love him."

"One more thing?"

"Yes."

"I'm not sorry I hit you."

Roland shifted the doctor's bag he'd been carrying to his other hand. "I know."

He was gone.

"What?" Dunk raced through the room. He checked the bathroom for the third time, even behind the shower curtain.

Gone.

"Check this hall, Mr. Rolls. I'll hit the lobby. Maybe he's there."

Not waiting for the elevator, Dunk literally sailed down the flights of stairs. The lobby was completely silent, except for the girl who checked them in earlier. He had to ask her. He tried to look and sound calm, even though he was not.

"My son, have you seen him?"

She was pretty. Her dark eyelashes were thick. "No, it's been quiet, very quiet, except for you and that gentleman you met here about four minutes ago."

"Nothing?"

She shook her head. "Nothing."

Dunk ran out to their car. The doors were unlocked. The keys rested on the driver's seat over a note on hotel stationery in Joe's handwriting that simply read, "I do love you, DOD. Always. Always."

The cash they'd left in the glove compartment was gone.

Dunk screamed and screamed. "Oh my God! Oh my God!"

"Then Jesus was led by the Spirit into the wilderness to be tempted by the devil."
— Matthew 4:1

PART II
THE SON

CHAPTER TWENTY

Earl owned only one suit and it was seventeen-years-old. Since he bought it off the sale rack, he has lost, ironically, seventeen pounds. It fit as he expected, but he didn't care. He rang his next door neighbor's doorbell. It had been one year to the day since Joe disappeared. Except for one postcard three months ago, Dunk hasn't heard from his son at all.

Anniversary dates like this one today were too familiar to Earl. Lately, he'd been watching Dunk closely. Today was a summer storm day.

Earl rang the doorbell again and realized that standing here alone on the front step could take a few minutes. Carefully, he ran his hand down one side his open jacket. Janet had been the one who insisted he buy this dark suit in the first place. He wore it to her funeral, and now he'll wear it to this one.

The quiet in the morning brought the pain. Through a sudden veil of tears, he mumbled to the cloudy, gray sky heaven, "This shouldn't end like this, dear Father. Not at all. This is the worst. The absolute worst."

His green gray eyes shifted and refocused as he studied his own house. He remembered when his girls were little and had asked questions that did not have good answers for sweethearts their age, like why the chipmunk in the street had died in the dark alone, or why, after taking their walloping cat Bunny home from the local animal shelter, they asked why everyone couldn't be kind enough to love a homeless kitty cat or dog.

As if speaking to his little angels again, his voice sounded uncharacteristically gentle as he began to pray. "Oh dear Father, if we knew how much you loved us, we wouldn't say the things we say, or do the things we do. If we just understood that you sent your Son to the cross to free us from our sins, then days like this wouldn't happen."

Before Earl said, "Amen," the pit in his stomach widened, flopped, and then ached. Why this upcoming funeral caught and spun Earl was obvious. The one who had died had a life that was too big, too bright, and too full. Death had won, and it was love not death that needed to win here.

Staring at Dunk's door for an opening or a way to understand this deep hurt, he recalled those long, strong legs and the Bible College tee shirt the big kid wore the day they met. Michael's wide-eyed expressions made it clear that he'd never been to the house before. As Earl moved closer to the newcomer that day, it was obvious that the college kid had never done anything like this before. Michael showed up here because he cared, because he loved, and because Joe obviously mattered. As awkward and as challenging as this was for Michael to get to this door, he had to do it.

Michael stood right where Earl kept his feet here on the stoop. This hurt Earl. Michael just couldn't be gone. He remembered how much the boy ate when they went out to the Dairy Barn. Firsthand, he saw how the theology guy's face changed when they talked about Joe. He felt how much Michael offered to the world. He knew there was so much goodness, so much potential, and so much hope within this one remarkable soul.

Earl turned toward the street and tasted bitterness in his mouth. No, he couldn't explain to a three and a five-year-old why chipmunks were hit by cars, or why more people couldn't care for a perfectly wonderful shelter pet, but if there was something he simply, truly did not understand, if there was a something he could swing and swing a baseball bat at and miss every single time, it was the word suicide.

His heart began to beat in a lopsided way even though he was not moving.

Yes, a storm brewed today.

Earl waited another ten minutes, and then walked around the house to Dunk's bedroom. He stood at the window cracked open three inches. Raising his hand to reach over the sill, he tapped on the glass. He tapped again.

"Earl, no."

"Dunk," Earl said as he leaned in close to the house. "No, this isn't good, and yes, this is going to hurt. But I'm here. I'm going to help you."

"I don't need help."

Earl waited. Sometimes no words were the best words.

He turned, placed one of his feet up against the siding, and leaned back. Dropping his head, he saw that Bible College tee shirt again. He wanted to kick himself as regret pressed against him. Maybe they should have had more ice cream. Maybe he should have asked him about his high school, his love life, his interests. Maybe he should have listened more closely to what Michael was saying in the car, especially in the moment when he looked sad, and then conflicted. Maybe he could have invited the newcomer into his house after time at the Dairy Barn.

But he didn't.

He wanted to destroy the wretched word suicide. To knock it down and turn it to powder under his feet was his desire. At the time Janet passed, death was the best thing that could have happened to her. It was never welcomed, and he didn't want to see it first, or even look at it, but it had been close long enough that Earl knew it was in the corners of the room, and then it right beside his wife. Death was necessary for Janet. It was a thief with Michael.

Quiet, he was not sure how many minutes passed. Eventually he heard Dunk's bare feet on the floor. They came close to the window.

"You're still here."

"Uh-huh."

Wearing only a pair of gym shorts, the Dunk O'Dell the world knew a year ago would look impressive in this private moment. But not now. Dunk had found the seventeen pounds Earl lost over seventeen years. He put that weight on in the first six months of Joe's absence. Seven more pounds padded their way to Dunk's middle over the last six months. Dunk's waist had grown five inches. He'd never weighed this much.

"Earl, I told you, I'm going to this funeral alone."

"And I told you, you are not going alone. I'll drive myself, if I have to. We'll take two cars. I may have to do just that so that I'm not late. But I'm going. I met him and I liked him. And I can hurt today, too. You don't have the market on that."

Dunk couldn't speak.

Earl glanced at his watch. It was almost half past eight. He looked back through Dunk's bedroom window. "Twenty minutes to shower, shave, and change. That should do it."

"Alright."

"I'll be back with a breakfast sandwich for you. And I just decided, I'm driving."

⋅———⋅

Earl's focus went right to the single large photo framed on top of the long coffin. He was glad for the distance between it and the seat he had just taken because he didn't want to get closer. He didn't need a picture. His memories of Michael were enough.

"No, he's here," he overhead Dunk say to a funeral director a few minutes later. "I found my friend, thank you. He's right here."

Earl and Dunk had parted at the door of the funeral home as soon as they had arrived. Earl wanted to quickly find a seat after he had passed the only two students here from the college. In the alcove of the wooden staircase, it was clear to Earl that the two stood united in their heterosexual location. As they sat in the corner furthest from the casket, it was also clear they believed that being odd was out, way out. It was obvious from their expressions that on their own they would not have come. Someone at the college had made their attendance mandatory.

Dunk sensed what Earl was thinking. "No," he said. "They were not involved in Mike's death. I don't think those two really knew him. They're here as representatives from the school. Official function only."

"How—?"

"A funeral director at the front door told a lady near me who had asked. Their grievance ambassadors."

As Earl began to wonder why the college would have grievance ambassadors but not care providers for someone hurting like Michael—and by no means was he the first young person to have a hard time—a clergyperson began her waddle toward the tiny lectern to the left of the casket. Plump and as pale as uncooked dough, the rent-a-pastor strictly read dry words from a little black book. The only interest were her pencil-lined eyebrows which arched from time to time. With awkward pauses and painstaking gaps where a page was turned or Michael's name was to be inserted into her dry script, she either had a reading impairment or grabbed the wrong reading glasses.

Bored senseless and way too hot, Earl was not used to wearing this many clothes, especially in the summertime. He glanced around the funeral home that maybe sat a hundred. How sad, he thought, that there were only a hundred people here. This was tragic. The service wasn't even in a church, and Mike loved God. Earl shook his head. Hello, the kid went to a BIBLE college.

Thoughts flooded his mind. Mike probably didn't tell too many people he was gay. Earl himself didn't know until Dunk had told him, and that was only after Earl did some serious coaxing the morning he saw the obituary on Dunk's kitchen table.

Earl kept staring ahead as the pastor droned on and on, never once giving pause or passion to her words. Earl checked the generic bulletin in his hand and noticed that no time was included for sharing thoughts or memories of the deceased. He crumbled the paper. He was going to speak. He was going to share what was on his heart. After a prayer that, without expression or warmth, broke his spirit, he found himself on his feet. Before he started talking, he waited patiently until he drew everyone's attention. Dunk, seated beside him, repositioned his chair and leaned away as far as he could.

"Now I mean a lot of respect here," Earl announced into what became an awkward silence, "and my friend Dunk and I have travelled just over two hours one way to make this service..."

Earl suddenly stopped. One of the stone looks he received made him realize many here thought he was gay and that the younger, overweight one beside him was his partner. Earl didn't have words for this, just anger.

Swallowing hard, he suddenly knew more of the dark world in which this big-hearted young man lived. He saw how Mike experienced no options, other than the one he took. Nervous and embarrassed, he started to sit back down, and then, by God's provision, rose and squared his shoulders.

"I met Mike once. He came out to my neighbor's house to check on his summer roommate, whose name is Joe. See, Mike *really* cared about Joe. Cared enough to drive out to see how he was doing. That taught me a lot—a lot about the power of care, and more so, about the power of love."

Earl moved to stand in the aisle. "I've come all this way to say that I get what love is, and I understand what love can do. And a whole lot of that is ruined now. See, this boy Mike, he loved....*he loved*. He loved God, Jesus, and the Holy Spirit. Why else would he go to *Bible* College? The campus? The food? No. He had such a tender soul, such a mighty heart. I'm not going to preach to you. I think I'm about a week too late for that, but a great light has gone out—a *great* light crafted expressly by God—and we are responsible. We are all responsible. When God made that young man, He didn't make a mistake. We did."

No one else in the room uttered a word, except a small voice from somewhere toward the front said from his heart, "Amen."

After the service, an alluring young woman walked toward Earl and Dunk. Through a face fatigued with inconsolable loss, she stood in front of them. "I know you don't know me. We have never been introduced. I...I was a friend of Mike's. His best friend, actually. My name is Betsy."

Earl shook the hand he'd been offered. Dunk nodded to this young lady who wore a simple yet stunning black dress not for herself, but for Mike.

"Sir, when I heard you say your friend's name is Dunk, well I knew there couldn't be *that* many forty-something men out there named Dunk."

She moved to stand in front of Joe's dad. The pain pressing on each of them kept them from really seeing each other. "I met Joe. Just once. Mike had taken Joe and me to this park one afternoon. It was an important time in Mike's life." Tears fill her eyes, first in sorrow for her own loss, and then in sorrow for Dunk's.

Earl watched as everything changed within Dunk. The younger of the two men reached for her hand. "You're Betsy?"

"Yes."

"My son..." Dunk swallowed. "My son mentioned you. We were about to bust glass at the time. I know, breaking glass, that's another story—totally another story." Dunk had to stay focused. This was his chance at information. "But he mentioned you. He just stopped everything for the moment and mentioned you. Joe said you were awesome."

A part of Betsy could not hear the words being spoken. They were just too much. Awkwardly, she nodded.

Dunk didn't waste time. "Do you know where he is?"

"I...I don't."

"But he mentioned you. He never contacted you?"

"No."

"Not even once? I mean, is it possible you missed his call?"

Earl slid his hand under Dunk's arm as Dunk gained a lot of volume in a small area.

"A note or a message or...or something? Anything? Yes?"

Betsy shook her head.

Dunk's eyes suddenly turned bright red. "Not at all?"

Betsy's eyes mirrored Dunk's pain. "I know your son has been missing for a year now. I just want to share that I found Joe to be one of the most remarkable guys I've ever had the chance to meet. I've thought of him a lot after meeting him, to be honest. He left a solid impression with me."

Though inches from her, Dunk couldn't quite understand what she was saying.

Betsy continued. "I know he called you DOD. I'm not sure I remember why, but here on this day of loss, I'm sorry for the hurting you've been doing not just here at this funeral—I know you didn't know Michael all that well—but for your heartbreak every day." She turned to go, and then stepped back. She waited for Dunk to look at her. It took a moment for his mind to look again through his eyes. "Joe is in my prayers. You are in my prayers."

"Nothing? Nothing at all? No calls to you? No message?"

"Dunk," was the only word Earl shared.

With the wound opened in a new place, if that could even be possible, the lost man's pain circled inward, faster and faster. Though people must have been around him, he was certain he was alone. He said to himself, "Nothing. Nothing at all."

❖⸺⸺⸺❖

Unlike Janet or his girls, Earl was not the impulsive one, yet he pulled alongside a roadside stand at the first chance he could turn into the parking lot.

Dunk looked out and up at the small, empty parking lot with a blank expression. That the car had stopped was fine. After all, he wasn't the one behind the wheel. When he pulled himself out of his thoughts, he read the large sign above the sliding windows of the little building right in front of him. He stared ahead and tried to be polite. "I don't want ice cream."

Earl opened the driver's side door. "Okay."

Quickly Earl returned with a bunch of napkins and two tall cones. Leaning through his open window, he handed Dunk one of them.

"I don't want this."

Earl nodded. "Oh, I know. I heard you when I stopped the car."

"Earl."

Carefully, Earl opened his car door. "This isn't about you, Dunk. This is about me. This moment is about me and Mike, and the ice cream he and I shared. That boy just really, really touched me. And I miss him."

Dunk moved his eyes but not his thoughts.

"Now, it's hot and you can just hold that thing until it drips down your hand and onto the floor mats under you. And I can gripe about you when I clean the mess up when I get home, but no, *this* moment isn't about you. *This* moment is about one boy lost."

"You mean another lost boy. This makes two."

"Dunk."

"Two young men lost. And do you want to know the saddest thing about this? The selfish thing? I don't know if Joe is alive or dead." He started to shake. "I just don't know, Earl. Where is my son? Is he dead or alive?" Dunk knew Joe wouldn't leave him like this, especially for this long, so something must have seriously happened to his boy. He started to cry, and then wail. Through the sobs and the breath he could not seem to catch, he sputtered, "I can't do this, Earl! I can't! All of this not knowing!"

When the surge of emotion to his right quieted down, Earl said flatly, "Joe is not dead."

"How would you know?"

"I just…" Earl knew he was about to say something crazy, and he never said anything crazy. Somehow he knew Joe was alive. The boy may not be well, but he was alive. "I just know. That doesn't make any sense, but I know."

"I just miss my buddy *so much*."

Earl's hand moved to rest on Dunk's damp shoulder. He didn't say anything, even when the sobbing started again.

Taking the melted cone out of Dunk's sticky hand, he left the car to throw both treats away in the tiny stand's single garbage can. He returned with both damp and dry paper towels from the men's room along the side of the narrow building.

Dunk couldn't face his driver. "I ruined this Mike moment for you."

"Nah," Earl handed his friend the first of a few damp paper towels. "Mike understands tears. Think about it."

———————

They sat on Dunk's back deck, side by side, each holding a beer that was a lot colder thirty minutes earlier. Dunk kept quiet, and Earl certainly didn't expect as much as a word. The man who had mentally mowed his neighbor's lawn twice now simply knew this single father of one had to get through these last aching hours of the day, this first year anniversary date.

Earl knew what was true. It was better, far, far better to do this with someone rather than alone.

CHAPTER TWENTY ONE

Betsy avoided romance novels for this reason: when parts of them came true in her life, it meant trouble. *Big trouble.*

Looking at the stunning black dress in her closet, she knew her best friend would want her to wear this man trap to more than just his completely impersonal and terribly dry funeral. Yes, Mike, who had always loved her and brought out the best in her, would not want to see what he called a "beautiful look" pushed against her closet wall. He would say that the sight of this stunner being ignored would kill him, and she didn't find that funny.

Having the dress back from the dry cleaner for weeks now, she stared at it. As one who regularly bought clothing only to return the unworn purchase a week or so later, she couldn't take this one back. It had been in her possession when Mike's parents called her with the news of Mike's death. It wasn't until the day of the funeral that she actually remembered she had the dress in a long plastic bag that hadn't been opened since she left the department store.

"Guess you're mine now," she had said as she held it up to her body and glanced down. "My dream," she added without looking at herself in the mirror, "to look good at a funeral."

Mike would make a joke about what she had said. In doing so, he'd pick her chin up with his words, maybe even make her laugh. He wasn't here with a quip though, so the silence ached until the pain swept in again. She found it hard to breathe.

Turning from her closet and more tears, Betsy thought the worst grieving she would do would have happened in the days leading up to the funeral and the event itself. During those first few sleepless days however, no one could have told her what to her was still incomprehensible, that grief changed daily. She wouldn't have understood her unending heartbreak was like water on a lake, sometimes it was flat and familiar and at other times it was dangerous and murky. What didn't change each day was this: she loved and missed her big lug, her jokester, her literal boy-next-door, and her childhood tree house partner for life.

The pain pressed on her chest. She could not wear this dress again. She pictured herself reaching back into her dorm room closet and sending that dress into the wastepaper basket. That would be crazy though, impractical. She was neither of these things. Instead, she realized, she was a girl who couldn't move well without this love in her life. Standing still in the middle of her long, narrow room that she shared with a roommate gone for the evening, Betsy couldn't move. She couldn't think. She couldn't be.

To survive, she tried to pretend what Mike would say. There were no words though. She closed her eyes and saw the picture she had of him on her desk, the same one that had been placed on top of the coffin.

Moving back to the open door of her closet, Betsy steeled her resolve which was what Mike would have demanded. For the second time, she pulled out the options she had laid out on her bed ten minutes ago. It wasn't that she didn't like Tad Matthew McGregor, the football player, the economics major, the charmer, and, of all things, a classical guitar player. He held doors open for her. He listened to her. He walked slowly when they were side by side as she dreamt out loud, or reverted to her nerdy, calculating herself. Tad knew how much she ached, or at least he was quiet while she fumbled through parts of her day. He also heard her insecurities and her self-sabotaging ways and, as if with a gentle, hand open, redirected her back to the better path.

He was also handsome. He had that perfect hair a prince would have in an animated movie. With all of the good qualities he had going for him, he just didn't seem to see her, at least not for who she really was. That single fact was enough to shut down this possible relationship, right? To her way of thinking, this one bad piece leveled all the good ones.

Or did it? She needed Mike to talk about this because she didn't know what to do. Sometimes Tad was wonderful; other times she couldn't wait to be apart from him. No past relationship had been this confusing to her. Maybe Mike's absence really did have something to do with this because she just could not decide where to put this guy.

She had said yes to something simple—just coffee at one of the campus' eateries, the *Cup Up*. It was just to be as casual meeting. When he called later that day—never give a Romeo your number—and had suggested dinner for two off campus, she couldn't think of an excuse fast enough. In her pause, the blue-eyed flirt just jumped to action.

So now, much to her dismay, this was their first serious date. To surprise her, he had sent to her dorm room three roses in a vase about an hour ago. The card read, "You press a smile into my lips. My heart beats fast when I think of you. I cannot wait for tonight. Tad."

Yeah, she thought, this was a big date. Yippee.

She sighed as she stared at the options in front of her: a sleek and simple blue dress, a silk blouse and jeans, or a flowery dress that when worn with a sweater old church ladies seemed to like. Which?

The idea of her life being like a romance novel came into her mind again. For a second—for one fast, fleeting second—she deeply wished her date tonight was not with this plastic Malibu Ken Doll, but Joe. The boy in the water. The one who somehow still held her attention. She had met him only once, and, in truth, most of that day didn't go so well because of what she had said and done. Especially on a night when she had what could be a Hollywood film star date, she should forget him. In fact, there were times when she succeeded in losing Joe's name and the obvious ways he cared about Mike.

Tonight, however, she did not want to succeed. As she had so often done since the funeral, she remembered meeting his DOD, a kind-looking man so obviously broken from the disappearance of his son. He was really hurting that day. His red eyes and numb expressions made his grief so big, so real.

She still felt a pull from within when she thought about Joe mentioning her to his DOD. The barechested wonder boy from the creek may have brought her name up only in passing, but he did remember her. Unlike her date tonight who looked at her, Joe looked through her. Tad held the spotlight on himself—and his monologues were often dazzling—whereas Joe used his soft, inviting, inward light only to find hers. Joe's goal had been to get to know her better, but she turned him down. No philosophy major would get close. That he'd disappear was her plan, but it troubled her that he had completely dropped off the map. Toward the end of the summer session, Joe just vanished for a reason even Mike didn't understand. When Mike had called with the news, Betsy couldn't believe it. This was not like the new roommate Mike had described, nor was this the Joe she had met. "Just gone?"

"Yep. There was one call from his dad, and it was awkward. He had said Joe had been hospitalized, but I never heard from Joe. Nothing."

At that point in their conversation, she went on about herself as Tad would do. She gave her Best Bud so little space, if any at all, as she began an egocentric speech about how she should have given Joe her number and stayed in touch with him. This became her loss, not Mike's.

She was so wrong to do that. Slumping down onto her bed, she discovered just how like Tad she was. This chilled her.

"I'll cancel," she said about tonight. I just won't go. Mike probably wouldn't like this guy. Sure, his long list of great accomplishments would hold Mike's attention for a moment—Tad was impressive—but, knowing her best friend, he would hear what she didn't say about him. This would bring on a discussion, maybe even an argument. In fact, that was what they were doing when they were alone together after she had met Joe—arguing. Mike had thought he would be good for her. While she had thought of Joe more than she should have, something in her tonight suddenly snapped. A new anger popped as she walked back to the black dress and lifted it out of her closet. "This Joe guy you wanted me to meet? Your Mr. Sensitive? Yeah, funny. Like what, a day after I meet him he disappears? This is your idea of a winner? Someone who just vanishes?"

Wearing the black dress, heels that challenged her every step, and a dangerous perfume she borrowed from a friend across the hall, she stood at her door ten minutes later. Staring at it, she said, "You're both gone, you and a guy I should stop thinking about."

She opened and then clicked closed the door behind her. She wouldn't wait for Tad in her room, or on the landing of the nearby open stairwell. She'd meet him in the lobby.

CHAPTER TWENTY TWO

At first, the swearing bothered Joe. The caustic, angry sounds made him grit his teeth. These days the acid words rolled off his tanned, muscled back. He hardened even more when he realized why. He regularly spit the poisons himself.

The foreman was a jerk. Everyone hated him. What he could do well was give the crew something specific to mouth off about, and that united them.

This was their third consecutive project where supplies came in late, or were faulty when they arrived. Subsequently, there would be a lot of standing around which led to long hours into the night, which irked Joe deeply since they were paid not by the hour, but by the day. When building materials failed, tension rose. Blame shifted fast if you were not fast on your feet. In the fifteen months he'd been with this company, Joe learned to be quick on his feet.

He despised this job. He absolutely hated working year-round for a shifty swimming pool installation company in the Deep South, but, because the job was very physical and stressful, many guys quit after a few weeks. The company also paid him in cash, which alleviated any records or a paper trail. That was not the best part, though. The company had him working in a six-state area. He spent three weeks in Georgia, South Carolina for two, and a week in Mississippi. He remembered spending a month in Louisiana, and two months at two different sites in Alabama. This meant no cameras. No recording devices were hidden, either. There wasn't enough time to set them up with Joe constantly on the move. Also, with the guys he worked with literally being so transient, that freak would be challenged to hire someone to spy on him long-term. It was impossible to know for certain who his coworkers had as their real employer, of course, but it was easy for him to stay quiet, especially around hardworking Mexicans who spoke only Spanish.

He liked this very much.

———•———

Reggie was forty and looked fifty-two. An alcoholic, he started drinking around 9 AM and didn't stop. His eyes were coated in an eggy yellow. His skin cracked like abused leather, especially over his hands. His hatred for God and himself ran so deep that those near him could smell something violent or vile when he sweated, which was often. Together with Joe, he had been on this miserable site for the past four days. Joe knew before the weekend rolled in, with forecasted record-breaking heat, that at least one guy would quit. He hoped it would be Reggie.

Odd or specialty-type pools were the worst to install. This particular job for a posh hotel in Jackson, Mississippi, maxed out all of them. The specs called for a large hot tub to be attached to a kidney-shaped pool. A twelve-foot waterfall, a wet bar, and a nearby fire pit laid in stone and dark granite completed the plans. This not-so legitimate pool company had never attempted anything this complex. Economically-priced residential pools were their specialty, which meant when customer complaints rolled in, and they did, the "you get what you pay for" line spilled into conversation. If the complaints persisted, the long-distance customer service rep needed only to point out all the places the customer signed or initialed, and like that, the gripes muted. To avoid lawsuits, the company has changed names four times.

This current job came from a friend of a friend. The money for this project enabled a summer in the Hamptons for the pool company owners. Along with this good news, there were a couple of inexperienced employees working in this hotel who were to be accountable for

expenditures. This meant new bills and added expenses could easily
be included almost daily without much interference or questions. On
the management end, this hotel deal was a dream. For those working
on the actual construction however, it was a continual struggle.

It was already one of those days. Reggie started with his first
thermos, and it was not quite half past eight. Looking for the best
tools to use for the job at hand which meant nabbing what wasn't his,
he muttered inflammatory words under his rancid breath. The biting
comments were aimed at Joe who had just broken a pipe meant for a
drain. Joe needed this job, but with too much anger and sweat now
in his own blood, he didn't need this. Staring at the broken pipe, he
realized this wasn't the only thing to break. Today was the day. "Ah,
what did you say, Reginald?"

Reggie repeated his spiked words.

Rubbing his chin with dirty hands, Joe wondered, "Now, is that
you talking, or is that the booze I hear in your thermos over there?"

Reggie glared at Joe. "Oh, it's me."

They stood about five feet apart.

Joe dropped the shovel in his hand. It splattered mud over his
already mud-caked jeans. "Still not clear with what you mean there,
sunshine. Drunks don't mumble though."

Reggie heard how Joe wasn't like the rest of them. That silver spoon
affected how the boy talked, and this hurt the broken man more than
the petty words Joe spit, or tried to spit. Joe ending up here was one
thing, but he could tell the kid had at least some college education,
which was so far above what anyone nearby had. That this mouthy
punk was here in this hell by choice busted him. "Calling me a drunk?
This is what you got?"

Joe tasted evil in his mouth. "What I have is a headache. You."

Out of habit, Reggie's foul language ripped. It burned right into
Joe who charged and knocked down the man who had already been
knocked down by life fifteen years ago when his wife, with a diagnosed
mental illness, took her life and the life of their nine-month-old baby boy.

"Fight! Fight! Fight!" The nearby crew started chanting.

"You stupid sh—" The older man swaggered to his feet and charged. Joe ducked. From behind, Joe kicked Reggie in the small of the back. The hit was hard, cruel. The bitter widower and father dropped again.

A flash memory of the movie on the wall in the lab rippled in front of the fighter on his feet. It was one where young Joe slammed a mentally handicapped student into a cinderblock school hallway. Fiery mad at the billionaire god he could not escape from even here in his thoughts, Joe kicked Reggie again, and again.

Not yet defeated, Reggie rose as an angry serpent ready to bite. When his fists started connecting, he fought the privilege Joe had. He fought the younger guy's age and the fact that Joe shouldn't even be here in these literally muddy pits. This kid with unbroken teeth and a disposition of some university frat boy shouldn't be throwing what could be a bright future away.

A broken metal pipe hit Joe in the ribs. Down he went. Straddling the kid, Reggie used the pipe to choke the mouthy underachiever.

Joe would not be undone. He fought the darkness he sucked himself into since he left that hotel room on the fourth floor. From the ground, he forced himself to become even further from the one he was a year-and-a-half-ago, an idealist with hope and happiness.

Using a short two-by-four, the foreman jumped in and broke up the action, but not after a lot of damage had been done to both men.

"Fired! The both of you!" He sputtered. Glad to see the drunk go, he immediately wondered how he could get that good worker back, the one with the strong back and the brains. He'd just have to play this right.

"Now go on, the both of you! Out!"

As the foreman made his way out of the muddy mess where the fight began, he caught sight of the latest shipment that had arrived yesterday afternoon. Without opening the crate, he knew the wrong materials had been delivered. This meant construction would be delayed by a day or two.

He turned to take in the scrap behind him that he had just broken up. Another bonus was that neither dirt bag in the fight would have to be paid today. If he was careful, he might even get away with cheating them out of yesterday's pay, too. That younger one—Joe was his name—he was promising. His shoulder didn't look quite right though. It was likely dislocated, and he heard that metal pipe hit those ribs of his square on.

"Yeah. Fired. The both of you!"

•————————•

Joe didn't know her name, even the fake one she used when he paid her cash up front. He just needed this.

It was the ugliest motel room he'd ever seen, and he'd been in real dives. Curtains nearly twice his age matched the faded carpet that literally could never be clean again. He knew the worn sheets hadn't been laundered, and he was not even going to think about the bathroom where she made him shower.

The sex wasn't good, of course. Why would it be? But there were no cameras. Nothing else was important except that there could be no more recordings. No more of his life would ever be projected onto a white wall.

As for the rest of his life, it simply didn't matter what happened. He told himself a minute after he met this woman who had first approached him in a bar that he wouldn't care about her, and he was doing his best to make sure that happened. He wouldn't think about Reggie either. Since their fight a few hours ago, he succeeded at forgetting what happened. When he closed his eyes for more than a second though, he could picture Reggie hurting, and this made him mad. Even though he could see Reggie in a sunlit hospital room under a soft blue blanket with a TV remote in his bandaged right hand and a nearby bedtray holding now cold vegetable soup, Joe knew he wasn't Jesus' clone. How could he be? Sure, he could picture Reggie clearly. The blinds in the room were half down, and his sleeping roommate didn't make a sound during one very long documentary on migrating whales. Joe knew these and other visions were no special power, no godly gift. He only had to look at what he has done to see who he really was, and that was no clone of the spotless, sinless Jesus Christ.

"Babe, you're quiet."

"What?"

The woman beside him stirred. "You look like you got something on your mind. You wanna talk?"

"No."

She called herself Daphne, and today's cash would make her car payment. Looking up at him, she saw something in his eyes that he tried to blur, if not lose altogether. Taking in the fresh cut on his face and the split lip from a fight she guessed happened hours ago, she started talking to him about her car, her kitten Bianca, and her boyfriend who often watched and enjoyed her having sex with strangers. Soft and low, her voice purred.

For a few minutes, Joe just listened. Unlike times with other clients, she knew this one heard. If she set this up good and right, it was possible this could be a two-sided conversation. That would be nice. She could tell from the sorrow behind his eyes that he hadn't had anything like a real connection for a long, long time. She kept talking, telling this stranger about her mom, her one and only semester at the junior college, and which shades of nail polish all women should avoid.

Suddenly, Joe realized Jesus spent time with prostitutes. Using irate, belittling words, he kicked her out of bed. Afraid of his anger and threats, she scrambled and started to cry. Most of her clothes filled her arms as she scurried out a door that, even with a repaired lock, still didn't close just right.

Securing the door, he approached the bed and slid even further from the space where she had been beside him. He forced his eyes closed and, in a lucid moment, recalled scripture he memorized in college, 1 Corinthian 6:15-16. *Don't you realize that your bodies are actually parts of Christ? Should a man take his body, which is part of Christ, and join it to a prostitute? Never! And don't you realize that if a man joins himself to a prostitute, he becomes one body with her?*

"I am nobody with no one," he said to himself, thinking what he tried so hard to avoid, and that was that he was a clone, a test tube creation, an experiment. "I am not even me."

He hated himself because he was not himself. Into stale air that still smelled like the empty sex he never should have had, he growled. "What a cruel joke you've created, Mr. Roland Rolls."

It doesn't take long to drink money. In less than two weeks, the wad of cash he kept blew away. But, he told himself, it had been a good two weeks. A numbing two weeks.

The homeless shelter was by far cleaner than most of the dumps he'd stayed in, and if he continued to drink just enough nearly all the time, he'd make it. *And that's not such a bad plan, is it?*

Just as he thought this, he saw from his place in the lunch line a clean-cut man his age serving part of the hot meal at the shelter this afternoon. The charitable young guy without head lice or bad breath wore a Bible College sweatshirt identical to one he once owned.

"Step up, doll," a woman behind him muttered. "Step up."

Joe couldn't move toward the food, at least not easily. He kept his head down as he came close to the counter because he was certain a handful of broken glass at the top of his stomach would cut him. Just ahead, Joe spotted the sweatshirt guy serving sweet smelling yellow corn in a big, stainless steel tub. Panicky, he opted out of line after a meat of some kind hit his tray. The fork, knife, and spoon he should get rested in large metal drinking glasses at the end of the line, just beyond an array of three day-old desserts. But he couldn't go back. Facing a wall at an empty table, he just licked what he had off the tray.

A moment later, hearing the guy in the sweatshirt make a joke with someone as he carried away a full trash bag through the corner doors to the dumpster, he wanted to cry. Oh, yes, he wanted to slide under the table and sob. But there were no tears.

Thinking now that he could really use a drink, he sealed his soul from its last vulnerable road. He wouldn't care anymore. There would be no more blue blankets or bandaged hands, and he would never be called "doll" again. With a determination he had never had before, he forced his eyes and heart to become the cold, sterile, hard plastic vial he'd come from.

•————————•

From a man who left his cot to go pee in the middle of the night, Joe stole the whiskey he'd spotted earlier in the guy's brand new, eco-friendly grocery bag. The last third of the liquid gold went down magically, wonderfully. When Joe's lips began to numb, he just stared into space. He knew what was true. There were no tears. With certainly, he said, "There is no God."

CHAPTER TWENTY THREE

Even though today's weather was miserable by even an optimist's standards, Betsy was determined to push and pound her way through today's five-mile run. She needed this escape, this release. The cadence of her feet and the rhythm of the run itself sent her to places she needed to escape to, and she was so grateful.

At first, Betsy was not sure whom she was talking with in her mind—it likely started as an inner conversation with just herself—but as the first mile stretched into the second, she realized to her surprise that she was talking to the seemingly simple yet deeply complicated philosophy major that she had met almost two years ago. She laughed at herself because thoughts of Joe had just snuck up on her. It was not that she hung on to a thread of hope with him. As a mechanical engineer graduating in just over two months, she was a realist: the odds of meeting this relative stranger again were truly next to none, and she was fine with that. She had moved on completely. The night she met Tad for their big date by choosing to wear her black dress made it clear that Joe was behind her. She was moving on with her life. Tad wasn't everything, but unlike Joe and Mike, he hadn't left her. He cared for her as he could, and in the six months that they had been seriously dating, she felt good around him. That was enough, right?

She told herself she shouldn't be thinking about Joe. Keeping that gentle, often charming worldly misfit out of her mind had been to her advantage because the truth was the truth: a girl can't look back on a guy who just wasn't there. Yet as she ran along, she realized she was able to find something in herself when she talked with Joe, something she liked and needed. As she was finishing a long stretch of road beside a muddy field of grass just turning green, she wasn't even sure if it was raining because Joe's spirit seemed to fill her with light and energy. Joe did see all of her, flaws included, yet only the best in her came forward in his company. Unlike Tad, Joe wanted to find out and enjoy the fun and quirky parts of her so that they could be brought out even more. She teared up as she remembered the little country store the three had visited after their time by the water. Mike had stayed in the car as the two went inside.

There in that store holding two cans of a blue soda, Joe stood still after he had been walking toward her. Motionless, he held her in his eyes for an instant, and then somehow gave her back to her own self — better, sweeter, and more complete than she had been before.

In having a conversation with Joe as she ran along, she was able to successfully vent the stresses of dating Mr. Football who could be difficult or demanding when she wasn't there to support him, or point out how great he was. Sure, when she was somehow "off," Tad would humor her as if she were acting goofy. At first this was a lighthearted part of their routine, their inner dialogue, but she was weary of the game because it masked this truth: she was his mirror, the one who was there so that he could take a better look at himself.

Tad had pushed for more intimacy as a way to connect them more completely. True, Betsy thought, sex can connect a couple, but it was becoming clearer to her that the relationship between the two of them wasn't right. It hadn't been good since they started.

She ran even faster to face what she had been hiding from herself, which was the voice inside telling her to quit the relationship. For a moment she thought she was running away from troubles, but she was actually racing toward them. She did not like who she was with Tad. Yes, everyone needed support at times. This certainly included herself with Mike now gone, but she wanted to be more than a cheerleader.

The very heavy rain that wasn't forecasted until midday arrived at the start of her third mile. She pressed on because in more ways than one she was not turning back. As far as those silly romance novels went, she wouldn't be the princess, duchess, or some fair maiden caught in some tragic story. Instead, she continued to realize that sharing her thoughts with Joe brought the release she needed. She told Joe about the everyday things she had been passing, like the push of tulips out of the mulch under a sign for a retirement village, or a girl and guy couple running side by side in the opposite direction, each wise enough to wear baseball caps that sheltered their eyes from the steady rain.

As Betsy entered a grove of tall trees that had not yet begun to leaf out, she also shared with Joe her deeper thoughts, her struggles. Anxiety inched closer as she came upon her graduation in two months. Interviews started next week and she wondered how they would go. Specifically, she wondered where she will go. While it would be alright to stay near her family here in the Midwest, the chance of a new city in a new area of the country made her smile at the possibility. Yes, she could see herself living far from here, at least for a while.

Her career situation, as she knew from listening to both her dad and two of her favorite professors who do or have worked in the mechanical engineering field, would take care of itself. She knew what to listen for, what to share, and how to navigate through interviewing conversations to get what she wanted professionally.

And then, like that, Betsy realized something odd. She wasn't talking with Joe anymore, she was talking with God. Without her knowing, thoughts of that guy with the attentive, gentle eyes rolled over somehow, or broadened. Yes, something changed, deepened, and blossomed. She sighed because if anyone could bring an analytically-minded person to God, it would be Joe.

"God," she said tentatively, "you gave me something there. You did. I know it." Betsy paused.

If this was a prayer, she knew she had never prayed like this in full stride. Respectfully, she continued. "And all of these gifts. My major. My great grades. This school itself. My mom and dad. My health."

Out of the trees now, she ran along a narrow sidewalk. "And oh, yes, let me state the obvious here too." She almost giggled. "I can't forget this rain. You've given me that, too."

Something within her rational, measured mind made her frown. She focused so hard that the oddest, smallest objects in front of her, like the actual raindrops themselves, appeared individually. This was impossible, she figured, yet it was true. She could see each raindrop. At this, her body suddenly warmed from within. The rain others would call miserable didn't change, she did. She was running toward him. She didn't question who was in front of her, encouraging her along. Amazingly free, she just continued to race, her feet barely touching the sidewalk beneath her. As she ran dead center down an athletic field toward her dorm building, she knew who she is racing toward. It was Jesus.

"Tad?"

"Yeah?"

Betsy took the overly-muscled arm of his that had been around her and brought it between them. She held his hand. She had pegged him as the bad guy out on her run and knew that wasn't entirely true. Yes, while he needed a sidekick to his being a superhero, he was faithful, consistent. He held on when she would try to sabotage herself or the two of them as couple.

He stared at the nearby napkin holder. "Uh-oh, this is serious."

Moving her chair so that they were face-to-face at a small table near the doors to the *Cup Up*, the place where they were supposed to have had their first date, she rubbed her thumbnail with her index finger. "It is serious."

Tad pouted. "You don't like me no more."

He could be boyish when scared, or controlling. She'd figured this out.

She thought about her run in the rain and did her best to respond. "I do like you."

"Okay."

"It's just—"

His look chilled the back of her neck. He would not make this easy on her. She realized he shouldn't. Since they started dating and had spent significant time together over Christmas and New Year's, he'd been upfront with her. Honest and open—or as open as he could be—he would be the rudder to her sail. He took that directional position now.

"Betsy." His eyes, always a cool blue, somehow warmed. He touched her soul without reaching across the table. "Say it."

She remembered the raindrops. *Am I sure about this? What happened out there in the rainstorm really did happen, right?*

Betsy wasn't certain where the next sentence she was about to share came from because it certainly did not sound like her. "Tad, I've changed."

"Of course you have."

She didn't expect this, not now. Uncertain of what she really wanted, she continued the line of thinking she started. "I'm…I'm just a different person now."

"Oh, so this isn't about me, or anything I've done wrong, like ask for *sex*. This is about you. *You've changed.*"

Tad set his fists on the table. He knew he shouldn't have pushed for sex, not with this one. Thinking about his status with the team, his words filled with pride, then anger. "Well, you know what? If you don't want it, baby, you don't have to get it."

"Tad, I'm glad we can *talk* about this."

"Girl, that's all we do—talk."

Knotted, she didn't know what to say. If she could quickly buy and read a manual on this, she would. Suddenly, she wished Mike were here. As a relationship master, he'd know how to respond. Helpful, he'd coach her through this.

"No worries." He tapped the table with his fingers. "I get it. I've slept with Pam."

Wait, who's Pam?

"It was just sex with her, so, whatever."

To save face, Tad actually lied here. While he knew it hasn't been good between the two of them lately, he did not spend the night with another woman. He desired Betsy, and he'll wait for her.

As he looked down at the table between them, he knew he had to be honest. "What I just said? Yeah. I wasn't honest with you. I don't know why I did that. Wait, I do." He swallowed. "I didn't—don't—want to be hurt." His eyes met hers. "I don't know why I said that about Pam. I didn't tell you the truth. Pam? Me? We did not have sex."

Betsy wanted to know who Pam was.

Trying to hear the woman who just drove him so positively crazy, Tad tried to guess what was really wrong. "I know. It's graduation. It's coming up, and you want to be free."

"That's not it."

"But it *is* a transition time."

Betsy folded her fingers. This was going to be challenging. "When I was out running today?"

"In that monsoon?"

"Yeah."

"Well, I had an epiphany."

Tad didn't know what an epiphany was. He'd never heard the word before.

"Running like that was just this transformative experience. It was like I was on this path."

"Uh, you had to have been on a path, right? You were running."

She knew he was trying to be funny. "Not like that. I just realized there is something out there. Something I have to do. Travel toward."

"You're not making any sense."

Betsy shook her head. "Trust me. This doesn't make much sense now to me, either."

"What are you saying?"

She knew she just had to say it. "I saw Jesus out there."

Carrying more hard feelings than he could admit from his rocky childhood, Tad *definitely* wanted no part of religion. Spirituality definitely made him want to find the fast exit door. From their start as a couple, he offhandedly made that very clear. "Jesus. Out where?"

"It was raining. Hard. And I didn't seem to mind it. In fact, and I know this will really come off as strange, I could see so many individual drops."

"Drops. You saw individual drops of rain."

"Yeah. My pace was awesome, and it wasn't a runner's high, though this was close. Trust me. He was just *there*."

"You're getting weird on me." Tad looked to see if anyone overheard him. "He, Jesus, was there?"

Betsy did not answer. She did not know how to answer. Something like this had never happened to her before. Maybe she was weird. Maybe this actually didn't really happen.

But it did.

Tad shook his hands. Leaning back against his chair, he tried to be levelheaded. "You are not making sense here. In fact, this is just really odd." Like he did just a moment earlier, he looked to see if anyone were listening in on their conversation. This really annoyed Betsy.

"I know. This is strange."

Tad stood. "Let's go. Let's get out of here and talk about something else."

Betsy realized something for the first time. Her voice had never quite sounded like she was not quite herself. She *had* changed. She did see and speak to a Savior out there, her Savior. "No, I need to talk about this."

"Not with me."

As soon as Tad said this, he wished to take it back.

He could change. He could change for her. Despite this moment, despite how uncomfortable he was now around her, this was only a moment. It was true that he could be understanding and patient. He'll wait this through. This epiphany deal, whatever that was, would be something he will walk with her.

Suddenly he stopped what he was thinking. While he was not honest with her about Pam—whatever that was—he had to be honest now. He would not—could not—go with her on this religious ride. God-talk? Jesus mess? Seriously?

With his once Catholic mom, and his dad who said he was a Presbyterian or a Protestant, or maybe being Presbyterian and Protestant were the same deal, Tad could not go there with her. Yes, he did want her. Of course, he did. But this? This? He took a step toward the double doors behind him.

Sitting still, Betsy frowned. She didn't have the slightest clue as to how to answer the question she was about to ask. "If I can't talk with you about this, then who do I talk to?"

CHAPTER TWENTY FOUR

He needed alcohol more than air. He couldn't breathe without it.

Beckoning, the liquor store had its door propped wide open. A store like this was the sanctuary he needed. It was medicine, after all. He learned as a boy with perfect attendance in Sunday school that only Jesus could turn water into wine. This didn't stop Joe from trying to make alcohol from a running faucet when in desperate need of a drink. After all, he told himself more than once that Jesus wanted him to show up to the wedding dressed nicely. Joe knew from scripture that Jesus was a winemaker, at least in this part of his narrative. If Joe could drink just enough—not be excessive, of course, but if he could maintain that buzz—then what was read in the Good Book would be true. He'd get good clothes.

A few problems came along with this. First, he didn't know where the wedding was taking place. Second, he didn't know who was getting married. Third, he didn't know exactly how drinking "just enough" would get him good, clean clothes. More and more details escaped him these days. In fact, nothing made a lot of sense.

From the pocket of the long coat some definitely "Christian" woman helped him find a few days ago, he looked for the knife he had stolen from another sleeping drunk. He patted down the jacket. The knife. Why couldn't he find the knife? His hands kept shaking. Just get the booze, he told himself. Just get the booze.

He found himself in the store. Walking away from him, the sales associate busied herself with a customer. Their eyes never met. "Now," the employee said in a voice a little too haughty to a customer who was a little high end, "what kind of a bouquet do you prefer? Something sweet, or..."

I don't need a knife. I don't need a knife! I can just take it. All of this, after all, was just for him. It was just what he needed.

Taking in the aisle perfectly lined with bottle after bottle, he knew this store was somehow a church because the Lord does provide. Yes, holy Jesus, the Lord does provide. One bottle, two bottles, three bottles, four.

"And God," Joe whispered, "will supply all your needs according to his glorious riches in Christ Jesus. Philippians 4:19." With the long coat loaded, he walked out of the store less than a minute later. He couldn't buy that porn magazine he dared himself to buy as a teenager faster than this.

•————————•

How he found himself standing on the roof of a five-story building he did not know. He was not sure he'd ever been here before, but yet he didn't remember having any difficulty climbing the stairs and jimmying the rusty door to the roof. Maybe he had started off to the wedding and was looking for the rooftop reception. At the edge of the tall building, Joe looked down. He was not sure what city this was at the moment, but, after he downed more booze to keep himself blurry, he heard himself say that he was at the pinnacle of the temple. Of course, he was here in Jerusalem. He stood on the top of the Temple in the Holy City, just as scripture indicated. In being somewhat rounded, the roof's tan tile edging looked like loaves of baked bread. Yes, the stones were turning into bread, but the Tempter wasn't here.

Joe turned. He waited. Another hit from his bottle seemed good and right, but it didn't work. The bottle was empty. When did that happen? Looking down at the tile—the loaves of bread—he suddenly remembered his line. "Man does not live by bread alone." He slipped the new bottle out from his long coat and, in being so precious, he cradled the lovely one in the fold of his arm. "Of course they don't live by bread alone. They can't."

The bottle was a baby, and the innkeeper was a high-end customer looking for bottles of wine to entertain the guests that had filled all the rooms.

Joe dropped to his knees. He was messing up this whole script. "The clone can't get this right, Jesus. He just can't get this right." Crawling, he looked in all directions. Joe couldn't find a little camera anywhere. But there had to be one here, right?

"You wouldn't want to miss recording this, would you, Tootsie?"

He suddenly remembered the cash he stole this morning from two corporately-dressed young women on their way to their offices. He had the knife then. He scared them.

"That money," he mumbled to a rooftop air conditioning unit that might be from Roland Rolls' lab. "It's somewhere. Yes. It's inside my chest pocket here." His fingers became numb after the new bottle somehow emptied, but with a little effort, he stood back up and pulled out a handful of bills.

"I don't need money to buy alcohol." He started back to the edge of the building. "I'm going to save the world with this. Yes, the world! And you, all my children in the world, can have this." So wonderfully drunk, he flung the cash into the air. Magnificently the money fluttered in the breeze.

◈┄┄┄┄┄┄┄┄┄┄┄┄┄◈

It was Mike. It *was* Mike. He'd become a police officer. *When did this happen?* Joe studied the officer's face.

"Mike?"

Not wanting to touch the drunk at his feet, the cop spoke into the radio at his shoulder. "We found him. He's here. On the roof."

"Mike? You sound different."

"You're under arrest for robbery. Anything you do or say can and will be used against you in a court of law."

"Mike, you're an angel who is a cop."

The police officer rolled his eyes. "So, I'm Mike today. That's great. It doesn't matter that my real name is Dan, does it?"

Joe's eyes flooded with tears. He missed his dear friend, his roommate. The book talks in their dorm. The philosophical and theological banter. And of course the boxers that must have been red, not maroon.

Mike. Thank God! It's Mike! Joe tried to focus. "You *are* a cop! And you wore that sweatshirt, the Bible College one. That was you, right? With the corn for lunch?"

"Yeah, I did. I did wear that very sweatshirt. Sure. On a date with my wife and kids. Wouldn't you know?"

The officer held his breath as the rancid smelling drunk sat up after having very recently wet his pants.

"He will order his angels to protect you," Joe said. "And they will hold you up with their hands, so you won't even hurt your foot on a stone."

Joe glanced down at his feet. He was not sure how one foot was bare and the other wore a boot.

"You're my angel, Mike."

"Oh, yeah," Dan replied. "I'm your angel, alright."

⚬────────────⚬

The fifty-year-old former business man in the cell with Joe might be a heroin addict, but he'd know Jesus if he saw him. This was Jesus.

In the middle of the night, the lights in this county jail were very low. Water dripped from a faucet nearby. The hem of his garment, Joe's cellmate thought. The hem of his garment.

The convict who broke his parole earlier that day slipped his hand under Joe's blanket. Joe, asleep in a pair of state issued coveralls he did not put on himself, suddenly scurried to the nearest corner.

It's Mr. Rolls! Joe was certain of this.

Only the Silver Man is in some disguise. Yes, this is all a trick. A test of some kind.

The mad scientist had touched Joe when Joe was naked on that table. Now this creep reached out and stroked his shoulder.

"Rolls," Joe hissed, "I know this is you."

"You have to heal me, Jesus, if it's your will."

Joe didn't understand.

"I'm blind to only the white lines, the white, powder lines. Dear Savior. Heal me."

Scrambling to get away, Joe tripped over his own feet.

"Yes, Savior. Lord Jesus, I know it's you. Heal me."

Joe screamed a blood-curling scream. He screamed again, and again. He couldn't be here again. He couldn't be back in the lab. No, no, no.

Grabbing the bars to the cell, he just shook.

"Heal me, Jesus!"

"*Help! Help!*" No one answered.

"Heal me!"

Too frightened, Joe fainted.

⊶────────⊷

When he rolled onto his back an hour later, he felt something creamy and sticky on his collar. More covered his shoulder.

He took a breath. *This wasn't...*

The man laughed sinisterly. "It is." He motioned toward his crotch.

Now Joe knew what was true. He was in hell.

⊶────────⊷

Joe's attorney was overworked. Fortunately, this case didn't present any real challenges. As they went to court that morning, Joe confided in his lawyer that he still did not remember the proprietor yelling after him, demanding he return to her liquor store with the bottles in his coat.

The second-career attorney who ate her way to comfort with cholesterol-laden pastries and sweetened coffee drinks wanted to push the judge for professional psychological care. There was a brand new, exploratory program being implemented in one of the state's rehab centers. As Joe would likely get sentenced to one of the centers, she'd negotiate, plead, or beg for this particular facility because, hands down, she knew this: the kid was nuts. Distraught, disoriented, non-responsive, and fearful were just some words to describe him. With a caseload like hers, she'd seen this before, but never as severe. A couple of personalities lived within the boy who muttered scripture when not terrified of breaking out of some mythical science lab. To prove he had seen his former roommate Mike and not the police officer on the afternoon of the arrest was her best angle.

———◦———

The case took twelve minutes. Sitting still at the table completely unaware of the proceedings, Joe casually glanced in her direction when she came back to him from the judge's bench. He looked at her as if she were a stranger. *Have I seen her before? Is she my next door neighbor, the spy who pretends to write novels?*

Sliding her chair up to his, she set her short, stubby fingers on the edge of the worn table. "Joe, you do understand the sentence the judge handed you?"

He didn't answer.

"Joe?"

She tried again to help him understand his sentence. Sometimes, when it was just the two of them, it did seem like he listened to her. She waited for those warm, caring eyes to meet hers.

"Joe, considering what you have done—and someone was watching over you because, thank God, you didn't have a knife with you when you entered that store—you've been handed a mandatory ninety-day sentence in a rehabilitation center."

When she finished phrases he didn't understand about a brand new, one-on-one counseling program he must attend with a psychologist, she motioned to the courtroom officer. Using a voice like a mother, a tone she'd never used in court before and vowed to never use again, she said, "And now you have to go with that gentleman there."

"Does he work for Mr. Rolls?" He rubbed his foreman, feeling under his fingers a bandage that wasn't there. "I am getting another ulmintin injection, aren't I?"

CHAPTER TWENTY FIVE

She wore the flowery dress.

Staring at the fabric over her lap, Betsy kept her head down and tried her best to tune out the two voices behind her by reading the thin church bulletin a guy on the college volleyball team handed her a minute ago. Even though Betsy tried to concentrate on the paper in her hand to get ready for the upcoming service which would start soon, she still heard them.

"She is a very pretty young girl."

"She's not Ralphie Gennson's granddaughter, is she?"

"No, Blanche. Ralphie Gennson's granddaughter is a *big* girl. And she's like thirty-years-old. This one here? Why, I'd say she's a teenager."

"You *do* remember what happened to Ralphie Gennson's granddaughter, don't you? That no good husband of hers had had that surgery, whatever *that* was, and Dorri there—is that the girl's name?"

"Yes, I think so."

"Yes, she was named after her mom, come to think of it."

"You know what happened to her, don't you? Spent all her money."

"Like a gambler."

"Well, little Dorri had to go and get a *second* job at a place Ralphie would *not* be proud of."

"Where? Tell!"

Betsy knew she should turn around, invite herself into some conversation by first introducing herself to the finely-dressed seniors who graced a pew several feet behind her, but she couldn't. Instead, she slipped off her seat, nodded to the two gossiping grannies who, with obvious hearing loss, must not mean to talk so loud. She walked right through even more of the musty smell of the sanctuary to sit closer to the still vacant pulpit.

From the back of the church where he had been an usher, the volleyball player watched her every move. With the stack of bulletins in his hand, he waved to her. She did not wave back. Two days ago, she had her final goodbye with Tad. With a month to go before graduation, she was not going to start anything new. No sooner did she think this than the organ music started like a breathy sounding merry-go-round in slow motion that couldn't quite keep a steady beat. Suddenly the volleyball player introduced himself as Alden. He stood in the aisle next to her pew, and, before she knew it, dropped down beside her.

Betsy glanced around. In a sanctuary that could easily seat one hundred and fifty worshippers, eleven people, including the elderly pastor who had now appeared, filled the stale space. Careful to show respect over the next hour, Betsy knew of rituals and their importance. Having attended a Methodist church somewhat regularly ten years ago with both her parents, she made it through most of the experience, including the Lord's Prayer, without too much difficulty. When the anemic service ended, however, she bolted out of there. Reverence and silence was one thing; sitting in that near-death environment for fifty-seven minutes was another.

Staring at the sidewalk just outside the church, she wondered again what that rainy day run meant. She wondered if people do experience Jesus in church. She glanced over her shoulder. Without much difficulty, she saw this white steepled building becoming another remodeled space for daycare or community offerings. Two other small-time churches in the area had been repurposed. This property may be next. As she picked up speed on her way back to her dorm, she tried to walk away from the knotted feeling in her stomach. It wasn't that she could find anything *wrong* with the sermon or the service in particular, but it definitely didn't feel right.

She heard someone calling behind her. "Oh, wait. Hey, wait!"

Betsy did not want to turn around.

It was the volleyball player. With long, easy strides, Alden caught up to her. The college junior broke into conversation when their strides fell into sync. "I knew you were a Christian. I could see it when I'd catch you around campus."

Betsy didn't know how to respond.

"I was saved when I was fifteen. When did you let Christ into your heart?"

"I...I'm not sure."

Alden's hopes suddenly crashed. While sitting beside her all that time, he had mapped out so many things because, he knew, God does provide. He'd been sending arrow prayers to God to bring him just the right one. And Betsy, wow, she sure was pretty, polite.

Alden wasn't sure what to do. He meant well. Making her comfortable around him was important. Quickly, he decided to ask the question again. "When were you saved?"

Betsy knew she needed to be honest. "I'm not sure. I don't know."

Alden, a guy who really did care and followed Christ as he knew him personally, tried to remember what his grandmother had said about putting people into boxes. He knew this was something he'd been particularly good at since middle school when he lost the eighth grade class presidency to the boy who rode two seats ahead of him on the school bus. This he could not take, however. There were sinners and there were the saved. His tone was curt, abrasive. "Not sure? You live for Christ, or you don't. It's not 'iffy' here. Our Lord calls us. He does not want so-so Christians."

"Oh."

"Christ Jesus is your personal Savior, or he's not. The Bible says we are not to be lukewarm."

Betsy's knees felt numb.

Alden purposefully walked a half a shoulder ahead of her, pinning her back in a way she was not comfortable. "The only way to get to heaven is through Jesus. John 3:16. Can I tell you what that scripture says?"

She remembered what she was running toward that afternoon in the rain. It didn't feel anything like this.

After that church experience and this conversation, she'd like to kick off her dressy shoes and run again. Just run. Very fast.

"Did you hear me?"

Betsy honestly didn't know that Alden had just been talking.

———

After three consecutive Sundays in a mega church which sported a praise band and full auditorium seating for a thousand, she walked down the steps outside her dorm and met Alden, as planned, on a park bench. Five minutes into their walk toward town and a new church for both of them, he picked up on the conversation they had had by phone a few days earlier.

"Betsy, I did the mega church route, too. For me, it was cool for couple of weeks."

She looked at him. "But it just wasn't right, was it?"

The two had begun a walk along the path toward the south end of their campus. Alden's walk was much slower now, more relaxed. The persona he had with Betsy when the two of them left that small church four Sundays ago disappeared.

Alden thought about his answer. "Nah, for me, it wasn't right." He breathed, which was hard to do. Nervous around this pretty girl, he slipped one of his hands into one of his back pockets hoping that move would make him keep walking slowly. "It was like this big concert. This stage show. I mean, it was exciting and all—and loud—and I'll go again sometimes, for sure, but I didn't connect."

Betsy hadn't shared this with anyone before. "It really is about connecting, isn't it?"

"Yeah, sure."

"One-on-one. Personally."

"Yeah."

Just ahead, nearing the large church they'd be attending this morning, Betsy caught a glimpse of a guy in a dark shirt and tie who looked a bit like Joe.

Alden noticed this. "That guy?"

"What guy?"

"The one you're looking at. He's going to hell."

"*What?*"

"He's gay. He's going to hell."

Betsy stopped. Both feet didn't move. Alden, now a few steps ahead, turned. He shook his head. "What? I'm not wrong here, babe."

"We judge not, lest we be judged."

"He can be saved, sure. But now he's a queer. He'll go to hell."

"What did Jesus say about being gay? I don't remember reading that."

"This comes from the Old Testament, which Jesus came to fulfill. And the Apostle Paul, he—" Alden took a step back. He could bring her around. Love the sinner, hate the sin.

Just before entering the church, the guy who reminded Betsy of Joe looked at her. The glance that took a full second seemed much longer. Instantly, she thought of Mike. Her heart pulled out of her chest. "I'm not so sure I can talk with you, Alden. At least not now."

He'd had enough. Love was one thing; tolerance was another. "Fine."

"Fine? That's it? Fine?"

Alden was not about to be late, and he certainly couldn't be seen with a girl who loved poofs. "Fags like that guy?"

"Again, somehow, you know he's gay?"

"Well, no. But—"

She was as angry as she was the day she met Joe. She'd been duped that day, tricked. On that big, honking rock, she fired off at Mike, now she'd fire for him. "You make me hurt. Did you hear that, Christian? You make me hurt. One of the two commandments Jesus raises as most important calls for me to love you, but that commandment does not say *anything* about liking you. Alden, I certainly don't like you, not now. The God I know is all about love. The God I hear from you isn't about love at all."

Defeated, deflated and frustrated, she kicked off her shoes, scooped them up, and, in the very dress she wore to Mike's funeral, she ran in the other direction as fast as she could.

The zipper along the back of her dress annoying rubbed her skin between her shoulder blades. At first she didn't care, she just raced up streets back toward campus. But then she stopped. As soon as she started walking, what immediately captured her attention was a little bridge and a low, quiet stream running under it. She didn't think she'd have any struggle at all. She'd just find a church. She'd just grow in her faith naturally and easily. No gossiping old ladies, no dry preacher, no dead church, no glitzy show with a band, no guys like Alden judging. Just love. And peace. Jesus himself.

A soft, well-worn path led to the water's edge. She took it. Not caring about the dress, she sat on a rock the size of a home plate on a baseball field. Folding her legs up to her chest, she rested her chin between her knees. A picture of Mike appeared in her mind. Eight or nine-years old, her Best Bud was with her in her beloved backyard tree house, the one with the wooden planks that led up to its hatch. She remembered the smell of summer. His floppy hair. His sweaty bangs. The treasure of letting her take his brand new Band-Aids off so that together they'd be the first to see the two stitches he had just received from the ER doctor after having slid hands first into home plate from a Little League game that very afternoon. Then she remembered Joe, lean and handsome and so full of life, shooting up out of the creek so long ago. He had that smile. That rush. That energy. The joy of the day was his. She looked down into the shallow water before her now. Maybe she was wrong about everything.

CHAPTER TWENTY SIX

Holding his arms, Joe sat quietly in front of her as he stared at her desk. While other times in this tight office truly scared him, this was the scariest.

Most everyone here called her the Doctor, even those who meticulously guarded the double locked exit doors, and these Michael-sized guys were far, far beefier than those his DOD took out the last time Rolls had him penned. Hiring all these actors—and this 'facility' itself was quite large—had to be a part of his greater trick. Of course, Rolls was watching him. While Joe couldn't see a sophisticated camera or recording device anywhere—was a button on a shirt really a button?—he knew someday a projector would drop from some ceiling and start showing his life again on a blank, white wall. This frightened him.

"Are you cold, Joe?"

Not quite meeting his captor in the eye, Joe tilted his head toward the sound of Dr. Blaine's voice.

"Are you cold?"

He shook his head no.

"You've been holding your arms for some time now."

Talented, compassionate, and dedicated, Dr. Meredith Blaine moved from her side of a short, strictly functional desk she used once a week while here. Crossing her long, shapely legs, she hoped this closer proximity would bring her complex twenty-two-year-old patient greater comfort.

Mandatory time with Dr. Blaine had been negotiated as a part of

Joe's sentence. Twice a week for thirty minutes, he shared one-on-one time with the doctor in a new, non-federally funded program she knew would be the first to fall when the budget tightened next year. Nevertheless, she was here now, and Joe presented classic symptoms of delusional disorder. This was their fifth week together, and Joe continued to share almost nothing. For example, the only time he mentioned the ulmintin injections was the day in court when he was sentenced to this rehabilitation center. Just like in their last session, Dr. Blaine noticed the swelling, defined muscles in Joe's arms. While to some this could mean he was health conscious, she was convinced he was building himself up for defense. New to this profession, she read about clients who had experienced severe trauma, like this one. Her hunch was that every day this once soft soul prepared to pack a punch, literally.

He knew she was eyeing him over as part of her job to report to Roland Rolls.

"I see you're wearing your running shoes all the time now."

Joe did not respond. Instead of the hiking boots at the bottom of his locker, he opted to wear the running shoes in case, at any time, he had to escape in seconds. The windows weren't glass this time; they were Plexiglas. The bars embedded in the Plexiglas were as wide and looked as strong as his wrists. The front exit—the only one he knew of—presented a daunting challenge as well. He might be able to take out one Michael-type guard on a good day, but not two, and a pair of gym rat linebackers always blocked the doors.

She thought about the miles he raced along the perimeter fence every day. "And I hear you run during your outdoor rec time. I mean, you *really* run."

"Who told you? How does the communication work between you employees?"

Dr. Blaine's eyes popped. This was the first time her patient had ever been involved in conversation, especially with questions.

Hopeful to get as much out of him as he would share, she considered how to respond. "Joe, I know this is taking time for you to trust me."

Crossing her arms just like he was doing, she waited to see if he'd add more.

He looked down to the edge of her desk again. "Do you watch through the cameras, too?"

"The cameras? You think someone is watching you all the time?"

Joe's look made one word clear, even though he didn't say it.

She understood. "Joe, here's where the cameras are. Look at me. I'm going to tell you. I think you should know what's here."

Joe's eyes dropped. He knew his direct glances could reveal info to Rolls.

"Alright. This is how this works. Look at me, and I'll tell you. Stay looking away and I won't. You have a few seconds to decide."

Joe didn't know how to play this part of the game. It was new. Reluctantly, his eyes met hers.

"Excluding the ones outdoors, there are twelve cameras total."

Joe glanced down again. *Twelve cameras?* Sure, in this office alone. *There's a weird pump in the carpet under my feet. Is there one in the floor?*

"Look at me."

He waited a moment.

"Look at me."

His eyes raised.

"Listen. There are two at the main entrance."

"By the guards."

"By those who watch the door. These are for all our safety. They monitor anyone who comes in."

Joe didn't respond.

"They are in place for all of our safety. We don't know if we'll get any surprises, like not-so welcomed visitors here. While there is no danger now, at some point we may have a guest with a very colorful past who has connections on the outside. The cameras are in place so that everyone is safe here, Joe. Everyone. That doesn't just mean you. It means me, too."

This is a good lie.

"Four cameras are positioned strategically at the end of every wing in this building. They are typical surveillance cameras. They are also for safety and the wellbeing of both residents and staff."

Again, Joe did not respond. Instead, he wondered again just how many people Roland Rolls had acting here.

"The remaining cameras are in the cafeteria, the nurse's ward, the exercise room and all the hallways."

Joe looked around for some of the cameras hidden here in her office.

Dr. Blaine moved back to her side of her desk. "No, we're not ripping apart this office to find what you think is here. This room has just been painted, and I like the color." She sat. "I'm also not a fan of moving while this place is demoed for you."

Joe kept quiet.

She kept the conversation moving. "One of the guards told me how you are quite the runner. And he told me this because I asked him how you were doing. And I asked him because you, as you may have noticed, haven't answered my question yourself. So, yes, the staffer told me how you run every day, rain or shine. Now I don't consider myself an 'employee' as I'm part of a medical staff not paid by this facility, but how we communicate—and this might surprise you, Mr. Quiet— is by talking." Dr. Blaine leaned forward. "You don't believe any of this, do you?"

His eyes narrowed.

"What do you believe, then? Before you were taken into our custody, your attorney noted you had said something about ulmintin injections there in the courtroom. I've asked you about these injections before. Is now the time we talk about them?"

Joe still kept silent.

In her softest voice, she seemed to ask herself the following question. "Do you think these shots will, or already have, happened?"

"You know the answer to this."

"No, Joe, I don't."

"Yes, you do! Why don't you just share your info with me first? It's only a matter of time before I see him again. Let's just get this moving along."

She backed Joe up. "Him…you mean, Roland Rolls? Along with the injections, you mentioned his name in the courtroom."

Joe knew she wasn't stupid. He also knew she was driving him, well, crazy.

She turned and opened a manila folder on her desk. "I hadn't heard about this Mr. Rolls." Out of the corner of her eye, she met his gaze. "So, you guessed it. I did some checking."

"Uh-huh."

"This is what I printed off the internet. Rolls made *Forbes Magazine's* list of one of the wealthiest in the world. He's number twenty-one. The information here reveals he's accrued his massive estate through inheritance and through science. It reads, "Rolls' grandmother is reported to have owned a renowned collection of religious artifacts, some dating back to the sixteen hundreds. And Roland Rolls himself, a deeply private person, has a brilliant mastermind in the field of genetics. His discoveries, though often not shared, advance the world of medicine in profound, remarkable ways." Dr. Blaine angled the computer printed papers in Joe's direction. "Would you like to see? There are two pictures posted, one of Rolls and another of one of his laboratories."

Covering most of his face, Joe rubbed his forehead with the palm of his hand. "How much longer, *doctor?* How much longer?"

"What, what do you mean?"

"How much longer does this charade last?"

Dr. Blaine's face blanked.

An idea suddenly flashed in front of him. He decided to go with it. "Oh, I understand this now. I do. This is an elaborate alcoholic treatment plan for me. Specifically for me." Joe thought about this. "That's what this is. There aren't other experiments going on, are there?"

Dr. Blaine just watched.

"Couldn't he just have orchestrated AA meetings somewhere? Set up the place and the players? Wouldn't that have been more authentic, *doctor?* This seems a little over the top, especially your being here. Keeping me dried out could have been more simply constructed, yeah?"

"Share more of what you're talking about."

He laughed. It was the first time she'd seen his perfect white teeth that miraculously escaped months and months of neglect unscathed.

"Joe? Why are you laughing?"

"Oh, sorry! I am sorry. I'm sure you're a nice lady somewhere, but you're not that good here. And, surprisingly, he isn't that good, either." Joe considered what he was about to say. "I'm a boozer. A lush. A drunk." And then—yes—it hit him. "You have all been waiting for me to say that I'm an alcoholic."

"Let me join you, Joe. Backup and share what you're talking about."

Remembering something that happened a couple of weeks ago in one of his regular small groups, he refused to hear her.

"Joe?"

"Wait. I did. I *did* say I was an alcoholic. I know how those meetings here are set up. I was paying attention. I did, I did say it."

"Joe, admitting you're an alcoholic is a huge step toward your wellbeing."

"I did say it. The group leader heard it. Mark or Markus, right? The guy's name? The leader dude with the..." Joe fluttered his fingers near his chin. "...with the long goatee."

Joe looked around the room in the long shot chance that he could actually say something directly into a camera. He paused, thinking that what he was going to share would enable him to see Roland Rolls sooner. And that was what Joe wanted. While a huge part of him dreaded seeing the freak again, he knew it was just a matter of time. He might as well get this over with now.

"I'm an alcoholic."

He waited. The *doctor* barely moved.

"Yes," Joe said again clearly, in case there was an issue with the recording devices. "I am an alcoholic."

Patiently, Joe continued to wait. Maybe Rolls wasn't here in his building, though that would just not make a whole lot of sense. Joe smiled. *It would be something if I wasn't the center of that guy's universe.*

If he were to believe that, then we would be out of his mind.

A few minutes passed. The doctor started reiterating what had happened in their time together so far and Joe tuned out. Finally, he sighed. She learned this was his way of wondering how much longer their session would be.

"We are just about finished here for the day." She looked at the papers that have not moved on her desk. "This Rolls is powerful, Joe. He doesn't look like anyone I'd want to mess with."

"Then why do you?"

"What?"

"Why do you mess with him?"

"I don't know what you mean."

Out of frustration, Joe slumped down. Leaning forward, he crossed his arms and dropped his forehead on the desk. There were no more words here. He would ride out the remainder of his time today in silence. When their session did end, the doctor said, "You can go now."

"Thank you."

At her door, he met her guard who took him back to his locked room.

Tired, he sat and then stretched out over his bed. He drew his blanket up over his head. While this was a little uncomfortable, he knew this hid his facial expressions. Of course, there were at least twelve cameras in his cell. Other monitoring systems were at play too, like his toothbrush did far more than reveal his temperature and determine his heart rate. It probably compiled info toward his physiological profile. He sighed like he did in the female actor's office. With the weight of the blanket over him, the rare and wonderful quiet comforted him. They won't let him stay this way for long, however. He was a circus performer moving through hoops by the command of bells and whistles.

His thoughts were different without the alcohol in his blood, like they used to be when he first started working with the swimming pool company. One at a time, he thought of Dunk, Earl, and Mike. He boxed each of them in longstanding cubes because he could not process his losses any further or any longer. If he did, he'd develop a crack. The crack would open, and he'd fall apart. No, he would not think of how much he missed and loved them, because that would only lead to a hole the freak will find, enter, and destroy.

He did think of Betsy since they really had no past and any future would be unlikely. With his breath warm about him, he wondered how she was, and where she was. He knew the date today. This was late August. She must have graduated college by now, probably back in May of this year. Good for her. Carefully, he let his imagination roam. Closing his eyes, he pretended she was beside him in a place that was somehow safe, or, even better, that they are far, *far* away, so distant from any watchful eye. Just like Joe was doing now, they nestled under the covers, side by side. Her arm, led by her attentive hand, slid over his chest, traced his ribs, traced around his stomach, and rested. There was closeness, tenderness. And a kiss. Oh, definitely. There would a kiss. And another.

And another.

CHAPTER TWENTY SEVEN

At the end of the school day, Jolie walked through Dunk's classroom door. She held fresh, warm copies of a quiz she'd give her students tomorrow morning during second period Health. This would be their first grade of the first marking period, and having drilled and grilled them for a week, she hoped they would do well.

Jolie had a way of starting a conversation as if it were the middle of a conversation. "Think of it this way, my friend," she announced as she made her way to his neat desk. "It's like an engagement present."

Looking up from his computer, Dunk stared into space as he tried to figure out the lines she could have said that would make the start of this conversation make more sense. While he could often figure out where his best friend was coming from, he had no luck this time. "The quizzes in your hand? These are an engagement present?"

"No, you goof."

"What do you mean?"

Jolie lowered her voice. "The news of Mr. Rolls telling you that Joe has just been found is like a present. And, since you've become engaged, I see this news that Joe has finally been located as an engagement present."

The connection Jolie just made wasn't quite there for Dunk, but he smiled anyway because after over two years of prayer, worry, wonder, and turning it over to God each and every day, it was true: Joe had been located. Five and a half weeks after Joe had entered a rehab center, he appeared on Roland Rolls' extensive screen which, having produced absolutely nothing for so long, finally began to shout information. With Joe's whereabouts known, Roland immediately called Dunk. The call came last night, exactly two weeks after Dunk had become engaged to Vanessa Marl, the fellow deacon he chatted with before a meeting at the church that also happened to be the night Roland's car first passed him.

Dunk remembered that meeting with the one he would marry. Vanessa had been with Viola, and the two were standing outside the fellowship hall when he approached. When Viola left to catch up with Pastor Smith, the two began to connect.

As he began to shut down his computer, Dunk smiled at the thought of Vanessa. He wasn't sure of her that first night. Right after meeting her, everything in his world had turned upside down, of course. In a luxury car that would smell of burnt plastic, he'd been taken to the lab. After seven days of calculated injections that Dunk still did not understand exactly how or why they had been administered, Joe disappeared.

It took Dunk half a year to really see Vanessa. When he returned with a swollen and bruised face, she was consistent with him, especially when his loss of Joe carried Dunk away for hours at a time. She was a friend, and then she became a good friend. An hour before worship one Sunday morning, when a great deacon plan slid to an average deacon plan and then climbed back again through Dunk O'Dell's willpower, she wanted to share what was true to her. "Listen, Dunk, I admire you."

He set her words aside, but she brought them around again as they were walking to her car after church. "You don't want to hear me, but I need to be heard."

Dunk wondered if there was a cost effective way to get rid of her dark-tinted windows, which he knew she didn't like.

"You're not listening, but I admire you because of your faith. You let God do what God does, and what God does is guide and love us" She stopped. Not moving made him do what she wanted him to do, and that was turn and face her. "I see who you really are."

Dunk knew that what she didn't see was his weight gain. She also didn't see his doors closing, his anger smoldering, or his faith hardening. Instead, she simply held to who he was deep inside, and that was a man who sometimes did the only thing he could do, hold onto his Savior by a thread.

A distant school bell rang. It was to alert students who were riding the late busses home to meet in the lobby. The sound of the bell didn't quite bring Dunk back from his thoughts of Vanessa.While Jolie was elated over the news that Joe has been found and would be released from the center in three months, she also remained excited over the engagement. As a result, she never heard the bell that didn't matter to either of them in the first place.

Having come out of her own thoughts on the woman she considered will one day be her "sort of" sister-in-law, Jolie sat on a corner of a long desk that would always be neater than hers. "Vanessa must be really happy, Dunk. I mean, really. This is an end to a really long, painful time in your life. She must be thrilled."

"Yeah. Thrilled."

Jolie read him. She waited for him to add more. When he didn't, she asked, "What is it?"

"What is what?" To a suburban high school science teacher so much was so new. First there was the engagement, which was huge in and of itself, and now here was yesterday's long-awaited news that Joe has been found. Granted, his son was in rehabilitation center—and the nightmare of what his son has been going through was too hard to swallow—but he has been found. Dunk still struggled to absorb it all. Joe had finally been found.

After repositioning herself on Dunk's desk, Jolie tried to bring her fellow teacher back from wherever his thoughts had taken him. "Vanessa. She is happy, right?"

The softness around Dunk's eyes hardened. "Happy? Oh. Yes. She is."

Jolie knew to watch his expressions closely. She didn't understand this reaction. Her friend, who had gained and then lost all those pounds, who once again looked like he could be on the cover of some fitness magazine under clothes that were often too baggy, shouldn't be this cautious, this nervous.

"Dunk," she set her papers down on his desk and softened her voice to a whisper. "I get it. You're worried. You're tied up about all of this. First, there's Vanessa. You are just two weeks into your engagement. On top of this you've just learned your son has been locked away with a serious addiction issue for the next few months. Oh, and Roland Rolls, let's not forget him. I know that while it seems like he's working with you now, you still have concern."

"You're right."

"Just take this moment by moment, Dunk, just as you have been doing. And love each one through this."

"And pray."

In the twenty-seven months Joe has been gone, Jolie was getting more comfortable with her best friend's faith. "Yes, Dunk, keep praying."

Knowing he will think about and then pray for his son as soon as she hops off his desk, she shared a quick prayer she felt awkward in giving and then marched out of his room just in time for her department meeting. Ever so faintly, she hummed the tune *Here Comes The Bride.*

About an hour after arriving home from school, Dunk enjoyed a long, slow walk around the nearby lake, which was his hiking trail every morning.

As relieved as he was that his prayers had been answered about where his son was, and again and again he thanked God for this, something still didn't feel quite right. It was as if he was wearing heavily insulated snow boots instead of what was really on his feet, which were his good, lightweight shoes on this warm, early autumn evening. A knotted feeling tightened just under this chest. He wrestled with why he had called from school and told Vanessa a white lie. He kept his head down as he tried to glide his thoughts over the fact that he had cancelled tonight's dinner date with her. But he wasn't feeling well. That was the truth.

Far from anyone except two former students named Madison and Kylie who circled past on their bikes ten minutes ago, Dunk pressed into why he had come here alone. Maybe when he returned two years ago without Joe he should have stayed silent. Telling Jolie and Earl *everything* may not have been the best course of action, but really, what options did he have? Fabricate another lie? And then another, and another, and another? That took too much energy. It also took too much time. And without Joe, he was hurting, really hurting. He didn't have the energy to live a fictitious life. Besides, his two friends were on to something. They knew about one camera. Other leaks would have happened, like why Dunk's other next door neighbors suddenly left.

He sighed and tried to refocus on the recent good news. Joe has been found. There would be no more wondering, no more guessing. Enormous relief ran with the blood in his veins, but this was a mixed blessing. Dunk tried to sigh again but found that he was just holding his breath. Joe has been in big trouble.

This open trail has been the one place he could really let his heart go. So far today, it didn't feel that way. Walking along further, he came upon a stream. The water in it moved quickly, even though there has been no rain for at least two weeks. Watching the late afternoon sun flicker in the babbling current, Dunk convinced himself that he will feel better soon. Everything will fall into place when he can see Joe face-to-face, if a meeting was something that Joe even wanted. Continuing on with the path before him, Dunk wouldn't think about that. Of course, Joe will want to see him. He'll want to be home with him. If not in the same house, and that made sense, then he'd at least want to be close.

Dunk swallowed. A locked rehab center. A three month sentence. He still couldn't quite wrap his head around this. But it will be okay. Of course, in a short amount of time, it will be okay.

He sighed. While he did not yet know everything his son had done, he knew Joe had been through too much pain. The clone of Christ? Who actually can live with *that* easily?

Moving on in his thoughts, he tried to convince himself all will go well when—or maybe if—Joe and Vanessa meet for the first time.

Joe might remember her because she had been a part of the church for about a year before she became a deacon. He would have been a high school senior when she joined the church.

Neither Joe nor Vanessa have ever met, even in passing. To that end, Dunk had never shared her name with Joe, and at some point when Joe was still at the Bible College, he could have mentioned the new deacon coming on at the church. Dunk just didn't want Joe to have more uncertainty, confusion, or instability in his life. What if Dunk had dated someone seriously and that relationship failed? What would that do to his son? No, he wouldn't put Joe through that. The truth was he didn't want to put himself through that.

He turned to God. With a deep, resounding breath, he brought in this verse from Jeremiah 29:11. *"For I know the plans I have for you,"* says the Lord. *"They are plans for good and not for disaster, to give you a future and a hope."*

CHAPTER TWENTY EIGHT

Driving straight home from the trails, he pulled into his driveway. Vanessa's car was parked on the street near his mailbox. They never gave each other keys to their places figuring that would be too tempting, especially since a real physical attraction heated their relationship. Still dressed from her day at work, she sat on his front step thumbing through a difficult file she had taken from her desk this afternoon. As a social worker within the county hospitals, her work often remained open just feet from her, even over the weekends.

Tucking some of her loose, soft, shoulder-length red curls behind her ear, she looked up at the man she would marry, even though no wedding date has been set. Her wonderfully blue eyes held one single tear each, which, in all of their dating, was something he saw only during the romance movies she watched so faithfully. Dunk was not sure what to make of this. As he came closer, uneasiness grew in his stomach.

Her expression showed great care yet she didn't say hello. Instead, when he stopped in front of her, she asked, "Are you okay?"

"Well, I'm—" Dunk hesitated. "I'm alright."

"Dunk?"

He didn't want to face whatever this was.

Vanessa sensed his hurt, confusion, and his guard. "Invite me inside, please. Let's talk for little while, okay?"

"Okay." Dunk immediately convinced himself that he'd like this time with her. Then again, a part of him would rather stay still, and quiet. Maybe they could stay outside for a bit, at least until he could get a sense of what she was thinking, or would like to share. His stomach suddenly flopped. Whatever this was meant trouble. A guy who said he was not feeling well and then was caught not being home? Yeah, this did not look good. He fumbled with his house keys. Four steps inside his house, he turned. She hadn't moved.

"You haven't invited me in."

A formality anchored her words. A seriousness he hadn't heard since their last disagreement over, of all things, how much to spend on Girl Scout cookies came through. With last night's news about Joe, everything that had been familiar, such as the simple, mundane act of walking into his house together, could no longer be taken for granted.

"Vanessa, would you like to come inside?"

"Yes."

She stepped around him. Even though she had passed inches from him, a part of her remained far away. Standing in his tiny foyer, she sighed.

"Vanessa, what is it?"

"I'll go first. I'll just get this petty hurt out. Okay?"

Dunk shut his door. "Okay."

She moved into his living room and sat on the couch in her favorite spot, the place that faced the picture window. "I heard you were at the park. Now it's not a big deal, and certainly I wasn't spying."

"Madison and Kylie."

"Yes. We both know it's such a small town, and with your being a teacher...*their* teacher, and the news of our engagement out in the community... Anyway, they didn't spill and I certainly didn't mean to find out, but I did."

"News travels fast."

"News travels fast."

Dunk sat beside her. "Vanessa—"

She set her hands on her lap. The bracelet he bought for her last Christmas caught his attention.

"It's not a big deal, Dunk. It's not. At least not really. I just wish you had said something first. That's all."

"You have a right to be upset."

Her eyes watered as they did on the steps a minute ago. "My issue isn't the biggest one here. Yes, you need to communicate better to me, even on the simple things. We can work on that. But Dunk, honestly, let me set this out right before you: you've been hurting since we've been longstanding friends, and as a couple. You've been crushed over the loss of Joe. What he's gone through. And you just learned last night what he is still going through. This is tremendous. I ache for him deeply. I do. And I get—I wholeheartedly get—that you need your quiet time."

Wow. Neither Earl nor Jolie knew him this well, and both had known him for so much longer than the woman here with him. He could feel his heart in his chest.

A tear fell from Vanessa's face. "I mean, he's been found. Found! After all this time, after all your heartbreak. That's one thing, for sure. But *where* he is. It must be a painful a place for him, and for you."

"Vanessa—"

"I don't mean to cut you off, Dunk, but you need to know that I understand this. Or I understand a part of this. You don't know how he is. You don't know if he's alright. And you don't know what state of mind he's in. Just out of the blue, Roland calls and everything changes for you."

"And you."

"And me."

The reason no wedding date had been set walked into the living room and sat between them. They both felt its presence, or, actually, its distance, between them.

Vanessa stared at her left hand. The ring sparkled. "Maybe we should have waited on the engagement, like we had once talked about."

"Vanessa, no."

"You have been honest with me, Dunk. You've never pulled any punches—any surprises—whatsoever. In fact, tonight was the first bobble, if we even want to call it that. And to me, tonight is water under the bridge. I do understand, and I'm not *that* sensitive. And I'm not going to be."

She stood. Having given this no thought in advance, she knew what she was about to do would be right in the long run.

Suddenly, silently, she thanked God. She would not have had this idea on her own. No, alone, she would have clutched what she had. She'd have held on to what she heard when he proposed on one knee and forged her own way right to the altar, come hell and high water. But one failed marriage behind her taught her a thing or two about love. It was patient. It was kind. It was not touchy or rude, and it certainly did not insist on its own way.

She knew she had just recited some verses found in 1 Corinthians 13 and smiled inside to her Lord. Since giving her life to Christ this past January, she loved and trusted Him.

"I know why you were there tonight, Dunk." She looked right at the man who made her heart fly sometimes. "I know what you thought about, and where you thought about it. You were at the water, weren't you?"

"Yes." Dunk stood beside her. Nervous, he wanted to cover what she kept unfolding. To keep her from finding what he himself didn't know he had kept hidden, he glanced into the kitchen. "Let me get you something to drink. How about dinner? Me, I'm starved."

As he headed off, she did not move. "I even know you really weren't feeling well. That is true."

He turned back to her. "Vanessa."

She stood and faced him. More tears spilled, but her expression did not change. "Joe is first. Joe has been first. You said this. I know this. I do. And that is one of the thousand reasons why I love you. Oh, Dunk O'Dell, I do. I do love you."

Knowing what he needed, her voice quaked. "We will not be engaged when you see him. When I meet him. No. The two of you need to be solid again."

He rushed toward her. He couldn't have heard what she just said. It had to be a trick in his ears.

She put a finger to his lips. "And then us. You and me."

Half angry, half scared, Dunk froze, even though he burned underneath. "You can't do this, Vanessa. No!"

She slipped the engagement ring off and set it his trembling hands.

"I am going to wear this again. I trust God and His perfect plan for us. And I love you forever. I do."

On her tiptoes, she kissed the man she deeply desired on the cheek. "Joe needs this, Dunk. Just as importantly, you need this, too."

Before she backtracked or said a single word she may regret, she opened the door. "You can ask me again. Hopefully, sometime soon. And I will say yes." She shot him a wry smile. "And, of course, I'll expect a nice dinner that night, too."

With a single, quiet click, she closed the door behind her.

Three full minutes passed. Just beside the driver's side door of her car, he knelt so that they were face-to-face. Vanessa was crying so hard she could not safely drive any further. Her car had moved no more than seventy yards from his house. She lowered the driver's side window.

Through his own tears, Dunk said, "I love you, Vanessa. You have to hear me. I do. I do."

Three cars passed in a row. This street was never this busy, ever.

Noisy neighbor Mrs. Eclara Eldo approached with her fluffy little dog, Fearsome, on his hot pink leash. Dunk glanced toward the one person he forced himself to intentionally spend time with every year during their block party. He closed his eyes. *Timing.*

Concerned he might get hit on a street that apparently was not quiet tonight—and he really did wind up in the middle of the road—he tilted his head just so and asked from a place of perfect candor, "I can still date you, right?"

Vanessa laughed. As she did this, tears on her face splattered her steering wheel. She repeated his question. "Can you still date me?"

Dunk leaned into the open window further. "Lady, is that a yes, or a no?"

She wiped her face with her fingers. "Now, I'll have to think about that."

Just as she said these words, a large work truck with its high beams on rolled toward them.

Dunk considered the situation. "Not to press you or anything, ma'am, but if I could have your answer soon? Otherwise, I'm not moving."

Not one for fifth grade math problems, Vanessa would rather not calculate the time she had to respond compared to the speed in which the truck rapidly approached. "Yes, goof! You can date me. Now get in this car!"

Dunk bolted around the car as the truck's driver offensively laid on the horn and cursed through her open window.

There, in the passenger's seat, Dunk sat still for a long, healing moment. Neither shared a word. Where their words split them as soon as they had both entered Dunk's house, this silence here, healing and familiar, brought them close again. Reaching for the seatbelt, he secured it and asked, "How about a hamburger at the Dairy Barn?"

"With a face like this?"

Not moving, Dunk reached deep into her eyes. "With a face like that."

"I must look like a mess."

"You look like a woman who knows love."

She stared through the windshield.

Mrs. Eclara Eldo had obviously walked Fearsome to the end of the street and turned back for more news. Both Dunk and Vanessa waved to her.

"Joe. Me. Truth on," Dunk continued into the silence. "You look like a woman who knows love."

Without realizing how or when it happened, the two held hands and, after talking for a few minutes about the everyday little things in their day like hot pink leashes, her new caseload and the experiment his low kids did well on this afternoon in biology, they kissed. When they moved apart just a bit, Dunk cupped the back of Vanessa's head with his hand. "I love you, Vanessa. Forever."

A moment later, she dropped her automatic car into gear. "Say all that nice stuff, whatever. But you're paying, and you're not the only one hungry."

At the stop sign at the end of the street, Vanessa spilled one more tear, but was careful to look out her side window as she did so. Meanwhile, Dunk slid his hand onto Vanessa's lap and tried his best to keep his heart from fluttering so fast.

It's going to be just fine, he told himself. He breathed silently through his nose. Joe's been in a drug and alcohol rehab center for nearly six weeks, his engagement to Vanessa has just fallen apart, but it's fine. It's all going to be just fine.

CHAPTER TWENTY NINE

Jolie slapped the menu onto the table for two. She didn't need to look at it, anyway. She couldn't focus because these past few days have been *just* too much. Whatever happened to a plain, boring, simple life? Looking at her dining mate who was still busy searching the meal options, she stared into space and pined for the old, mundane days of cameras, spies for neighbors, some mysterious if not all out creepy rich dude, and a Jesus clone. In comparison, Joe's three-month sentence in a rehab center almost rolled in on the verge of ordinary. This brand new news about a 'temporarily' broken engagement, however, now *this* definitely deserved some comfort food.

Neither Jolie nor Vanessa would ever know that this was the very booth where Earl and Mike shared dinner and dessert, and Jolie didn't know that Vanessa and Dunk came here just over two weeks ago, the night the engagement was put on hold.

"Ice cream!" Jolie announced to their server as he sauntered toward them with his order pad opened in his hand just below his waist. "A lot of it!"

Too aware that he was handsome, the server smirked. "Okay, what flavor or flavors would you—"

"And yes," Jolie interrupted, looking at Vanessa. "The ring is off this girl's finger, so we are celebrating with calories—*a lot* of them. To freedom! She is no longer engaged."

"Yes," Vanessa shared mildly, hoping that saying this out loud would make this easier. "I'm a free woman."

"Now tell me, fine looking man," Jolie jokingly purred because he was obviously not one of her students, "you're what? Twenty? Twenty-two?"

"Twenty-two."

"Out of college?"

"Yep. Graduated this past May."

"Applications in?"

"All over the place."

Something in the way the young man answered enabled Jolie to catch on to what their server studied. A click simply went off inside her. "A teacher, huh?"

"Yeah."

"Me, too." While anything could happen within the school year, she realized that it was well past the hiring season for a fulltime job. He would likely have to wait until the middle of next summer when most new teaching positions opened, which stressed everyone. "And you're subbing now, yes?"

"Yep."

Jolie and their server talked frankly for a minute or two. In this time, Jolie dropped her overt flirtatiousness to help out a fellow in the field in an incredibly tight job market. Vanessa could tell Jolie would rather be free-spirited and a bit edgy tonight, but, true to herself, the seasoned teacher offered advice on upcoming interviews.

Now and again Vanessa looked at their very good looking server who, sporting just the right haircut with just the right amount of hair product, carried a charisma very few knew about, let alone had.

In the sudden silence between them, their server turned to Vanessa. "And what can I get you?"

She had once heard Jolie say that dessert could actually be a meal. "Ice cream too."

"How about those flavors now? What would you both like?"

Jolie collected both menus with a quick slide of her hand. "A combo of the best ones. You surprise us."

"Alright."

"And two spoons."

"Sure thing." Turning quickly, their server moved toward the kitchen.

When the ladies faced each other, a moment of awkwardness bounced between them because neither knew the other woman very well. Jolie reached for her iced tea and changed her tone from the unfamiliar one Vanessa heard when their server first arrived to the familiar one she had heard before. "Now, tell me, really, how are you?"

Vanessa would rather have the Lady Cheetah back then answer because, truthfully, she didn't know how to answer. She was just thankful for this invitation to be here. While it was true that she didn't know Jolie the way she'd like to, she could really use a friend with candor.

Jolie filled the quiet between them. "This has to be hard."

"Well…"

Looking to see that no one was around, Jolie lifted and set her drink down without taking a sip. "Maybe if we didn't live in a small town, things would be different. Better. And your church life. That is tough. While Dunk has decided not to share with your congregation where Joe is, at least for now, everyone knows that the senior deacon has a broken engagement with a woman once divorced. Those old, crabby ladies, they must be all abuzz!"

"They're not crabby."

"Vanessa."

Vanessa thought of Viola Munson. "They're not. They are not crabby."

"But they are talkative."

Vanessa opted for silence.

Jolie met Vanessa's eyes.

"The ladies at church are trying to be helpful." Vanessa considered all she had heard since she and Dunk shared their news. "They're prayerful."

"Good, and don't mind me saying this, but you don't need prayers as much as you need Joe home."

Vanessa swallowed. The outspokenness from the woman sitting across from her was wonderful, and a bit startling.

"You do. And so does Dunk. You all just need to move on—or move through—this."

Vanessa sensed Jolie had more to say. One look encouraged Jolie to continue.

Jolie repositioned herself in her seat. "Okay. I'll just say it, or I'll try to, anyway. This connection between Dunk and Joe. Now I get father/son things, and what has been between the two of them has been great, it has. I've seen it firsthand through the years. And Dunk, you know we've been tight for a long, long time. Yet *this*, I don't know..."

"You have a funny feeling?"

"Yes, kind of. Do you?"

"I have a funny feeling about Joe sometimes. It's just...well, tell me. What is he like?"

Jolie guessed at what Vanessa didn't actually come out and say. "You mean..."

"Yeah."

"Dunk told you all about the...?"

"He did. Dunk shared everything with me one night before our engagement. He told me about Roland Rolls and the movie on the wall."

Jolie had heard about what that film showed, but was confident in what she was about to share. "Well, Vanessa, honestly, despite what unfolded on that wall by that creep, Joey is remarkable. He's always seemed to know and care for me, very, very deeply. And he sees things the way that most people don't. That's a definite. In ways well beyond his years, that special one has been smart, curious, and bold. Since Dunk came back without him and told Earl and me about the cloning, well, I jumped right into scripture. My Bible has everything that Jesus said in red. Unfortunately, except for the part of a twelve-year-old Jesus at the Temple with his parents, he doesn't say much until his public ministry starts."

"When he's thirty-three."

"Not twenty-two."

"But is he divine, or *could* he be divine? I don't know. Is this clone actually Jesus Christ, or just some happenstance two-thousand-year-old dead guy in Jerusalem?"

Vanessa looked down at the table and then back toward her new friend. "I just know this. There is only one Jesus Christ, our Lord. He's sitting at the right hand of God, the Father, in heaven."

Jolie took a long sip of her iced tea and thought, *whose double, divine or not, is in a dark place somewhere wrestling with more demons than the devil himself knows what to do with.*

Suddenly a new, different server brought their ice cream dessert. A complete opposite of the one who had taken their order, this young man would rather cower than serve ice cream at the counter, which was the job he had been pulled from a minute ago. As a social worker, Vanessa noticed more of this young man than her teacher companion. She still didn't understand how Jolie pegged their first server as a teacher, but there was something she could see with this young man—something loud, something clear. She knew the word. It was pain.

She noticed that his nametag said "Ben" and immediately she wished she could find and touch his darkness in some way. She had never had something even close to this sensation happen to her before, but it was clear. She felt moved by him. No one should be this sad, this troubled.

Jolie wondered about all the thoughts Vanessa was thinking. She could see the burn scar on his neck more easily than her desert mate. Focusing on the creation on the tray in Ben's arm, she tried for a joke. "This is for the two of us *and* for everyone else here tonight, right?"

Ben didn't like conversation. Ben didn't even like being here. Anxiousness and apprehension sparked within his dark eyes. Nervously, he set between them a small mountain of ice cream covered with delicious sauces. Just as he stepped away, his thumb caught the lip of the serving bowl. Because of his speed in wanting to exit, the dessert toppled face down on their table. Ben was fast, however. He needed to get out of this proximity. Everyone was staring. Eyes were on him and it was all he could do not to panic. Fortunately, he made the mess disappear quickly, but as he went to work cleaning the table, Vanessa now noticed the long burn mark on the side of his neck. She also noticed something deeper and far more painful than the pain of that old wound: no one really saw Ben for who he was. No one reached him. Unlike their first fast and fun server, this young man had a shadow of a soul. The sorrow twisted her heart.

Jolie asked her desert partner, "What is it?"

With Ben nearby, Vanessa wasn't sure how to answer. She thought again of her caseloads, of the thousand hard and sad stories she knew of firsthand. Never had anything moved her as obviously as this one young man. She couldn't explain why she felt the way she did.

When two small sundaes arrived a few minutes later because they had both reordered after seeing how much came the first time, Vanessa saw that this teen could be as confident as the first if someone steady and secure in his wobbling world had said out loud these three words: *I love you.* She didn't know how she knew this, and of course, she could be completely wrong. Maybe this was a need in her. She was different before she had met Dunk, and different wasn't better. She thought about the time she had arrived early to her first deacon's meeting and hid behind the dark windows of her car.

Sensing how distance Vanessa had become, Jolie asked her question again. "What is it?"

Vanessa didn't immediately answer. "I'm not sure. I'm honestly not sure."

• • •

Neither woman ate much. While the conversation continued, Jolie wondered when, or even if, Joe would be coming home, and Vanessa, for a reason she still could not shake, kept wondering about this server Ben.

Everyone needs someone, Vanessa thought while Jolie visited the women's room ten minutes later. Because her mind and her heart seemed to be in one blur, she was not sure if she was thinking of Joe and

Dunk before she said it, or if she was thinking of Ben whom she had not seen in minutes. Glancing out the window, she studied the parking lot and the light traffic on the road beyond it. An old pick-up truck passed carrying a load of pumpkins. A young farmer and his kids filled the cab.

She realized she had been rolling her fingers over where the engagement ring had been. Yes, she thought again, everyone needs someone.

———————

The two ladies said goodbye to each other at the door since they'd parked in different directions. Pausing a moment, Vanessa suddenly had an idea. Without thinking any more on it, she walked back quickly to their table. She set extra money on her napkin in addition to the tip she'd already left that was more than the cost of both sundaes. When she spotted Ben walking toward her from the kitchen, she moved in front of him, which was an act she had never done in her lifetime. It was challenging for him to look up, but he did. Vanessa had not planned this moment—she couldn't actually believe it was happening—but she came right to the point. She heard her own voice come out warmly, tenderly. "The extra money on our table is not a mistake. It's a generous tip because I see a generous heart within you. Now I don't mean to sound all weird on you, and I know that I might, but I want you to remember this, okay?"

Ben connected with her instantly, something he rarely did, especially with a stranger. A warmth in her eyes told him to trust her. "Okay."

"You're going to be loved someday—loved so wonderfully well."

He nodded. It was not so much a nod of agreement, but one where he acknowledged that he heard her.

"You're loved now. Right now." She handed him a card. "No pressure, no pulls. Just consider coming."

"What—?"

Her words were not her own; she was not even sure how she was talking. In the moment, she was so grateful to God that this wasn't being received as some hard line pitch. Vanessa Marl didn't do those. "It's my church, and you matter. *You matter.*"

Ben nodded.

"No hard sell. Just consider you're loved."

Vanessa left. She had never done anything like this before, ever. It was the deacon in her. Then, as she reached her car, she knew that was not quite true. It was God in her.

CHAPTER THIRTY

That woman, the beautiful one with the loud friend, who gave me such a huge tip? It's like she could see me. No one sees me. No one ever really sees me. And she spoke to me. And the card wasn't some hard sell. It wasn't some weird pressure thing like I know some religious soldiers force.

She just heard me—and I barely said a thing. But she heard me. He almost smiled. *I was heard.*

"Ben!" It was the manager standing at the double kitchen doors. "You gonna move sometime soon? Plates don't actually walk into the dishwasher."

"Right. Sorry."

From the super-sized gray plastic tub filled with dirty dishes that he set on the counter near the sink a minute ago, he began to clear what he just carried. He tried to ignore the funny feeling down the back of his arms and along his inner thighs as he quickly worked at a job he was actually good at doing. A good worker, he glanced at the double doors again. As he washed the pile in front of him, he had a daydream that the woman with the church card had dropped by again—only this time two girls in a booth nearby overheard how wonderful he was. One of the two girls smiled that smile at him. She came back the next day alone, and the Dairy Barn was so quiet. And they talked and they laughed.

"Ben!" It was his boss.

"Yeah?

"Never mind."

Ben returned to his work, remembering again how his daydream started with the woman with red hair.

He smirked. *It's true. She could see me. Really see me.*

———————

He never took his clothes off near the mirror attached to the top his dresser. In fact, if he could have it his way, he would have no mirror in his bedroom at all. His mom really laid into him when he covered the glass with all sorts of icons, labels and tags from what he pulled from magazines in the school library, but the truth was this: he didn't want to see himself, especially with his shirt off. It was not just the burn scar that splattered down one side of his upper torso. He was used to the permanent memory his grandmother made on his skin when as a boy she suddenly lost her temper because he couldn't follow directions. It was his hollow chest, and his scrawny, pale body that made him keep his eyes low.

No one would want to see this. Worse, now that so many of his classmates were dating, he realized something colder: no one would want him. There was no girl at the Dairy Barn who smiled at him. There would be no more silly daydreams either because here alone—so painfully alone—he knew no one would want him. Quickly, he peeled off his white, ice cream splattered white dress shirt and threw on an extra, extra-large hooded sweatshirt.

Turning toward his closet, he dropped the black dress pants all employees were required to wear at the Dairy Barn, and, in a flash, slipped on thick, baggy sweatpants a man twice his width could wear. These sweat bottoms were his favorite because in being so heavy they never revealed how thin he felt, or how much trouble he had eating sometimes. Feeling his stomach, he had to eat though. The gym jocks at school couldn't get him for being skinny.

Actually, no one at school could get him because, despite meeting that woman today who gave him such a huge tip, he usually wasn't seen, and he wasn't seen because he didn't matter. He was random, an extra. While his mom did rag on him about his decorated dresser, she didn't care. She could care, she just didn't. At first he was to be seen and not heard, now she made it clear that he wasn't to be seen either. Yes, the days when he was a mildly amusing toy for a few minutes ended when the odd, nerdy looking kid who could somehow be entertaining as a boy met a completely awkward puberty. His problems became his own when his random cuteness faded. Life became his own.

During lunch, he was destined to the Loser's Table in the cafeteria. Even though he kept to himself, he knew that even the down on their luck kids had dreams. He just didn't. If he wished anything, it would be that he could be more invisible. Even at school, what he did say didn't really matter. What he thought didn't really matter, either. His regular teachers left him alone, and when some random, overachieving sub came in for the day, he learned to give just enough of an answer as to not draw attention to himself. He wasn't dark or devilish, he was just his own quiet world.

What made this all surface was that lady who came in today. Returning to his room from the kitchen where he took out a brand new jar of peanut butter he'd eat with a spoon alone in his room, he again wondered why she had shared what she did when each day he just disappeared a little more, no matter how many thirty-six ounce jars of Mylomay's Crunchy Peanut Butter he ate a month.

He stared at the wall in front of him. Why did she notice him? Who was she? He knew the encounter with her was a fluke of some kind. It could never happen again. There would be no way this kind and gracious woman would stop to spend time with him again.

But what if she did? What if she came back? Without realizing what he was doing at first, Ben pretended the two of them were in some high-end kitchen together on a bright, cheerful morning. Sunlight poured in from a wall of eastern windows, and, as only women can do—as only kind women can do—she tussled his hair. An enormous breakfast appeared from her arms in front of him. Big food. Sausage, eggs, and home fries with barely a trace of red pepper and onion filled his heavy plate. The pancakes were served next. In the midst of all of this, she asked about last night's homework and the chess club outing after school that night. Would he join the track team this spring? She also wanted to know about his girlfriend, the one he met at the Dairy Barn. Together they sat and they ate and talked. And there was that word, the word she mentioned. *Love.*

Suddenly, she was gone. As fast as he let his mind create this, she disappeared. He was going to eat that peanut butter, though. Yes, he was going to eat that meal in a jar. Dropping down in the narrow area between his twin bed and the closet door, he set his headset over his ears, raised the hood of his sweatshirt over his head and, in the final part of his too familiar routine, hit the power button to his angry music. He won't hear his mom come home later, and she'll barely know he was here.

This was just as it should be. Yes, it was so much easier this way.

In his routine, something was different this time. It was not the tender woman at the restaurant he thought of when he closed his eyes; it was the one with her. He realized the other woman was a teacher in the school. He thought she taught health or something like that. He'd never had her in class, and tonight was the first time they'd ever been face-to-face. Yes, she was a health teacher. Ms. Walkers. Second floor. Her room was right near that handsome science guy, Mr. O'Dell, the one who gained and lost all that weight. He was missing his son, or something like that.

Ben thought about the poor guy for a while. He had sad eyes and a broken part that only someone like Ben would be able to see. He had guessed Mr. O'Dell and Ms. Walker were friends by the way they would stand side by side while classes changed. They'd even done a skit together on stage during an assembly about school safety when he was a freshman. They were quite a team, and in what they said and did, Mr. O'Dell seemed to be a star.

His memories returned to the restaurant. How did he not recognize Ms. Walker at first? Sometimes he overheard her students talk about her in school. She was funny, they said. He knew her to be loud and bossy.

Speaking of loud, the music against his ears wasn't working as it should. He'd been thinking of school too much—which he never, ever wanted to do. He was usually able to blur away the crushing insults with the beat of the songs in his head, but tonight he couldn't escape that he wasn't funny. He wasn't loud. He wasn't bossy. It felt as though he had swallowed a rock when he realized he was none of these things. If someone were to ask him who he was—not that anyone ever had— he'd answer, "I'm nothing."

Tonight, he will not eat that peanut butter. Instead, he curled into a ball which allowed his shoulders to sink closer to the floor. He hid, even from himself.

CHAPTER THIRTY ONE

"It's your father, Dunkin O' Dell, who will meet you on the other side of the doors."

Joe had completed his sentence. As a final part of his rehab recommended by that psychologist, if she actually was one, he spent a month in a halfway house.

"My dad? He's here?"

"You asked us to contact him when you entered here thirty days ago. We cleared him and your one-year probationary period has been transferred from Mississippi to Indiana, as you requested. He's your safe person." Barely looking at the sheets in her hand, the bureaucratic house manager kept filling out the necessary release paperwork. "He's here."

"Here?" Joe felt mad and excited—mad that he didn't know that he'd see his DOD until this very moment, and excited to finally, finally be free. He checked his wallet again, a habit he established not because it held money—he was broke, of course—but because it held a keepsake that tied him to Betsy. "Here, my DOD is—"

"Yes."

"When can I —"

"Now. I'm finished with this file. The door is not locked."

"It isn't?"

"You take care of yourself, Joe. You take care."

"The door isn't…"

"Go on. And don't come back."

⦁————————⦁

Joe heard the fresh gravel move under the running shoes he wore so faithfully, and, when he looked away from the building, there were no fences. Here in the early November light, everything looked different. Everything was different. And there. There he was!

From a distance, Joe could see his DOD hadn't aged. He was somehow taller too. His shoulders were even more square, his waist tight and trim. It was a fact that Dunk O'Dell was handsome. Why had Joe never realized this before?

At first sight, Joe understood what was true in his heart: he loved his DOD. He needed his DOD. He also knew the energy—the force—he had used to keep this well-intentioned man locked at a distance had been too much, too great. And this was his doing.

Joe teared up because keeping his DOD away had been so wrong, and so cruel, to both of them. Too much time had passed. Too much heartache and heartbreak had been carried over the years. Too much hurt and too much unhappiness—too much hell on earth—had buried them both. But it was over.

With the halfway house far enough behind him, Joe bolted. All those months of running made him fluid and fast. He had to get there. He had to get close. Finally, fully, and completely, the damage and the distance between them ended before they even touched.

Their embrace was powerful, incredible. The motion and emotion of their hug didn't stop after they bonded body to body. Instead, it somehow kept expanding, creating a barrier of protection around them. All of the stupid things Joe had done before seeped into the ground under his feet. He ran from Roland Rolls when he could have been reinforcing what he knew, and that was the love he had for this bold employee who dared to steal an eighteen-month-old from some sterile science lab.

"I love you, DOD."

Dunk's words crumbled. "I love you, son. I love you." Shaking, he set one of his hands on the back of Joe's head. His forehead dropped to Joe's shoulder as he said, "Dear God, how I thank you. How I praise you. How you did not fail me." Their eyes met. The connection was perfect and complete.

When death does come for Joe—and, after all of the complete and utter sin he has done, the twenty-two-year-old Joe knew he was just a human and will die as other humans die—maybe he'd be lucky enough to remember certain points or certain feelings of his life along the way from here to there. If so, this was one he would remember. Oh yes, this was one he would definitely remember forever.

"DOD," he said quivering into one rock hard shoulder, "don't let me go. Please don't let me go."

———

Joe was thankful DOD actually didn't ask to see his driver's license when they traded seats after a pit stop because while he did somehow keep his wallet over the past few years, he hadn't seen that credit card sized license issued from the state of Indiana since the early days of working for the pool company.

He would need a new license, for sure. That was number twelve in his Action Plan, which was a paper he had to include in his release along with receiving two hundred and fifty dollars he earned by doing extra community service. What his Action Plan didn't include was seeing Roland Rolls, of course. Joe was not about to write *that* one down. He needed to see him though. There would be no more recording devices, no more monitoring.

"DOD, I'm going to visit Rolls."

Maybe because it dropped in from nowhere, Dunk thought Joe was joking. He looked to his son.

"I'm serious."

"You want to go back to the lab? To Rolls himself?" In the passenger seat, Dunk crossed his left ankle over his right knee. This took a little doing given the size of his car, but Dunk was flexible. Curiously, he looked over to his son. "Shouldn't we just stay home for a few days? Get used to this?"

When Joe realized Rolls wasn't going to show, he not only spoke up where he should have, but also he shut up when he should have. That psychologist may or may not have been an actress. Perhaps she never knew who her actual her employer was, but Joe knew to pull himself together to get out of there. He had to face Rolls again to make sure there were no more recording devices, no more movies. Joe picked up from the pause in the conversation. "I'd like you to come with me when I see him."

Dunk's heart could not beating this loudly, could it? He tried to sound calm. "I think we should just go home. We can have a great meal tonight and kick back." He focused on a small farm out in the distance to his right. "Yeah, let's chill for a few days, and then we can think about bringing Rolls into this."

"I don't know about the 'chill' part, DOD. There were recording devices at home."

Looking back to the highway, Dunk considered what the two of them had already talked about in the car. There were no recording devices. Joe has not been monitored since he left the lab with a bandage on his arm.

Joe adjusted the rearview mirror. "Just like there weren't any in the rehab center. I get you."

"You are not being recorded. You have not been recorded."

Joe kept his eye on the same white car had been following them for miles. Was one of Rolls' employees trailing them?

Dunk watched Joe's eyes. "And we're not being followed."

"Yeah."

"I've talked to Roland. No, we are not 'buddy buddy,' but we've been somewhat connected since you've been gone."

"The two of you have had conversations?"

Dunk hesitated.

"DOD?"

"He is trying, Joe."

"Uh-huh."

"You don't trust Roland. I get that. But let me ask you outright. Do you trust me?"

"DOD."

"Do you?"

Joe didn't answer.

"You've been through hell. I see it in your eyes. Sometimes I hear it in your voice." Dunk let his heart speak. "I don't understand how hard this has been on you. I may never get how hard this has been, but I can try."

Joe thought on this. "No cameras?"

"No recording devices, either. They are gone."

A quiet slipped in between them. With time to think, Dunk revisited just what that the movie on the lab wall had done to Joe's health and wellbeing. Both angry at Roland and still protective of his son, he revisited for the four-thousandth time why he didn't take Joe, the toddler, further. Sure, he had the idea about burning a boat off the coast of some ocean only to come back by a lifeboat for a new life in Europe, but what if, after leaving the lab, he had kept driving to the Pacific Northwest and somehow slipped off to Alaska, or Hawaii? They have schools there. A way to change his last name and even his appearance was certainly possible, or he didn't have to teach at all. With a new name and face, he could have learned a trade. Dunk pressed the back of his head into the headrest. He could have picked up odd jobs here and there. Life in one or two bedroom apartments could have been manageable, maybe even exciting. Firsthand, they could have seen so much of the world, experienced new cultures, and learned new ways of living. Had he chosen this life for the two of them, his son wouldn't look and sound like he'd been through a war. Dunk turned toward his window. A tear of regret spilled down this cheek. He chose to stay stateside, keep his name, and teach in a public school. So much for even trying to hide from Roland.

Joe knew where his DOD's thoughts had been. "It's okay."

Dunk still couldn't face his son. "What is okay? Joe, what, of any of this, is okay?"

"You did what you could. The Mastermind would have always been a step ahead of us, even if you put our lives in danger. And you couldn't have done that, DOD. That is not you, that is not who you are. You always wanted stability for me, love. A great church, a house, and friends." Joe felt his DOD's pain. "I've had time to think on this, too. I've also had a few years with this."

"Joe."

The white car behind them took the exit they just passed. A low-flying helicopter that suddenly passed overhead had to be a military craft because two more identical to the first buzzed by a moment later.

Dunk thought about the last time he heard a helicopter when he was with his son. "Buddy, this wanting to meet Rolls. I don't know. What if you after meeting him you disappear again? What if you run off from another hotel to vanish for two years, or twelve, or twenty?" While communication with Roland was in fact better, everything could change tomorrow.

"You said you've talked with Rolls."

"I have."

"I get that things are better now."

"Things are better. They are. But son, let me be clear. I don't want to go with you to Roland Rolls' lab."

"Okay."

"But if you go, then I'm deciding now that I'm not going to be a part of whatever falls between you and Roland Rolls." The foot he had crossed some time ago came down now. "I'm not going to be a part of it."

"Okay. I hear you. You don't have to go with me."

"And if you want to get to Roland, you're going to have to finance it. This car goes home."

Joe didn't mean they'd shoot off to the lab now. "Finance it? I have two-hundred and fifty bucks on me. In two weeks, that same amount comes again."

"This is supposed to be news to me?"

Joe couldn't believe his DOD was sounding like a tough cop. When he realized why, he immediately understood all the hardships his DOD had been through. Holding the wheel loosely with both hands, his shoulders dropped. Without touching the man he so deeply and so dearly loved, he understood the pain of prolonged hurt and intense loss. There should have been no pool company, no fight with Reggie, no woman whose name he did not know.

"There was *a lot* of paperwork sent to me a month ago when your three months in rehab rolled into another one at a halfway house. There aren't a lot of surprises here, except your wanting to immediately see Roland Rolls."

Joe's voice tightened. "You knew about the two-fifty?"

"You have four installments of that amount coming to you. It's to help you establish a new routine."

"And not drink it away."

"And not drink it away."

At slightly different times, both father and son realized the recent words and the emotions between them were truly filled with fear and with pain. In their happy lives together—and despite some dead goldfish and an occasional heated moment here and there—they were happy, both came to understand that something had closed between them, and something else had opened. They realized what neither wanted to face. There was so much heartbreak between them, so much mess, and so much loss. The neat and tidy lives they knew as a twosome would never return, at least not completely.

Dunk gripped the door's armrest with all his strength. There should have been an 'accident.' The two should be in the Middle East now, or Asia, or maybe even Australia. Why did he stop where he did with an eighteen-month-old? With the whirl of emotions still circling fast, he wondered if God truly wanted this for the two of them.

The next thirty three miles rolled on in silence. Even when the sun broke out through the clouds now and again, everything through their windows looked gray, worn, or neglected. As if ready for a long winter, the road was hard, unforgiving. The landscape braced itself for cold and stormy weather.

———————

They turned onto their street. Keeping calm, Dunk didn't look at the driver. "Earl knows."

Joe turned. "What?"

Dunk took this carefully. "I have to share this with you, buddy. Earl knows. In the last days when Rolls was recording, Earl actually found a camera. He found it while you were getting those ulmintin injections. When I came back from the lab by myself, it was a pretty tough time. I knew that alone—and I didn't know where you were—that I couldn't keep lying."

Joe considered this. "Earl knows."

Dunk nodded.

"Everything?"

"Everything."

Joe kept both hands on the wheel.

"There's a little more. Earl told Jolie about the camera while we were gone. She knows everything, too. And they're behind you, Joe. They are. They are with you and they love you."

"DOD."

Joe didn't know what to think. Telling Earl and Jolie about Roland Rolls, sure, he could sort of understand that—but telling them both *everything?*

"And Earl said this to me before I left to pick you up this afternoon. 'Tell him I'm his number one fan, always.'"

Joe slipped the car into their driveway as snow flurries hit the windshield. Earl's house looked empty. "Where is he?"

"He's giving you time, Joe. He came up with this idea on his own. He's at his daughter's house for a few days. He's there so you can have space to get your feet on the ground. But there's a note on his door for you. Read it when you're ready."

Amazed, Joe shook his head. "He really cares that much."

"Joe, he's Earl."

"And Jolie?"

"She has a dinner ready for you when you say 'go.'"

Dunk thought of Vanessa. That, as planned, was going to remain quiet for a little while.

Suddenly weary, Joe stepped out of the car. "And the neighbors over here? They are new?"

"You'll like them. Their names are Galvin and Kristen. They have a daughter. She's four. Her name is Iris."

"They named a four-year-old Iris? Like the flower?"

Dunk stood in the driveway. "It's a funny story. They'll have to tell you about it."

"They don't know that I ..."

"No, just Earl and Jolie." *And Vanessa.*

Joe took in the scene before him, including the approaching sight of Fearsome being walked with his hot pink leash by Mrs. Eldo. His voice was scared, hollow. "Can I do this, DOD?"

"With me, you can."

"DOD."

"With me you can. I love you, Joe. I love you so much."

They met at the back of the car a moment later. Their embrace was as intense as it was when they first hugged hours ago. Again, Dunk thanked God. His son was standing in the driveway, a dream come true.

"I see you are home from school, Joey," Mrs. Eldo said as she passed. "I haven't seen you in *forever.* Have you graduated yet?"

"No, I haven't, Mrs. Eldo. There are some things I needed to clear up first."

"Oh."

It's now or never, Joe. "Mrs. E.? I have a drinking problem. I had to take some time to face some bad choices and consequences, and clean up my drinking."

Mrs. Eldo could not believe what she just heard. The man who embodied some holier than thou church, that gooey and goody goody Christian has a drunk for a son? Really? While it was true that she hadn't seen that modern-day hippie boy around much, thank God, was it true? He was some off the deep end alcoholic? Score one for the other side. Church really doesn't save people from wickedness and sin.

Joe knew where she was. "Mrs. Eldo?"

"Oh yes, dear." Their neighbor needed to hear more of this directly, of course, and she definitely couldn't wait to share this immediately. First things first though. She planted her feet firmly on the cold ground to gather even more information. She was going nowhere.

"So, no, I haven't been in school for a while. But, in time, it will be good to get back. Yeah, it will be good." He took a breath in the chilly air, even though he didn't seem to be breathing. "How are you? How's Fearsome?"

Adjusting her frilly winter scarf and hat, she added up everything she had just heard, afraid she'd forget a single word later when on the phone.

The snow came down a bit heavier now. Joe asked again. "How are you? How is your dog?"

"Oh, he's fine. My little Trooper and I? We're just fine."

"Well," Joe said, taking a moment to let her words settle, "that's nice."

Dunk knew the only way to move Mrs. Eldo along was to invite her to dinner. She never said yes because she always felt she'd have to return the invitation, and that was just too much, especially with two grown men and the amount of food they would certainly eat. The price of ground beef just went up thirty cents a pound at the grocery store.

When she was well out of earshot, Dunk set his hand on his son's shoulder. "I'm proud of you. That wasn't easy."

Joe watched Mrs. Eldo's backside. "I don't know how I'm going to do this."

"I'm right beside you."

From the trunk, Joe grabbed the book bag he carried with him out of the halfway house. Its simple contents were the only things Joe owned: toothbrush, toothpaste, shaving cream, razor, a clean t-shirt, socks, boxers, and a second pair of jeans. That was it.

With eyes wide open, he stared at the world around him. *How am I going to make it here? This isn't the same place. I'm not the same person. Maybe I should run. Run away again.*

Knowing his son and sensing his fear, Dunk nudged Joe's shoulder with his own. "No, you stay. You stay put. This is your home for as long as you need it to be."

"DOD, I —"

"And those running shoes on your feet? Well, they can do laps. Many laps. From the looks of them, they're not built for a one-way run."

Thinking of where every bone in his body, every muscle, every organ, and every single cell came from and what an almost normal, typical tomorrow could be like, Joe said, "I'm scared."

"I know."

Standing here, back in his old world again with so much and so little changing, Joe found it hard to fill his lungs with air.

Dunk bumped Joe's shoulder again. "I love you, Joe. I do. And son, I will love you through this. I will love you through this."

"Come with me when I meet Rolls."

Dunk paused. "I'll think about it."

"DOD."

"We'll see, Joe. We'll see."

CHAPTER THIRTY TWO

Betsy turned toward the door she just closed. Extending her hand, she twisted the doorknob lock. As a part of her nighttime routine, she also made sure to deadbolt the door near her shoulder. When finished, she sighed.

Tossing her purse on a nearby chair in a random act of drama or foolishness a mechanical engineer like her would never do, Betsy sighed again. Neither sigh released anything. Instead, she remained tight. When she looked back to the door she had just locked, she realized she was still locked, still inaccessible. This didn't make sense because her job was great. Her coworkers were great. Even her boss was great. She couldn't beat the easy commute or the fact that her salary enabled her this great space *plus* monthly money she could put away to buy a condo of her own somewhere not so far down the road. Still, something felt boxed in, closed. After a date like the one she just had tonight with someone who reminded her too much of Tad, she realized something was missing, or lost.

To fill her empty self with something, she went to her cupboard for chocolate. After taking several nibbles from a candy bar she bought at a chocolatier's shoppe—ah, to have an expendable income—she realized she was never tasting the sweet treat. Did that stop her? No. She just ate more. An hour later, dressed for bed in a sleeveless t-shirt and old running shorts, Betsy stood in front of her bathroom mirror. Her expression meant business. "Okay, chocolate breath," she stared at herself. "It's time you and I had a serious talk. Just the two of us. Ready?"

Ready.

She set both hands on either side of the bathroom sink. "I don't get you. I don't get what you want. The bells? The whistles? Isn't that something for a fairytale? You've dated a couple of really good guys, not perfect guys, but guys even your dad would like. They've cared about you. They've reached out to you. They've even respected you, and guys today, um, yeah, they want sex fairly early."

Like on the first date.

"Not necessarily the first date, but…but the one thing in common with your guys from the past, even Mr. Football Tad, was that each was kind of different. "They all had something in common though." She stared at herself. "What they have in common is you. You are the one common denominator in all of these relationships. And you know what? You want too much. You expect too much. There is no such thing as star-in-the-sky romance. There's just what is real, and what is real is life, and life is what it is: confusing, sweet, gritty, messy, sometimes happy but always, always real. So take it. Take the plate offered you and start filling it up. Call this Antonio guy back…"

Anthony.

"Yes, Anthony. Remember that. Anthony. Call him back. Tell him you were just in some weird, funky, off mood tonight and that yes, you did have a good time with him, *and you did,* and tell him you'd like to see him again. Soon. Very soon."

She tucked her hair behind her ear. "You're going to laugh at his jokes, however lame they are. And you're going to learn five facts about golf and five facts about lacrosse—whatever that really is—and you're going to like it, girl. You are going to like it."

I am. I am going to like it.

"Now you're pretty and you're smart and this is going to work out very well."

His name is Anthony. His name is Anthony. I got it. I got it.

"Now stop talking to yourself and get on that phone."

A minute later, she tapped out his number. With one hand holding her phone, the other reached for the cross around her neck.

One ring. Two.

"Hello?"

"Anthony?"

"Yeah."

"It's Betsy. Listen, about tonight…I was just a mess. I mean, I had a good time and it was nice. You are nice. You're funny and I was just in this weird space, maybe from work, I guess. I just wanted to let you know—"

"It's not going to work out."

"Anthony, what?"

"You? Me? Nah. It's not a match."

A silence seeped through the phone.

"Yeah," he said a moment later. "It's just not going to go."

She'd never been so forward so fast. She'd also never been this angry this fast. Really? *He* was dumping *her*? "Can I ask you why?"

"You're in love with someone else."

Suddenly, she let the cross in her fingers go.

"So, yeah, Betty-Boop, good luck with that."

Click.

◈————————————◈

After Betsy slipped into bed, she turned her face toward her pillow and took a slow, quiet breath. Immediately, she popped her eyes open because she was certain she smelled the inviting fragrance from a creek. Turning to get comfortable after what had been a long day, she remembered she had washed and changed her bedding this morning before work to get a jump on her Saturday morning tasks. She had used a new laundry detergent, but that couldn't explain this, could it? When she closed her eyes again however, the refreshing scent of nature from a fast-moving current through the woods returned. All of a sudden, he was there. His white toes bobbed in the water. Joe was laughing and splashing.

How many months had she pushed him toward the back of her mind where she thought he belonged? She didn't wish him any ill will of course; she actually hoped he was doing well wherever he was. As she tried to fight her way to sleep over the next hour though, she kept seeing Mike's roommate in the water, on shore, or there beside her when Mike had told them he was gay.

When she started missing Mike again, she knew it was no use struggling to stay in bed. Reaching into the darkness, she turned on her nightstand light and knew what she must do. Out from the covers and on the floor, she pulled out the dressed up box she had kept under her bed. It was made only of cardboard and, for its age, still appeared almost new. She had said she would open this only when it was time, and by 'time' she meant it would take years for her to even lift its sturdy lid.

She wouldn't open the box tonight, of course. Doing so would dishonor the place where she was in now, and while she'd like to leave her ache to the upcoming winter wind and have it carried far away, she knew she needed to hold on to this last, wonderful piece from her dearest, longest friend just as it was now, unopened. Her fingers traced the box's edges over and over. She knew the contents under the lid, of course. She filled the box over the years with childhood and teenage memories and mementos of Michael. She remembered one treasure was a list of candy on a piece of pink paper.

"You should marry me," she could hear herself say when they were both ten.

"Of course I should," he answered, not missing a beat.

"And our wedding will be big, with lots of candy."

They were huddled in her tree house at the time, the best hangout for both of them.

Mikey was an expert on candy and this, quite understandably, would take much consideration.

"Jars of candy," Betsy said after a long moment. "Glass jars with fancy ribbons near the top. White and not too long, like my dress."

Mikey corrected her. "Buckets of candy. *Big* buckets."

"At each table."

"Of course."

After they filled out the pink paper, their conversation moved on, probably to something they had not finished earlier, like their endless debate as to which was better: lakes or swimming pools, caramel or peanut butter filled candy bars, the *Screamin' Demon* or the *Pharaoh's Revenge* carnival ride. In what had obviously been routine for them, Mikey's look seemed so far away in that moment, almost as if he was in the place where they would marry.

She asked, "What are you thinking?

"You know, we are going to have to say the words."

Betsy didn't understand. "What words?"

"The words the married boy says to the married girl."

Dropping to her side and then turning to her back, Betsy remembered saying what seemed like a practical solution. "Maybe we can just write them out."

Betsy did not remember what Mike said after that, but whatever happened next, the two had a plan.

Her fingers continued to trace the box between her hands. She knew her vows to Mike filled another paper inside, this one a pale, soft yellow. She swallowed. She could not cry again, at least not now. She would simply have to wait for another time for more tears, which she realized since the funeral all those months ago, was still something she'd become quite good at doing. Quietly, she bowed her head and listened as her heart ached, twisted and squeezed. Then, from nowhere, she rallied. *Enough.* Tomorrow was a new day, and the start of a relationship around the upcoming holidays might be something good for her. She would forget again wet boys and creeks, football players who could learn what the word epiphany means, and blind dates from anyone calling her Betty-Boop.

With her back against her bed, she stared at her ceiling. A new relationship? What was she thinking? She simply could do anything of this without her soulmate, her backbone, her life.

"Michael," she whispered as she kept holding the box that would not leave her hands. "Michael, come back."

CHAPTER THIRTY THREE

He hasn't worn pajama bottoms since he was fourteen. The soft, loose fabric felt good against his ankles and bare feet. As he stood at the door to his father's bedroom, he gathered some of the soft cotton near his thigh. "Thanks for thinking to buy these for me, DOD. They're comfortable."

With his reading lamp lit on the nightstand beside him, Dunk had just crawled into bed. Tired, he set a men's devotional on his chest. "No sweat."

"DOD? That conversation in the car?"

"Yeah?"

"I said I wanted to see Mr. Rolls."

Dunk remained quiet.

"And I wanted you to come with me." Joe hesitated. "The cameras? Even before I knew about them, I thought there were times I was being watched."

Dunk looked at the empty side of his bed. "Sit."

Joe sat facing the wall, not his DOD. "So, there are no cameras now. No recording equipment."

With a deep sigh, Dunk set a bookmark in his book, one Vanessa bought for him just over a month ago. "Mr. Rolls and I...Roland...how do I say this? Well, he's changed. We've changed. The two of us are different now. See, when you were gone, when you were missing, we had something very crucial in common. We didn't know where you were. We had no clue. No way of finding you. Think about it. You could have died up there on that roof."

"You knew about the roof?"

"And the liquor store robbery. But we learned of that long, long after the fact. Roland would not have let you hurt yourself. It was all he could do *not* to bring in an experienced, highly-trained psychologist to the rehab center for you, instead of the rookie you had. He cares that much. Really. The one you still call the mad scientist would have sent staff to try and maneuver you into better health faster had he known your whereabouts. Think about it."

Joe would rather not.

Dunk continued. "When you popped up on a screen weeks after your arrest, he shared with me your blood alcohol level. Joe, buddy, you were so drunk that you could have walked right off the top of that building. Now, this is true: his reasons for your safety and my reasons for your safety are different. And this is also true: he is a scientist through and through. That won't change." He glanced over the edge of his bed for a second. "I doubt that can change."

Joe thought about this.

"All the while you were gone, he didn't know where you were. The night you left the hotel is the night you slipped out of his amazingly webbed system. That was a first for him."

Joe turned to face his DOD.

"So, yes, we shared something in common—our concern for your safety. Our worry about you. I know Roland a little differently now."

"It is better you mean?"

"To some extent, yes."

"You and Roland Rolls?"

Dunk nodded. "Yes, me and Roland Rolls."

"This keeps turning and turning, doesn't it?"

"You can say that."

Joe's stomach felt better now that he sent two slices of marble cake down there an hour earlier. The longstanding treat was one of his homecoming gifts waiting for him on the kitchen counter, but even more comforting than the feeling of cake in his stomach was the fact that he had slipped away—completely—from Roland Rolls.

Dunk guessed what Joe was thinking. "You're solo, bud."

Joe remained quiet. He had missed this space with his DOD. This felt so good, so right. He looked at a large photo of himself on his DOD's dresser. It was a school picture framed in a dark wood. With a pencil neck and his first 'grown up' haircut, Joe was an eighth grader.

Watching his son, Dunk knew a question was forming. He waited.

"Why did he show me that movie on the wall?"

Dunk sat up and folded his hands in his lap. "I asked him that question once."

"And?"

"I didn't completely buy into his answer, though I think he was trying to be as honest as he could be with me at the time."

"DOD?"

"I think he showed that movie because he wanted to prove to you, without a shadow of doubt, that you were his special project and that you had been monitored so closely."

Joe rolled his eyes. "Project."

"Yeah. Joe, without question, he wanted you to know where you came from. Who you are."

"The clone of the Son of God."

"The clone of the Son of God."

Joe considered all he had heard. "DOD, after all this time, it's still just really weird."

"But you are so like Jesus."

"A drunk."

"Joe, no. You have this soul. This way of thinking. This way of seeing things, of reaching people."

"But I'm sinful."

"You're human. And to me, *that's* what this is all about. Did Roland clone divinity? I don't know. Or I should say as a scientist myself that we don't know yet. Yes, scripture says Jesus was perfect, sinless. But this is clear to me, Joe. You have Jesus' nature. You have his human heart. I know this. You have his human side, and, as humans, we live in a fallen world."

Joe considered his sins.

"You most definitely have Jesus within you."

In the quiet, Joe thought about some of those he met and touched over the past months. Lost souls. Broken souls. The lonely. The weak. The marginalized. There was a woman who lost her family. A man who lost his arm. A guy his age who couldn't go home. They all knew Joe by name, and he knew all of them. He met a man with a mental impairment who found a new life just by sitting near Joe at every meeting. Another soul was blind in one eye and unable to see what was before him with another. He knew of a modern day Samaritan woman at the well, and he did know her history without her sharing it first. Joe knew her past because, like him, she had a point of drinking hers away. All those touches. All those conversations.

The two business women he robbed on their way to work did not respond, but he wrote a letter to the woman who owned the liquor store. In it, he apologized for the robbery. She came to the halfway house, as invited, so he could see her and make both restitution and amends.

Joe frowned. "I've done so many things wrong. I threw Miles Nolan, that childhood classmate of mine, up against the wall. We saw that in the movie. And I killed those goldfish. Cheated on tests. I broke those windows on the side of the house."

"Yeah, you did."

"Jesus is the spotless Lamb of God. I have spots—a lot of spots."

"You have a fully human side, Joe. So did Jesus."

"But I'm not divine."

Dunk remembered what he had said a couple of minutes ago. "Maybe. And maybe not."

"DOD."

"This life, like anybody's life, is not about what you are not. This life is about who you are. And God, we know, chose you as as He chose us all to be His children."

"That may not be true. I'm a clone. Did God have God's hand in that, or was that Roland's move alone?"

Dunk barely smiled. "God is the creator of the entire expanding cosmos. I think His awareness includes what Roland is up to."

"But of out of His love, God gave us free choice. Roland acted on that free choice when he cloned those funeral linens."

"Maybe. Yes."

"DOD, maybe?"

"Yes, Roland did act on his own. You, too, act on your own. All of us do. But the Crafter of the heavens and the earth and the stars above gives and takes, we know. Yes, God allows the rain to fall on the just and the unjust, but He also blesses."

Joe knew where his DOD was headed. "If God had wanted, God would have taken me out. He would not have let this 'experiment' happen, or proceed."

Dunk pressed his shoulders into the pillow behind him. He didn't realize how much he had missed times like this with Joe. "His hand was in the cloning. He was present to you in your creation as much as he was present to me in mine."

Joe's heart swelled.

Rubbing them gently, Dunk held his own hands. "It's a lot to take in, I know. And we both know—at least for now—that we don't understand all of God or God's nature, or God's being. But buddy, we do know this…"

Joe finished his DOD's thought. "God loves us."

"He created us out of His master design to love Him back, if we so choose."

Joe felt tired. All he really came in here to say was that he had changed his mind since the car ride. He didn't need to see Roland Rolls, at least not anytime soon.

"So," Joe scratched his chin, "I'm on my own?"

"Pretty much."

Joe frowned.

"Well, no matter how old you get there, I am your DOD."

"Speaking of that, I'm sorry."

"Sorry for?"

Joe thought about the tough cop voice he heard earlier in the car today. "I am really sorry for putting you through all that I did. I didn't leave you on purpose, DOD. I left myself, whatever that was, or whoever that was. But I left a hole for you here."

"A big hole."

"I...I..." Joe stopped. "I hurt you."

"You did what you had to do."

"And what I had to do was find myself." Joe looked back on his eighth grade school picture. "Did I succeed?"

"Yes and no. I don't think any of us really find who we are until we find God within."

"You're pretty smart for some muscle guy."

Dunk shrugged.

"I am sorry, DOD. For everything."

"I know."

Unlike those last silences in the car, this quiet between them felt so, so good. It healed.

In peace, Joe moved toward the door. "Hey, I'm going to go to bed now. Good night."

"Yeah, good night."

Joe crossed the threshold, stopped, turned and walked back. "Oh, I'm going to give Mike a call tomorrow, if I can find a number for him that works."

Dunk nodded.

"I've missed him. A lot."

"Hey," Dunk said, drawing his covers up to somehow avoid any more on this one subject, at least for now. He kept his lips tight so that his son could get what he needed, which was a good night's sleep. "We'll talk about this tomorrow morning, okay?"

Joe sounded suspicious, but stopped. When he thought of Mike, everything went blank, void, quiet. "Have...have you talked with him, DOD?

"Goodnight, Joe."

"Goodnight."

In the dark, Dunk reached out and kissed a religious book on church growth that Vanessa gave him, as if somehow the book was her. For over an hour, he couldn't sleep. Instead, his thoughts and prayers kept churning, looping on the subjects of Mike and Vanessa. Joe was going to have a long day tomorrow.

When Dunk could close his eyes for more than thirty seconds in a row, he replayed a part of what he and Joe had talked about here in his bedroom. Maybe Joe really was just human, like Roland Rolls believed. And Christ's second coming, as he always believed from scripture, would *not* be like this—through a clone. Christ's second coming happening through Joe *was* crazy. The signs from scripture *clearly* didn't support this, at all.

While he was certain the rapture would not happen through a man two doors down the hall wearing solid blue pajama bottoms, Dunk paused for a moment. The Son of God came as a baby in Bethlehem and the world didn't stop. The world didn't bow. According to Luke's version of the birth narrative, throngs didn't follow the bright star, only a handful.

But God was here. In the baby. And God was here in Joe, as God was here with the rest of us.

If humanity could learn anything from Moses and other wonderful, biblical souls present to the Great I AM, Dunk knew this: we don't know God. We can't know God.

"But we do know this," Dunk said softly, "God is present, and God is good." He looked out his bedroom window. "And God is love. All the time. Always and forever eternal love."

As Dunk had done before on the countless nights when he did not know where his son was, he thought of the remote possibility that Jesus, in his early twenties, also had deep struggles. Scripture told Dunk that Jesus certainly had trying times in the wilderness where Satan tempted him. The painful story taking place in the Garden of Gethsemane also showed Dunk that Jesus begged his Father for a different fate. Both of these scriptural accounts made Dunk aware of the very human side to the Son of God. Jesus certainly understood human hardships because Jesus was here as flesh and blood.

Dunk shook his head. He closed his eyes. Joe was here. Joe was home. This was the first time in what felt like a decade that the two were under the same roof again. As sleep came close, Dunk did not protectively clutch one of his pillows to his side. Instead, he did what he has never done before and will likely never do again—he sprawled out completely over the well-worn mattress.

CHAPTER THIRTY FOUR

Joe fumbled for the coffee, which, as always, could be tricky to get to behind the tall cereal boxes over the refrigerator. Why DOD never moved the coffee to an easier, more accessible place...a mystery of biblical proportions.

"What's this?" Joe asked himself as he reached for a high-end bag of something completely unfamiliar to him. "French Almond Vanilla?"

With a question on his face, he held the new coffee brand in his hand. "DOD doesn't like vanilla anything." He moved to the sink to get water in the filter. Standing there, with the water running, he frowned, squinted. *What's this scented liquid soap in this New Age bottle? Whatever happened to that gooey bar in the old soap dish?* Speaking of soap, some expensive stuff adorned the half bath where there had always been average bars in the past. Joe smiled. *Maybe Jolie's interior design tips were finally reaching the bachelor pad.*

A few minutes later, he listened down the hall for DOD and heard nothing. Not wanting to sit inside at the table with his coffee, he knew just where he wanted to go, and this cold, quiet, early morning was just the right time to get there. He left DOD a quick note on the kitchen table. Dressed in old boots from the basement with a long coat and gloves, Joe wandered over to Earl's empty house. Before he even came close to Earl's front door, he spotted the note Earl had left for him.

Holding the envelope, he sat down on Earl's top step. Looking up and down the street, he realized he should have combed his hair, but the messy look, he told himself, helped promote his boyish charm.

After all, he was just about a month and a half from turning twenty-three. Time to start thinking about preserving that youthful look. He smiled. At this rate, he would need reading glasses soon. Carefully, he opened the letter.

Dear Joe,

You're home now. I couldn't be happier. This is where you belong as long as you choose to stay here (which I hope is a long, long time). I imagine you're right on my front step as you read this. I also imagine it's fairly early in the morning. Unlike your dad, you and me start the day right.

Joe, a lot has happened to your dad since you've been gone. This distance between the two of you hit him real hard. At one point, and he won't tell you this, he gained and then lost thirty pounds.

Your dad knows you've served some time, but he doesn't know <u>exactly</u> where you've been, not like I do. How do I know? This may surprise you, but I'm going to come right out and say it. I have a prison record. I spent two years in the Indiana State Penitentiary because I sure didn't have the best friends a guy could have. I did wrong, and I paid for it.

Now Janet and both our daughters know about this. No one else. I haven't shared this with your dad, who, as you know, is like a son to me.

And you are like a grandson to me. You and me may never get into what set you off, and I'm not talking about your time with that Rolls guy as much as I am talking about your own wrestling match with who you are. Listen up, boy. I love you. I love you for who you are, and I love you for how you are. I always, always will. Know that. But I do want to share with you, right off, that walking back into life after where you have been is not easy. In fact, it's hard, confusing, and overwhelming sometimes. You're going to need someone to hear you, and I'm going to be right…

Before Joe could finish, and the letter ended in another paragraph, DOD stood in front of him. Barefoot and wearing only what he wore to sleep last night, he held his phone in one hand. His voice was locked with tension.

"That was Earl's daughter, the one he's been staying with. She just called. Earl is in the hospital there. The ER. It might be a stroke, and it doesn't look good. We have to go. Now."

CHAPTER THIRTY FIVE

He didn't even think of asking DOD if he could drive. From the passenger seat, he just stared ahead. Earl. This couldn't be happening. This just couldn't be happening.

The letter Earl wrote was tucked in the front pocket of Joe's jeans. He rested his fingers over it. The letter changed everything he'd known about the man who seemed to always be working on something. He recalled what he had read an hour ago. *I do want to share with you, right off, that walking back into life after where you have been is not easy. In fact, it's hard, confusing, and overwhelming sometimes. You're going to need someone to hear you...*

Pulled by worry, Joe remembered a time, shortly after the baseball bat incident and the broken windows on the side of the house, when Earl overheard another one of his tirades. This rant was just verbal; nothing smashed this time. Joe could still hear the backdoor slamming behind him and, in his meanest ten-year-old voice, he spurted sharply, "And I hate you, DOD. I hate you!"

Earl overheard the angry words. Using a wheelbarrow and some long clippers, he was quietly manicuring one of his berry producing bushes in his backyard. Unlike the neighbors on the other side, there was never a fence between the properties, and so Earl, leaving his gardening tools just where they were, sauntered over to Joe.

"You don't hate, son. Now you can be angry with someone, and you may need to step away sometimes, but you don't hate."

At the moment, Joe thought Earl was not helping. "Yes, I do!"

Earl placed his warm hands on the front and back of Joe's narrow shoulders, and that was enough. Joe just needed to be held still because he had been moving too fast all morning long.

"Get the lemonade and the glasses. Two of them. Set them on my table. I'll be inside in two minutes."

"I don't want lemonade."

"I didn't ask you what you wanted, Joey. Just go and get the lemonade from the fridge. Get out two glasses. Set them on the table."

"But I can't reach the glasses. You keep yours too high."

"Then use a chair."

"But they're glass."

"Use a chair."

Tracing the note in his jeans pocket with this finger, Joe didn't remember a single word shared when he went into Earl's house. While Earl's counsel to an angry, restless boy about a single, not quite perfect parent may have been pure pearls of wisdom, Joe couldn't recall what they had talked about. He knew Earl listened to him, though. Earl always heard Joe. Never too busy, and most often with cookies or lemonade on hand, Earl always heard Joe's every word.

"I'm thinking about him, too," Dunk said through the longstanding quiet between them. "And you know, he's one of the toughest birds out there. He really is."

"DOD, I don't remember three quarters of the things he has said to me," Joe looked out the passenger side window, knowing that he was not really seeing a thing before him, "but I remember how he could make me feel."

About a dozen clean white paper napkins scattered along the edge of the road just ahead. A moment later, as their car passed, they took off in a short, low flight. Joe turned his neck to see them scurry, roll, and land.

He made me feel loved.

⋅━━━⋅

Jenna and Jackie, Earl's daughters, flanked Dunk in a waiting area.

Together for the first time, the trio shared all the right things. Both women found relief in retelling what had happened so far this morning. Just within earshot both Jenna and Jackie's spouses paced on what looked like numb legs.

It was a stroke, and yes, it had been caught early on. The prognosis, while still not set, looked very promising. Earl may well have a full recovery.

Both women thanked God over and over that their dad had been staying with Jenna when it happened. The older of the two daughters actually heard him fall in the middle of the night, and the ambulance and immediate treatment could not have been more prompt. None of them ventured to think what could have happened if Jenna didn't hear her dad, or if Earl were home.

"Girls," Dunk said, even though they were just a few years younger than he was, "I really don't know how long it would have taken me to notice, had this happened when he was next door. Maybe a couple of hours. Maybe more."

Without warning, all three looked up to Joe. He still hadn't combed his hair.

He should say something. His voice caught though and his mind blanked. When it came to Earl, he was just not good at things like this. "Yeah," he finally said, "it's just a really good thing."

Without a word, all three settled their eyes into empty spaces in front of them. With a weird, almost nauseous feeling in his gut, Joe knew he was no comfort at all. He didn't even think to pray. It was Jenna who bowed her head and spoke with tightly closed eyes a prayer that echoed what Dunk had shared in the chair he still occupied. "Dear Heavenly Father, we ask that you be with our dad and his treatment. Restore him by your will as we keep our faith in you. This we ask in your Son's name, amen."

Dunk's eyes stayed low, but Joe knew what he was thinking.

In your Son's name.

Earl's ICU room was down a long hall. Just beyond his wide, sliding glass door was a small, open area with nearly floor to ceiling windows that were completely covered with closed blinds. Quietly, Joe sat in what seemed like an out of the way spot. With his knees nearly to his shoulders, he sat near a towering a beige machine. If the big metal monster had been stripped of all of its paddles, curly cords, switches, screens and monitors, Joe thought his companion could be a Zamboni, the machine used to make ice rinks smooth.

Like the big box beside him, he couldn't move. He couldn't think. Dropping his forehead to his knees, he wished he could taste lemonade.

———

Hours passed. More tests. More waiting. No good news came. No bad news had arrived, either.

Alone with Earl for the first time as this was the first 'shift' he could volunteer for solo, Joe wrapped his fingers around the silver rail to the bed. He could not lose this man. He could not lose this friend, grandfather, and indelible support system, nor could he stand to see this ageless man who was always, *always* on the move be motionless like this.

Plugged into beeping or humming machines in at least three places, Earl's eyes had not opened since his fall fourteen hours ago.

Joe closed his own eyes. He remembered he brought Earl's golden retriever back to life. He had been alone with the dog on Earl's deck. Joe had just put his hand over Buster's hard, stiff, and cool side. With what had been a simple rush of energy from within his own body, he just said quietly, "Live." There was no more to it. Dunk and Earl, who had been inside to find a sheet to wrap the dog in before burial, quickly slid open the nearby patio door a moment after Buster came to his feet. Nothing strange happened. Nothing odd had taken place, at least in Joe's mind.

"I had the faith of a child," Joe said into the quiet. "I loved Buster. He was a good friend, a great buddy. And it just happened." Joe looked at Earl. "And now so much has happened. There was that pool company, the months of hell on those job sites. There was that guy who reminded me of Mike in that he wore a Bible College sweatshirt while serving corn in a food line."

As he had done yesterday in the car with his DOD, he thought of Reggie and the woman he should not have met after he was fired. The man in that jail cell also stirred his memory. With all of this weight, in all of this darkness, Joe knew he couldn't get back to who he was. In longing to be that boy again, he suddenly wondered what would have happened had he never been told of the cloning. He did share last night that he has had the feeling of being watched from time to time, but what if there had been no lab, or no announcement? What if he never knew? It was likely he wouldn't have run off. With Mike, he'd be a college grad. He'd know where Betsy was, and he would have had more time with Earl.

Joe tried again to find a piece of Mike in his thoughts, but failed just like he did last night. There would be time for that later. He looked to the man beside him. "You have to wake up, Earl. You have to come back. I have your letter, and I need you."

There has to be something here, he told himself, thinking of his own DNA and the lab that put him in a bed similar to this one. *There has to be something within me. There has to be.*

He tapped his toes within his running shoes, moved to the balls of his feet to first flex his calves, then his hamstrings, and finally his quadriceps muscles. He thought of his arms, his chest, his lungs, and his own blood. He experienced nothing, absolutely nothing.

You have to try harder, Joe.

Not really knowing what he was doing, Joe checked the door. It was clear. He raised his hand from his side. He remembered the story of Jesus healing Simon's mother-in-law in the Gospel of Mark and the Gospel of Luke, and the healing of Peter's mother-in-law in the Gospel of Matthew.

Leaning forward, he set his hand on Earl's shoulder. He thought of the woman who grabbed onto the hem of Jesus' clothes, the parallelized man on the mat, the healing of a man's hand on the Sabbath. He even considered Zacchaeus and how Jesus had changed his heart.

It has to be here. It has to be here. In the stillness, nothing happened. Absolutely nothing happened.

Try, Joe. Try!

Still nothing.

A nurse of some kind passed close behind him. "Excuse me," she said, "I don't need you to move, I just need to…got it." As quickly as she arrived, she was gone. In the wake of her absence, Joe didn't move. He didn't breathe.

There was still no change. No voice. No connection. No power. No healing. He didn't know what he was doing—or not doing—and he felt completely stupid. He should move his hand because this just must look weird. But this was Earl.

Pray. Now.

Joe had not talked with God since…had it been that long? Joe swallowed. He hadn't talked with God since the day he and Dunk left Roland Rolls' lab.

I don't know who I am. I don't know if I'm a mistake, like I think I am—or I thought I was during my rough and sinful years away. I don't know if I'm anything like your Son.

Sometimes I don't even know how or why You've kept me here, a wreck that I am, a failure to Your sight, but I do know Earl, dear Father. I know his love for You, and I plead that he is made well, should this be Your will. Let this be. Amen.

As he removed his hand from Earl's shoulder and turned, an aid holding a tray of covered food came up behind him.

"I didn't want to interrupt you there," she said, a little nervous because she knew the guy in front of her was cute, especially when he looked at her, or changed one of his tender expressions. His face carried such warmth and kindness.

Like what I did or said really matters?

"Well," she continued, walking into a space that felt odd to her. "Here's his dinner. He's ordered chicken pot pie with cherry cobbler."

"Um, there must be some mistake here. Earl here hasn't been here long enough to order food." He motioned to the bed. "And he hasn't said a word since he's been admitted to this hospital."

The aid looked at Earl. It was clear this man did not order anything. "Oop-sies! I'm so sorry! I clearly have the wrong room."

As the aid turned to leave, that odd feeling she began having did not dissipate, though she noticed that it wasn't as strong as when she was facing the gentle guy with the tee shirt that fit him so well. She turned back at the door. Usually so shy, she just blurted, "Do I know you?"

Though he has heard strangers say this to him often, Joe shook his head.

She thought about that feeling she had. It was strongest when she was standing closer to him. "You just seem really familiar, that's all."

Keeping the tray well-balanced, she moved into the hall and smiled at a friendly nurse she often sees.

"Yes," she repeated to herself as she moved toward her cart to check how she goofed up this food order. "Very familiar."

Three doors down, the weirdest thing popped into her mind. In the Catholic Bookstore on the corners of Blakely and Roselyn Streets downtown, she remembered seeing a plate painted of Jesus on his feet, his arms open at his sides. Even though she saw the plate about a month ago, she pictured this clearly because the plate was on the sale table with a handmade sign that read, "All items fifty percent off."

Yes, she thought, Jesus was wearing an off-white robe with a soft blue sash. He was holding the hand of a man on his knees dressed in jeans, brown leather shoes, and a hooded sweatshirt.

She dismissed this picture quickly because chicken pot pies do not taste good cold, and she had a job to do.

CHAPTER THIRTY SIX

The teen stopped in his tracks. *It's her! The woman who left me an enormous tip after I spilled all that ice cream at her table in The Dairy Barn!* Ben took a big step back from the little coffee house's plate glass window where he just noticed her inside sitting alone at a table for two. *Did she see me? Can she?*

To be sure he was invisible, he retreated another step from the direction he'd been walking. He turned. Standing against the building, he faced the busy street right around the corner from a large hospital some two hours from home. *Maybe it wasn't her.*

Ben stared at his designer knockoff shoes and felt the weight of what he knew to be true in his core. He was invisible to the world. This kind, generous woman had been one of the few who actually saw him, and he realized the irony in that he was trying to hide from her. Feeling foolish, he tried to peel himself off the side of the building, but couldn't. He was safer here.

His mind spun. This was just such a surprise. Sure, she had given him some card about a church, but didn't all church wackos hand out stuff like that? Maybe she was different. She seemed genuine, but he didn't know. Jesus people were weird, and her time with him may have been an act, a lure. The only thing certain was that it had been roughly two months since she was in The Dairy Barn. His stomach felt funny. He didn't want to see her again. Then again, he did.

He thought for a second. He could be mistaken. After all, a lot of beautiful women were out there. Quickly, he took another look. *It was her!*

He jumped back to the nearest safe place, which was an alcove that almost left him as exposed as he was the moment he saw her. A mother and early teenage daughter who approached from the opposite direction gave him a lot of room as they stepped off the sidewalk to pass. A young dad pushing a baby carriage followed. He had been talking to his little one until he saw Ben, and then awkwardly kept his mouth closed as his feet moved more quickly. Ben knew it. He looked ridiculous pressed up against a building. He swallowed. Obviously, he wasn't invisible now. This was crazy, but maybe she did have something to do with him being seen.

Ben wasn't quite sure what to do, or how to move. He considered his options—to stay or to go. His feet didn't move. It was true that he has thought of this beautiful lady behind the window a few times since they stood face-to-face during that one very odd meeting. She was a one shot deal though, a passing fluke. Of course he would remember her, but would she remember him?

This was crazy. He was crazy. He didn't think this way. He had never been stirred or moved in these weird, confusing thoughts. Things like this just did not happen to him. What was clear were his feelings. The oldest girl he could possibly *consider* dating would be twenty-one, so it was obvious that he didn't have a thing for older women. That didn't mean he didn't notice how the thoughts he had of her made him feel, however. She was pretty, poised, and elegant—yes, elegant was the word. But there was more to it. There was some odd or wrong connection here. In the fairytale never told, she was royalty; he was a poor barn boy, an unwanted and unnoticed child of someone who couldn't care. While he knew many little girls dreamed of princes, castles and kingdoms, there was no far-fetched tale of what this was, an invisible young scruff who was suddenly made visible by a kind-hearted queen.

Ben pressed into the building. Doing his best, he tried to make sense of this. He knew he was no dreamer, yet this mystery woman represented a world he knew very little about. From what he was born into with his mom and his grandmother, and both women were

Siberian tanks in the coldest of all winters ever, this wonderful woman behind the glass offered a glance at what he had only seen from a distance. Though this was whimsical, it was something he wanted. He certainly didn't want the fluff or the pretend stories—that was just crazy stuff—but he did want dignity and kindness in his everyday life, and this woman represented both.

He almost laughed, but it wasn't funny. He was literally on the outside looking in. Standing away from the building with a courage he likely borrowed from the pages of someone else's dream, he watched her. With her open, kind, expressive face, he guessed she was a woman too many men fell in love with, maybe for the wrong reasons. She couldn't save them all. Then again, after having spoken to her face-to-face, Ben thought differently. Maybe she could.

Though he hoped he'd never be caught, Ben continued to look at her from the middle of the sidewalk. Papers flooded the little table where she remained alone. The empty chair across from her held her open briefcase. Even during a coffee break, she was working. While he knew she was obviously busy, he should talk with her. He should just walk through that old, pockmarked door, pull up a nearby vacant chair, sit down, and tell her that he needed help. He needed someone to listen to his thoughts. He needed someone to hear about the places within him that were dark and getting darker. They could talk about his mom, or how he just didn't want to be seen. He could also tell her his chilliest thought. He didn't want to be here.

Ben was imagining things, of course. Talking with her—with anyone—would never happen. Even as more people passed him on the sidewalk, his eyes didn't leave her, and fortunately she never looked up from her paperwork. He watched as she read what she held. The pen in her hand glided over something she needed to mark or sign. In all of these common, everyday movements, something remained so bright about her. He wasn't sure how he knew this, but he was certain of it. It could be that she was a doctor here. Maybe she was a therapist, a real woman of care. He smiled. It could be that he'll see her by chance in one of the four elevators, or even on the fourth floor after he goes back into the hospital to check on his grandmother recovering from her gall bladder surgery.

He *could* see her again. Maybe she'd make a difference like she did the first time. For one second, he hoped. But he knew how life worked. He knew how his life worked, anyway. With the exception of a mom and a daughter and then the young dad pushing a baby stroller, he was not seen. He was not heard. He was not loved. Some guy somewhere could dream of meeting a woman like her someday. After high school graduation, maybe with a good job somewhere far from here, he could find a girl who would become like this one. She would be his world, his everything.

She stood. While organizing her papers back into her briefcase, her phone rang. Ben watched even more closely. Good news from the caller reached through the phone to touch her face. For a second her eyes that sparkled landed right on him, but he could tell from what she was hearing that she did not see him.

Even now he was a dull and dated wallpaper covering someone else's room. He was fringe in someone else's life, a basic, boring frame to a picture that showed interest, life, and spark. He didn't matter, really. No story would be written about him, even if it was a sad one. He was not a focus, even once. He would never be the center of attention. He was someone overlooked. Of course this stunning woman could not see him because he was just not here. He was just not important.

CHAPTER THIRTY SEVEN

Even though he found the quietest corridor with no one in sight, Dunk still turned his back from the nearby vending machines as he started his private call with Vanessa. After he filled her in on the news that Earl was awake and able to share a handful of words with slurred but understandable speech, she planned to meet him soon because, as a surprise to him, Vanessa was in a nearby coffee house. They said quick goodbyes with "I love you."

Before Dunk took his phone away from his face, he heard over his shoulder, "Who's Vanessa?"

Knowing it was Joe's voice behind him, Dunk's face blanked. *Joe didn't hear this last part of the conversation, did he? Of course not.*

Joe crossed in front of Dunk and shoved his free hand into the front pocket of his jeans. He shrugged one shoulder. "So, hi."

"Hi."

To have fun with this, Joe awkwardly nodded. "Yeah."

Dunk turned his phone off. "I didn't see you, Joe. You came up pretty quickly."

"Must be all my running." He handed his DOD a wrapped sandwich from the cafeteria two floors below. Holding the turkey on rye where he'll only eat the turkey, Dunk could not move.

"I didn't mean to interrupt you and...Vanessa? Is that her name? Yes, Vanessa." Joe tilted his head as if he could see a photo of her in his mind. He raised his forearm to his shoulder. "I'll go check on Earl's daughters."

"Earl's daughters. Yes."

With the slightest smirk, Joe paced off to the corner of the short corridor and turned. "Bye."

Dunk closed his eyes and thought of his not so private goodbye with Vanessa. Maybe his sandwich delivery boy didn't hear much.

But of course he did.

"Bye, Joe."

Ten minutes later, Dunk found his son and sheepishly stood beside him in a wing of the waiting area. The section was completely vacant. To tease the man he loved, Joe started right away. "So, Vanessa? Right, Vanessa. She seems nice."

Dunk frowned. He was not a good actor. "You're such an on-the-go-guy, Joe. We should talk about how you're doing with running these days, yes? I mean, when is the last time we had time for that?"

"I'm not so sure."

"Are you getting in good miles?"

Joe knew Dunk was joking, or, more accurately, trying to joke. In the car yesterday, they had talked about Joe's running. Deciding to have more fun, Joe started pacing. "I had a classmate named Vanessa in second grade."

"Yes, running. That's always a good thing."

"She was really a lot of fun, and really pretty—you know, for a seven-year-old. I bet your Vanessa has these qualities, too."

Dunk tried to stay on one subject. "All those miles. How healthy for you."

Joe tapped the sides of his legs with his fingers. "She would let me share her crayons on special projects."

"Yeah, it must keep you in great shape."

"Especially the ones she broke. She was always passing me those."

Dunk would not be outdone. He tried to keep up with his questions. "Curious here, Joe, how many miles do you average a week?"

"I was always a fan of one particular color she had. She liked it, too."

"Um, do you like to run alone, or with others?"

"Um..." Joe gently mocked the sound he'd just heard. "It was a blue one."

Dunk stared at the floor in front of him. "I had an uncle who used to run. It was track and field, I think. Yeah. He was a sprinter."

"DOD."

"What?"

"Spill. Who is this Vanessa?

"A friend of yours from third grade?"

"Second grade." To stop him, Joe held up his hand. "And now you're done."

Dunk wasn't sure if he swallowed or nodded. He may have done a haphazard combination of both of them.

When Dunk tried for another tangent, Joe put his hand back up. "Done."

"Joe."

"Still done."

Dunk swallowed successfully. He has had friends around his son, and that was what his few dates were called—friends—but Joe was right: Dunk was so not ready for this, especially now. A cool feeling slid down his back as he realized in front of his son this truth: he will never be ready.

Joe filled the quiet space. "So, Vanessa?"

Dunk wrinkled his brow as if he'd been thinking. "Vanessa."

"Yeah."

Dunk tried again to avoid this. "Nice of her to share her crayons."

Joe's fingers found his chin. "Not that Vanessa, your Vanessa."

If Earl were with them now, he would say that Joe needs a shave. The neighbor they knew to be steel abided by the simple mantra that a good, clean share was to be done every morning. Dunk agreed with Earl on daily shaving now that a few of his own whiskers were gray, but the middle-aged man thought a bit of fuzz on Joe's chin added character. The look made the young man seem thoughtful, casual, somehow more grounded.

Joe continued. "Yes, your Vanessa. The one just on the phone with you. You know, the woman you were engaged to."

Dunk's eye sprang open.

Joe pulled a phone out of his back pocket. "I haven't had a cell phone since...you know...it's been awhile. So I borrowed this one. It's Jenna's husband's. I just used it to call your buddy, Jolie."

Dunk couldn't speak.

Joe enjoyed this. "Yeah, I got a hold of Jolie easily. In fact, she answered on the first ring. She knew that Earl is awake now and talking. She thanks you for your call about an hour ago."

"Joe."

"Yeah, and when I just happened to tell her Vanessa just seems like the best thing to come along into your life, well, she just opened right up."

"Joe."

"She didn't quite tell me everything."

"Joe."

"But I did get a lot."

Dunk was out of options. It was time to speak. "You weren't to find out about what happened like this. There was going to be a different time. A different way. With no jokes. Okay, maybe a crayon or two— broken or not—but Joe, Joseph..." Dunk paused. He blinked. His throat closed and his eyes watered. "No, son. It just wasn't supposed to go like this."

"And you're not supposed to love me this much. It's illegal in thirteen states."

"What? What are you talking about?"

Joe met Dunk in the eye. "I'm talking about you, dad. Yes, *dad*. That you love me this much? That you wanted to make sure I'd be alright before you committed like this? That you've put your own heart and life on hold for me?" He paused. "That you and Vanessa did this for me?" Tears began to fall from Joe's eyes.

Dunk heard everything Joe had just said, but he backed up a bit. He knew the nickname DOD had happened by chance. It was no big moment between the two of them when it came up, but it stuck. And he'd been called that for years. His lips trembled. "dad?"

Joe's tears continued. All he could do now was nod.

Dunk shook his head. Tears began to form in his eyes, too.

"I just don't know that there are many dads out there as thoughtful as you, as thorough, as wonderful. And probably as sappy. Really? You were going to wait and tell me?"

A long, strong hug followed. Wrestling free for only a moment, Joe set his palms on his dad's shoulders so they could be eye to eye. "I am your son. *I am your son.* Isn't it time I call you who you are?"

Muscle met muscle again. In this second hug, their ears danced together playfully yet neither noticed. From the floor under their feet, what Joe did sense was that the world around the two of them seemed right and true, and then something shifted. Something warm, something wonderful. Joe thought of Jesus. All of a sudden, he thought of the times young Jesus hugged his dad, Joseph the carpenter. Here, through this embrace in a quiet hospital corridor, he knew Joseph and Jesus had moments like this. Joe was certain of these times because he knew the love between a father and a son could be so profound, so strong, and so aligning man to man. It went far beyond gene to gene and generation to generation. Joe was not sure just how he knew the Savior and his father connected like this in and around what might have been a humble wood shop, but he was certain they did. Yes, the two connected, and loved.

Before leaving this quiet hospital space, Joe dropped coins into a nearby vending machine identical to the one near Dunk when he had called Vanessa. With two bottles of water in one hand, he passed one to his dad before raising the one remaining. "To my dad, and to Vanessa. To long lives together, and to happiness."

Pausing a second to remember a wonderful second grader and the crayons she so willing shared, Joe thought about his own prospects of being with someone so special. He raised his bottle a bit higher. "To love itself."

Flesh gives birth to flesh, but the Spirit gives birth to the spirit. You should not be surprised at my saying, 'You must be born again.' The wind blows wherever it pleases. You hear its sound, but you cannot tell where it comes from or where it is going. So it is with everyone born of the Spirit.

—John 3:6-8

PART III
THE HOLY SPIRIT

CHAPTER THIRTY EIGHT

The organist swelled the music as the pair entered through the wide double doors at the rear of the large church sanctuary. Holding a single red rose, a tradition started by her grandmother, Vanessa slowly made her way down the long aisle with Earl at her side. Thankful that he said yes to giving her away, she leaned into him and smiled. Still so mindful of the rehab he pushed himself through following his stroke just five months ago, she started to ask, "This pace, is it...?"

Having walked both his daughters down the aisle, he knew how important this was not only to Vanessa, but also to him. He tapped the top of her hand. "It's just fine."

Standing at the altar in jeans, a blue dress shirt and a dress jacket—which was typical Dunk style—Vanessa smiled as she watched Joe lean into his dad's ear and whisper something that made Dunk's face completely effervesce. As they had just practiced, she passed her bridesmaids, starting with Jolie who had a tear in her eye. Then, with Dunk now beside her, she handed her rose to her matron of honor and linked hands with her husband-to-be.

"Dearly beloved," Pastor Smith began.

Suddenly, the twin gold-plated candelabras Earl's daughters had set up just minutes ago collapsed on themselves, one after the other. The clanking sounds made such a ruckus on the marble chancel floor that the pastor backed into the altar table which, having been moved for the wedding, was usually never right behind him. The heirloom crystal vase on the table that was to hold the flowers tomorrow teetered toward the floor. From a distance of ten feet, Joe dove to catch the antique that would surely break. Coming in like a batter sliding toward home plate, he was successful in the save except he ripped his shorts in the process. A moment of calm followed when no one moved, let alone dared to breathe.

When he came to his feet in what he considered the bridesmaid's section, Joe unknowingly revealed to everyone a good part of his colorful boxers. Having everyone's attention, he said to the couple of the hour, "And this is the part where I think you two are supposed to say, 'I do.'"

Everyone laughed.

Just then, Betsy slipped through the heavy wooden doors Vanessa and Earl had taken just ninety seconds earlier. Five months pregnant, she wore a stylish maternity top for the first time. She looked absolutely beautiful in a sharp fuchsia blouse with its crisp scarf.

Walking quickly down the aisle, she said, "I could hear the noise in the parking lot. *What* was that? Is everyone alright?"

Moving to stand beside Joe, she gave him a quick kiss on the lips. "Hey honey," she whispered, yet everyone could hear her. "Do you know you're showing a lot down there?"

Everyone laughed again.

"Alright," Vanessa said, still smiling. "Alright! Let's gain some composure here."

Joe glanced down at the torn side seam in his shorts. His heavy bangs flopped over his forehead as his hair had grown out considerably since his return from the halfway house. "I don't know. Composure. It's a little too drafty for that, don't you think?"

Vanessa still smiled. "Okay, this is how this goes. Bad dress rehearsal tonight, good ceremony tomorrow." She looked around her. Her bridal party had been here at the church for about twenty minutes now. "Everyone has that, right?"

Dunk reached for his future bride's hand and looked at Pastor Smith, the man he has shared his faith journey with for years. "Maybe we should do this now. Let's go for the Real Deal tonight, just in case something worse happens tomorrow."

Vanessa laughed. "We should definitely be practicing the kissing part."

Dunk looked at his love and then Pastor Smith. Before he set a warm, gentle kiss on the lips of the bride-to-be, he said, "Yeah, Vanessa and I? We really don't want to mess up that kissing part."

Laughter from the catastrophe in the church spilled into the rehearsal dinner, which was a catered meal spread out casually yet elegantly over Earl's backyard. Still not one to profess any knowledge of bows, wedding bells, or brides on the night before they marry, Earl, who had five grandsons, welcomed all the things that dressed up this celebration. In fact, he purposefully invited his daughters to do what they did best: bedazzle. From festive table linens to candlelit sconces glowing low in his tree limbs, they made their mark. Soft white sheers lifted slowly and easily now and then to welcome the early August breeze. The goblets of scented garden flowers at every turn made him smile. He couldn't believe what love could do.

In a peaceful moment where Earl found himself standing alone, he thought of his late wife, Janet. He kissed his fingers to her, which was something he hasn't done in a long, long time. It was a gesture they had started early in their marriage because the romance between them was something they said they could often taste on their lips.

Earl smiled inwardly. Janet would be enamored with this night and that handsome neighbor of theirs, far too long a bachelor, who was getting married tomorrow to a woman as gentle and as glowing as a single candle flame.

As they passed their dad, Earl's daughters continued to debate why those candelabras fell. "It's totally your fault," Jenna joked to Jackie.

"Totally yours," Jackie returned.

Their eyes lit at the same time as they said together, "Cinderblocks!"

They turned back to their dad. "No."

"But the bases just need more weight for the flowers," Jenna pleaded. "And we'll spray paint the blocks gold. And there's superglue and appliqués we can find or make."

Earl appreciated diehard dedication, even on such things as flower fortitude, but still shook his head no. Playing the old grump, which has been a role he has enjoyed these past few years, served him well. He grumbled, "And before you ask, I do not have gold spray paint in my garage to match the color of the candelabras."

"Oh yes, you do."

He pretended not to hear Jackie. "And I don't know what an appliqué is."

"Dad," Jenna tilted her head, ready for what could be round two. "Sure you do."

He ignored both girls, even though all three of them knew he had a wide, well-organized array of spray paints in the basement and had heard of an appliqué, even if he couldn't spell the word or guess how such a frilly thing could enhance a rough cinderblock. A pragmatist, he envisioned the candelabras toppling tomorrow, this time with the candles lit. "And no—and I'll say this just once—you two are not running any risk of burning down the church."

Jackie shook her head. "Burning down the church? Like sending the sanctuary up in flames could happen."

Jenna gained an inward focus and seemed to speak to herself. "We could make up dad's corsage to carry a fire extinguisher!"

"Yes!" Jackie agreed. "We do have extra greenery. It hasn't all gone into Vanessa's bouquet."

Both women, who could so clearly be seen by anyone as sisters, started looking at their father's chest in a very particular way.

Earl put his hand over his jacket's lapel. "No."

Before moving on to make sure everyone was doing well with after dinner drinks now that the meal had been served and cleared away, each daughter patted her dad's arm.

From two table lengths away, Jenna turned. "You used to be fun, you know."

"Those were in the days when, with you two, I was glad I could carry extra fire insurance on the house."

She wrinkled her nose.

"And I didn't have to even think about having extra gold spray paint on hand."

Jenna's eyes lit with what she just heard. "So, you do have it?"

"In the basement. There should be at least most of a can. You know where."

"And dad?"

"No, Jenna. No more ideas."

"Wait, you didn't know what I was going to say or do." To Earl's great surprise, she took her fingers, kissed them, and waved them toward her dad.

Taken back, he had no idea she knew his and Janet's gesture.

"I love you, dad."

He frowned theatrically. "No fires."

※

"No what, Earl?" Viola Munson cooed. Self-proclaiming that she was the one who first made it possible for Dunk and Vanessa to get to know one another because she was, after all, there on the church ramp when the two met before that first fateful deacon's meeting, she would be one of the scripture readers for tomorrow's service. Overhearing just the tail end of the banter between dad and daughter, she moved in her dainty way to stand beside Earl, who, much to her delight, turned out to have a lot more class than she gave the old gruff credit. Tilting her head just so, she repeated her question. "No more what, Earl? Come on, tell."

"How about this, Viola, I'll tell you that I'm happy for my neighbor here."

"Ah, yes."

"And Vanessa, too."

Viola tilted her chin. "I have to say, this is interesting, isn't it? Vanessa will be moving into that lovely house next door. You'll be a neighbor to the newlyweds." Her socially phony voice rose to its climax. "How wonderful."

Earl took a step back. He had perfected talking to single women his age in such a way that they would scurry. "And property values?"

Flirting, Viola blinked. "Yes, property values?"

"They will go up as a result of her being here on the block, for sure. That's what really matters here. Real estate."

"Oh."

Earl continued smoothly. "A good woman like Vanessa? Why, she increases the value of a home."

Completely shocked, Viola didn't quite know what to think—and this may have been a first. Having been near her for many, many church coffee hours, Earl knew this silence was a rare and wonderful treat. "Yes, Viola, it's all about simple economics. The mighty dollar, you understand. Net worth, value, that sort of thing." He opened his hand. "Can I refresh your drink?" Her open jaw expression was priceless. "Viola?"

In all of her polished perfection tonight, she was not certain how to get away from this obviously misguided host other than to run, and at her age she feared she'd lose some necessary support item secured under her dress if she darted off too quickly. "Well, Viola? Would you like your drink refreshed?"

To all out flee from this behemoth was something she couldn't consider, at least fully. "Oh no, no. I'm fine."

Dunk, the diplomat, caught Viola's need for speed. He met her as she scurried toward the dessert table. He repositioned his wine glass as he said in the stuffed shirt way he was beginning to learn, "I'm very glad you were able to join us here for the dinner, too. It's nice to have you at this party as well as at the church." Vanessa, equal if not greater in charm than her future spouse, slipped her hand around Dunk's back. She smiled at the one who had wiggled her way into their wedding. "Yes, Viola, we are both glad you could juggle your evening for us. This is a big night for Dunk and me, and we're happy you could free your schedule."

Freeing Viola's schedule meant she wasn't home now to watch her favorite TV game show, *Spin, Spin, or Lose.*

"Yes, me too. It's breathtaking to see you two lovebirds on this lovely summer night. It sure has taken enough time, though."

Both nodded. Vanessa came up with a polite response first. "Well, the good things are worth the wait."

Joe and Betsy, on the dance floor Earl built, started dancing when a new, fun, fast song began. Vanessa and Dunk had the first song on the floor to themselves ten minutes earlier, and that tender piece was the last slow song the five piece string band played before turning the night over to dance music.

"Why, look at them go," Viola remarked, smiling less than sincerely. "She's a beautiful girl, that one."

"She is," Vanessa answered.

"And they met where?" She made the same ever so subtle facial expression as when she had to eat another woman's lemon bars at a fundraiser. "A cemetery of all places?"

Dunk and Vanessa exchanged a glance. As only couples who have been close together can do, they non-verbally agreed that Vanessa was to answer this one.

"Yes, both Betsy and Joe had a mutual friend, a wonderful friend. His name was Mike. In fact, it was Mike who introduced them."

"Just like I introduced you two."

"Ah, yes."

Viola made a face. "But a cemetery? That seems like an odd place to start, doesn't it?"

Vanessa nodded. "Well, I have to tell you, Mike meant a lot to both of them. It had been years since Betsy and Joe saw each other. In that time, however, each thought of the other person now and again."

"That is sweet."

"And yes, they did meet at the entrance gate by a memorial garden, a short walk from Mike's grave. Betsy was there for one reason, Joe another. Neither expected to see the other, it just happened." Vanessa noticed one of her co-workers waiting to talk with her, but she wanted to finish this part of the story.

"Viola, their meeting happened just after Earl's stroke. Joe really needed to see where his friend and college roommate was, and Betsy, well, she and Mike literally grew up together."

Viola considered all of this and lied. "There near all those headstones. An historic site, I imagine. It is *kind of* romantic, I suppose."

Vanessa excused herself to answer a question her co-worker had about a food allergy and the menu for the reception tomorrow. With Dunk still at her side, Viola eyed all the pretty desserts. Pies, cheesecakes and fancy sweets artistically covered the little table. Not wanting to be seen eating too much, for heaven's sake, she picked up a little Lenox plate. "Earl's stroke was nearly half a year ago, if I have that right. And she's how far along?"

"Who? Betsy?"

"Yes, she must be about, what, four months into her pregnancy?"

"Actually, five."

Viola knew exactly what she'd like to say here, but remained careful. "Well, it is nice to see a future mom and dad together."

To field this one, Dunk wished Vanessa was back. She could handle the phrasing on these things so much better than he could. "You should ask them about that, Viola."

"Oh? Something I should know?"

By the grace of God, Jolie stole her best friend away at just the right time. "Come on, bachelor boy. There's some dancin' you and I will be doin'."

Dunk turned back to Viola who would pile more pie onto her plate now that she had a moment to herself. He smiled at his fellow deacon. "All you need to know, bottom line, is that I'm going to be a grand dad, and I couldn't be happier."

Viola needed to know more. Oh, yes, she needed to know more. It was her responsibility, after all.

CHAPTER THIRTY NINE

Jolie could be considered a hazard to others on the dance floor that Earl was clearly glad he reinforced. Elbows here. Knees there. She did hit her best friend in the face, but it wasn't a direct hit, so the red mark would be nothing by tomorrow morning. She danced. She totally, happily, let loose without any inhibitions. It was time to celebrate and get it on down, down, down. After all, this was her best friend's rehearsal dinner party, and the music was good and loud. A hand flew here. A hip toss landed there. A chugga-chugga boom-boom like a deranged chicken came next. Another chugga-chugga boom-boom followed, and another, and another. Dunk tried his best to keep up with the dance machine—and he could move on the floor—but this time was hers. Anyone could think she'd had one too many, but Jolie only sipped half a glass of wine after the prayer and her toast tonight. After years of seeing his loneliness firsthand, she knew how long it had taken this man to find the one he loved so deeply and truly. She was not going to let this moment go without *a lot* of joy released.

From their seats, Joe and Betsy watched the fun. Tired from a day of work and new weight on her feet, she leaned against his shoulder, and, since it was getting cooler, his arm covered the top of hers. Viola seized this opportunity. She blindsided them.

"Oh," Joe said with a bit of surprise, when the senior plunked herself down. "Viola."

"Hello, Joe."

Joe sat up, but kept his arm around Betsy. "I know you two met in the church after the rehearsal, but again, Viola, this is Betsy. Betsy, this is Viola. Viola is one my dad sincerely enjoys working with in church."

Betsy appreciated Viola's directness. "You're a deacon along with Dunk and Vanessa, isn't that right?"

"Yes, dear." Viola leaned in closer to Betsy because the music—if you could call it that—was far too loud. "How wonderful to see you two dancing earlier. Exercise for a mommy is really healthy for an unborn baby."

Betsy wasn't quite sure she liked the word *mommy*. It was babyish. Then again, this swell in her stomach was a baby, not five months of voracious dining twice a day at an all-you-can-eat buffet.

"Yes," Betsy agreed, "the exercise is good."

From the dance floor, Jolie hooted and the three turned to watch her and Dunk laughing as they tried some limbo moves without a limbo stick. Viola found their foolishness to be too much. Motorcycle driving Jolie just needed to ride off on her bike before she embarrassed herself any further. Back to the subject at hand, Viola played with the lobe of her ear only to draw attention to how her earrings exquisitely complimented her outfit which was a formal garden dress she had worn years ago to an art reception. "You are going to be a beautiful mother, darling."

"Thank you."

She turned to Joe. "And you're going to be a great dad, Joseph. You've had a great dad, so this is going to come easily." She winked at Betsy. "If you don't butter them up, then all the baby changing will be yours, princess."

The word *mommy* may have passed. *Princess* was another story.

The flab under Viola's jaw wiggled when she laughed. "Yes, changing a diaper. Daddies say they have no clue!"

Betsy raised her shoulders away from Joe and set her athletic arms on the table. "Joe is not the father of my baby. Five months ago, I became pregnant with someone else."

Viola's double chin solidified.

Betsy continued in a candor neither Viola nor Joe had heard before.

"Yes, Joe's not the baby's dad. I did what I shouldn't have done with someone I had moved on from. It was a mistake. A one time mistake, but nevertheless...that man knows about this child, and is choosing not to be in the picture at this time."

Viola's eyes widened. "Oh. I see."

Thinking of Viola whom he did respect even with her penchant for sharing other people's business a little too often, Joe looked at Betsy. "She certainly does see it *all* now."

"Joe," Betsy asked, "what's that supposed to mean?"

If Joe opened the lid on what he was feeling in front of a church mouth here like Viola Munson, then that would make this hot story all the hotter. "We can talk about it later."

Innocently, Betsy shrugged. "Why not now?"

"Viola, would you excuse us?"

"Joey dear, you can say whatever you need to in front of me. You know that."

Joe swallowed. He had learned a lot from his dad in situations like this. "You're always right, Viola."

"I am? Really?"

Joe's words were perfectly shellacked, which was something that surprised him since he never put on airs before tonight. He faced Viola with the look of a dignitary able to negotiate an unsettling situation. "I know from you, dear friend, that manners are used to make people comfortable. And, of course, you definitely want us two to be comfortable, don't you, Viola?"

The senior's face sank. She'd been caught by her own old words and reputation. Viola was forced to retreat, for now. With enough information for the moment, she began her long exit. "I was the one who intruded upon you."

"Oh Viola," Betsy disagreed. "That's not it at all."

While Viola wanted all the specific details including names and dates, she also valued the high pedestal on which she placed herself. Slowly, she came to stand. It was a process. She made it clear from her exaggerated movements that she really did not like these ill-equipped chairs on grass no less. On her feet, she offered her hand to them both. "I should be going, anyway. It's been quite an evening, as you know." She reminded herself of the recent misfortune of seeing Joe's underwear.

"So, if I could just find the happy couple of the evening, then I'll be on my..." she glanced toward the dance floor and made just enough of a face of disapproval toward Dunk and his buddy, that manish woman. "There's one. Now, where can I find Vanessa, the poor thing?"

Betsy still missed the nuances and social slights. "She's *not* a poor thing, Viola. She has a wonderful guy in her life, Joe's dad."

Despite decades at the Presswater United Church of Christ, where she knew she needed her Jesus, Viola also knew she had moments where she wasn't as Christ-like as she would want the world to think. This was one of those moments. She certainly would not be ruffled by an unmarried pregnant woman with an open mouth, nor would she come undone by a booze boy, who, rumor had it, did time in jail. Her feet were done. She was done. She'd said too much, loved too little. Tired, she found her tin can car on the street in front of the house of Dunk's neighbors, who, with their daughter, were away at an anniversary party tonight.

She sat behind the steering wheel. All of a sudden, it hit her. What she had said was wrong. What she did was unkind. She had her own past, of course, that included her own family secrets. She also knew what it meant to be an authentic follower of Christ, which she wasn't tonight. She knew she needed to go back and try to fix what might fester between Joe and Betsy.

Lumbering back through the side yard, she immediately noticed Vanessa with other guests.

"Viola, did you forget something?"

Her look was far away, but it came back. "No, I think I found something that's been missing."

Vanessa made an inquisitive face. "Care to share?"

"Yes, I will, but only after I find Joe and Betsy."

"What?"

Joe turned to Betsy. Side by side, they were walking around the block a few minutes after having said goodnight to Viola a second time. The most seasoned deacon had come back to apologize to the young couple for being too nosey. Betsy let the whole scene go, even before Viola's return. Joe, however, did not. It was his suggestion to take a walk after seeing Viola to her car and watching her drive off. "You don't know, do you?"

"You're upset now, Joe. That's all I know."

"Viola Munson?"

"She's sweet, isn't she?"

Joe could not believe this. Between the two of them, Betsy was the one he thought who would be the least likely to put up with Viola's behavior.

"Joe, what? She is sweet! She just wanted to talk with us."

"She just wanted to find out about the baby."

Betsy patted the slight curve of her stomach. "Well, that's a natural thing to do."

"She wanted to know about us, too."

They came to the first turn at the end of the street. Awkwardly, they bumped shoulders as they each saw a different direction in front of them.

"Joe, we've talked about this. We are not keeping secrets."

"We have talked about this. And apparently we need to talk more."

Betsy didn't like the sound of Joe's voice. She also didn't like that she somehow messed something up with Viola at the party and wasn't quite sure what that was.

"Yeah, Bets, I think we need to talk *a lot* more."

His tone triggered her own spark. "We? This is my baby, Joe."

"We do not need to shout to the whole world whose baby you are carrying, Betsy. Yes, key people should know, like your close family and mine. Future doctors. Maybe even her first and second school bus drivers. I get that. I get that loud and clear. And the baby should know who her father is. That's good. That's right. And it's fair."

"But—"

"But the Viola Munsons of this world do not need to know every little detail. They don't."

"I'm not hiding anything."

"You don't need to broadcast everything, either."

Betsy could not believe what she was hearing. She didn't figure her easygoing, supportive, and tender boyfriend could be anything like this.

"All I'm saying, Betsy, is that the whole world doesn't need to know everything."

Control, she thought. *That is what this is about. Joe is coming at this with a need for control. He wants some prideful male ownership over this situation. And over me.* She looked at him as if for the first time. "Who are you?"

Joe couldn't speak. He couldn't put into words that his life has been so open for so long with those cameras and recordings, that if anything could be closed, he'd not only welcome it, but also he would fiercely protect it. He'd do anything not to have an ongoing newsfeed on the baby he already loved more than he could say.

Misreading Joe by thinking he was someone who wanted to corral her, Betsy rebelled. She was not going to be maneuvered or manipulated. "Speaking of not broadcasting everything, maybe you don't want to know this. Tad? He didn't use a condom like he said he did."

"What?"

"He said he had, of course. At first."

Joe could not believe he was hearing this.

"But he told me just a few days ago that when we had sex that one time, it wasn't safe."

"You—you had unprotected sex?"

"I didn't know it at the time. It was dark, and he took a moment to reach into a nightstand drawer. He said he put one on." Actually, Betsy realized, she had never asked him. It wasn't exactly the time for conversation. She just assumed.

Joe was numb. "You had unprotected sex." *No wonder you're pregnant. Where's Mrs. Eldo?* He wondered. *With her little dog, she'd love to overhear this.*

Betsy continued. "We are not continuing this conversation about the one and only time I've had sex. It was my choice. I didn't make the right decision that night, but we're here now, my baby and me."

Joe stopped. This shouldn't be happening, at least not tonight, not on the eve of his dad's wedding. Maybe this conversation should just wait.

"Joe?"

Yes, Joe thought, this should wait. As a couple, and that was what they've been since they met at Mike's grave, they would need to work this through. Not tonight though, and not in anger.

"Joe?" Betsy didn't like the faraway look in Joe's eyes.

Staring at full-bloom marigolds that lined a sidewalk, she sighed. She was not good at this. She was simply not good at dancing in a relationship without one steady beat. She should have been smart enough to catch the slights Viola dished out as perfectly as a pretty piece of cake from tonight's dessert table, but she wasn't. By no means was she naïve; she was born into a social world quite similar to the one she had experienced tonight; but she wasn't handling this well because she was only thinking of herself. This was her pregnancy, her baby.

She thought Joe wanted control, when in fact she did. Her life, including her love life, had to be a certain way and meet certain expectations. She rolled back to the first time she met Joe. The fight she'd had with Michael there on that big boulder near the water happened because Joe wasn't what she wanted. He didn't measure up; he wasn't enough. This may have had something to do with her being an engineer, but that wasn't all of it. Everything had to be a particular way. Everything had to have a particular order.

Michael would have coached her here. He would have smoothed out all of her sharp places. She knew through experience that grief was a process of stages and sometimes what she had passed would loop around again. She also knew she couldn't keep going back to thoughts of Michael when her relationships wobbled. She had to do things on her own now. Still, without her best bud, and she could not replace him, she wanted to tear up a little or pout because she truly was just not good at situations like this.

With Joe still looking so far off, she tried to breathe. She tried to think. She could do this. She could hear her boyfriend, adapt, or at least show some flexibility. While it was true that she loved consistency, not surprises, she looked at her life. Over these past months, Joe had been almost a daily part of this pregnancy, whereas Tad had not only been distant, but also carried through with his engagement to another woman. Living in Florida, he was now married, and he and his pregnant bride were expecting their baby any day. But it was true. Her old college boyfriend, the football player, slipped in between the sheets when a lonely and broken Betsy called on him. Tad knew his then fiancée was a few months pregnant at the time, but that detail didn't matter when Betsy offered him her bed for the night. Only when Betsy found out that she was pregnant did Tad tell her that he just married a woman also carrying his child. Betsy had called Tad because of that guy named Anthony, who, after just one date, sent her off to Tad. The day after she slept with him, she went for the best comfort she could get, and that was at Mike's grave. It was there that she met Joe.

Stalled on what had been a walk around the block with the man she loved, Betsy realized she had to stop making a mess of her life, and the lives of those around her. One look into Joe's murky eyes told her he was lost in his thoughts. She vowed to listen, just listen. "Joe, what is it?"

"I love you, Betsy. I do. And my once forever single father is getting married tomorrow. I am his best man. Understand something. This conversation can wait."

"I don't see why. This doesn't have to wait. We can talk."

Anxious for everything to go well for his dad tomorrow, Joe snapped. "He is my dad. He has been there for me a gazillion times. This night, and tomorrow, they are *huge* for him. They are huge for Vanessa, too. We shouldn't have left on this walk here. That was my idea, and it wasn't a good one. I'm sorry about that. I need to get back to that party and be there for them in their happiness."

"Joe, wait. We can talk."

"*We?* What is this *we*, Bets? Isn't it just you and your baby?"

She wanted to say he was right. She was being self-centered. This was the time to share with him where her thoughts had just been, but she couldn't do it. She couldn't speak.

Joe looked in the direction of tonight's party, then, lowering his voice, faced her. "You just talked with Tad. Recently, right? You found out about him not wearing a condom."

"Yes."

"Why didn't you tell me?"

"I—I don't know."

Joe's voice softened. "I invite you to get the answer to this one. And I'll need the answer to this big question, too. Where am I in this?"

She wanted a script. She wanted her lines, or, more accurately, she wanted her monologue.

"Bets," Joe asked again. "Where am I in this?"

This was too big, too much. She had made a mess she couldn't clean up.

"Bets?"

She couldn't answer.

Hurt, Joe built sudden defenses around what he needed to protect so that, like his time in the rehab center, he had a way out, if needed. "You should understand something here. I love my dad. He is my number one this weekend. And you, you are *not* to upstage my father's wedding by sharing your whole sordid story. Out of respect for the couple of the day, please silence that you're pregnant from a then engaged and now married man who's expecting a child any day with his new wife. Do you understand?"

The chance to speak was right there. She could do this. She could share how she felt.

He turned back toward his dad's house after a moment. Over his shoulder he said, "I just have to go now. I need some time alone."

Only when he was out of earshot could she say, "I love you. Joseph, I love you."

CHAPTER FORTY

Holding a piece of decadent chocolate chiffon cake that could easily serve two, Jolie shrugged and shook her head. "Men are just stupid."

Betsy, who was wearing one of Earl's midweight work shirts over her dress, didn't say a word as she sat on his washing machine in a room she believed was way too small for a closet, let alone a laundry area.

"Yes, stupid," Jolie continued, her focus shifting from men in general to the cake in her hand. "And yes, I've burned off enough calories on that dance floor tonight that I can eat this whole thing, even the crumbs, step on the scale tomorrow morning, and still have lost weight. And yes, oh yes, this is obvious: I will look so fine in my dress for this wedding." Jolie looked at her current laundry roommate who had the sad eyes of a puppy needing to be rescued from an animal shelter. "Did you hear me about my dress?"

"Yes."

"Then don't be so sullen, beautiful one." Jolie was glad the doors in this laundry area were open because this space was really tight. As she kicked out one of her legs from her seat on the dryer, she forked more cake into her mouth. Between bites, she asked, "Have I told you about it?"

"It?"

Jolie sighed. "The dress! Now we have to get past this 'men are stupid' part so that we—and by 'we' I mean you—can move on to more important things, like this dress. I'm telling you something right now. It's stunning." Jolie, with fork in hand, started sliding her arm high and low. "Well, it's all fitted up and through here. It's not tight, but it's, you know, *good*. And it swirls a little here and here and here. It's this greeny-limey color that makes my skin look all good—I mean really good—like it has been done up by those commissioned makeup sales women in department stores." Jolie shimmied closer to her conversation partner. "You know the ones behind the counter who always tell you what colors work for you before handing you the cost of what you need to look all beautiful."

Betsy always avoided those women.

"And listen. Just you listen to this, Miss Betsy Ross. Or let me just call you Ross Betsy because it slides better for me. In all my years, I have never, *never* worn anything that sparkles. *Ever.* This number? This oh-the-boys-are-going-to-drop number, why, it's just so fine."

Betsy's expression did not change.

"And I'm wearing this because I love my friend. I love him, bad. I mean, this is such a special time. That cute man has found the love of his life, and tomorrow? Well, I can hardly wait. I'm so happy for Dunk-ba-dunk." Jolie, who noticed her words had no effect on the dishrag doll beside her, kept trying. "And my nails, do you want me to tell you about my nails?"

"No."

"I actually had another teacher friend shop with me, and we found just the right shade. It's a lighter limey-green color, like you'd find in a cucumber sliced. And the manicures are at ten tomorrow morning with Vanessa. You'll be there."

Like Jolie, Betsy had never had her nails professionally done. "I'm not sure that's going to happen."

Jolie gasped. "Drama!" She took another bite of her cake, this one much smaller than the last. "And there will be none of that."

That's what Joe said.

"You still don't get this, do you Ross Betsy?"

Tearing up, Betsy raised her hand to her face, but Earl's shirtsleeves were so long that she couldn't see her hand. "I don't think, honestly, that I get any of this."

Jolie set her cake plate down. She would like to eat more but won't. Despite what she had just said about having no fear in consuming calories, there was a wedding tomorrow and with or without that stupid, way overpriced dress she truly struggled to buy—really, *sparkles?*—she was going to look good. "This is what it is, okay?"

"Okay."

Jolie accidently kicked the dryer under her. It made a familiar empty metal sound. "No, you have to listen to me, and listen good. Do you get what I'm asking for here?"

"Yes."

"Joe loves you. He loves *you*. You also have to understand that he *loves* that baby. I've seen him when you're not watching. He *loves* your belly buddy. And he doesn't want anything—or anyone—messing that up, including you, Miss Ross."

"I thought you were going to call me Ross Betsy."

Jolie considered this for half a second. "Things evolve."

"Jolie, why, why is this so hard?"

"It isn't. *It* isn't hard at all. *You* two are making it hard, and that's because you care so much. And you're scared about that care. Now, it's true, I've never been married, and I'm not saying you and Joe are going to go down Wedding World Road, but I have been around, and I'm not talking about my weight. You put him first, Miss Ross. Well, right behind God, Joe is first. *First.* Do you hear me? Think about him. Think about what's best for him. Move what you need to move, say what you need to say, praise what you need to praise, bend what you need to bend so that directly *and* indirectly, that young man gets it. He gets that you love him, support him, and care for him like I know you do."

Betsy considered what she was hearing.

"And he'll do the same for you. Actually, and you know this, he's *doing* the same for you now. He has you way up here." She raised her hand above her head. "And here's the truth. While that baby down there is not his baby, no one—no one—would ever know it. He is hot for you, girl. Hot. That kind of love you don't want to mess up."

Betsy swallowed hard. Her heart burned. "But I'm messing this up, Jolie."

Immediately Jolie wanted to disagree with her, but didn't. "You just go slowly, and you listen to him. Listen to him *hard*. And know this deep down. It's what I started with here, if you remember. Men are stupid. Stupid. They never say what they really mean. You just have to read 'em, and you can."

Starting to cry, Betsy knew Jolie likely meant well, but she was wrong, especially about Joe. The one she loved was not stupid, and he meant what he had said. Thinking about when she was with him last, she used Earl's sleeve to catch her tears.

"Oh," Jolie said, "I know Earl. He'd be happy to have that old shirt of his catch some of your drops, darling. Go ahead, let loose."

"I am scared."

"No, you're not scared."

Betsy shot a glance at her newfound friend.

"Okay, you're sort of scared." Jolie started to tear up herself. "But you're in love, Miss Ross. And love is always good, always. Even at times like this, or especially at times like this. You'll see. You'll see."

"It's either ice cream or alcohol," Vanessa said, holding an ice cream scoop in front of Earl's chest freezer. "Both have calories, and since one of us is pregnant, ladies, is it going to be chocolate almond crunch, French vanilla, or some of both?"

Jenna, Jackie, Jolie and Betsy sat at the small kitchen table that remained piled high with surplus goods from the dinner party that wound down about an hour ago. It was a small house and everyone at the table quickly figured a meeting in the kitchen was necessary for the youngest in their company. Even Earl caught wind of it, and he was out in the garage at the time making sure all the filled garbage bags were secure for the night. While he had never seen or even heard of a raccoon in the neighborhood, he could be never too careful.

"Dad," Jenna said when she heard her father at the garage door. "Stay. Join us."

Earl made his way to the kitchen. One look at all those faces and he knew where he should go. "No ladies, I'll be back. This time is for you."

Jenna checked the clock over the sink. It was 9:35 PM. "You've taken your medicine, right dad?"

Earl headed out the back door. "Yes, and don't worry. I won't be long."

When the door closed behind him, Vanessa set the ice cream containers on the counter. Tucking a heavy, long, loose curl behind her ear, she smiled. "Your orders ladies, I didn't get them. Who wants chocolate almond crunch?"

※

Jolie called it like she saw it. "This is the lamest impromptu bachelorette party known to womankind."

Vanessa laughed. "It is. Just my style!"

They'd all had dessert earlier. The ice cream Vanessa offered did not sell. With not so much as a single dish or glass in front of any of them, they talked about everything and nothing. The rehearsal itself. Dunk. The upcoming manicures. The schedule tomorrow. Earl's health. That chiffon cake.

Vanessa, who sat beside Betsy, set her hand over her new friend's forearm. "And now Joe. Let's talk about him."

Betsy sighed.

Vanessa asked, "Does anyone here think that Joe is in love?'

Each woman exchanged a glance and answered affirmatively at one time.

"So Betsy," Vanessa confided, "the day I met Joe? I was nervous. I knew from our start how much Joe means to Dunk. They make such a great one-on-one team. So to sit down across the table from him, especially after all this time had passed and say hello for the first time? Honestly, I was just in a knot."

Betsy looked closely at the bride beside her. Vanessa wore such a calm expression. In thinking about make-up for the second time tonight, she realized it wasn't the foundation on her face that hid any difficulty that had come along her way, it was her faith. In fact, in the few months since she had met the re-engaged woman, Betsy noticed that nothing seemed to really shake Vanessa, including two candelabras that crashed in front of her just hours ago.

Still wearing Earl's shirt, she held her nervous fingers still. "But you had a wonderful lunch that first time. Joe has always been taken by you."

Vanessa looked knowingly at the woman who did glow with this pregnancy. "You missed the part that I was nervous about this. It wasn't so easy."

"So, what did you do?"

"I did what I'm asking you to do. Give this to God. That's what I did before I met Joe. I could have been a wreck. I could have worried and fretted. But I didn't. I just trusted love. I didn't always. I have a failed marriage to prove that. I made mistakes. Big ones."

Betsy thought about Tad. So much of that relationship had been so wrong.

Vanessa's voice lowered to a place of perfect peace. "But here's the truth I've come to know through Christ: God gives us such guidelines on love. Sure, we fail sometimes. We all have egos and arguments— sometimes loud, sharp arguments—but His Word guides us each time, every time."

Betsy gave an open look that said she needed to know more.

Vanessa glanced at the clock over the sink and then to the door Earl had walked through twenty minutes earlier. She knew what had worked for her and Dunk. "Ephesians 4:26. Don't let the sun go down on your anger."

Betsy considered what she had just heard.

"Yes," Vanessa said, sensing Betsy's doubt and worry. "Just trust love."

"But I've made a mess of the night before your wedding."

Vanessa smiled. "Oh, no, you haven't. No, not at all. I love to share what I've learned about God in this relationship with Dunk. Oh, and this a great truth, too. When Joe is happy, I'm happy."

"But Joe isn't happy."

Vanessa checked the clock again.

Betsy asked, "Now?"

Vanessa nodded. "Now."

CHAPTER FORTY ONE

The bottle of whiskey sat quietly. Gin kept it company. Together they centered on the top shelf of a clearly outdated cabinet in an odd, open space at one end of the mostly remodeled kitchen. As balm to a wound or oil to a seized motor, their labels stared at him. Though he stood ten feet away, Joe tasted both of them, wet and wonderful. He looked down. He looked away. They were still there.

Remembering why he was in his next door neighbor's kitchen, he set off to complete his task which, as it turned out, was a simple errand. When he had come back from his walk with Betsy and asked what he could do to help with the clean-up, one of the church ladies who was about to head home asked him to return the borrowed pie servers used tonight. Easy.

He set the washed and clean servers on a neatly folded tan towel beside the neighbor's sink. Done. So neatly done. And he was fine. He will be on his way. Before he moved though, before he even thought to breathe, the booze began to call.

Joe thought about how good it was to live a life like those in this neighborhood. The little, everyday experiences, like borrowing from a neighbor what you needed and then returning it, made him appreciate the life of normalcy he'd like to have. He didn't have that yet. Instead, he felt he was looking through a plate glass wall when he considered that this was where regular people do typical, run-of-the-mill, common things. But he was not typical. He was not normal. Sure, he could pretend. He could hold down two part-time jobs that paid nearly nothing and would go nowhere. He could rescue heirloom vases that may crash from time to time, joke about a huge tear in his shorts and make it socially through a backyard party the night before a wedding. Yes, he could fit in most of the time. But he wasn't even real. At least not completely.

Something hollowed inside him as the booze kept calling. He could throw a pity party for himself about the cameras and the recordings from his past—but the truth was he did not have his own self. He was actually someone else. Someone who was not here. Someone who was two-thousand-years-old. Someone who—and there could be no question of this now—was Jesus.

He stared at the kitchen around him. A calendar on the nearby wall showcased some of the things the people who lived here liked to do as a family. Joe read some of the interests that were completely unique to them. A garden club party, a humane society fun run, a sandbox date and tickets to a National League baseball game were *their* interests, not someone else's. A glossy, open travel folder with upcoming vacation plans sat on a nearby desk that fit what they authentically enjoyed. They were not copied people.

To all of this, Joe was numb. Lost. Maybe Dolly the sheep did alright through her life as a clone, but he couldn't do this. He couldn't fit in. He could not find himself because there was an inescapable truth: he was not himself. He was a copy. And the booze kept calling.

He swallowed and tried to focus. This was fine. He was fine. And he could do this. He could just turn from this kitchen sink, walk back through the sliding glass kitchen doors, head down the neighbor's paved drive, loop around their mailbox and his dad's mailbox, and meander up his dad's similarly paved drive. He'll be home in an instant. He would kiss the cheek of the church lady who sent him on this errand if she was still there, make a joke, and move on.

Of course, he could get out of here. He was practically on his way. "Just walk," he heard himself whisper. "Just leave this house."

The catering company understandably forgot to bring more serving utensils as they did not furnish the rich array of desserts tonight, and

Kristen, in whose kitchen he now stood, quickly offered her cake and pie servers before heading out this afternoon. Both she and her husband Galvin, along with their daughter Iris, would be back in time for the wedding tomorrow. Tonight they were celebrating Kristen's parents' fortieth wedding anniversary out of state. Joe realized how orchestrated his being here was. How perfect. The bottles actually said his name now. Their call was necessary after the last angry words he had shot at Betsy.

Yes, the bottles were necessary, needed. After all, he was just a shadow of sorts, a shell not just of anyone but of the Son of God—perfect, incredible, flawless Jesus. And imperfect, faulty Joe just ripped into Betsy. So this here would just be a little alcohol, a swallow or two. Half a glass at most. Just enough so that he could numb this. With the simple sliding glass kitchen door so far away, he realized there was more he had to numb than one dumb fight with his girlfriend. Despite all that white icing on the wedding cake tomorrow—and he and Earl picked up the snow mountain of fondant flowers and frills this morning—nothing could cover up what was obvious: he was a failure, a loser. It was true. Joe could not do this life any other way.

Closing his eyes, he saw the rejection letter in his mind. Two weeks old today, it sat on his desk, hidden, of course, from his dad and Betsy. The administration at the Bible College, after much serious consideration, *certainly* couldn't let him return to school after a robbery, mandatory time in a locked rehab center, and a probation. That just couldn't be done.

The words of the second paragraph still echoed. *The moral character of our well established institution cannot be breached. Our hearts and our prayers go out to you at this time, and we sincerely applaud your interest in furthering your education, however we maintain the highest decorum society expects from all our fine graduates. We wish you well...*

He laughed a laugh that would cut him if the sound itself could hold a blade.

Fine graduates wouldn't rip their shorts tonight. What good son, for that matter, would even wears shorts to his dad's wedding rehearsal in a church? And old shorts at that? *They are old because you I can't afford new ones.*

The booze kept speaking, louder and louder.

He thought about the rent due on his one-bedroom apartment over a two-car garage three streets from here. Making fifty cents over minimum wage at Dell's Landscaping wasn't getting him very far ahead, nor were the extra hours in the kitchen with a quiet guy named Ben at the ice cream shop downtown.

But they are good jobs, dad said over and over again. *It's a restart, and it's good.* He sighed. He knew his dad had a direct hand in both these small businesses hiring him, especially since he could walk to both. And Joe walked over to this kitchen, which too was serendipitous. Just like it was supposed to happen. That good, loving God of his must have mapped this all out: his love for Betsy, her becoming pregnant one single day before they met, his mishandling of all of *that* tonight, and, lest he forget, the college rejection letter he cannot share with anyone. It stood to reason then that God, the master planner, must have even made sure that Joe would see the alcohol, and have this house empty.

The alcohol. Close. Unguarded. Private. He already smelled the whiskey, even with its cap on. The latch on the cabinet was chest high. At four-and-a-half, Iris was far too short to reach it. It could not be locked.

Is it?

Opened.

He could not do this. He could not.

It was too late.

⟡

He winced with the first swallow. Acid seeped through his esophagus. He could not take a new breath. But why would he need to do that? He had no future. Betsy will see through him soon enough. She will have to at some point. She was going to be a mom, after all. She doesn't need two babies, especially a big one who by this point in his life should be able to handle more than himself. Sooner or later, she will see he is a failure. This? This will help her see that. Staring at the ceiling, Joe told himself that it would just take time, a little time, before the wonder warmed in his stomach and mixed with his blood. Then he'd be loose. Then he'd be free, totally free. This really was his only ticket. Another hit on the bottle melted his lips.

He slid down the wall behind him and, with his feet awkwardly tucked under his legs, he glanced at his muscular, vein-laced arms. He stared at his skin, its contours. No one has yet to realize that the permanent, soft, red swell on his forearm marked the unhealed sight of the ulmintin injections.

"Mr. Rolls would notice," he said as he rubbed his thumb over the red mark. "He'd see this right away." The sound of that man's name made Joe's middle collapse. He fell into himself.

This is the house where the spies lived. This is one of the rooms where the two processed information on their little neighbor, the clone. Hunched and hiding, he took another swig. Another. More burning, burning, burning. The alcohol was mad at him because it had been too long since he'd been back to where he belonged. Nevertheless, they'd be friends again. Yes, friends.

In the deep quiet, he thought of his greatest heartbreak, Mike. He realized this was the first time he has had his liquid savior since he found out about the suicide, and the whiskey, now speaking up, told him the truth: it was his fault Mike was dead. After all, it was obvious. Had Joe been there, had he come back from that lab and stayed close, Mike would not have faced so many walls alone. If Joe had returned to finish that summer semester, Mike wouldn't have been by himself. They would have roomed together again that fall and someone would have been in Mike's corner. Someone would have understood. Someone would have spoken out against homophobic policies and punishments. Someone would have loved him. Someone would have held him. Someone would have found the light in his soul and guarded it until it glowed again. And that could have been him. But it wasn't. Joe closed his eyes. The surfboard scene from his first days in college came to him.

"Did you know you were a surfer?" That upperclassman on the orientation board had asked before he hopped onto that board in the campus beach scene.

"I do now."

Then there was Mike. Big, incredible Mike stood right in front of him. That was their beginning, their perfect start.

"Encore," Mike had said. His first word to Joe.

Joe was not there long enough to do anything more than once. The pain became a hole. At the bottom, the alcohol found what Joe had been hiding. On his knees with his torso doubled over, he shouted the deep, lacerating words he'd kept from himself all this time. "I wasn't there! I wasn't there!" Spit splattered the tiles under him. His fists pounded and punched the shiny surface. "I wasn't there for you, Mike!"

He shook his head. It was not life that did this; he did this himself. He did this all himself. A stillness slipped into all this thoughts and quieted him until he heard his own words. *I am not even a real person. I am a copy. And I can't even do that well.* He cried and cried and cried. He failed himself. Worse, he failed his friend. Mike might be here tonight, here beside him, if Joe, this stupid, failing freak with a well-recorded life, had been there.

His forehead banged against the floor. "I love you, Mike!" With his hair covering his face, he yelled from the wounds of his broken soul. The sobs could not stop.

"Be here so that I can tell you that I love you!"

CHAPTER FORTY TWO

Without knowing how it happened, Earl suddenly fell toward his car, his backside against the passenger side window. One of the trash bags he'd been carrying from tonight's party was in his bad hand and sunk to the garage floor. It was the lingering affects from the stroke. He knew he had overdone it these past few days. The lawn didn't have to be perfect, the bushes could have been trimmed back in the fall at the time of the year when he always did it, and he didn't need to put in all the stakes around the dessert table tent by himself. He held his chest. He felt winded, tired. His heart wasn't beating the way it should. This happened two weeks ago. He was in the grocery store, aisle seven, baking supplies and canned goods. How he knocked over more than a dozen cans of peaches was a mystery, but they toppled and rolled. One can made a beeline for a teenager who only had peanut butter in his big cart.

"Sir," the boy had asked, "are you okay?"

Earl was familiar with the boy's scar on his neck. He had seen it somewhere before.

"Sir, are you alright?"

Earl couldn't speak. This had never happened before. A part of him felt completely fine. Another part was completely immobile. As quickly as it came on, it was gone.

"Here I am rolling peaches at you."

The boy was shy. "Let's just get these peaches back where they belong."

They met again two aisles later. The boy was so fast with getting all the cans tidied up that Earl really didn't get a chance to properly thank him. Earl wanted to change that now. "You need to eat more than peanut butter, young man."

Ben looked into his own cart.

"I have some dented cans of fruit to go with your meal there. Tell you what, I'll buy them for you as a way of saying thanks, bud."

"Did some dent? I didn't notice."

"No, I just put some peaches in my cart because I felt guilty about my one man crash."

Ben smiled, but it was guarded.

"You're from the Dairy Barn. That is how I know you."

Ben nodded.

"I do want to give you these cans. I can meet you at your car in the parking lot. It is my way of saying thanks, unless there's something else here you would like."

Earl knew the kid agreed to the peaches just to keep this moving along. Ten minutes later, Earl looked over the car Ben drove to the grocery store. He could take care of that rust, and easily bump out the dings in the driver's side door.

When the peach cans were placed in the back seat, Earl said what was true. "You look like you could use a friend."

"I'm okay."

"Well then, maybe I could use a friend." He stepped into the quiet between them. "I had a stroke a while back." He would say anything to build a bridge with a lost young person, including what was about to catch in his throat. "I could use a hand sometimes."

Ben was stuck. He wanted to run again but didn't know how. He folded his fingers around the car keys which were in the front pocket of his jeans.

"You are the age of my grandsons. And you're almost as handsome as they are." Earl laughed. "That was supposed to be funny."

Ben nodded.

"How about we just say hi again sometime? Maybe eat some peaches."

It was clear the boy wanted to go. When he did drive off, Earl was hit with a sad feeling. It took a few minutes to pull this together, but he realized Ben somehow reminded him of Mike. The two didn't look, act or sound the same, but maybe Ben was gay. How would Earl know? He knew no gay people, or, more specifically, he knew no one who identified themselves with this sexual identity. He had learned that there were TV and movie stars who were out, but Earl wasn't a fan of watching the world on a screen; he wanted to live the world out loud and in living color. When Jackie and Jenna were in elementary school, there would be a boy or two in their tap or Irish Dancing classes. Not that that meant anything, but the thought of any young boy or girl being lost, neglected, ignored, or misunderstood pulled at him.

Realizing he had to keep moving along here after tonight's party, he stooped to pick up the trash bag that had fallen to the floor by his car. The garage doors were open. He stared out into the night. Ben was out there, somewhere.

As if on cue, the ladies in the kitchen burst into laughter again. Either that one thick wall had somehow became thinner tonight, or they were just that loud. He smiled as he picked up the last of the trash. They were that loud.

Suddenly, Earl thought of Joe. He had been standing in Dunk's kitchen to say goodnight to the groom when he overheard one of the church ladies asking Joe if he would please return those stupid, completely unnecessary dessert servers to Kristen and Galvin's house. That was fine, of course, until Earl remembered his neighbors had a liquor cabinet. It was stocked. The alcohol. He couldn't find Ben tonight, but knew where Joe was. He had to hurry and beat the devil who, in that perfect timing, chose tonight to strike.

"Dang these old bones," he muttered as he crossed Dunk's front lawn. "Move!"

He was too late, of course. The mess had already spilled.

CHAPTER FORTY THREE

This water pressure was something he wished he had in his own bathroom. Should he replace his old tub and shower with one like Galvin and Kristen have here?

"Stop! Stop!"

Earl continued his thinking as if he hadn't heard anything. *No wonder Jackie and Jenna don't shower that often when they visit.*

"Earl, stop!"

"Not for another minute yet."

"Let me go, you crazy old man. Get me out of here!"

Earl smiled to himself. While he may have knocked off a few fruit cans in the grocery store a few days ago, his good arm had a great grip on Joe. Hanging on tightly to Joe's shoulder and shirt collar, Earl still couldn't believe he was thinking of how to improve his own plumbing.

"It's ice cold! Stop!"

Satisfied that his own fingers felt numb, Earl let go, thanking God for all that blasted physical therapy he had been through since the stroke. Joe slipped and stumbled against the far wall of this great looking, mini spa-like center, and then hurried out of the way of the spray that still splattered.

Shivering and soaked, Joe growled, but there was light in his voice. "I think I hate you."

"You hate yourself. But those are the devil's lies. We're going to work on that together, you and me, a little bit later on." Turning off the water before tossing Joe a towel, he reached for the bathrobe he had found in Kristen's closet. It was white, heavy, and not too effeminate. Since he didn't think Galvin had a robe, this would work.

"Strip and wear this." Earl moved toward the bathroom door. "Also, get this water up off the floor and meet me in the kitchen. A little coffee is next, and then water, lots of glasses of water."

Folding his arms over his chest as he pressed his freezing fingers under his underarms, Joe shook. His teeth chattered, and, by the grace of God, he did a good and necessary thing. He lifted the lid to the toilet and threw up.

"Less in the system," Earl muttered to himself as he readied himself to handle one of those newfangled coffee machines in a kitchen not as familiar to him as his own. "That's a blessing."

Earl left the bathroom and immediately returned. "Oh, and the judges just shared their final tally. The wet tee shirt competition? Yeah, you lost that."

The distant sound could be an air conditioner, but it was not especially cool in here. Taking another step, Betsy called out again. No response. She knew Earl was here somewhere with him. He wore one of those aftershave lotions old men wear on big nights like this, just like her grandfather did. The scent was just inside the sliding glass door.

Betsy turned and stopped. There it was on the counter. Her eyes watered. Her mouth quaked. *Oh no.* She stared at the sight as if it was an unwelcomed guest, and then realized exactly what the open bottle was—the enemy. Keeping her front to it as if it was a dead rat she'd never want to touch, she didn't know what to do with it until she realized she was angry at it and, dead rat or not, she marched up to it, grabbed its neck and poured the remainder of the evil down the sink. As she stood at the sink, she understood the strange sound she heard when she walked in was coming from a shower in another part of a house.

Joe, what have I done to you? She set her hand to her forehead and wanted to cry out but little sound escaped. The knot in her chest tightened while her knees wobbled. There was no time for this.

Think. Rinse the bottle. Yes. There was a strong scent of the alcohol right here, and it had to be gone by the time he came out of the shower. The water that had been running in another part of the house stopped while she was rinsing the sink. The house was now completely silent. From someplace behind her, Earl's sudden footfalls startled her. She gasped.

He, too, was surprised to see her. Slowly, he brought his hand to his chin as a flicker of light played within his eyes. "Say, isn't that my shirt?"

She wrapped its very long sleeves around her wrists. "I've been wearing it for a while now."

"I know," he offered.

She was scared to ask this question, so she just locked down more pain and worry in her heart.

Earl's voice was clear. "He will be fine."

"I know this is my fault. We, we had this big fight. It was over the baby. Well, not over the baby, but over us."

Earl moved toward her and she fell into his arms.

"I've made a mess of things."

Rocking her back and forth, he tried to reassure her. "No, alcohol itself made a mess of things. Joe can't blame himself." He met her in the eye. Not until he saw them in this light did he realize they were the exact same blue color Janet's were. "And you can't blame yourself either. It just happened. No fault. No finger pointing. This is just a lifelong mess, and we are all going to have to live with it."

"But—"

"No. Just no. He's going to need us in a few minutes. And we have to be honest with him and for him. If you are going to walk this with him, Betsy, then you have to be strong."

She was not sure she could do that.

Earl thought of his time in prison, and then that first year free again. He loved Joe. Oh, how he loved that boy. He loved Betsy, too, and needed to be clear because these next few minutes really mattered.

"I suggest you listen closely to your heart right now, little lady. If you stay here in this kitchen, you're in. If you can't handle times like this, I'll help you to the door."

For the first time in a long time—maybe ever—she understood what she had to do in a relationship with a person she loved.

"It's yes or no, Betsy."

She met the man she admired squarely in the eye. Her voice, like her backbone, did not wobble. "I'm going to be strong. I'm going to be strong."

"Atta girl."

⊶————————⊷

Ironically, Joe bought towels as a wedding gift for his dad and Vanessa to celebrate the bathroom the couple had resurfaced and repainted. The towels complimented the mini make-over Dunk and Joe did to make Vanessa feel welcome in a house once lived in by father and son, and soon to be enjoyed by husband and wife. As he was on his hands and knees mopping up excess water with a towel nicer than the ones he wrapped earlier today, he doubted the gift he bought the newlyweds would be good enough. He should have spent more, but couldn't. His head sunk. His heart stung. Earlier he had told Betsy not to make a scene by bringing up her past, and what was absolutely clear here was that he had made a complete mess of *everything*. Tonight, of all nights, he lost it to drinking right here in the neighborhood. There would be no keeping this quiet. All he wanted was one perfect day for his dad, and he couldn't even do that.

Rising to his feet with the alcohol still moving within him, an idea sparked. The best present he could give the couple would be to run away again. Yes. The two dated without him around. They should have a life free and clear of the messes and mistakes he has made, and will make. He couldn't stay here. He couldn't be 'normal.' As testimony to that, he should take this opportunity to find some long ago hidden recording device aimed at his dad's house. Rolls was no fool. With a flip of a switch, a camera's eye could return to life and ruin the life he himself was wrecking. Had it not been for the drinking, he could have continued working for the swimming pool company. Without a degree, he was destined to work at blue collar jobs for the rest of his life, so why not give Mr. and Mrs. Dunkin O'Dell a brand new start? Yes, he would leave. He'd be gone by the time they returned from their honeymoon. It was the perfect plan.

Stepping back, wondering where to leave a very wet towel, he stepped on something sharp under the plush area rug in front of the bathroom sink. Raising a corner of the soft rug, he saw that it was one of Irises' little toys. He knew Betsy was carrying a girl. A mechanical engineer liked very few surprises in her world, so she found out her baby's gender as soon as she could. Swallowing hard, he realized there was no life he could really give mother or daughter. As an engineer, she would help design buildings he would lay block for at an hourly wage. What mutual friends could they possibly have? And alcoholism, robbery, and a year's probation aside, he stared at the red scar on his forearm. He was too weird, too different.

Yes, he had a plan. Before the honeymooners returned, he'd be gone.

CHAPTER FORTY FOUR

"I do. I really do."

Vanessa's smile beamed so brightly when she heard her husband say these long-awaited words. They kissed without the signal from Pastor Smith after Dunk raised her short, white veil. With gusto, the congregation immediately came to their feet. Applause followed. The couple was pronounced husband and wife, but no one heard the pastor because the cheers, hoots, and hollering had escalated. Since Mr. and Mrs. Dunkin O'Dell were both so vitally active in this church family, the pews on this picture perfect afternoon were overflowing with four-hundred and fifty guests. Joy rang in the air with the steeple's clanging bells that Pastor Smith had his nine-year-old son set off in a clamor only a boy could create.

Rather than wait until the couple left the sanctuary, Jolie surprised Dunk and Vanessa by seeing to it that each guest had a small can of spray confetti that they could actually launch at the newlyweds as they marched back up the aisle. The effect was amazing. High, middle and low, streamers of white and silver papers fluttered or floated. Between this moment and tomorrow morning at nine when the first service started, Jolie had about five hours of vacuuming to do, but this sight—her best friend getting *married*—was the best in the world. She'd vacuum for a week for this great guy.

Realizing the organ music had already begun, she met her groomsman at the base of the chancel steps. Following the couple in front of them, she basked in her walk up the aisle. A day this happy has been such a long time coming. Like the bride herself, Jolie radiated. She completely effervesced in happiness, and didn't need stupid sparkles in her dress to do it.

———————

Vanessa's gown not only flattered the beautiful woman, but also it showed where she was at this place in her life. Nothing in the flowing cascades was too much, or too little. With beadwork here and flares there, it was perfect not because of the dress, but because she was in love. Dunk, her striking complement, never wore a tuxedo so well. In the pictures of the wedding ceremony and the reception both in the church hall and the immediate west garden of the property—where else could four hundred and fifty people sit?—the photographer captured every detail, including Jolie's cucumber colored fingernails.

The color of each dress in the bridal party varied from emerald to a soft celery shade. Each dress design was also uniquely different to the woman wearing it. In a dark dress that hid her baby bump better than she thought it would, Betsy stood at a great distance while the wedding party photos were taken. With Earl as their counselor last night, the conversation with Joe went alright, but there was still more she'd like to share. Perhaps when the reception winds down, she would have that chance. If not tonight, then she hoped it would be soon.

She heard someone behind her and turned. It was a wedding guest she saw sitting on the groom's side of the church during the wedding.

"I'm Kristen," a pretty, dark-haired woman said as she held out her hand. "With my husband and daughter Iris, I live next door to Dunk, and now Vanessa."

After introducing herself, Betsy shared a bit of confusion. "I thought Earl was their neighbor."

"Oh, he is. Galvin and I are on the other side of the newlyweds. We couldn't make the party last night because my parents were celebrating their fortieth anniversary out of state."

Betsy saw this polite person who was about ten years her senior as someone so genuine, kind and friendly. Given the right circumstances, they might be friends. "You have a nice neighborhood."

Kristen took in the whole bridal party as the photographer positioned Vanessa with just the groomsmen. "Oh, thank you. We feel lucky. It's the people who make up the best part of the neighborhood, for sure."

Betsy thought of those nearest her in her condo. She sometimes heard but never saw them.

Kristen continued. "I heard your wedding was as lovely as this one."

Betsy felt pressure against her face. She used it to keep her expression still. "My wedding? Oh, I'm not married."

Kristen carried a look of complete professionalism. It was just a part of her nature. When she did make a mistake, she was quick to correct it. Touching Betsy's forearm, she made sure they met eye to eye. "You'll have to excuse me for that, please. I must have misheard something earlier."

"It's quite alright." From the groomsmen who were in a pack as they waited to be positioned for a new photo, she heard Joe burst into a sudden laugh. This would not be a big deal; Joe laughed often. Something happened however, something small that immediately became big for Betsy. Maybe it was her hormones. Perhaps the pregnancy itself was doing something weird for the first time. But there, in his tux at the front of the church, Joe seemed so far away. Betsy swallowed. He was so far away.

Sensing her screw up about being married went deeper than Betsy admitted a second ago, Kristen's held genuine remorse. "Well, again, I am sorry."

"What? No! It's really no big deal." She stared at Joe. She lied to herself. *It is no big deal.*

Kristen guessed correctly. "You and one of Dunk's groomsmen?"

"Excuse me?"

"You and Joe, are you two together?"

Betsy didn't know how to respond. She simply shrugged.

The sparkling cider in his glass trembled. When standing in front of all these people, he didn't think he'd be so nervous! The microphone sat in a stand just to the left of the bride and groom's table. From his tux pocket, Joe reached for the short speech he had written out weeks ago.

"May I have your attention, please? My name is Joe. Many of you know that. Some of you who are here to celebrate this husband and wife's commitment may not know that I'm not Dunkin O'Dell's biological son." Joe looked out into the overwhelming crowd. Some were surprised at what he had just said.

"Now an adoptive mother can be overheard saying that her baby was born in her heart, not in her womb, but what does a single, adoptive father like my dad get to say?" Looking left and right, Joe paused. Tears already began to run down Vanessa's face.

"I will tell you, my dad had the chance to say a lot of things. A lot of wonderful things. He said things like, 'I love you, Joe,' when I'd screw up or when I'd break something like the windows on the side of our house." Joe closed his eyes tightly. "Wait, I'm *not sure* dad said he loved me *that* day."

Polite laughter spilled over those nearby.

With his eyes open again, Joe focused on something that was not quite before him. "For the longest, longest time, I used to call Dunk O'Dell 'dod' because his initials are, as you know, 'D – O – D.' That was the name I had called him once as a boy, and the name kinda stuck. So, while other kids my age had a dad, I had a DOD." Thinking of how Earl would often joke about his dad when the two would enjoy a beer together after a day in their yards, he added, "That's not to be confused with a dud."

A few people laughed. One groomsman cheered. Joe paused before he continued. "My dad was, and is, awesome. Always present. Always caring. Always loving. He wanted only the best for me, and that included anyone he would bring into our household. He didn't date very much, or very actively, because he only wanted *just* the right woman not only for himself, but also for me."

Dunk held his wife's hand.

"Today, you know, he married that woman. God has blessed them, and will bless them in their years ahead."

Joe's eyes met the bride's. "I know this blessing from God is real and true because my dad, Vanessa, is capable of unconditional love." Joe closed and suddenly opened his eyes. "My life has not been perfect. There have been years I've caused my dad loneliness and pain, and as he never gave up on me, I see, in his eyes, that he will not give up on you, your marriage, or any hurdle that comes your way. You light and lift his soul, and we are all better—each of us—with you in our lives." He turned to the guests who filled every inch of space around him. "So, ladies and gentlemen, raise your glasses. Join me in what both Vanessa and my dad know is the most powerful gift we have with God, and that is prayer."

Joe felt a bit like Pastor Smith and the sensation did not feel odd to him. "Oh Creator of the stars and of all the lights above, continue to guide and teach this man and this woman in Your Word, Your way, and in their lives together. Be their rock, their shield, and their great comforter now and always. Amen."

Joe took one step away from the microphone. "To Vanessa and Dunk O'Dell, cheers."

Vanessa spun Betsy by the arm and swung the pregnant woman through the double-doors. The kitchen and volunteer wait staff stopped in their tracks as a woman in a flowing white gown dashed down the food prep area, past refrigerators and the cake carving station with a pregnant blonde in a dark dress in tow. She parted a new Red Sea. "You're all fine everyone. The food is *great*. Love you."

One exit door led absolutely nowhere and it was here, in private, that Vanessa faced Betsy. The bride's expression was firm yet caring. "Well, have you talked with him?"

A part of Betsy was still back in the kitchen they had just raced through. "Talked to him? Your husband?"

"Yes, isn't he handsome?" Even though her shoes were comfortable on her feet, and the issue of *Bridal* magazine she read months ago said to give her footwear several practice runs, she stepped out her soft white heels for a minute. She took two steps so she could stand in the cool, thick shaded grass. "No, you wonderful thing. Have you gotten very far with Joe?"

She couldn't believe Vanessa would take the time, least of all now, to talk with her. "You stole me out here to talk about this? It's your wedding day. Shouldn't you be..." Betsy motioned behind her.

Vanessa's eyes did not move from Betsy's. "Since you didn't answer my question, I'm going to go with the hunch that you haven't talked with him. I base this in large part because you are trying to carry off a polished expression."

The door opened an inch and then closed. Vanessa nodded. "We have ninety-seconds before someone in the kitchen broadcasts my location. We have to make the most of this. Yes, you did talk with him. You must have, right?"

Betsy hesitated.

"But nothing really happened. Is that it?"

"Well—"

Vanessa lifted her gown allowing air to circulate over her feet. "I know about the liquor cabinet. This is my wedding day, but I refuse to be isolated, or insulated. The immediate good news, and yes, there is good news, is that he didn't go that far for that long."

The door popped open. "Vanessa, you are wanted in the—"

"I know." She smiled warmly. "I'll be right there."

The door closed.

"Did I say ninety seconds? I meant thirty-five."

The door opened again. This time Vanessa caught it, held up her index finger indicating just another second to someone Betsy could not see, and turned back. "Please listen. Life is not complicated, it's perfect." Stretching a bit like a contortionist because her hand remained on the door, her silky, narrow feet stepped into her shoes. "I'm not Cinderella, it's not even close to midnight, and I know, despite this fairy tale dress and some very handsome prince with a new ring on his finger, that I'm not riding out of here in a horse-drawn carriage. I'm going to see a bunch of scared little mice and a lopsided pumpkin just ahead of me." She walked through the door, turned and stopped. "But it is perfect, Betsy. It is perfect when you wipe off that perfectly fake smile you've been wearing since I've seen you today, and make it real. Be open and honest and true with Joe."

"But I don't like mice."

"I never said I did either." She held one of Betsy's hands and changed directions just a bit. "You are sure about all of this, sweetie. I've known it since the two of us met."

Betsy held a question in her eyes. "I am?"

"Let me take you back in time a bit. We were on Dunk's back deck, remember? You and I were messing around with those flower pots, the big ones that are gray ceramic battleships. Joe had shared with us that you just found out you were going to have a baby. When he went inside for something—maybe it was the plant food—you were still beside me, but your heart followed him right back into the house."

Betsy looked away.

"You remember that?"

"Yes."

The woman of the hour left the door open and started making her way back through the kitchen. "It is that perfect."

"Just no to mice, okay?"

Over the clatter in the kitchen, Vanessa didn't hear her. Alone now, she thought about the whiskey bottle and what she had said to Earl last night. "But the rats I can handle."

———————————

"I owe you a bottle of whiskey," Joe said to Galvin as the two stepped away from the refreshment table with tall glasses of water with lemon. "And I'll get your wife Kristen's bathrobe laundered and back to you tonight."

Galvin, who was so much better one-on-one than at huge events like this, shook his head no. Even though he had seen Joe a lot lately around his dad's and Earl's properties with all the pre-wedding landscaping work the two pulled off, Galvin still remained a bit shy, a condition he's had since he was Iris's age. Kristen should be the one to talk with Joe. In fact, as the lawn care specialist around their home, she already had a rapport with the young twenty-something. More than once she has tapped into their local pro gardener for all the insights Joe could share. When a rose bush seemed destined to die, for example, Kristen cornered Joe. For twenty minutes, she engaged him in conversation about her wet soil and drainage. Left alone, Galvin would kill Astroturf.

"Yes," Joe said again into the quiet, "I'll get that robe right back to you."

"Joe, really, no worries."

While Galvin cared about Joe and wanted to share that any place but in a crowd, it was Kristen who stepped in to alleviate the awkwardness her husband felt. "Galvin's right, Joseph. I'll get that old robe whenever, and the bottle was a re-gift from my brother. We've had it since the days before Iris."

"But I owe you."

"And we owe you," Kristen said quickly, not allowing Joe to go further. She wasn't sweeping Joe's alcoholism under the rug. She wasn't going to let it bring him down, either. "Your speech there about your dad? Your toast, I mean. Well, yeah…I was right the first time. It felt like a speech, a good speech, because it taught the two of us a thing or two."

Joe was embarrassed. "I, I don't know what you mean."

"I'll be honest with you," Kristen lowered her already low voice as if she was about to say something no one should miss. "No one has a charmed life. Galvin and I struggle sometimes. We do. But no way are we taking any payment for a bottle we don't even appreciate because what we do appreciate is hearing your words." She made sure she caught Joe's eye. "Now we all have problems, and hurdles. Every one of us. What you said there in your toast made a difference. We are the ones who owe you."

When Kristen saw Betsy approaching, she nodded and started to step away with her husband because she sensed Betsy and Joe needed time alone. "Now, before I go, you need to hang out with us. Soon. Iris misses you." When Betsy was close enough, Kristen announced, "And you, too, Betsy. Come over. We have lots of coloring book pages to work on."

As Kristen and Galvin waved goodbye, Joe turned to Betsy. Knowing Iris really did love to color, in fact, she recently invited him to a one-on-one coloring book party, Joe frowned. "I have trouble staying within the lines."

"No, I'd say you know exactly what you're doing." Betsy would not be uncomfortable here. She would not mess this up. "I think you have a pretty good idea of the way things should look."

"You're not talking about coloring book pages, are you?"

CHAPTER FORTY FIVE

The baby grew over night. The dress she wore to the wedding last week would not fit today. As she made her way through the aisles at the bus station, people noticed her now obvious swell and gave her an open path. She smiled on the inside, not because she came across like some Arctic icebreaker, even though she believed she weighed as much as one; she smiled because the not so little bun in the oven could very well be carrying a sign that read, "Give us space!" She had never considered the advantage that being this pregnant was a great way to clear a pathway. In fact, when two men her age cleared away the luggage at their feet—and the two were not close to her—she realized this wide load had its perks.

"Do you need a seat, young lady?" It was a senior gentleman, dressed so thoughtfully, who asked.

Gosh, I'm just over five months along. How pregnant do I look?

"No, no, thank you, I'm fine."

"You're looking for someone then?"

For the third time in less than a minute, she nervously glanced about the large room. "Well, yes."

"And you love him?"

Surprised, Betsy's jaw dropped. *How many signs am I carrying today? Does everyone here know what I ate for lunch?*

The dignified gentleman of African descent repositioned his cane from one hand to the other. "You just have that love look, that's all." He glanced toward the ladies room as a woman his age with rich, warm skin walked out slowly from it.

Seeing care and warmth in his soft hazel eyes, Betsy knew what the traveler seated meant by 'love look.' She studied the senior lady and then met his eye again. She asked, "How long have you two been married?"

"Who? Us?" He teetered left and right just a bit and, just as any other experienced storyteller would do, barely licked his lips. "Child, I've just met this hot number today. I think she likes my style. I'm going to get the courage and ask her for a dance. Think I should?"

The woman inched up beside Betsy. "Oh, don't let this most handsome man spoof you, my darling. Meeting me today? Hardly! We'll be married sixty-three years next month." She sat beside her husband, met Betsy's eyes with her own, and said what to her was obvious. "Oh, you're in love."

Unlike Mike who could talk with a passerby as if they were long lost friends, Betsy rarely talked with strangers, especially like this. She struggled because, in being new at this, her words felt funny in her mouth. "That's what your husband sort of said."

"Don't listen to him. He's a flirt. He mentioned dancing, didn't he? There's no music going on in a bus station now, is there?"

"You have a point."

"But *I* know. You're in love."

Wondering how she was going to do what she had to do here in this strange place, if, in fact, she hadn't already missed the one she was trying to find, her eyes suddenly teared up. "How? How do you know?"

"Because I'm in love myself. And when you're there, child, you just know. There's nothing more to it. You just know." The woman repositioned her purse on her lap. She leaned a little toward her husband, looked around Betsy and said, "And there he is. He's behind you."

Betsy turned. The woman was right. Joe, who was wearing sunglasses and a stiff expression, made his way through the door. He was carrying a stuffed duffel bag that could easily hold two full-sized vacuum cleaners.

Betsy breathed. *Thank you, God.* She turned back to the woman. "How did you—?"

The senior just smiled, and then bowed her head. Solemnly, her husband joined her when she prayed, "Dear Heavenly Father, bless this couple as you have blessed us old souls. They have something in front of them. This I know in my heart. Allow Your love, oh God, to see them through today. May they hear You through each other."

After a pause, the gentleman said, "Amen."

Before turning to Joe who had not yet seen her in this crowd, Betsy asked again, "How did you—?"

The gentleman tapped his wife's leg, just above knee. "Not all angels have wings, little girl. Not all angels have wings."

———————————————

With the duffel bag at his feet, he set his sunglasses on his head the moment before he saw her. There must have been twenty people between them but neither Betsy nor Joe moved any closer. From that distance, the two shared a great deal with their eyes only. Silently, they told each other their stories of guilt and shame, worry and relief, and loss and gain.

It was Betsy who took a step first. Unlike all the other awkward conversations she has had with men she had dated, this time she would not mess up at all. No, she was clear. She remembered Earl's words in Kristen and Galvin's kitchen. She also remembered what Vanessa had said about mice. She did not wait one second more. She would do this. When they were a few feet apart, she jumped in. "I was wrong. This baby is yours. She's ours. I just got messed up. Scared. The night before the wedding, on that walk after the rehearsal dinner. I was scared."

"Betsy."

"I'm not finished. I know you want to run. I know you think you've messed up everything, or will mess up everything. But it's just a bottle, Joe. *It's just a bottle.* Alcohol has a power, or a pull, and I know I can never break that for you, but I can tell you that I will always stand beside you."

Moving inches toward her, Joe shook his head.

She continued. "Since the wedding, I've been asking a lot of questions, Joe." Her eyes watered as she stood inches away from him. "I know about the lab and the ulmintin injections. It was Earl who finally broke down and told me about who you are, and actually, how you are. He did it because, like me, he loves you."

"Betsy."

She could not hear him, at least not now. She could not stop until she had said it all. "But I knew long before. I knew something, something I couldn't name. The day at the park when Mike told us who he was, I knew who you were, too. I *knew it, Joe.* The resemblance between you and Jesus was there then—and that was before you ever met that scientist guy, Roland Rolls." She touched his hand. "And I know what you were thinking the night before the wedding. I know what you had on your mind when you were on the floor with that bottle. You were thinking about Michael. You love my childhood bud, and I know you miss him. And I know you wish you had been there for him. I know this because…" Her fingers shook. "I wish I had been there for him, too. She swallowed. Emotion would not run over her. "But the telltale sign— the one I could finally see so clearly, much like the two on the road to Emmaus—was you coming out into Kristen and Galvin's kitchen with that white robe on. Yes, with my eyes open, I could finally see that you *are* him, and that is not the curse you have believed it to be."

"But I am not him."

Betsy thought of the angels without wings she had just met. "He came as both fully human and fully divine."

"I am not—"

"Divine?" She reached for and caressed his face. Closing her eyes, she felt so thankful that he wasn't gone, that she was here in time, and that she could share what she needed to share. She did love Joe O'Dell. She did. Completely.

Joe set his hand around her forearm. She didn't stop caressing the side of his face as she spoke. "I believe Christ, or some part of Christ, is within us all. He is, Joe, he is within us; and we can choose to let him into our lives. So, alcoholic, ice cream server, gardner, and one potential undergraduate rejected from the Bible College—I saw your hidden letter—I see who you are. You are a man who gets angry, protective, possessive and worried. You are a soul who cleared out your one bedroom apartment early this morning and wants to run because he doesn't have all the answers, but you are you divine. You are divine to me. You have been. In all the years we were apart, I never let you go. And you—the thoughts I had of you—brought me to Christ."

Joe looked down. "Bets, I'm not divine."

"Yes. Yes, you are. You are divine like the rest of us, maybe a little more so. Can you make the blind see? In a way. Will you feed five thousand? You gave a lot to four-hundred and fifty with your toast, so....maybe." Just as Joe started to shake his head in disagreement, she stopped his chin from moving, and lifted it. "You are also human. Broken. Imperfect. Sinful. You are that, too."

Joe suddenly felt the prayers from two people nearby he had never met before. He tried to make sense of what he was receiving, but only wanted to give in to one new thought. "You do love me, don't you?"

She nodded.

"And you're not going to let me run."

She took a breath. "Well, you do like those running shoes. I happen to like mine, too." She looked straight down at the growing mound blocking the view of her feet. "That is, when I can see them."

He raised his duffel bag and in so doing brought everything back to where it had been before. "Can I kiss you?"

"Yeah, I think that would be good."

CHAPTER FORTY SIX

The newlyweds would be home late tonight. He had to get the note back. In a crisp white envelope, it rested right beside the little houseplant and twin candles Vanessa had set out as a centerpiece on their kitchen table. Joe smiled. *Centerpiece. This house is really going to change.* Fumbling with the key in the side door which hadn't worked well in a month or so, he turned to the two who were coming back from a sidewalk leaf collecting excursion.

"Oh, hi Kristen. Hi Iris."

Iris whispered something to her mommy. Kristen looked at Joe and then nodded to her daughter. As only a little one can, Iris rocketed toward the man she adored. "Joe, Joe! I want to show you all my leaves! We've been collecting them and everything!"

The man receiving all this affection bent down and scooped up the little tike the way he had done since the day they met. They spun a full circle. Iris smelled like summertime when he set her down.

"I love you, Joe."

Before he answered, he saw his note again through the glass door, the one that said he was leaving and, with love, wished them a bright future, one they could only truly have without him.

Iris touched his nose. Her eyes studied all of his soul in one simple glance, and with the tone of someone many times her age she said what she was thinking. "And you're never going to leave me."

Joe swallowed. "Oh, Iris."

She presented her fist. "Now, eat me up."

This was a game the two often played. Joe pretended to eat all of Iris, starting with her hands. Noisily, he started gobbling.

"Joe," Kristen called as she worried they were overstaying their welcome, "we didn't mean to interrupt you."

"It's okay."

"Iris, we should let Joe get going."

"He's coming with us. I'm going to show him all my leaves!"

Pulling their small red wagon containing about a dozen green leaves behind her, Kristen started up Dunk and Vanessa's drive. "We're working on this, Joe. Iris, honey, we have to *ask* if people want to do things with us. We have to invite them. We don't know if they can join us unless we ask."

"Oh."

"Well, Iris, sweetie. Ask."

"Joe, I want you to see all my leaves. Come to my house."

Kristen said, "Would you come to my house?"

Iris echoed. "Would you come to my house, please?"

Joe swallowed again—hard and dry. His face flushed. He would have missed this, all of this simple, true goodness, had he been on a bus somewhere heading far from here. "Why, I'd love to. Iris, I'd love to see your leaves." He squeezed the house keys that had been in his front pocket. "I just need to check something in my dad's house—my dad's and Vanessa's house—and I'll be right over, okay?"

Kristen deftly turned the wagon around. "That will give us some time to set up all of your leaves, Iris."

"We have *a lot*."

"We display them on a board, Joe. This is all highly organized and scientific. Come on, Iris. Let's get started. Joe has something he needs to do."

Iris spun and pointed her little index finger at him. In a low, soft voice only he could hear, she made her point clear. "And you 'member. You are *not* leaving me, Joey Joe."

Joe's face warmed even more. *Joey Joe. This little girl. Her insistence. Her love.*

"I am not leaving you."

———————

Kristen opened her front door ten minutes later. "You're okay with this?"

"Yes," Joe smiled. "Sure."

The board was as tall as Iris and was one and a half times as long. It took up a whole corner in the kitchen. Filled with ceramic plates Iris had painted at the Painting Palace, the alcohol in the cabinet was gone. Joe tried to ignore the memory. "Iris, wow! This board is huge!"

She giggled. "I know."

"Galvin can get these matting boards from work. They're one-sided, but if you ever need something like this for anything, they're great. Galvin would be glad to hook you up." Kristen bent down, showing a hint of her pale, toned lower back. "We used these pushpins, right, Iris? They are holding all of our leaves."

"I see this, Iris."

"Honey, tell him how we have the leaves arranged."

Suddenly shy, a trait *rarely* exhibited by this little one, Iris took a moment to answer. In the quiet, Joe stared at the floor under his feet. Heartbroken and sobbing over the loss of Mike, he was inches from this tile a week ago.

Setting some of her straight, silky, shiny black hair behind her ears, Kristen said, "You know what the word 'arranged' means. We talked about it."

The nursery school student was playing for attention. "Oh, yeah."

As Iris started pointing to how the leaves were categorized by color and size, Joe sat beside her so that they were face-to-face. He half listened as his friend went on and on about dark and lighter colors, shapes and sizes, because the fingers of one of his hands stroked the tile.

"And this one is really green. And this one is really, really green."

When Iris absently leaned back into Joe, he realized Mike was here, somehow. Joe couldn't explain it, but he could see one single leaf flutter and skip across a parking lot. Maybe it was at the Bible College. He wasn't sure. Deep inside, against Joe's bones, and with the tickle of Iris's hair against Joe's face, Mike sent his friend one clear message: "It's okay. It's really going to be okay."

With Iris reluctantly down for the start of her nap, Kristen and Joe took a short walk along the back of her house. On this pristine afternoon, the two had been walking along the border of her flowerbed, and Joe, with his own meandering pace, made his way to asking Kristen how Galvin had proposed to her. She didn't answer. Instead, she gasped with a question of her own. "You're going to ask Betsy, aren't you?"

Joe stayed serious. "Just answer my question."

"Answer the question," Kristen repeated. "Okay. How Galvin asked me to marry him. Well, Mr. Romantic was very factual when he asked me. That's just the way he is. We went to one of our favorite restaurants. I kind of knew it was coming, which honestly made it nice." She smiled. "My husband and I are a lot alike. We're low on the surprise scale."

"Really?" The two rounded a corner to her side yard.

"Yeah. We had shopped for rings a little bit. I don't care much about a rock." She frowned with her pencil-line eyebrows all furrowed. "I know, not very materialistic of me. I should have held out, negotiated for a bigger stone." She fanned the fingers of her left hand. "Not to get off the subject, but I swelled so much from carrying that little chatter box in there that, during the last two months of my pregnancy, I couldn't wear any ring."

Joe wondered if Betsy will get that way. In so many ways, despite what Betsy said, she was not very large at all. And the two women, Kristen and Betsy, were very alike in size and in mannerisms, which always made Joe comfortable around the woman who lived next to his dad. As they came to the front of the house, they sat on the front steps.

The space between them felt good and right. Joe wanted to get back to how Galvin popped the question. "So, what? He just asked you?"

"He did. He went down on one knee when, on cue, the waiter brought a single red rose. It was simple, sweet, and yes, romantic."

"Oh."

"What matters is not the cost of the ring, or even how it's presented. Now a thousand women within a ten mile radius will argue that, but it's the words you say from the intentionality of your heart, that's the beauty. That's the part that matters forever."

Realizing in Iris's company today that he will ask Betsy for her hand, Joe suddenly wondered and worried. Days ago he was in a bus station, packed and ready to leave. He knew he had exit skills, but could he stay in place? Of course it was not a question of his love for Betsy. What he felt for her was obvious, clear, and wonderful. He knew what was true. He had thought of—and even dreamed of—her since the day they were introduced at the state park by a guy who knew what he was doing. He took a deep breath. *The big guy would have us married by now.* Time with Iris didn't tell him anything he didn't already know; he loved kids. It was the thought of Joe O'Dell being a husband that chilled him.

Kristen read him. "Oh, you can do this!"

Joe took in all of the woman seated beside him. "Who are you?"

"Just someone who knows."

Staring at the tree limbs above them, Joe remembered his dad telling him about his new neighbors. It was at the time father and son were heading home after Joe had left the halfway house all those months ago. There, in the car, Dunk had shared that there was a funny story about how Iris was named.

"You know, Kristen, I never heard how Iris became Iris."

"Changing the subject?"

Joe easily raised one shoulder.

Kristen promised to herself that what she was about to say out loud, even after all this time, would make it easier. For the darkness to turn to light, she told herself she needed to share more of what had happened. "I'll tell you, Joe." For a moment she didn't say anything.

"Kristen?"

"I lost my first three pregnancies. Three different miscarriages."

"Oh, wow. Kristen, I'm so—"

She would not stop. She told herself to keep going, keep sharing. "Three different stages. The last I carried full-term. He was stillborn."

"Kristen, what an impossibly dark, heartbreaking time. That must have been crushing. You must have sunk with such loss."

"We named him Galvin Russell. My husband is Galvin Roger. You know how my husband and I don't like surprises. Each baby was named early on." Kristen continued, determined not to stop. "We had the two girls first, Sarah Anne and Michelle Adele. They also carried family names. Even though Sarah Anne was just fifteen weeks old, we named her. Same with Michelle Adele, who was within me for five-and-a-half months."

Joe swallowed the pain because Kristen couldn't anymore.

"And then, we...we had stopped trying for a while. We just took a rest. And my cycle was irregular then, so we didn't know I was even with our little flower until I was a full three months along. That, in and of itself, was a blessing." She stared into space. "After nearly carrying my son until the end of my term, I couldn't...couldn't...we couldn't name this one. It was my way of being angry with God for another round, this one unplanned. I didn't recognize that anger then, that lack of trust and faith. I do see it now. Every day I'd wonder and wait. Tell me, would she stay, or would she go?"

Kristen barely shook her head. "And she came, right on time. She arrived on her due date of all things. She's just like her mom and dad—a meticulous planner!"

Joe smiled.

"She was healthy and beautiful...and we were awed and humbled, and, trust me on this, we were so deeply, *deeply* thankful."

"And you two were without a name for your baby."

"That's right. Both our mother's and our grandmother's names had been taken with our first girls. And we didn't just want to name her *anything*. She had to have meaning, great meaning."

"What did you do?"

"We looked in the Bible. She was a gift, this complete, unplanned, surprise gift. And we had to thank Him."

"Yeah, Iris isn't..."

Kristen nodded. What she was about to share she never said to anyone else, let alone thought it. The Holy Spirit just spoke to her. "You, Joe, you have a way about you. I don't know what it is, but this story feels different when I share it with you. It's healing, somehow. Blessed."

Embarrassed, Joe looked away.

She continued. "But no, you're right. Iris is not a biblical name. And Galvin and I were stumped because Priscilla, Rachel, Ruth, Marion, Debra, Mary, and Elizabeth didn't fit our wee sprout, who, even then, was a talker. She had quite the set of lungs on her."

Remembering their last one-on-one coloring date, one where Iris discussed in detail the particular importance of the pink crayon, Joe silently agreed.

"We were so busy trying to name our little blossom here that we completely missed the rainstorm right outside my hospital window. And then the rainbow. The sign of the covenant. See, Galvin always knew that this pregnancy would be the one. He didn't tell me this until he saw the rainbow."

"But," Joe frowned, "her name isn't Rainbow."

"Iris means rainbow. See, just as we were at that point, Vanessa, who had just joined your dad's church without so much as a glint in her eye of becoming a future deacon, shows up at my door with what kind of flowers?"

"Irises." Joe nodded. He sat silently for awhile. "I don't know if that's a funny story."

Kristen agreed. "But it's a good one."

CHAPTER FORTY SEVEN

Betsy shook her head. "Do you know how much I weigh?"

"Oh, come on." Joe set his foot on the first rung of the ladder to her girlhood tree house in her parents' old backyard. "It's totally safe."

She checked. The wooden planks were brand new. Still not quite understanding all of this, she glanced back to the house she grew up in as a girl.

"Bets, it's totally safe. Come on. Don't you want to see it again?"

She remembered the cherished hours she and Mike spent here in her tree house. In spite of the fear that it may be ruined or in great disrepair, she did want to see it again. "Are you sure?"

"Yeah, it looks pretty good." He tugged on a rung about chest high. "You'll be fine."

She would be fine. He had done this work himself without her knowing, including widening the hatch to accommodate a woman almost seven months pregnant. The weekend she went out of town for work was the weekend he showed up here with fresh wood, Earl's tools, and a strange question to ask the couple who now owned the house Betsy grew up in years ago.

"The two who bought this house must have just refurbished this," Joe said. "Look, this is really sturdy."

After having been on the market for some time, Betsy's parents had just sold this house a year ago to a couple in their late twenties.

"You're right," She agreed. "They must have just done this. But they don't have any children yet. Why do you think they'd do this now? If anything, I would have repainted the back porch first."

In all his planning, Joe didn't anticipate this question. "I...I don't know. Maybe they have a niece or nephew?"

She bought into it. "Could be." Looking back up, she admired the old wooden structure directly over her. "It is a *great* house."

"It is."

Over the fence and across the neighbor's yard, she looked at the bedroom window that used to be Michael's. She only looked; she didn't want to remember everything as it was too painful. There was a different child who slept between those walls now, and she prayed—she just stopped and prayed that his or her world would be so different from Mikey's, that there would always be love, not fear.

Joe watched her. He knew what she was doing.

She knew his eyes rested on her. "But this is trespassing."

From his front pocket, Joe produced the note the two of them found a few minutes ago on the front door. He read it again out loud. "Dear Betsy, thank you for coming. As we talked about, we put the boxes we found in the attic that had been marked with your name out in the tree house. Since we're refinishing the hardwood floors, storage space is tight, especially in the attic. We hope you enjoy what you find in your boxes. Best, Carlos and Efficia."

Betsy stared at the paper. "I still can't believe my mom wouldn't have checked the attic before moving. That is so unlike her. It's really strange."

"But don't you want to see your treasure?"

She patted her belly. "My junior high cheerleading outfit *might* not fit at the moment. And I wonder why they just didn't leave the boxes in the garage. Carlos and Efficia must really have a lot of stuff."

"I bet they do."

Betsy squinted and stared at the one she loved. "You're being—I don't know. You're being funny."

"I ate your pickle and potato salad sandwich on pumpernickel on the ride here, remember? Maybe that could explain this 'funny' thing, Bets. Come on! Let's climb! You go first."

"Uh-oh. You test this out. I'm climbing for two, you know. You, muscles, make sure it's safe."

"Good point." Joe scrambled easily up and then back down.

"The boxes," she asked when he stood beside her again. "They're there?"

"Yep."

"How could you see them? You were up and down that tree in two seconds."

"They're there."

She reconsidered what she said a minute ago. "You *are* being weird, you know that, right?"

"Kiss me."

She did set her lips on his, a little more reluctantly than he had hoped. "Funny."

Joe leaned back. "You kiss me and it's funny?"

She shook her head and smiled. "I taste pickle."

"Climb!"

⊶───────⊷

Once inside, and this took *a lot* more maneuvering than the last time she was here before the house was sold, she turned back. "The hatch is wider. It's like they knew a wide load would be coming through." She noticed the two cardboard boxes but immediately went to one of the three windows. Joe watched her eyes move through the memories of the countless hours she had spent here. She started to get teary-eyed. "This. This is one of the best places on earth, Joe. This was my safe place. My world. So much life was spent up here. Me and Mike…" Her eyes held a faraway expression as if the only thing in front of her was a wall of pain and tears. "I miss him *so much*." She looked at Joe and swallowed. "But I'm so glad I'm here again. To remember him. And now to be here with you."

She stared at the two boxes. "That's funny. Yes, my name is on these boxes, but it's not in my mother's handwriting."

"Maybe it's your grandmother's."

Betsy frowned. "I don't think so."

She lowered herself onto one to the two simple benches her father had built so long ago. "It's tough for me to bend over there, Joe. And my lap is shrinking fast. Would you open one of the boxes for me?"

"Me?"

"Yeah."

"Okay."

Joe pulled out several strands of Christmas lights. "Your favorite holiday."

"Yeah."

Joe had wired a receptacle in the floor and plugged the lights in.

Betsy beamed. "Electricity! What a great touch!"

After easily stringing most of the lights overhead, Joe pulled out a new cushion. There was a name embroidered on one side, but Joe kept that down as he ushered Betsy up and then back down on the softer surface.

"Me, a princess in my castle. Nice touch there, mom." Betsy set her hands on her knees. "What's next?"

He pulled a rose out of the box. It was housed in a vase with a ribbon around its stem.

"Wait a minute!"

Moving quickly, he unfolded a tablecloth that, when opened, Betsy could see was a baby's blanket.

"Joe."

From food containers that emptied the first box, Joe opened what would be a lovely lunch for a kid—peanut butter and apple jelly sandwiches which were one of Betsy's childhood favorites. Also included were juice boxes, animal crackers and two candy bars.

"You remembered," she said, smiling at the desserts. "I told you at the wedding Mike and I were planning when we were kids that we'd have buckets of candy at each table."

"I love you."

"I love you, too."

Joe stared at Betsy's stomach. "I'm just getting ready for lunches like this with the next little girl in my life."

From the second box, Joe pulled out the empty whiskey bottle. He reached for her hand. "This stays empty. And if it's alright with you, we keep it around to remember."

"We?"

He nodded.

"Oh, Joe." Now she knew what he would be asking her.

He filled his hands with all the little things he had saved since they started dating—movie stubs, ice cream sticks, a napkin from the hot dog stand in the street where they grabbed a bite to eat after her first ultrasound, a broken paddle from a time they played table tennis with her old college roommate and her boyfriend, sunscreen from their day at the beach, the ribbon that had been around a simple present Betsy had given Joe, and the tick-tack-toe paper they had played on when coloring together with Iris.

"This kind of tells our story, Bets. Well, pieces of our story, anyway."

"You saved all of this?"

"It was packed to go with me when I had planned to leave."

"And you planned all this?"

"Yeah, Carlos and Effecia are conveniently out for the day. Maybe they are looking at hardwood floor stains for the flooring they may refinish someday."

"You refurbished this tree house?"

"Yes."

She reached over and played with a strong curl behind his ear. When she let it go, it brushed up against the base of his neck. "You did all of this?"

"Betsy, you've told me how special this place has been to you. From one of our very first dates, you've talked about this tree house. It's one of your very happy places."

"A part of Mike is still here. You left that."

That was his cue. Now was the time. Joe lowered himself on one knee. Betsy didn't realize it at first because she had been listening to

Joe so closely. "He brought us together. He's a part of us, love. And his love, great as it is—and it is great—is here today."

"Oh, Joe."

"He was your best friend. Now I'd like to ask you if you will be my best friend forever. I want to have and hold you, Betsy, in sickness and in health, in plenty and in want, for richer or for poorer, forsaking all others until death parts us."

"Joseph."

Joe found the box that held the engagement ring. He presented it to her.

"Bets, I've realized again and again and again, since we've been together that my life is home with you, no matter where we are. I love your baby as my own. You know this. You are light and laughter to my spirit. I promise to love you and cherish you, now and always. All I want to know is this: will you marry me?"

"Yes, Joseph. I will marry you."

She gently slid off the cushion when she kissed him.

Turning it over, she read the name embroidered on the pillow. "Janet Elizabeth." Betsy knew exactly what this meant.

Joe said, "It's just a suggestion. I thought she could have your middle name, Bets. You're a hero for choosing to carry her through. And Janet?"

"Earl's wife's name."

"Yes."

"It's perfect. It's absolutely perfect."

CHAPTER FORTY EIGHT

It was one thing to see it on camera for all these years from the comfort of his climate-controlled lab, it was quite another to walk through it. As he walked through Larry's side yard, Roland felt a sense of frustration that his high tech equipment couldn't reveal and record even more data. The brush of the breeze against his face coupled with the scent from the lawn that Earl had just mowed nearby almost overwhelmed him. Dunk's side yard was also far more uneven than he was aware of, and, while this had no notable consequence over the years, the glare from the sun against the house's siding never occurred to him.

Roland felt weak in the stomach. It had been one hundred and nineteen days since he'd last been outside. From birds fluttering to distant music playing, he found the distractions intolerable. His stomach continued to splash in discomfort because this visit was completely unplanned. He forced himself not to do any calculations prior to his unexpected arrival. This was going to be pure happenstance, a "pop in" as neighbors on this block would say.

Out in his backyard trying to determine the best place to plant a hardwood tree given to the newlyweds as a gift, Dunk stared in disbelief as soon as he spotted his former employer rounding the corner of his house.

"Larry, before you can say anything, I believe Joe is fine."

Roland continued toward his destination, even though his left knee suddenly ached from the car ride. The billionaire went so far as to buy a brand new car to get himself here alone. He did this so that he could experience what it would be like to actually be behind the wheel of a vehicle like everyday people drive. To his surprise, he actually felt fatigue from the bumper-to-bumper traffic he experienced through an eleven and three quarter mile construction zone on the highway exactly thirty-nine minutes ago.

Shocked, Dunk still processed Roland Rolls standing in his backyard. He came back to what Roland had said a moment ago. "Well, that's good." He nodded. "That you believe Joe is fine."

Roland nodded. He felt it was more important to share vital information first—the presumed wellbeing of Joseph—than to start with mundane small talk. Gauging the interaction so far as awkward, he forced himself into the vernacular. His face tightened for one and a half seconds, but he could do this casual greeting. "Well, hi, Larry. I just thought I'd stop by."

Dunk nodded broadly. He ignored how funny the next words sounded. "Hi Roland. It's nice to see you."

"You're not expecting me."

"Yeah, this is a pop in." The exchange in glances made it clear that Dunk knew Roland would have thought about the phrase used so often on this block. Roland awkwardly tried more small talk. "This is nice weather."

Dunk grinned. He was certain Roland knew the exact temperature, including the humidity level. "It is nice. It is definitely nice." Dunk paused. He stopped just for the fun of it. "And Roland? You can be finished with the small talk now if you like. You did a good job."

"Did I?"

Dunk squeezed the handle of the shovel he'd been holding. Still wanting to tease his unexpected guest a little, he answered, "You were fine."

"Fine." Roland ignored how completely vague the word was.

"Very fine."

Roland pushed through one of his barriers. "I just wanted to see you, and to come unannounced. I didn't want to surprise you in a bad way. I ran that risk."

"No, I'm okay. I trust you. We've been through a good deal together. And I am glad to see you." Dunk motioned toward the back deck. "Would you like to sit?"

Having been seated behind the wheel of the car for three hours and nine minutes after a rather disturbing public restroom experience, Roland would rather not. He knew this was a social courtesy, however. He lied. "Yes, I would. Thank you."

"Can I get you something to drink?"

Roland projected that he could say no to this question, and did. Just as the two sat on deck furniture that Roland observed has been exposed to nature and has not ever been thoroughly sanitized, he slipped his hand into the inside pocket of his jacket and presented Larry with a small white box secured with a fine white bow. "This is a wedding present for you and your wife, Vanessa."

Dunk was taken aback, even though as a recent groom he had received many gifts wrapped similarly to the one now in his hand. "Ah, thank you."

"You are welcome. Open it."

"Ah, Vanessa is not here right now."

"I didn't know that."

"You didn't?"

Roland gave Dunk a look. "Open it."

After a short wrestling match with a box that Joseph at eighteen months could have opened easily, Dunk jingled car keys.

"It's the vehicle I drove from the lab. Except for the six hundred, sixty seven miles it took between locations, it's brand new, and it's yours."

"You're giving us a car?"

"Yes."

"A brand new car."

"Yes."

"You know, a lobster pot would have been within normal parameters."

Roland sat back awkwardly. Everything he wore would be laundered soon and this alone gave him slight solace. "You know, you're beginning to sound like me."

Dunk's heart warmed. He knew how challenging all of this was for his special guest. That Roland was here, sitting on furniture he had already processed as being unclean, after having engaged in some small talk? Well, this said a lot.

"Now you're going to give me a speech about how proud you are of me, or how pleased you are that I'm actually here at your house."

"You're processing."

"Old habit."

"No, I'm going to say, 'Buddy, let's take it for a test drive.'"

It took a great deal to surprise Roland Rolls. "Seriously? You and me, in the car?"

"It's parked out front, right?"

"Larry."

Dunk stood.

"Larry. Let's not—"

"I'll drive."

Roland did not move as Dunk stepped off the deck.

Dunk tossed the keys high in the air and caught them easily. "Adventure waits."

"No."

Dunk sauntered around the side of the house and did not turn back. "Yes."

⸻

It was not a *car*; it was a high-performance dream machine. At first sight, Dunk had every intention of not keeping this *way* over-the-top gift. Seeing this latest model sports car all shined and sparkling with the top down and the mammoth red bow secured across the hood made what Dunk was about to say all the easier. "We can't keep this car. Thank you, thank you. But no."

Dunk figured Roland must have put this wonderful four-wheel

rocket through Ron's Car Wash on Oyster and Main and set the bow in place before walking around the side of the house to find his former employee in the backyard. "Oh," Dunk shook his head, "this is a definite no."

"I was the one just saying no, remember? Just a minute ago in your backyard, that was me."

Longingly Dunk stared at all the metal muscle.

"Now you know I know you. And I know what this car means to you."

It was true. Dunk was a car guy, but only in his secret dreams. Even Vanessa didn't know how he longed for open rides with machines so finely tuned that driving was not just an experience; it was a joy. Dunk avoided the car dealerships on the strip in the city for this reason alone: it was best not even to see them.

"This is your mid-life crisis," Roland paused in an attempt at humor. "Early."

"No."

"You're going to say this will feed twenty villages in a third world nation for a year, and that you cannot justify driving such a luxury. You're also going to say that you're a teacher and a public school educator doesn't own—or even value—this status symbol."

"You're right."

"You're going to think this gift is too grand and that I'm buying you somehow—either as a thank you, or as a lure to make you do something you do not want to do."

"Again, you're right."

"Take this car, Larry. Live this dream."

"For all the reasons you just mentioned, and then some, I can't."

Roland knew he had about two minutes before Larry became resolute in his decision. "You had the keys in your hand and hustled around to the street here. Before you saw this automotive work of art, you were all set to take me for a drive. Well?"

"Your gesture is kind, even grand. Okay, your gesture is very grand.

But I can't. Even if this were an economy car, Vanessa and I couldn't accept such a gift."

"This car speaks to you somehow. I know this. I know this, because I know you. Think of what it would be like to soar down Route 71, or Interstate 80, or take a corner where the car knows the turn before you do."

Dunk knew real gifts, and real gifts were people and time. Still holding the keys in his hand, he realized with Roland here now that he could open up something that could never be tied with a bow, the question that had been on his heart for many, many years. Roland struggled to predict what Larry was thinking because he knew his friend could no longer see the car, even though he was staring right at it. The possibility of Dunk using this time to gain more insight into the past was probable, but Roland decided to try with this gift because, in truth, he did want to acknowledge and celebrate his friend's marriage to Vanessa.

"Let's take a walk, Roland."

"Only if on this walk you'll consider keeping the car."

"Deal."

When they set off down the block, Dunk reconsidered the car for one or two steps and then asked, "Roland, this has been on my mind for a long time."

Roland knew what he'd bring up now. He also knew the car will likely go back with him to the lab.

"I want to know why you chose me to raise Joe. I was a single guy."

"Yes, you were."

"Well? Why me?"

"There was a 19 percent chance you'd ask that question today."

"Roland."

"It went to 93 percent when you suggested we walk."

"Roland."

"Okay. Conventionally, I should have chosen a male/female married couple so that the cl—, so that Joe would benefit from two parents not one."

"But you didn't do that."

"I didn't do that."

They walked around Iris's wagon and her new rock collection which Roland immediately recognized as being categorized. Dunk thought of that amazing little girl. "Her leaf display would impress even you."

Roland saw more to the collection than Dunk. "A future scientist. Wonderful."

The breeze swept around them from behind and after looping once, settled in front of them. Walking into a space that felt filled with God's goodness, Dunk knew it was time. "So, Roland, I've had this question since you told me I was specifically hired to take Joe away from the lab. Why not someone else? You said I 'tested well.' There has to be more to it."

"There was."

"Well?"

The senior of the two looked off into the distance and tried to notice his feelings, not the objects in front of him. This, of course, was difficult to do.

"Roland?"

"Alright. I'll answer. I wanted to see what it would be like..." Roland paused, and Roland never paused. "I wanted to see what it would be like for me."

Dunk didn't understand.

"I could never marry, of course."

Dunk interrupted. "Don't follow that thought through. You can marry."

"Larry," Roland continued, unappreciative of the distraction. "You were my substitute, my surrogate. You did what I could never do. You loved."

Dunk suddenly couldn't move. What he just heard crushed him.

"Don't offer sympathy. It won't work."

"No matter how robotic you say you are Roland, you are a human."

Dunk's guest continued walking, unfamiliar with why emotion would stop his partner. As the distance between them grew wider, he reluctantly took five steps back. "I chose a single father because I could not do what you've been gifted to do—and the gift, Larry, is so obvious. You love. Secretly and privately, I wanted to see into a life I could never have. That is why you were chosen, so that I could vicariously live your life."

"Roland."

"I saw it all so very, very close."

Dunk tried to meet Roland eye to eye, but Roland turned away.

"Don't just see this life. Feel it. Live it."

There was only so much right-brain guru garbage Roland Rolls could take every decade. He'd reached its max in the last four seconds. "What?"

Thankfully unaware of what his friend was currently thinking, an idea popped into Dunk's head. He turned back the way they'd come. Over his shoulder he said, "We're heading in the wrong direction."

Unable to predict even three likely outcomes, Roland was perplexed. "What are you doing?"

"You, Roland, are not a machine. I'll show you what a machine is."

⚫━━━━━⚫

Earl would be so angry at him if he got caught. He'd experience at least seven days of glares and heat. Vanessa, of course, would kill him dead. He would be cold and six feet under before clothes on a line would have time to dry. But he did it. He opened that sports car up on the interstate and they flew. The speed thrilled. The adrenaline rushed. Two stomachs turned. Only two of the four hands shook though. Making a sudden right hand turn, they took the exit at top speed. In seconds Dunk was sure Roland was unable to count, they zoomed around the lake where he hiked daily. Familiar with the area, Dunk knew every turn and curve on this scenic route. He could do this drive blindfolded, but this was far more fun with his eyes wide open.

As Dunk yielded at an intersection, Roland said something about nausea. Two fast turns later and, just like that, the two stopped in front of a new home construction site. A large landscaping truck was parked in front of them. Roland was pale. His eyes had difficulty focusing. "I get it," he said to his driver. "I am human."

"Precisely."

Roland looked over his right shoulder. "Why, why are we here?"

"This is what Joe does now. You know he works for this landscaping company. This is his latest project."

Bushes, shrubs, ornate rocks and mulch comprised the view.

"Oh." Roland couldn't think of what else to say because, while arranged neatly, all he observed were bushes, shrubs, ornate rocks and mulch. "This is very nice."

Dunk smiled. He knew his companion was trying. He knew that what he would say next would change things. "Joe is here."

Roland didn't make a sound.

"Come on." Dunk slid out of the car easily. "Let's say hello."

Roland couldn't move. He couldn't do this. It was one hurdle to show up unscheduled and unannounced. Another barrier was even getting into this car with Dunk. He did not drive the way Dunk did, or, more accurately, *could not* drive the way Dunk just did. Now this? No, he could not meet Joe here. He was unprepared. His hair felt as if it had been blown out by a hairdryer, his skin burned from the pure rush of speed of the last twenty minutes and his stomach was ever so slowly finding its way back to where it belonged. *No, not Joe. Not now.* He sat still. No one was in sight.

Of all the extremely odd sensations he has had in the last forty one minutes, a strange thought came to him. This might be what it would be like to live a full, busy, and exciting life. One could find oneself suddenly parked outside a new place that, if the architect simplified just a few of the many angles on this new house and added some stained glass windows, could be a New England country church. Curious, Roland pressed past his reluctance. He had a strangely sad thought about churches, and the people who attended them. After a fast and fun ride through life, few wanted to meet Jesus. The three-in-one God was awesome through the thrills and awesome chills, but to suddenly, abruptly stop and meet their Savior—to actually step on the brakes and get out of a car—well, that just demanded too much.

Roland continued to sit still. He heard Larry talking in the distance. As his finger slid along the side of the door to unlock his side of the car, he felt an urge to use a colorful phrase or two, only it was beneath him. That he could not take this guttural step into vernacular phraseology was unfortunate, because he would really like to let loose. He opened the car door. Firmly closing the car door behind him was not enough, but it would have to do.

CHAPTER FORTY NINE

Roland ventured up the rough incline that would someday be the front walk to the new, high-end home. Just inside the wide, unfinished foyer, he glanced up the open staircase and noticed the second floor walls had not yet been sheetrocked. The scent of freshly cut wood shavings, nearby exposed insulation, and what must be a lingering glue product made him long for a handkerchief he could use to cover his mouth and nose. A barely bent nail the size and shape of a very pointed tack rested plainly in a walkway. This messy, chaotic process could be summarized in one word: dreadful.

Overhead, he heard someone hammering and calculated the weight of the worker to be one hundred and seventy-six pounds, the weight he predicted Joe would be. After Roland took three steps further into the home, he inspected a room he could not easily identify. Perhaps it would be an office. Through an open area that would likely include French doors showcasing the backyard, a man stood outside on an unfinished deck. He looked like Jesus Christ, complete with carpenter's hands and sawdust on his knees. How Roland knew this baffled him completely, but there he was, Jesus cloned.

Roland reconsidered Isaiah 53. The ancient text stated nothing was beautiful or majestic about the servant's appearance. Nothing would attract people to him. While no one knew what Jesus looked like beyond firsthand experiences, something tugged within Roland, something odd, something off. He actually—honestly—felt uncomfortable in

Joe's presence. He held his stomach. His fingers felt like ice. It was a challenge to swallow.

He observed Joe's build which naturally widened from a young man to a grown man's musculature. Engaging a ratio of muscle building and calorie intake, Roland predicted Joe would gain a pound this year alone. However, Joe's longer hair accentuated such a softer, kinder looking face that was not just startling; it was somehow amazing. So much stirred within Roland. It wasn't just the sight of Joe's build or his soft brown curls—and it certainly wasn't the nausea he experienced from having Dunk behind the wheel. This also wasn't the afternoon sunlight per se, though the diffused golden cast flickering through the trees certainly helped. Yes, it could have been all these new construction smells, but there was much, much more.

Roland was reluctant to think further on what flashed through his mind because there could be no empirical measure of what he was considering. He tried to scan his thought processes to determine what, if anything, was quantifiable. Nothing registered. No old channels provided new information. Suddenly, an informational source within himself that had never given him any input before presented what he could not deny: Joe had an unexplainable aura around him. Looking away, Roland returned with his full attention to what was irrefutable. *Joe had an aura.*

Immediately the same urge overtook him as it did when they were in the same space for the first time. There in the lab, shortly after the initial ulmintin shot had been administered, he had wanted to touch Joe, and Roland Rolls never wanted to touch anyone. Forcing himself to stand still on subflooring that somehow seemed to be moving, the scientist tried to discern this new data a second and third time. Familiar processing routes jammed, much like what had happened during their initial face-to-face encounter. He could not unblock them. With the exception of the flu touching him once as an adult, causing five employees to be immediately dismissed, a complete malfunction like this has never happened. His breath became shallow. His skin tingled.

The complete opposite of his guest, Joe was at peace within his space because this had been one truly productive, remarkable day. His sense of wellbeing wavered when he sensed Mr. Rolls' discomfort, however. Trying to set his unexpected companion at ease, he said warmly, "It's good to see you, sir."

Stepping out onto the deck that, when finished, will make an inviting deck even by a billionaire's standards, Roland could not register what he just heard, at least fully. What came to his mind was scripture from the Gospel of Matthew, and then also from the Gospels of Mark and Luke which told of the woman healed simply when she touched Jesus' robe as he passed by.

"Mr. Rolls, are you alright?"

Roland answered indirectly by commenting on the scripture that had just popped into to his mind. "The well-recorded story of the woman touching the hem of Jesus' garment seemed exaggerated to me, excessive." He barely shook his head. "Why someone would do that— why she reached out like that—just didn't make sense, until now."

Joe nodded. "She saw something."

"She felt something."

Roland tried to do what he did best, and that was dissect this encounter into smaller, manageable components. Stepping out further from the house, he tried to level what had been out of balance. "I knew about your involvement with landscaping, of course. But here's the surprise. You're a carpenter."

Joe's heavy eyes lit up as he shrugged. "Hey, it's in the blood."

It is in the blood.

Still disoriented, Roland felt like he was not standing on anything secure, even though what looked like plywood did not bend under either of them. As he raised his focus from his feet to Joe's face, he scanned the scar on Joe's forearm. Thinking of himself, and then of the passions a builder has when finished with their work, he said, "It's nice to leave your mark."

Joe missed what Roland saw on his forearm because, from this vantage point, he was captured by how the afternoon sun brought depth to the faces of the rocks out front. With his attention directed toward the road, Joe noticed the shiny new car behind the landscaping truck. Its sharp lines and shiny surfaces did nothing for Joe. "My dad has a way of moving people."

"Larry is quite the driver."

Joe met Roland's eyes.

"Oh, you meant your other Father."

Joe knew he had somehow been ahead of the scientist, a small miracle in itself. "I'm not divine, Mr. Rolls, if that is what you're thinking or seeing. I'm just a guy, a total, sort of normal guy. I need my Father—my Lord and God—because, well, to put it bluntly, I'm a screw up."

After establishing a new mental operating system cobbled from pieces of his well-established thinking patterns, Roland thought about Jesus' need for His Father. According to scripture, there were times Jesus escaped from the crowds. There was also Gethsemane itself, when Jesus, on the eve of His crucifixion, cried out to His Father.

Roland was suddenly shocked when he recalled scripture where Jesus stood with His disciples and asked them, "Who do you say I am?" He could hear Peter's response. "You are the Messiah."

Roland wondered how Peter knew this. What did Jesus reveal in that moment, or, considering what he was feeling in this moment, what was revealed within Peter? Maybe it wasn't Jesus who changed in front of Peter; maybe something changed within Peter that enabled the disciple to truly see the Son of God before him.

Overloaded, Roland could not engage any more in the moment and took a different direction. "Joseph, you may not know this—how could you, really?—but for years the question I asked centered on whether you were—or would be—divine. Even when it became more and more apparent that I had cloned Jesus Christ's DNA and not someone else who was buried in a stone tomb in Jerusalem, the focus question remained. Did I clone the divinity of Christ?"

"Mr. Rolls," Joe said again, "I am not divine."

"Let's not be too quick to rule this out completely. Instead, let's remain open to what God can do. After all, you knew about my grandmother. You mentioned her when we first met. You even knew about the long dining room table and the titanium box on it."

Joe shrugged.

"You even knew the contents of that box."

Joe looked at Mr. Rolls differently. As he did, the breeze quickly shifted from south to northeast.

Roland continued. "The question isn't about divinity entirely, though it's a part of this equation. The question unfolding for us is humankind's sinful nature, and the God who is present to us through our sins. Joseph, listen. You let us see through your very human side what Jesus was like when Jesus showed us his human nature."

In all of what he just heard, the carpenter with the calloused hands honed in on one key word. *"Us?"*

"Yes."

"Us." Joe's face beamed.

"Yes."

"That's plural."

"I see that."

Joe played. "You do? You, Roland Rolls, you see that?"

Roland realized that divinity, at least by this scientist, could not be contained or calculated by any humanly known measure. He smiled. From a place where he has never been before, Roland said, "Today I see you differently."

"Maybe you are different today."

"What do you mean?"

Joe continued slowly but deliberately. "After all this time, maybe you are beginning to see God's love. And before you deny it, I can tell you this. Some people take one glance at me and get a sensation like you had when you first saw me today. I also can show you other people who don't notice anything peculiar or unusual about me at all. Usually they are the people who have a dozen items in the grocery store checkout lane clearly marked for shoppers with eight or less items."

"You're kidding."

"I'm serious."

Roland smirked. "Like I have been."

"Like you have always been."

"Joseph, you have a way of knowing me. Are you sure you're not divine?"

Joe's expression changed as quickly as the breeze did a few minutes ago. "There are people who don't see me as anything more than just a guy in front of or behind them in that line. They are not looking, or they do not see that God is in everyone. Then there are people who walk in the ways of Christ's love. They see me like you saw me as you stepped out onto this deck."

"So, you think I've changed. I went from not seeing Christ at all, to seeing Christ in you?"

"God reveals God's self to those who are looking."

Roland didn't make a sound.

"Mr. Rolls, the people who don't see anything Christ-like in me are not the ones with too many items in the express lane grocery store lines necessarily; the people who don't see me aglow are the ones who do not want to see me or Christ."

Again, Roland was silent.

"They are the ones who curse through heavy traffic when, pressed for time, four wide open lanes suddenly shrink to one."

"That happened today."

"It did?"

"Yes, on my ride here."

"You drove yourself?"

"Sure."

Joe paused. "You don't have a license."

"You don't know that."

Roland's heart opened and he suddenly laughed. It was a deep laugh, wonderful and rich. It carried him back sixty-one years to the memories he had with his grandmother. He wished that what he was doing now, he could have done with her—and that was experience and express joy.

When the laughter subsided, Joe waited for Roland to wipe the good tears from his eyes.

Roland nodded and then beamed. "We did clone Jesus."

When Roland said 'we,' Joe knew he meant just one other person—the one he had been thinking of—not a team from his lab. "Mr. Rolls, you're talking about your grandmother."

"Yes, I wish she could experience this today. I really do."

Joe stared in front of him seeing something that wasn't quite there, and then coming back, he tucked his fingers into his back pockets. "Tell me more."

Roland easily shared. In fact, the words spilled. "It was her passion that, pun intended, birthed this. The ancient funeral linens were hers—my grandmother's. She valued them so dearly. Now of course, I was just a boy when she showed them to me for the very first time, but their reverence, through her very eyes, has stayed with me for so many years."

Joe tilted his head. He was in love with the sound of Mr. Rolls' laughter that, not so far gone, still resonated between them. "Tell me about your grandmother."

"You know about her."

"But I await to hear what you'll say about her."

When their eyes met again, sweet emotions found Roland, good feelings. An experience like this had never, ever happened to him before. Maybe his burst of laughter opened something because everything in and around them was now different, better. The wobbly floor was solid now, and in a strange way, Roland was completely secure.

"She wasn't a religious person in her later years. None in my family were known to profess any faith, let alone practice it. I remember she said a church tradition was for the disenfranchised. Nevertheless, she kept this truly priceless treasure in a titanium-encased box and was so very excited the first time she showed the burial linens to me there on her twenty-four foot long dining table."

"It must have been quite the moment."

Roland recalibrated. "Absolutely. It changed everything."

"It changed everything for you."

Roland slowly nodded. "The cloning—a technological advancement she never knew of—began at that point in time for me. She had shared that the linens were traced back to the Middle Ages, and I remember thinking about the Battle of Hastings and the ninety facts I knew about the event. I know just ten more now." Roland slightly smiled. "Her hands shook in Morse code, the words *blue bonnets* and *chocolate*. It didn't seem like I was paying attention to her. In fact, I wasn't. As oppositional as I was with her then, I had to know. Was this Christ's cloth?"

Joe listened silently.

"I do wish Grand was here. I wish she could not only see what I see today, but also feel what I feel. I hear you, Joe, oh, I hear you say that you are not divine—but you are not standing where I am. You are not experiencing what I am experiencing."

"She would be proud of you."

Roland was completely taken aback. New tears suddenly filled his eyes. Hollowed, he asked, "Would she? Would she?"

"You weren't a computer. You were her grandson."

"Science has been my life. It is what I do."

"And it is a gift."

"A gift from God."

"You're sounding religious, Mr. Rolls."

Through his tears, he suddenly lit from within. "Maybe this whole 'experiment' wasn't for the world."

"Maybe this cloning was for you."

"And Grand."

Joe returned to something he had sensed when he looked out into the open space, with Roland standing here beside him. "You know, it's not too late to say you love her."

A moment fell when nothing happened—it would actually have been seven seconds if Roland was counting, then tears really spilled. "I don't know how."

"You do. You did this cloning for yourself, but you also did this cloning for her. You honored her curiosity."

"And curiosity is not disrespectful to God?"

"She loved you. You love her back."

So many times today, Roland had to realign or reconfigure himself. As they moved off the deck, the two could hear Dunk in the distance. "And the proof is here in you, you Joseph, telling me this."

"Yeah. I think so."

They slowed down at the base of the stairs. When they stood still, Roland no longer thought of Peter. He considered the disciple Thomas. "I did doubt."

"And you did touch me."

Roland was quick. "Yes, I did do that when we first met in my lab."

Joe laughed.

"Don't laugh. That was not so funny."

"But we can laugh now."

Roland set his words out carefully. "You are love. I see what Dunk sees, and Betsy too. And the others—Mike, Earl, Vanessa, Jolie, your new neighbors Kristen and Galvin." He smiled. "And Iris."

"God is love."

"And you are God."

"And so are you a part of God, by being built in His image."

Roland sensed Dunk and his former student getting closer. The time was coming for the two of them to leave Joe to his labor, whatever that may be. He would get those keys, so that he could drive that race car back at a meandering, great grandpa speed, and he'd do this without Dunk ever knowing he did not have a license. "I'm not close enough to admitting that all of this is God's universal plan just yet, Joseph."

"I know. But you're closer."

◆

Seven hours and seventeen minutes after his conversation with Joseph, Roland stood beside the table where the linens were first presented to him. Staring at the seat Grand once occupied at the head of the long, stately table, he realized again what was true. It had been quite a day, one he never anticipated.

The sports car he offered the newlyweds sat in one of the distant garages, likely still warm under the hood. Dunk would not accept the gift. A garden dish Vanessa insisted on sending back with him rested alone on a shelf in a refrigerator on this floor.

"You're going to taste homemade goodness," Dunk had said as he set a loaded cooler on the floor of the passenger's side of the car he would dream about owning for the rest of his life. "You enjoy it, Roland."

From the living quarters, Roland moved down a long, wide hall. He left that wing of the mansion one hundred and nineteen seconds later, descended two staircases and opened the door to one of his labs. He studied everything there. It was perfect and orderly. It was also lonely. Given the day, and how odd it had become, Roland wanted to believe Grand was somehow not so far away—at least in this very moment. He paused a long and painful moment, and then said into the silence, "I love you, Grand."

CHAPTER FIFTY

Neither the lemonade nor the cookies had changed over the years, and now as Joe thought about it, neither had the tablecloth. As he watched Earl turn back for the pitcher on the counter for a second round, he hid a smile. The summer before he started his freshman year at the Bible College, Joe had walked in on a debate between Jenna and her dad about tablecloths and the need, about every decade or so, to replace them. As Joe looked down, he saw Jenna still hadn't won.

"Well, of course I tipped her off," Earl stayed on the subject at hand as he sat down beside him again. They'd been talking about Betsy, only Earl didn't know about the engagement yet. Joe and Betsy had planned to share their news with everyone later tonight. "What is that saying?" Earl asked, "Behind every good woman is a man?"

Joe bit into a cookie. "I think you have that switched around."

After taking a big gulp from the glass in his big hand, Earl sighed. "It doesn't matter how that saying works. I just know I sent in the big guns, and I knew she could get the job done." He took another hit from the sweaty glass in front of him. "Big guns? Sorry, I meant to say big belly. I sent the big belly in to get the job done."

Joe laughed with Earl.

"But how did you know? I mean, I could have taken off at any time after the wedding, and it didn't have to be by bus."

Earl set his elbows on his table. "Let me ask you something, Joe. Do you know how big God is?"

Thinking about two cardboard boxes in a tree house and how, at several low points in his life his engagement proposal may actually not have happened, Joe paused for a long moment. In doing so, he also thought of Roland and his dad together in a sports car. "I have an idea."

"Good answer. That's all I think any of us get in this life about God. An idea. How Betsy was to find you, and when? I just gave it to Him."

Still in awe, Joe slightly shook his head. "She was there for twenty minutes before I was to catch a bus. It was perfect timing."

Earl met Joe with a serious, teary-eyed expression Joe was not used to seeing. "Buddy, let me tell you something. There were two ways I could have gone when Janet started dying, when we really knew this was it. I could spin a web of hate and sorrow fueled by pity—and for a few days there, honestly, I gave that a shot—or I could reach up and reach out. I took the second route, Joe. I gave it all to Him. And I remember I didn't give it all to Him for me alone. The girls, if you remember, were teenagers then. I couldn't fall apart on them. If it weren't for Jackie and Jenna, I might have stayed in that pool of hate because she died in such pain. There was *so much* suffering. But I turned it over. He forgave me for all that anger, all that deep, raw, nasty anger which all went to Him."

Joe had never shared this with anyone. "I know about that kind of anger."

"I know you do, son. Your dad will never know its depths. My daughters, thank God, they won't get it, either."

"Betsy."

Earl nodded. "No, she won't get it."

Joe thought about his time with the swimming pool company. "It was white hot anger, Earl. Really pure." He remembered what Kristen had told him about not naming Iris early. "Me? I fought with and distanced myself from God."

"And succeeded."

"And succeeded."

"But God stayed with you as God has stayed with me. I knew about you and that bus terminal because I reached in and reached down and I didn't find that old pit of pain. I found direction. I thought about what you'd been going through that night, with your spat with Betsy, and then the whiskey. All of this plus the wedding itself, where we all wished Dunk and Vanessa a new and bright start...well, it came together for me. You had an escape plan. And I knew—I just knew—I had to get Betsy to that bus terminal on that day, at that time."

"That doesn't make sense, Earl."

"Of course it doesn't."

"Our God is bigger than we realize."

Earl laced his fingers together. "I never shared this with you, but I met Mike once. Yeah, it was when you and your dad were at the lab. That big buck drove up here from college wondering where you were."

"He did that?"

"Yeah, this college kid had just gotten out of this little car and I could tell from his boyish expression that he was not certain about anything. He was wearing a Bible College shirt and I put two and two together."

"He came up here looking for me."

"That's what love does, Joe. It makes us move or respond in ways we wouldn't on our own. Now hear this today, like you have not before, okay?"

Joe took a moment. His eyes met Earl's. "Okay."

Earl felt the spirit of God through him when he said, "Don't hurt yourself any more over this—*all of this*. Mr. Rolls, the cloning, your life with its highs and its lows. Just know this." Earl's voice became both richer and softer. "Love always heals."

Joe experienced this of course. He lived this. Still, it was good to hear. Thinking of Mike, he said, "I miss him."

"That's what love does, too."

Joe swished his lemonade around in the glass but didn't drink any more. "How'd you get so smart?"

"Behind every good man is an even greater woman."

Side by side at Earl's kitchen sink, which was the specific spot the two of them hadn't been in since Joe was in elementary school, Earl took a deep breath as he dried the last plate they used for the cookies.

"Earl, what?"

As if Joe were indeed his grandson, he realized he shouldn't wait. This was the time to tell Joe what he has been holding for a long time. Patting his front pocket for his car keys, he said, "Come on, let's get some chicken pot pie and cherry cobbler."

Joe looked to the drying plates in the rack beside him. He thought about the surprise dinner he and Betsy were throwing tonight.

"Yes, chicken pot pie and cherry cobbler. Let's go and find some somewhere."

"You can't really be hungry now, are you?"

Earl recalled his time in the ICU. "I wasn't quite in the mood the last time I heard that dinner option, either."

"Earl, what, what are you saying?"

"Chicken pot pie and cherry cobbler."

Joe's face blanked. "I don't get it." Knowing Earl had an odd appetite, he added, "If you want to go out and find some, I'm in."

"Years ago, when you were just a sprout, you sang to me a part of a song you had no way of knowing about. It was the perfect gift at the most painful time."

"What?"

"The two of us were having dinner together. Spaghetti, it was. And you knew the first song I danced to with my wife at our wedding."

"I remember."

Earl glanced at the basket of fall gourds in the center of his table. Vanessa had gifted this centerpiece to him just yesterday. "You don't know this. Eight months ago, I heard your prayer. I heard every word."

"What prayer?"

"The one you prayed when you were alone with me in the ICU. I don't know how I heard your words, but I did. Your hand was on my chest, and in all that time I was unconscious—your voice was the only voice I heard. Well, it was the only voice I heard until that aid came in and said…"

"Chicken pot pie and cherry cobbler."

As he shook his keys for a second in his hand, he nodded.

"You were out then! Completely out! Earl you were like…"

"Close to dying." He stood and turned toward his back door. "We're just going to call the lemonade and cookies an appetizer. Come on, this is still the lunch hour. Let's eat. All this talk of food makes me hungry."

CHAPTER FIFTY ONE

At first, no one said anything.

"Well, when?" Vanessa asked, rising from the awkward silence to excitedly hug the future bride and groom. "When?"

Betsy looked at Joe. She wrapped her arm around her fiancé's waist as the two stood in the open space between her dining area and living room. "We were thinking not this weekend, but the following one. Saturday, October first."

Dunk had never used an obviously fake response before. He didn't know it was in him. After nodding, he said, "Well, that will work."

Joe hugged Betsy from the side. "We want to do it before the baby is born."

Betsy added, "And we really shouldn't wait all that much longer."

Earl set his hand on the back of Jolie's chair. He couldn't be more joyful. "That's wonderful!"

Jolie and Kristen echoed. "Wonderful!"

Wiggling in her booster seat, Iris asked, "Why is everyone so happy?"

Galvin whispered into his daughter's ear, "Because love is here to stay."

⋅────────⋅

Vanessa reminded herself of what she had heard hours earlier. While waiting for Dunk to join her in their bedroom, she gently whispered, "Love is here to stay."

She didn't have to convince herself of this; she knew it. She also knew that Dunk seemed to be happy about the upcoming wedding. True to his character, he said the right things with the right inflections at the right times through the dinner party—even his final words at the door were sweet and affirming—but his concerns about this marriage began to weigh heavily on him during their nearly silent ride home. Vanessa did not press the subject after they started off in their car because her husband needed this time to let the big announcement settle. It wasn't the engagement itself that set off his alarms; Dunk had clearly seen and had even said that Joe and Betsy were on track to get married; it was that the wedding date was literally just days away. That in itself was pressure to a guy who typically moved slowly. He had shifted from being a single man to a sudden father, and from working in a lab to working in a school, but all of this happened so long ago. Yes, Joe and Betsy's timing did truly rock him, but what really rattled Dunk was what he didn't want to face: he was losing his son again.

Vanessa sat on her side of the bed and considered the last few months from Dunk's perspective. Joe had returned in a 'back door' sort of way. He didn't actively seek Dunk; instead, Dunk was the safe person Joe needed in order to leave the halfway house. To Dunk, Joe didn't have a stable, financially secure job. There was also no prospect of one in the foreseeable future. The child Betsy was carrying wasn't Joe's, and Betsy, while employed in her dream job, had some baggage of her own. Neither Dunk nor Vanessa had ever heard too much about Tad.

Through the closed bathroom door, she heard a drawer shut loudly. It opened again, and then after a sharp expletive, it shut even louder. Dunk muttered under his breath words she was glad she couldn't hear. Her husband's face was tense when he walked into their bedroom. She hadn't seen that expression before, at least not to this degree.

Knowing her husband, and the verse about the sun not going down on your anger, she said softly, "We should talk about it."

"Talk about what?"

"What's troubling you."

Dunk moved to his dresser as if to retreat. "It's nothing."

She waited a moment. With his dress shirt between his hands, he wadded it and tossed it into the hamper just inside his closet. How he never missed amazed her. "Vanessa, there's nothing to say."

"Wait. No."

Dunk snapped. "Wait? No? What is *that* supposed to mean?"

Vanessa stayed both calm and level-headed. "It means that there is a lot to say. You can either hold it and stay all worked up, or you can let it out."

"Let what out?"

She thought that maybe levity would work. "Twenty questions is not a game I want to play tonight, unless there's a prize."

"Honey?"

She turned to him after she could sense she was having no affect. "You're upset at your son. You're upset that he's rushing into things. You're even upset that he didn't come to you first about this fast approaching wedding. But far more than being mad, you're scared. You're scared that the relationship between Joe and Betsy isn't secure enough."

He slipped off his undershirt. "No, I'm not."

"We're not doing this. You may not want to talk about this now, and I can understand that. I can certainly give you more space, but we will talk about this at some point."

The sight of this well-built man impressed her. After all, she still felt that she was on her honeymoon, at least in part. But not tonight. When he began to take off his pants, she glanced away.

"What are you talking about?"

She stayed silent.

"Vanessa?"

"I love you. I do. This said, there's a lot of pressure here in this room. A lot of hurt. Maybe I shouldn't have brought this up with you tonight. When you're ready, we'll talk."

He slid into bed beside her. "Good night, then."

"Good night."

He didn't kiss her. She didn't reach for him, either. When he turned down his light, she switched off hers. They were quiet in the dark for a couple of minutes.

Suddenly, he turned toward her. "I still don't know what you mean."

"Dunk," she said warmly, "you do. Be honest with me."

"I am."

"You are not."

"Babe, it's all good."

"You're not being truthful with me, and that's not going to go down between us. This is not all good. Not by the way you see things. Admit to me that the Perfect Guy is troubled by the less than perfect scenario here."

"I'm not the perfect guy."

"But you try to be."

Dunk didn't want to hear her or see himself. "I'm just going to say goodnight."

She drew up the covers on her side of the bed, stared into the darkness and said softly, "Good night, Dunk."

⊗⸻⊗

Ten minutes passed. "What?" He asked sharply. "I just don't get you! I'm not the perfect guy!"

She was nearly asleep.

He lifted his head up off his pillow. "God has all of this. It will all be fine."

She turned. "God does have all of this, but you don't. You have worries."

"You are putting words into my mouth."

"I'm admitting how you really feel."

"So, I'm mad."

"Right."

"And I'm scared."

"You are."

He turned back to the wall, only after wrestling with the sheet. "You know, Pastor Smith isn't going to marry them. He's not. He likes to plan these things out after counselling couples for weeks if not months on end. There is no way he is going to go for this fly-by-the-seat-of-their-pants wedding. What are they going to do? Hire an Elvis impersonator?"

"Maybe."

His voice growled. "All you have to say to this is 'maybe'?"

She added nothing.

"I am not mad."

She waited.

He sat up and then threw the covers off. "I am hungry. Do you need anything?" He didn't wait for her to answer as he padded down the hall toward the kitchen. She couldn't hear him in the refrigerator and the cabinets making a massive sandwich he didn't need.

Here in the quiet, Vanessa realized nothing like this would have happened if her ex husband had been in a similar situation. If she were still in her first marriage, she would have either jumped right in and pressed until he popped, or, even worse, she would not have read any of his signs. She would not have heard what he was thinking when he didn't say anything at all.

She sighed. Everything was different with Dunk, better. Sure, he was struggling with tonight's big announcement, and he was doing it for some good reasons, but she knew when the time was right he'd think about what she said. She didn't know when exactly the conversation would happen between the two of them, but they would talk more on his feelings about Joe's upcoming wedding, and on what she saw in Dunk that he had yet to see himself, and that was this need to be the perfect guy.

She knew this was tough. More heated words may come, but she used the fingers of her right hand to gently twist her wedding band. "Thank you, God," she said. "Love is here to stay."

CHAPTER FIFTY TWO

In his bed alone, Ben knew no one really should be talking to their pillow. His pretend companionship—ah, this was a *pillow*—was all he had though, and he wasn't sure when he actually started talking out loud to it. Yes, it was pathetic. Yes, it was sad, but since no one was looking at him, especially in school, how could he ever find someone to share a night like this? He stared out his nearby bedroom window again. The stars seemed pasted in place by a child's hand. The moon, which was just rising from the southeast, lit the few puffy clouds that skimmed over the dark sky. He had learned the name of those clouds in junior high, but forgot now what they were called. All he knew was that this was a perfect night for love. He raised his shoulder and looked down at his pillow which had been beside him. "What?" He asked, "I thought you were sleeping."

Ben ignored that his hair smelled like chocolate marshmallow ice cream from the Dairy Barn as he stroked his imaginary friend. Quizzically, he frowned. "What is this?" He pretended his companion was the soft shoulder of the woman who loved him, who needed him, and who, on this very night, had to be so very close to him. "You'd like what? A kiss?"

He dreamed of having company here. Someone to talk with, laugh with. But this was a pillow, this was a single bed, and he was the only one at home in the house. After turning to the wall, he closed his eyes. The familiar silence around him brought him the isolation he knew too well.

There was too much noise at work sometimes, too much turbulence. He should find another job, something where he didn't have to interact with so many people. The Dairy Barn was familiar though. Every now and then someone in the kitchen would make a fuss over him, but usually he was left alone. He liked that.

Then again, maybe he didn't.

His mind drifted. Unusually restless, he turned back toward the window. The sky was a bit clearer now, and the stars spread out by the hundreds. Some seemed to twinkle when he squinted at them. Others were so strong and bright. Then there were some like him, small and dim. Closing his eyes even more tightly, he hoped someone would find these little ones. He hoped someone who cared enough and who looked hard enough would find the ones so many never see.

He drew the pillow up over his head. It was warm with his breath and, continuing into his imagination, he could feel someone touching him. This was someone who never felt the gross, scarred skin—and the damage certainly didn't show here in the starlight. In fact, his skin wasn't burned at all. It was perfect. The fingers over his body were saying only what his soul needed to hear—things like I love you... come closer to me...I just want to kiss you...I want to hold you, stay near you all night.

Ben slid to the edge of his mattress and, with his long arm, reached under the bed to find his old trigonometry notebook—the one he hardly used in class last year. He found the last page he worked on a few nights ago.

It was too dark in here, even with moonlight streaming over his lap. Angling the page just so against his thighs toward the window helped only so much. There was no way he could read what he had written, but he remembered most of the poem. He thought the words could be song lyrics someday. He traced his fingertips over the page, feeling the indentions from his pen as if the heavily pressed letters were somehow Braille in reverse. Surprisingly, he could make out the words.

Darkness find me. Cover me. Hide me so well that I am found, found by you who only sees what is inside me, and what is inside me, you know, is not broken or bruised.

He could not make out the rest of his work and by no means did he want to slip out from under his covers to turn on the only light in his room, a glaring overhead fixture in the middle of his ceiling. His fingers ran over the words he had already memorized. *Yes, darkness, find me. Cover me. Hide me so well that I am found. See me because you are me. There is no distance.*

Ben turned back to the window. He made up more than what was on his page in front of him. *Starlight,* he thought. *Hear me. Listen to me sing low and soft, low and soft. Dance your diamonds with me. Dance your diamonds with me.*

———————————

His pillow. His notebook. His thoughts. His lyrics. His soul. If only someone would find him. If only someone would see him. Hear him. He knew this was weird. Really. What teenage guy did this? What teenage guy felt this? Yet it was there. Here. There will be a day, he knew, when he wouldn't be alone. When he wouldn't hurt. He closed his eyes to the memory of one distant, dim star. The soul he waited for. The girl of his dreams. The love of his life.

Just find me.

CHAPTER FIFTY THREE

She found—what was this?—a rose petal?

"Joe?"

Holding her full roundness with both hands, she realized there was absolutely no way she could get down on the ground to see if, in fact, this little pale pink thing was, in fact, what it appeared to be, a rose petal.

Moving back inside from her tiny yard space, she made her way to the kitchen. The large bowls Joe left on the sink after their pasta dinner for two tonight were now dry. She knew he planned to come back downstairs to tuck them into the cupboards, but with some interesting maneuvering, she accomplished putting them away herself. Those that were clean in the dishwasher could wait until morning. She was done. Her ankles, just a little swollen, told her she was finished for the day. Wondering where Joe went, she lumbered her way through the living room.

As she came upon her open foyer, she stopped. Rose petals. Dozens of them. They were the same color as the one she spotted outdoors. They made a narrow, winding trail up the stairs. "Joe? Joe? I'm onto you. Where...?" She started climbing. At the top of the steps, taped to her closed bedroom door was a plain piece of copy paper that read, 'Welcome to Betsy's Night Spa and Massage Center. Now serving: one.'

She opened the door. More rose petals layered her bed. From her walk-in closet, Joe came out wearing a getup she had never seen before: a tight white t-shirt and equally white dress pants, neither of which he would ever wear in front of anyone but her. The clincher was the peel and stick nametag on his chest that read, "Joe, manservant and massage expert." A white towel was draped over his forearm.

"Welcome, madam. My name is José, and I'll be at your disposal tonight."

Never had anyone come even close to doing something like this for her. She laughed, until she realized she was ruining the mood.

She eyed her man. "Does that shirt come off, José? It looks tight."

"Madam, that's a strange request so soon. But whatever you desire will be granted."

She chuckled at what he said and how he said it. "No, no. Leave it. I just want to see how long you can stand keeping that on. Where'd you get it, anyway?"

"Madam?"

"Where did you pick up your look, sir?"

"The Thrift Store."

"Along with the pants."

"Yes, along with the pants."

"They good look on you."

Joe bowed. She noticed he had mousse or gel in his once wavy hair that was now straight and rested at the top of his shoulders. Like his clothes tonight, the hair goop was something he never wore and probably wouldn't again.

"Whatever you say, madam." He extended his hand and, as a novice actor, tried to start over. "Welcome to your night spa and massage center. I have sparkling cider on ice for you, and can draw your spa when you're ready."

"You mean the bathtub."

Joe boyishly rolled his eyes. He tucked his lips to one side because he was not sure how to respond.

Oh, he's just so cute.

Betsy kicked off her slippers. "I actually like your hair that way, manservant. What are the odds of seeing that look tomorrow when we—"

"No."

Betsy pouted.

"Now, as for your massage, we have your space ready for you right over here." Joe motioned to her bed. She noticed a few expensive looking bottles on her nightstand.

"Yes," she said, "let's start there. The bath and the booze—the cider—can wait. Start with my ankles."

As ordered, Joe did exactly what she said.

<hr>

The shirt did come off. She rested her head against his bare chest. Tired, she said, "I love the bath idea. The spa idea. It's just going to have to wait. I'm really tired."

"Though moderately disappointed, your manservant can handle that."

Betsy laughed. "Manservant. Where did you come up with that?"

"I have my resources."

"Hey, Joe? José?"

"Yeah?"

"What's that?" She was looking at the mark on his forearm. "You know, I've never asked you this before. Where did you get that, or how did you get that?"

Joe closed his eyes. "I don't know. It's just a mark or something. Maybe I was born with it."

Betsy kept her voice flat. "Maybe you were born with it." Playing a waiting game, she thought of the word secret but didn't say another word.

Finally, after almost two minutes of silence, she blurted, "Oh, come on, tell me! Maybe you were born with it? Maybe? Is that a yes, or a no?" She faced him. "And 'I don't know' is not your third option, manservant."

"Bets."

"Wait. I'm remembering, remembering. I heard this. 'Whatever you desire will be granted.' I desire to know where this mark came from, Joe. It looks like it probably hurt when it happened."

Tired himself, he sighed a deep sigh. He circled his fingertips over her knuckles and swallowed. "It was a painful skiing accident."

"You don't ski."

"Snorkeling."

"You don't snorkel."

"My early days as a NASCAR driver. It's a burn mark from the Daytona Four Hundred."

Joe thought of Ben, the guy he worked with at the Dairy Barn. He had a burn mark on his neck. He tried a few times to invite him over because he sensed something sad within his co-worker. So far, Ben had declined. Joe prayed that would change.

"Joe, it's five hundred." She reached for and holds his hand. "It's the Daytona Five Hundred. Now seriously?"

"Windsurfing? High school chemistry explosion? Giving a poor, homeless dog a bath? A bite from a vampire?"

"Joe."

His head sunk into a pillow. "An ice pick. An anchor. Acid rain. On my fourth grade field trip, I was bitten by an Emperor Penguin. Hey, you know, cute and cuddly as they are, they are *mean*."

"Joe."

"As an inquisitive child scientist, I set an Uncle Jerry's Cosmic ice cream pop on my forearm until it melted. The scar from the ice cream pop's aggressive preservatives on a boy's skin was huge indeed, yet, through the miracles of modern technology, plastic surgeons have successfully reduced the hideousness to this."

She raised her head. "I *loved* Uncle Jerry's Cosmic ice cream pops! They could really burn your tongue."

"Or your forearm."

Betsy settled back down. "Joe. Seriously now. What happened?"

He swallowed. His thoughts were numb, distant and isolated. The part of him that mattered, the part he has tried to protect since he was in that rehab center, successfully locked itself away. In a voice that sounded similar to his own, someone else skimmed over the story of the injections, and the lab itself. When the words stopped, he stopped.

She did not like the silence. "That must have been awful. That must have been so *awful*."

He turned and rolled away from her. "It's past, that's all. I really don't want to talk about it."

"Joe?"

Keeping his back to her, he closed his eyes.

◆━━━━━━◆

She stared into the darkness. Certain he was asleep and regrettably so far from her, even though they shared the same soft, mid-autumn blanket, she didn't move. The baby, who typically stirred when she was first trying to get to sleep, pressed on her bladder. She dreaded having to slide out of bed and go to the bathroom because she may wake him. Yet sure enough, Janet Elizabeth elbowed here and kicked there. Betsy didn't move herself though. Joe needed his sleep. He needed time and distance from his story.

Maybe she shouldn't have asked. Maybe she shouldn't have been all up in his face about it. Spouses of police officers learn not to ask, and soldiers who've seen combat never tell their stories, at least completely. She was wrong to pry, but she didn't know. Now she didn't want to look at what could pass as a birth mark, at least for a long, long while. Her forehead wrinkled. *The body of Jesus cloned.* How many people out there, if they knew who he was, would be so wonderfully fascinated to see him like this, shirtless beside her, sleeping so calmly and quietly? More questions would circle from those outside her immediate life. *How warm are his hands? What does he smell like? Are his hugs strong? Can he hold you with his eyes? And just what color are his eyes, anyway?*

Her heart caught in her chest. She fretted. Overheated. Was there any normalcy to any of this? How many people needed to know about this? Everyone? No one? What if that Roland Rolls guy showed up?

This mark really began to unnerve her. She had known about

Joe's past. She knew about him before she ever went to the bus station. Knowing it was one thing; seeing it was another. This body beside her, with its low, nearly silent breathing, was *exactly* the image of Christ seated at the right hand of God at this very moment. She tried to think. Calm herself. Breathe. But everything spun.

Maybe no one would ever leak this to the whole world. Maybe the two of them will grow old together like the two she met at the bus station.

And maybe not.

Her mind raced. She knew, deep down, that Tad loved her. Even though he was married and by now had a baby with his new wife, she knew his heart was with her, or could be with her again, and she could get him back. She slipped her hand over her stomach. If that were to happen, they would be a real, complete family—mother, father, and daughter. She faced a fact that she had pushed away until now. She actually did like having sex with Tad. This was not something she would ever want to shout, let alone share, especially to her boyfriend now fiancé, but together with him and the way he held her, touched her… It *was* complete.

She bolted straight up in bed. How could she ever be *that* close to Jesus' body? Thankfully, Joe didn't move when she did, so she took this opportunity to slide out of bed carefully, visit the bathroom, and pad her way downstairs. Standing in front of the refrigerator, she remembered what she had promised Earl. The two of them were in Kristen and Galvin's kitchen that fateful night with Joe and the whiskey. She said she'd be tough. She'd take this through. But this is Jesus' body upstairs in her bed. Would it be sacrilegious to make love to it? *It would have to be.*

A cold thought caught inside of her. She lusted after Joe's body. It was true, and maybe it was weird or warped. Wondering this, she slumped down with bubble gum ice cream which she had dabbled with jelly beans and chocolate sprinkles. Diving into her creation, she tried to get it out of her mind that a gazillion nuns would probably detest her for the steamy thoughts she has had. Although she had never even been close to being Catholic, she imagined a thousand priests would cast her into hell for the times her eyes have wandered where they should not have wandered when with Joe. She shoveled the ice cream, jelly bean and chocolate sprinkle combo into her mouth as her mind raced. She was pregnant—obviously!—and the two of them have not even come close to having sex. In fact, she hadn't *seen* all of her fiancé yet. The flash thought of Joe naked sent her to her feet. Everything was okay until she had asked about that red mark. Again, why did she ask about that? She ran her fingers through her hair. This should be troubling, right?

But this is Joe, not Jesus.

Sitting still on a high chair at her kitchen island with her midnight snack deserted on the opposite end of the counter, she could only be calm when she pictured herself with her old college boyfriend. Maybe this was a sign. Maybe this was a message, God's message. She didn't want to do wrong. Reaching for and opening her kitchen Bible, the one she used when she ate alone, she traced through scriptures she had highlighted.

God, she found herself praying, *what do you want me to do?*

She waited. She listened. Nothing was written scripturally about Jesus being intimate with anyone. No book, chapter, or verse opened even a hint of Jesus himself being sexual in the least. In Luke 7:38, a woman washed his feet with her tears, and wiped them away with her hair. She proceeded to kiss and anoint his feet, but, Betsy realized, that was it. This? Her and Joe? It can't be done, shouldn't be done.

All she saw when she shut her eyes was how she and Tad would look good together as husband and wife. Confident and ambitious, Tad was also handsome, and he was caring, or caring in his own way. He'd work hard to see his family happy. There'd be no clone talk and no possibility of an interfering camera. There'd be no TV news reporting team in her life. Ever. Even her dad would approve. From the day they met, her warhorse of a father had a warm spot for Tad—and that was before they even spent their first of many afternoons together in front of the TV watching football games. Joe, on the other hand, well, not having a college degree was the first place her dad would start, and it would only get worse from there. Closing her eyes, she could see herself with Tad on a white sand beach. Just in front of them, their daughter would be wearing one of those fun, silly hats. Photo albums would depict this perfectly sun-kissed, content threesome.

Why did she ever leave him? He was enough. Wasn't he?

CHAPTER FIFTY FOUR

Betsy lengthened her stride. Walking briskly like this in the early morning was one thing, sure, but she missed running. This would be the perfect hour of the day to run this out, or through. There was just so much to think about, and suddenly, with this wedding date now set, there was no time. Her heart literally jumped into her throat. This ridiculous delusion—panic?—last night was just cold feet. In the light of day, she realized the truth, when with Tad, she thought of Joe. What she had been experiencing over the past few hours was just nerves, *big* nerves. She rounded a corner.

Suddenly, she stopped. The note she left for Joe had to be intercepted. "Janet," she said as she held her belly, "we have to hurry."

———•———

Quietly he stared at the note on the counter just under the cabinet that held her juice glasses. Without picking it up, he knew what this meant. She wanted to leave him. She couldn't marry him. Of course not. He was too weird, too different. He will never be normal, and she deserved the best life she can get. Maybe if he hadn't been there at the grave the day she showed up, she would actually be with Tad, the father of her baby. Maybe it was still possible they could be together now. Whatever differences or difficulties they have had could be worked through.

His being in the picture kept the two of them apart. Without him, they could at least *try* to have a relationship. He should go, not for himself, but for her. Immediately he pictured the bus station. He could get another duffel bag. They weren't married. He could walk away to save her. There was time. His wallet was tucked away in a drawer upstairs. The landscaping job just paid yesterday. It was not much of a start at all. The engagement ring really set his already low finances even lower. It would be okay though.

He tried to reverse his thoughts. He didn't want to go. He loved her so much, but she needed more. This future life with her had been a dream; now it was time to look at the big picture. When he does leave her, she'll get pity votes. The community will just see him as some loser, some low-life. Victimized, she'd have honor or allure in the eyes of men who will want to date her in the future, that is, if it didn't work out with Tad.

Tears formed in his eyes. *God, no, I don't want to leave her. Ever. I love her. I love her so much.* He swallowed and shook his head. This could not be about himself. She made the choice with what was behind this note. He loved her. He wanted what was best for her. He'll go. His heart shattered. He'll go. As he trotted down the stairs with his wallet in hand, the front door suddenly opened and caused a near collision in her narrow foyer. She was back too soon. Even if they were on opposite sides of the planet, the proximity between them would still be too close.

"Hi."

"Hi."

"Did you have a good walk?"

"Yeah. Did you?"

Joe frowned. "Betsy, I didn't go anywhere."

She set her hands on the small of her back. "Yeah. Right. What was I thinking?"

What were you thinking?

She sensed his question, but avoided it. Stepping toward the living room without thinking why she was moving, she quickly turned back. "We...we should talk."

Joe's voice was high and dry. "We *should* talk."

She just needed to say it. Tell him everything. She loved him. She so deeply truly loved him, all of him. She has just been afraid. Even now, she felt scared to share her thoughts.

Into the painful, heartbreaking silence, Joe asked, "What?"

Just say it.

"Betsy, what?"

"I thought about leaving you."

With his hands shaking, Joe dropped his wallet that he hadn't yet had time to put in his back pocket. "Look at me, fumbling fingers."

She took three steps toward him and knew she had to say it again. "Joe, I thought about leaving you. I just got really scared."

"That was why you left the note."

"Yeah."

"I didn't read it, but knew what it said."

"The note only said that I'd like to talk with you."

"Talk with me about this."

Her shoulders dropped.

He should have been quicker, maybe even left in the middle of the night. He was knotting and twisting her. No one should talk like this before their wedding. She would be better off with Tad. He wanted to reach for the doorknob but couldn't move.

Over the past few weeks, the top of her stomach had become a convenient little tray for holding things, like both of her hands. "This cloning thing. Earl told me everything just after Dunk and Vanessa's wedding." She won't look anywhere near his forearm. Instead, she stayed steady by looking straight into his eyes that looked wild if she truly noticed. "But I was okay. It was just like, 'Alright. I can deal with this, sure. This is not really a big deal.'"

Joe bent down to pick up his wallet. "It is a big deal."

Wanting to make sure that what she wanted to say made it out uninterrupted, she kept on talking. "And I did what I needed to do. I did what my heart told me to do. I met you at the bus station."

He stood. "Bets, you're not hearing me. It is a big deal."

"No, it isn't!"

"Betsy."

"This is what we make it, Joe. *We*. Us. If we want to let this be a big deal, you know, we just may be successful at it."

He held out a flicker of hope, though he didn't even realize it. "What, what are you saying?"

"I'm saying that we can handle this. We. You and me. Us. I'm unclear what all of this means, or could mean in the future. You are, too. For all we know, you may just need another ulminmin injection."

"Ulmintin."

Angered by science on top of a sleepless night, she snapped not at him, but at what has happened to him. "Whatever!"

Joe offered a surprised, funny look.

Taking a breath, she continued. "Here's the truth. No future is secure for any couple. And no two are exempt from being confused every once in awhile. Including us. We'll just take it day by day."

"You thought of leaving me."

"I got scared, yes. Maybe some of this—or even a lot of this—is because I'm carrying the baby, and yes, I'm eating ice cream with jelly beans, but I am not using this pregnancy as an excuse. This is just me, and yes, love of my life, here is what we need to hear together: I did get scared."

"What if this really is too much?" the doorknob was in clear sight now. "It is too much."

She took a step back as she added up the following: his wallet, him standing at the front door, and the time of the day. He wouldn't need his wallet for anything at this hour, and he didn't keep it here by the front door. *He went upstairs to get it. That is why he was standing by the door when she came home.*

His knees felt weak. He couldn't face her in the moment. Truly, he only wanted what was best for her. Would she understand that?

"Listen, Joe. Maybe I shouldn't have said anything to you. Maybe I should have kept this quiet. But it's important to talk, whenever anything comes up—good or bad. I'm going to love you. I will always love you. That is enough for us to live together forever. Over any mountain. Through any hurdle. Yes, I did get scared. But that's just nerves, fear. And I'm not giving into that today. Hopefully not ever."

Joe heard her words in his head, but they did not come close to his heart.

Betsy sensed this and lowered her voice. "If Vanessa has taught me one thing in going through not one but two engagements to Dunk, it's this: love takes trust, and it takes work, a lot of work." Holding both of his hands, she lowered herself to one knee.

Joe squinted. "What, what are you doing?"

Nuns and priests could either love or hate her since her eyes rested right below Joe's waist, but she knew what was clear. "My commitment is with you. My future is with you, now and always."

"Betsy."

"Will you marry me?"

Everything fleeting and fearful thought he had—and there had been so many—changed when he realized just how much he was loved. Her face told him everything. If there were more bus stations or even an airport, she'd find him. He knew what she thought about the possibility of cameras everywhere, or news reporters camped out at their door. She was that devoted. Her love was here to stay.

Overwhelmed, Joe also dropped down on one knee. Betsy loved him, and he loved her. It was that simple. It was also that wonderful. His hands trembled. "I want to make my promise to you, too. And to do it with God's blessing on us. My answer to your question is yes." Clumsily, he handed her his wallet.

"What?"

He watched her beautiful fingers. "Inside."

"Your driver's license?"

"Bets."

She turned to sit down on the floor. Holding his license, she admired it. "Good picture. You are definitely cute enough, for sure."

Joining her on the floor, he rolled his eyes.

She continued studying what is in her hand. *How can anyone look so good on their driver's license photo? And I would actually think of leaving this guy? Really? Look at that wide neck. Look at that smile. The depth of his eyes says if you ride this life with me, we'll have romance, fun, closeness.*

"Betsy. That's not what I wanted you to see."

She kept looking. "Your grocery store shopping card?"

"Babe."

"You have three dollars in here. How do you live with so little cash?"

"Budget."

"Joe, I don't see what I'm—"

His warm hands held hers as he reached for his wallet. The simple, casual touch, as always, felt right and good. It connected them, united them. "Here."

He pulled out two aluminum can tabs.

"What?"

"Check to see how they're inscribed."

The two tabs had clearly been in his wallet for a long time. They were neatly pressed, but she could make out, in the tiniest letters, *SS*.

She gasped. "Spark Shark? That's a soda! I remember, it was blue." She smiled brightly. "It was pretty bad, remember? They stopped making that…when?"

"The year we met."

"Yeah." She was not connecting why these tabs were in her hand. "Why do you have these two tabs in your wallet?"

"Bets, think about it."

She frowned until she realized how long Joe has had these tabs. Her fingers shook. "Oh my stars, no!"

"That little store."

"On our way back to campus. You saved these all this time?"

"It was the first thing I bought you. It was the first thing we'd done together."

Her voice trembled. "Mike, he, he stayed in the car, remember? He said he was fine. Always polite. He was probably wise enough not to drink this stuff. But you and I…"

He took her hands, rubbed the tip of his nose against them, and moved her to her couch which was feet from where they had been. They sat slowly and carefully. He faced her. It may never cross her mind that he was able to hold onto his wallet during the darkest months he spent as a drunk. She may also never realize that for a long, long time there, those two tabs were the only things he had in that wallet.

His voice held the warmth she remembered from the first day they met there at the state park. "Please listen, Bets. Please. I love you so much. From the start, our start, you've been here, with me."

"Joe. I can't let you go. Ever. *Ever.*"

His face held expressions she had never seen before. "I get scared sometimes, too. I try not to. I try to think, 'You know, this is a pretty normal life you're living here, buddy,' and it doesn't matter where I came from. I try to shrug this off. I try to make this not such a big deal and say that it doesn't really matter all that much about Mary, and about her husband, Joseph—and, I don't know—I think offhandedly sometimes, and this might sound crazy, but I think, virgin birth and all, that carpenter, that amazing man, just like that amazing woman who heard the message from Gabriel, is all a part of this." He glanced down toward his body. "Yeah, somehow, I just think Joseph is here."

Betsy looked at his forearm now.

"Roland Rolls named me Joseph. Dad changed my last name to his. Rolls gave me the last name Messiah."

"I didn't know that."

"Dad told me this the first night we came home from visiting Earl in the hospital after his stroke. I think you should know that I'm glad for my first name. I think Mr. Rolls did well there. Joseph."

Betsy nodded. "Yeah, I think so, too."

Tired from all of this, Joe rubbed his eyes. Neither said a word for a few minutes. Instead, they stretched out further on the couch. Without realizing it, they let all that had been said settle and find a way to rest deep into their bones. Joe turned toward Betsy. In a voice he never would have thought possible ten minutes earlier, he said, "This wedding thing. I think the date we chose is good. How about you?"

She stroked his chest. "Yeah, I think that will work."

"I love you." *I love you more than I can say.*

She felt God against her backbone, and knew this man and this wedding was totally right. "I love you, too."

CHAPTER FIFTY FIVE

She wore her hair piled high on her head. Maybe she'd opt for some curls later—on the big wedding day, of course—but that didn't matter now. This was just the dress shopping day. But oh, how she had been looking forward to trying on gowns of all shapes, shades and sizes. The instant she set her eyes on this dress, she just totally, completely knew. "That one."

Standing on a heavy wooden box to give her height, she positioned herself in front of a well-lit three-way mirror. As she waited for her mom and the shopkeeper to bring her the dress so that it could be held up in front of her, Iris took an appreciative glance at her long, slender neck. The little pearl necklace that showcased a garnet flanked by diamonds, a must have on her last birthday, was just the right touch today. Yes, she liked what she saw.

"Ready?" The shopkeeper asked as she entered the dressing area with the dress Iris chose draped over both arms.

"Yes!"

The shopkeeper presented the little lady with what had been showcased in one of the little shop's two front windows, an elegant, soft lace A-line dress with a beaded bodice. The owner of the store, a young mom herself, shared what was true: the pale yellow shade with the miniature cluster of dainty yellow roses centered just below the neckline highlighted the little girl's coloring perfectly.

Iris would hear none of this flattery. She turned to the one person whose opinion mattered.

"Joe," she asked, her voice coming across as surprisingly firm, "What do you think? Is this pretty enough for you?"

From a seat against the wall, Joe answered. "It's absolutely, positively pretty. You, gorgeous, will look wonderful in this dress."

Excited, Iris turned and jumped. "Can I try it on? Can I try it on?"

"Look," Vanessa said as she studied the flowing fabric, "There's just a little bit of a twinkle in this long dress part."

Iris stated matter-of-factly, "They are my diamonds. My dress has diamonds."

"Well, we have to see how this dress will fit you, my darling." Kristen started to walk back to a dressing room with her daughter. "It has to be comfortable on you, right?"

Iris answered like any girl who was in love with Joe would answer. "No, it doesn't."

"Iris, you have to wear the dress for *the whole day.*"

"This is the dress for the whole day."

When Iris and Kristen closed the dressing room door, Vanessa sat beside Joe and smiled. "Even if that dress with its crinoline feels like a burlap sack when it is on, I bet that little girl will say it's comfortable."

Joe, who at first felt roped into this all girl outing, agreed.

"Anything for you." Vanessa tapped his arm. "She adores you."

Knowing the feeling was mutual, Joe nodded. Settling further into a chair built more for looks than comfort, he folded his fingers over his lap. He decided to joke. "Now who is Carolyn?"

Not following, Vanessa barely shook her head.

"You said Carolyn. 'Even if that dress with all its Carolyn feels like a burlap sack when it is on…'"

Vanessa now knew Joe was kidding.

Joe asked again. "Who is Carolyn?"

She rolled her eyes. "It's crinoline. The fluffy stuff under the dress that makes it full is called crinoline."

"Yeah." Joe pretended he didn't hear her. "Who is Carolyn?"

"The one who makes dresses fluffy."

Joe crossed his leg over his knee. "This sounds complicated."

Thinking men like Joe should never be in places like this, she added, "Oh, it is. It really is."

"Every fluffy dress?"

"Every fluffy dress."

"Fluffed."

"Fluffed."

"Wow." Joe's eyes popped in astonishment. "That's a lot, isn't it?"

Happy to be included today, even if it did mean enduring conversations with the goofball beside her, Vanessa glanced at her watch. "Maybe by the time Iris comes out, Betsy will be here. Yes? Did she say why she is running late?"

"Betsy told me that Carolyn needs a little help."

"The future Mrs. Joseph O'Dell is not a fluffer. Everyone knows that."

"But everyone can at least *try*."

"Everyone but Betsy."

"You have a point."

The two paused to listen to Iris giggle excitedly through the closed changing room door.

When it was quiet again, Joe chuckled. "My girl."

Vanessa turned to Joe. "So, did Betsy say what's keeping her?"

"No, not really. She said she's run into someone she hasn't seen in a long while, and will talk with me about it when she catches up to us. We're to head on to lunch if this dress passes."

Vanessa remembered her own dress shopping. The feeling here was what she experienced herself all those months ago. "Oh, this will pass."

Joe sat back and failed to hide a tight-lipped grin.

"What?"

He remembered the look in Iris's eyes when the dress was held up in front of her. "She does love that dress."

"She loves you."

"Yeah?"

"Yeah."

Joe leaned forward and looked at Vanessa before he stared at the space in front of him. "And you know what?"

Vanessa smiled because she could feel what he was going to say next. "I love her."

"I know. It's pretty obvious."

Reaching into his pocket, he pulled out his phone and sent a message to Betsy. *In love with another woman. If you still want me, hurry. She makes me look tall.*

It was a perfect fit and the late summer sale price helped. Vanessa offered to buy the dress, but Kristen wouldn't hear of this. "Even if this were over budget, I see us getting a lot of wear out of this dress. It's well-made, hand washable, and the autumn tea party season is in full swing."

They both looked down the hall behind the cash register. Iris had been in the bathroom for a long time.

Some soft yellow headpieces on a nearby counter caught Kristen's and Vanessa's eyes. As Vanessa bought one as a later surprise for Iris, Joe sat down again, wondering where Betsy could be. An uneasy feeling turned his stomach. Joe sensed she was with a guy, and the conversation between them jarred Betsy. And then Joe knew, he just knew.

She was with Tad.

Too many minutes passed. Kristen knocked on the bathroom door. There was no response from Iris. Since the door was unlocked, she entered and found it empty.

"Oh, no."

Kristen's voice didn't raise the greatest alarm, but it was enough to rush Joe into standing right beside her.

Don't panic, Kristen told herself. *Iris is a good, smart girl.*

Standing nearest the dressing rooms, Vanessa said she'd check there.

Joe moved past the cash register. "I'll look through the store."

A minute later, an exit door near the bathroom was the only place left to look. According to Kristen, Iris wouldn't use that door because the little girl knows the word 'exit' and not to leave a store without her mom. Kristen pushed on the exterior door with some difficulty. Iris couldn't have used this. It was too difficult to open. Nevertheless, Kristen walked through the door just to check. Nothing prepared Kristen for what she was about to see. The blood curling scream from the back alley rocketed Joe through the rear door. Kristen screamed again and again.

"No, no, no, no, no!" She shouted. This was a nightmare she couldn't be seeing.

But it was.

"Oh God, no! You can't take my daughter!"

By a large green Dumpster, a half dozen bees swarmed over her lifeless daughter whose neck already had swelled to the size of a softball. Kristen sank to her knees and, doubling over, slapped the blacktop. "No! I cannot lose another baby! I cannot!"

Joe spotted the bee's nest. It was no significant threat. Bending over the little girl however, he couldn't hear Iris's breath.

Of all of the things to think of now, Kristen remembered sitting with Joe on her front step. They were talking about how he'd ask Betsy to marry him. Suddenly, she knew who Joe *really* was. "You save her!"

Joe shot her a look of fear.

"You save her. I cannot lose this one, Joseph. SAVE HER!"

He felt for her pulse. Iris had one, yet the swelling had increased in the fifteen seconds he had been leaning over her. He could not get air into her four-year-old lungs.

"SAVE HER, JOE!"

Joe heard his own heartbeat, steady and strong. For a second, it was as if he was watching this scene from a slight distance. A voice within or above said, *Go back inside the store. Under the cash register is an emergency kit. It contains an EpiPen. Get it. Stab Iris in the thigh with it quickly. Go now.* Like a robot, Joe did exactly what he had been told to do. When the swelling receded just a bit, Joe breathed into Iris's mouth successfully this time. He tilted his head to bring his ear to her mouth. Faintly, she began breathing on her own. Though he could make out that the shopkeeper and Vanessa were talking wildly, and could see that Kristen was crying, the wail of the approaching ambulance siren was the next sound he heard.

⸻

Dunk knew exactly what had happened. He heard the full report from Vanessa before he arrived at the hospital. With Iris now admitted upstairs, he walked outside the ER's sliding glass doors where he met Joe. "You saved her."

"God did."

Dunk set his hands into his front pockets. "You both did."

Joe stopped in front of little yellow mums and mini pumpkins that were a new part of the well-maintained landscaping around this momentarily quiet entrance. Thinking of Iris's dress, Joe could barely feel the words come out from his mouth. "He just told me, dad. He just told me what to do. He sent me right to where that kit is kept, and to that EpiPen."

Dunk shared what he had heard from Vanessa. "Even the shopkeeper didn't know that emergency kit contained an EpiPen. Another minute or two more and…"

Staring at the flowers, Joe knelt down. "He talked to me, dad. He did. He even told me how to use the EpiPen."

Dunk turned and, facing the opposite direction from his son, sat on the sidewalk. Holding his hands, he said, "Praise God from whom all blessings flow."

"He really did talk to me, dad."

Quietly Dunk repeated what he had just said. "Praise God from whom all blessings flow."

Joe dropped down on a nearby metal park bench. When his dad moved to sit beside him, Joe knew he wasn't going to share where Betsy was, or who she had spent time with today. Joe could see Tad's face through Betsy's eyes. They were at the Dairy Barn, and he was suddenly telling her about love.

Dunk was surprised when Joe suddenly popped up.

"We should go, dad."

"You just sat down."

Joe started walking toward where he had parked his car.

"Joe, you okay?"

Holding his keys, he turned. "I should go, I mean."

"You're not making sense."

Neither is what Tad is saying.

CHAPTER FIFTY SIX

She picked up her phone message and read the following out loud. *In love with another woman. If you still want me, hurry. She makes me look tall.*

The man with Betsy considered this. "Are you going to hurry?"

Betsy considered this.

She thought about sending Joe a message back and wondered if she should give the one she loved a clue about this sudden, unexpected surprise guest. Quickly, she decided it would wait until they were face-to-face. With speed she typed: *You sure you can afford her?* Then she deleted the message, and started again. *So sorry to miss the dress shopping. Catch you at the restaurant. Will explain ASAP.*

After watching their nearly invisible server pass by, Tad noticed she was still looking at her phone. "You okay?"

"Am I okay with the message I just sent, or with you being here?"

"I meant with the message, but I guess with my being here, too."

Betsy nodded. Nervous, she still wasn't sure why Tad had unexpectedly come all this way from Florida to talk with her. "Yes."

Tad nodded. "Yes, to which?"

Before Betsy could answer, Tad shook his head. He still couldn't believe how beautiful she looked. Pregnancy made her glow. All his desires were even greater now. "And you told him it was me you're meeting."

She lied. "Yes."

"Well, thank you. Thank you for meeting with me. I know this is *really* a surprise."

Wondering why Tad wanted to come to a restaurant rather than talk outside her condo where they had met ten minutes ago, Betsy folded her hands over the Dairy Barn menu. She hoped it made her appear calm and composed.

"Yeah, right." Tad shifted in his seat. "Well, I said I wouldn't take much time, so I won't. I also said I'm glad for this face-to-face time. Again, thank you."

"You're welcome."

His fingers actually shook, which he had hoped wouldn't happen. "I said I would *not* be nervous for this. I have this all practiced out, too. On the flight, I went over this a million times."

Truly looking at him, she realized so little time had passed since she'd seen him last. Somehow, pieces of the two of them together had not changed at all. "Tad, we've known each other for a long time. And we've been close, so just speak. I'm listening."

Gracious, even now.

"Okay, I'll just say it, all of it. My wife Fiona and I will be getting a divorce. Her baby isn't my baby. Now, it could have been, but a paternity test is conclusive. The man she wants to be with asked for the test, and, sure enough, he is the father of her four-month-old baby boy. They are together now, and they plan to get married as soon as the divorce is finalized."

Betsy couldn't believe what she was hearing. "Oh, my."

"This is for the best, Betsy. Fiona and I were not working. We tried. We did. In that time, honest and committed, I've learned a lot about her and a lot from her, and she's just great, she is; but I'm in love with another woman. I have always been in love with another woman."

Setting her hands on the top of her stomach, she could feel what he was talking about. From the way he couldn't meet her in the eyes, she knew who he was talking about.

"I tried to forget you. I tried to move on. It was the right thing to do, right? We had broken up. We were over. Done. Finished. That one night we were together shouldn't have happened. But I needed you. Need you. And, like that, you were there. That night for me was a dream, a dream come true."

Tad looked straight at her. His bright green eyes seemed to open in a way that startled her. The college playboy disappeared. "I know I come across as some Casanova, some hot shot, some guy who juggles women for sport, but this is what I did: I tried with Fiona. I did. I shouldn't have slept with her. I *definitely* shouldn't have married her. But she was hurting too, deep down. And like me, she was lonely. When we met, Fiona and I were two broken hearts learning and moving on from our pasts. We were going to make it work."

Betsy didn't know what to say. This wasn't really happening, was it? She wanted to reach across and touch him at the elbow, but she kept her hands still.

"You don't have to say anything, Betsy. I know. I mean, I can see it. You and Joe? You're really together now."

"Yes."

He locked his heart in a tight box. It couldn't break in front of her. "I think it was right to tell you this, from my side. She's our baby, and someday she needs to know all of this."

"Tad, how do you know she's a girl?"

"Fiona, when pregnant, always honed in on clues. She did teach me a lot." He suddenly realized that a passerby here in this ice cream place could think—even for a moment—that they are the couple, and he was happy. He looked at her in a way he had never done before. "And Betsy, let me tell you, you are all pink inside."

"We are all pink inside."

At twenty-five, Tad frowned the first permanent wrinkle on his forehead.

"Yes, Tad, someday she will need to know about this year in our lives. I don't think we should keep this from her."

"Thank you."

"And I won't keep you from her, either. We talked about this months ago. For her wellbeing, she will know who her father is. No secrets. No surprises."

Tad changed directions. He couldn't have too much hope for being back in Betsy's life too soon, but he had to ask this question. "Are you going to marry Joe?"

"We are engaged."

He tried not to slump like he had been shot, but his strong, wide shoulders sank. "You two have the date set?"

"It's soon."

"Before the baby arrives?"

She worried how to answer.

"You can keep it factual here, Bets."

Bets. The name Joe calls me. "Yes. We are getting married in nine days."

"This doesn't have to be hard on you. You didn't know I was coming. It's a complete shock. I just didn't want to tell you any of this over the phone."

"So you flew up from Florida."

"Yes. You needed to see my face when I tell you this. I married a woman I didn't love."

Betsy still could not believe this.

Tad had to make this right. He had to be man about it, and let her finally go. "Betsy, as the mother of our child, marry the one you love. And take my blessing on that marriage."

He could not look her in the eye. "You also need to hear what you already know, and that is I love you, that I have always loved you, and will always love you. Joe or no Joe, that won't change here for me."

"Tad."

"I want to wish you the best, Betsy. I do. Marriage can be a wonderful thing. There are a few surprises coming your way when you realize this isn't for wimps, but you'll be a great wife. I know this."

Betsy couldn't say a word. She knew Tad, of course she did, but this was a new guy, a changed guy.

Keeping all his emotions under his control, Tad pressed on hoping to make this well with Betsy for her sake. "I'm not surprised that you are with Joe. The wedding in a week and a half? That's a little…well, I actually understand that, too. Had I known you were getting married,

I would have waited. This might have been easier for you after the wedding."

"I just can't quite see how you can be so caring. I imagine a lot of guys would be bitter, or angry, or..."

He leaned forward and flashed the most charming smile she had ever seen him wear. "I love you. I want what is best for you. I will always want what is best for you. If that was to be with me, if you were to be with me, wow, my world would soar. Literally, I would fly. And fly forever. But that's not how this is to be. Love is always good, Bets. Always. From every angle. Including mine here today. I'm going to be a great dad."

"You are not the man you were."

"No, I'm not. These months have taught me a lot." He set his elbows on the table and lowered both his head and his voice. "At one point two months ago, I was married and the brand new father of a baby boy. Now that's all gone."

"It is gone?"

"Yes. Fiona and her husband-to-be are off in Seattle."

"Oh."

"But I have a daughter. You need to know that's really important to me. And I'm not jumping from one situation to the other—from one baby to the other. I have learned a lot. I have changed. Love can do that." Tad opened his sports jacket and from an inside pocket handed Betsy a white envelope.

"What?" she asked.

"It's either a really big wedding present, or it's security for our daughter's future."

"Tad."

"Look inside."

"Tad?"

Before a flash of pain showed, he nodded.

She opened the envelope. It was a check for thirty thousand dollars.

"Tad."

"Except for those first three checks I gave you—checks which you have not cashed—I haven't given you a cent since you've been pregnant. It's yours. All four checks are yours. Use them for whatever you need."

She felt completely overwhelmed, but she couldn't be now. Setting her fingers just on her eyebrows, she took a deep breath. "Tad."

"Yeah?"

Betsy wanted her life to be simpler, clearer. "What I need is peace between you and Joe. I don't know how he's going to take all of this. The courtship he and I have had, from both sides, hasn't always been easy."

He looked at his check that she set on the table. "Maybe this will help then. I want what is best for you." With that, he stood. "Remember, I said I wasn't going to take up a lot of your time. I meant that. We just needed to have this conversation face-to-face."

"Tad, don't go."

"For me, I have to. At least for a while. I have more things I need to settle in my life after hearing what I have today. But it will be okay." He bent down and kissed her on the forehead. "I will call you in a few weeks. Same number, right?"

"Yes."

"Okay, we'll talk more after your wedding, which I trust is going to be one great event for all times. Now, I need to get out of your way."

"I'm not taking this check."

"Then don't. Give it to our baby."

"Tad!"

He pivoted and stepped away quickly. From a space of about ten feet, she could see his tears when he turned back one last time. "You be a beautiful bride."

With that, he was gone. As fast as he arrived today, he was gone.

CHAPTER FIFTY SEVEN

Distracted before, Betsy now realized she recognized the name of the server. It was Ben, a young man Joe had mentioned. Several times Joe shared with Betsy a feeling he had around Ben, who had started working almost a year before he did. It was one of deep sorrow. Looking at him standing across the dining area, she picked up the same sensation. She glanced back at the empty chair Tad had left. So much had just happened, and she didn't know where she'd begin to tell Joe about this afternoon's meeting.

Putting everything on a shelf for the time being—really, how would she walk through all of this?—she knew what she had to do right now. She double-checked her emotions through a quick prayer. *God, you've given me this thought. It isn't one I would have come up with on my own. Guide me through this. May it bring light to what I've just seen and realized. Amen.*

Not waiting a moment, she caught Ben's attention. When he was standing in front of her, she forced her eyes away from the burn scar on his neck. She strengthened herself within so she could be clear with him. "Ben, listen. I know you work with Joe sometimes."

"Hi."

"Yes, hi." Betsy rolled her eyes. She had heard that Jolie jumped into the middle of conversations sometimes. Now she had done it, too. "Yes, hi. I should have lead with that."

"That's okay."

Betsy shook her head. She backed up by introducing herself, but

Ben, who could not ignore the large swell of her belly, figured out who she was immediately.

Small talk was not Ben's strength, so after a minute of talking about Joe, the weather, and the day, Betsy moved to her point. "I have a question for you. If, if I give you a big tip, I mean enough gas money to get you to our wedding and back, would you please come to the wedding?"

The nineteen-year-old, who hid between his twin bed and the wall again last night, did not expect her question at all. Something in the way he reacted struck her. It made her realize why she suddenly invited this stranger to something as small and as intimate as her wedding. Without quite knowing why, she realized Ben reminded her of Mike in some way. She sensed what she had missed too many years ago: there was a deep hurting under the surface, and she wanted—no, she needed—to do what was right.

"Oh," she said, "you have to come. I'm so pregnant and not many people are going to support this spur of the moment thing, like my parents. I want you there. Please say yes."

Shy, he wanted to back away fast. "I…I…"

From her seat, she reached up and touched his hand. This was something she had never done before. An unfamiliar person she just met? Invited to her wedding? But the Holy Spirit was right. "Will you come? Please?"

She swallowed. What she was doing here was right, and yes, there certainly was a piece or part of Michael here. She was even more clear of that now. As she gave room for Ben to respond, she pictured the special box she kept under her bed. It was her Mike box. In it were details of her wedding that they had planned together in her treehouse. After a little time had passed, she gently tried her question again. "Ben, yes, you will come?"

Ben thought he would rather have a thousand pound rock on his chest. Table seventeen's order will be up any second. He still had to refill the drinks at table six. Then he remembered his pillow. Life was passing him by. "I…I don't know."

Nodding, she looked down and then wobbled to stand. She knew she was about to sound like a very big sister. "When a woman eight months pregnant asks you for something, what do you think you should do?"

"I don't know."

She smiled warmly and the kindness she extended landed somewhere within him. In a place inside of him that he didn't know too much about, he discovered something unfamiliar and new. The two connected.

"You've given the same response twice now."

"I have?"

Three twenty dollar bills filled his hand. "It's such short notice, I know, but it's also a sincere invitation. And Joe and I don't want a gift. No, not at all. This here is just gas money. We want you there." She reached for her phone. "I want you there."

Except for that redheaded woman who also gave him a super huge tip, he hadn't been touched like this before. It was odd, uncomfortable. "I'll think about it."

"Ben, thank you."

Outside the ice cream shop, she still clutched her phone. Looking for Tad's rental car which she knew was long gone, she thought of Joe and said out loud, "What am I going to say?"

CHAPTER FIFTY EIGHT

"The wedding is a yes, right?"

"What?"

Joe passed Ben who stood just out of the steam cloud from the Dairy Barn's boisterously loud, "don't-mess-with-me" dishwasher.

Ben spoke up. "What did you say?"

When Joe returned with jumbo mayonnaise jars in each arm, he made his question clearer. "The wedding and your being there for us? That's a yes, right?"

Ben's face flushed, and it wasn't from the heat of clean dishes. He hadn't answered affirmatively when Betsy invited him yesterday.

"Ben—"

"Yeah."

Joe stood with his backside to the double doors leading into the dining area. He waited an intentional moment before Ben's eyes met his. "Here it is, Ben. You do what you need to do. Seriously. We think it would be great if you shared the day with us, but whatever works for you—truth now—that's best. Just know how sincerely you are invited."

Ben didn't know what to think, let alone how to answer. Somewhere deep inside, he knew he was the problematic pup in the dog pound, the one not one wanted. This hardened him. He knew he was less trusting and even more unseen. Even now, next to the cool guy the waitresses all swarmed over, he was familiar only with being passed by, looked over.

He didn't remember shifting his glance or turning away for even half a second, but, just like that, Joe was gone. The only sign that the guy getting married actually stopped for a second to talk with him was that one of the double doors still swung open and closed.

Ben stared into nothing. Not so uneasy anymore—which was a first—he didn't stop thinking about Joe and Betsy's invitation as he stacked plates and filed silverware away for the next thirty minutes. Yes, he should just go for this. He should say 'yes' to this wedding, after all, he was sincerely invited not once but twice. Both the future bride and the future groom made it clear he was actually wanted. They seemed to see him. They seemed to be kind, too. Forcing himself to talk with people he didn't know and having a good time just might be a distant possibility. Okay, it was an unlikely and distant possibility, but why not?

Holding a single ice cream sundae glass, something suddenly dawned on him. He swallowed at what he realized—he liked his workmate Joe. Of course, he'd have a good time at this wedding. As he understood the invitation, there really wouldn't be a lot of people there, but maybe he'd meet someone, someone who would understand him. Maybe he could really talk to a new face about all the darkness he has been experiencing—or ignore the darkness altogether because this was, after all, a celebration. He almost smiled. Maybe this would be good. Yes, maybe this could be very good.

Joe popped back in as quickly as he did when fetching the mayonnaise. While out with the lunch time crowd who had packed the place today, he knew he was coming on all 'big brother' to his co-worker, but like Betsy, he could almost touch Ben's deep pain and loneliness. Joe only had a minute before he had to get back out there. He wanted to make the most of this time. He leaned against the stainless steel counter. "So, I want to ask you something."

"I'm thinking about the wedding."

Joe crossed his forearms just over his waist. "Something else."

"Something else? What?"

Joe thought of Tad, and while he was comfortable with the 'ex' meeting his fiancée, he found an angle where he could hopefully open Ben a bit more. Being theatrical, Joe frowned just a bit.

Ben took a bite into the set up. "What is it, Joe?"

"Yesterday, when Betsy was here, you saw the guy."

"What…what guy?"

"What guy?" Joe tried to be light and fun. "The guy Betsy was here with. Kinda big. Strong. Was he good looking?"

"Oh, him."

"Yeah, him."

"Is he competition?"

"You mean, should you be worried?"

"Yeah."

"Yes."

Joe unfolded his arms. "Don't hesitate there, buddy. Just lay it out."

Both turned their attention to the dishwasher because the grumpy metal monster spat as if really angry. When it quieted down, Ben, who had heard the machine curse at its contents many times before, leaned against the counter. "Very worried."

Joe played into this further. "While we're being so honest Ben, I have to say that I'm not so sure I like this open, candid quality you're wearin' here."

Ben stayed on task. "You should be very, very worried."

"Yeah, a bit more with me not liking the you-being-so-blunt thing."

"The truth hurts."

"Ouch."

Ben knew the truth here. He had seen how Betsy would sometimes pick Joe up from the Dairy Barn after work. He saw how she looked at him, how she kissed him. He did notice the other guy here yesterday, and he was big, broad, and handsome. Whatever he shared with her was intense. Ben knew the guy left broken-hearted because she was in love with Joe. Granted, Ben didn't know a whole lot about these things—and he certainly didn't listen as the ladies who worked here rambled on about their man troubles—but with Betsy it was clear. She wanted to be with the one she was going to marry.

Aware of the time, Ben started to wipe down the counter as Joe headed back to the double doors. Joe left and then immediately looped back into the kitchen. "Think I could take him, if, you know, there was trouble?"

"No."

"Ben, let me do this again. This deal with your being so honest here?"

"Yeah?"

Joe exited the door again but called out over his shoulder before it closed, "You may wanna curb that."

A pretty waitress named Wanda entered the kitchen through the door Joe didn't use. With that door open, Joe, who stood at the nearby cash register called back into the kitchen. "Yeah, you may just wanna let that one go."

⸻

Having clocked out, the two waited for their rides under a small, flat roof over the rear service door to the Dairy Barn. Puddles close to the size of Lake Ontario had begun to form in the back parking lot. It had been pouring for hours. Both were tired because customers never let up once the rain started around noon. "After all," their boss had said earlier, "what can young families do in a mini monsoon except watch a movie or have an ice cream outing?"

Standing just out of the rain now, Ben took a deep breath. He felt glad their shift had ended. He was also glad to see Wanda today. She was kind and attentive, and seemed like someone to get to know. And he was also glad to be close to Joe here in this private spot. Remembering the dishwasher's temper tantrum earlier, he realized this was the first easy feeling he has had in days.

Joe noticed. "That's nice to see."

"What is?"

Joe simply shrugged.

Ben found sharing space with someone uncomfortable, but Joe was different. The slightly older guy not only gave him just enough space, but also let him be who he was. Without thinking, Ben wondered about what Joe started. "What's nice to see?"

Turning to grab two hard plastic milk crates, Joe had planned for Ben's question. "You smiling, just being you."

Ben made a face like he didn't understand.

"You. When you're you, it's just a good thing to see." Joe moved two more crates so that a pair of makeshift seats were available to both of them. He took one. Both were damp from the rain blowing in under their cover, but he knew Ben had been on his feet all day. Hopefully, he would take the open seat. He wouldn't push it, though. Instead, he just prayed about it.

"I don't know what you mean, Joe."

Joe finished his time with God and rested his forearms on his thighs. "When you are you—when you are yourself—it's just…"

"It's just what?"

Joe glowed inside. *Keep him talking. Keep those words coming.* "It's just a blessing to watch."

Ben knew Joe went to the Bible College, though Joe himself never mentioned it. In fact, Joe didn't talk about his school, which Ben guessed Joe didn't finish. After all, what college graduate worked as a server or a busboy in a local ice cream shop? It was true Ben wasn't too sure of Joe. He couldn't figure the engaged guy out. For example, Joe didn't cram Jesus stuff down people's throats like he knew some of those church freaks did when they came to the Barn for dinner or dessert. Maybe Joe was one of those turned off by religion.

He frowned and barely shook his chin. "A *blessing?*"

"Yeah. You're a blessing. A gift."

"Okay, now you sound like that college you went to."

"What college?"

Ben kept his voice quiet and low. "That Bible one."

"You knew I went there? You checked me out?"

"Nah."

"You did! You checked me out!"

Ben looked down at his shoes which were getting wet. "No one talks like this. Blessing. Gift. You're weird, man."

Joe nodded. "From you, that means a lot." He checked Ben's

reaction, and before Ben could respond, Joe continued. "Seriously. From you, Ben, it means a lot."

"What do you mean?"

"You know, I'm an outcast."

Ben considered the seat beside his partner, but didn't take it. "Yeah, sure you are."

"I mean, there are a whole lot of people who do not get me. Who don't see me for who I am."

"You got a girl. You're getting married. That's pretty easy to see."

"Maybe I should say it this way. There was a time I didn't see who I was."

Ben drew his arms close to his sides. They warmed his upper body which was chilled by the rain that showed no signs of stopping. A warm feeling was also growing inside, if he paid attention to it.

"Yeah, I didn't see who I was. I didn't know who I was." Joe didn't move too fast. He just let his words settle.

Out of the habit of knowing how to retreat, Ben kept his eye in the direction of where cars would enter to pick them up back here. He was waiting for his mom. Yes, he had the chance to connect here, to make a new friend which was what that old guy with the peaches in the grocery store wanted, but he wanted what he knew—and what he knew was that he could go home and be alone, deeply alone.

Knowing this, Joe continued. "I hurt myself, Ben. I just did bad things because I thought I was a freak. Seriously. Who would want me if they *really* knew me?"

Ben listened. No one had talked with him like this. No one had made this much sense, either.

"I pushed people away. To do so, I actually hid for a long, long time. I especially hid from myself because, honestly, I didn't like who I was. I didn't like how I was made. I was different." Joe thought of showing Ben his scarred forearm, but knew Ben's scars were far deeper and far different on his soul. Joe closed his eyes to see all of his friend's damaged skin. He also saw the years of neglect from his mother and his grandmother. When he looked out again he said, "I see your scars, buddy. Not just the burn damaged skin on your neck and down under your shirt, but those scars you carry inside, too. You can say it in front of me. You're different."

Tears swelled. No one had been this present to Ben before. No one had been this blunt, this honest. That joke of a high school counselor could take a lesson off this guy who, as Ben could now see, had his own scar which, like his burns, still changed him, still hurt him.

"I am different." Ben continued. This time the words seeped down deeper, even more gently. "I am different."

Joe gave Ben's words all the space they'd never had, and the reverence they'd never received. He leaned forward, glanced at his comrade in the shallow shelter of the rainstorm, and then into the parking lot which was now filling up like a swimming pool.

"Yeah," Ben said a third time, "I am different."

"And that's cool. You are you. And again, when I get to see that? It makes me happy."

Ben was skeptical.

Joe paused before changing directions. "Favor?"

"What?"

"Can we talk more?"

"You wanna do the God stuff."

"Yeah. He loves you. And yeah, I would like to talk with you about being loved, plugged in, connected, at peace. I also like this time with you. We can talk God stuff; we can also just talk. Just us. Let's do it again soon. Alright? Now that I'm gonna be a married guy, I have to hang with someone on the free and single side."

Ben knew all about being single, detached.

Joe didn't look at him. "I have to be with someone who has known pain."

"Why?"

"So that it can be shared."

"Why?"

"So that it can be made better."

Through what was now a shallow ocean, Ben's mom arrived. Before getting into the car that had hard and mean edges like its driver, Ben stood still for a second at the passenger's side door. "And I'm coming to your wedding."

CHAPTER FIFTY NINE

Dunk raised his rented putter. Water rolled down his arm as he shook his head and hair free from the rain for only a moment. Triumphant, he stood at the final hole on the miniature golf course in what had been a steady downpour since Earl had picked up Joe at the ice cream shop for the start of this surprise bachelor party. Galvin stood beside him. Of the four, he was the only one wearing a baseball cap which made it a little easier to see the holes. This didn't help his game though. He finished third. Before the scorecard completely disintegrated, he rechecked the score with a little blue pencil and confirmed Dunk the winner. All four looked over the completely vacant miniature course and nearby parking area. Obviously, they were the only ones out here.

"One more time?" Joe offered, pulling his drenched shirt away from his chest. "This time we do it extreme. One hit after the other, no stopping. Fast. We just go. What do you say?"

Dunk laughed. "Extreme mini-golf? Is that a first?"

"I'm in," Earl said as he studied Dunk's smile. "Someone has to beat this clown."

The four started at four different holes in what truly was a great looking mini course with slopes, slants, two windmills, river rocks, two handsome wooden bridges and top-notch landscaping. For the next ten minutes, they just swung and swung, one hit after the other. Perhaps the only winner during this round was the one who laughed the most during the game, and that would make Galvin the victor.

Standing under the awning to return the rented putters and balls,

Joe admitted to the attendant who was Ben's age, "It's my surprise bachelor party tonight. We went twice. I hope you don't mind."

The teenage employee barely seemed awake. "We haven't been exactly busy, so that's okay."

A bead of rainwater ran down Joe's nose. "Thanks."

After handing Joe coupons for another outing here, the employee closed the short glass window after saying flatly, "I hope you enjoyed your bachelor party."

Dunk stood behind his son. "There's more."

Joe mopped his brow and beamed. "Really? We can go wash your car now?"

⸻

The rain had not stopped. All four stood in single file on Galvin's family's dock over a large lake an hour north of the miniature golf course. Soaking wet from their short walk from the cabin to the long, narrow dock, they had not yet been in the water. All four—Dunk, Earl, Galvin and Joe—were wearing similar navy swimming trunks.

Looking out over the six-acre private, spring-fed lake that was nearly polar bear cold as each day moved to close the chilling month of October, Joe shook his head at the three who were crazy enough to stand out here with him. He asked, "Did one of you plan on all this blue, or was this coincidence?"

"This is a tightly planned event," Dunk answered.

"Down to the finest detail," Galvin added.

"And the blue is symbolic of…of…what's the blue symbolic of again, Galvin?"

"Bachelorhood." Galvin tried to be quick on his feet.

"Bachelorhood?" Dunk asked before pointing out the obvious. "Uh, Joe is *getting married.*"

"So let's take the plunge," Earl said. "Jump!"

On the most senior's count of three, the four hit the air. One dove in, one somersaulted, and two cannonballed into the water.

———————

The roaring fire in the stone hearth of the family cabin felt good to all of them. The three had waited on the dock for Joe to finally get out of the water. Enough was enough. They needed to fill their bellies. The feast they had prepared succeeded at being simple yet delicious: tossed salad, London Broil, baked potatoes and late season squash, compliments of Jolie who planned the menu and prepped this meal and the following breakfast. Along with dessert tonight, which still remained a secret to the guys, she had filled two coolers in the back of Dunk's car.

Over the round table in one corner of the nine-hundred square foot cabin, Earl raised his mug of root beer a few minutes after Dunk shared grace. "To Joe. To his future wife. To many, many, many long and happy years together."

After they all drank, Galvin bumped Dunk's shoulder with his own, looked down and sounded both inward and reflective. "That was beautiful, Earl."

Sensing the humor, Dunk kept his eyes low and added, "I am truly fighting back the tears here, guys. The words of that toast? The phrasing? The emotion? It was all so genuinely, openly, unquestionably heartfelt."

Galvin nodded in agreement.

Dunk dabbed a finger under one of his dry eyes. "I'm...I'm nothing—absolutely nothing—shy of being verklempt."

"Yes," Galvin echoed. "That's it. Verklempt."

Holding his mug by its heavy handle, Earl stared at the guys and waited just the right amount of time before saying, "There is something to be said for getting to the point."

"What's that?" Galvin asked.

Earl frowned. "What? And use more words trying to explain?"

•————————————•

The fire glowed with low, red embers. All four swim suits, on a nearby indoor drying rack, remained damp. Dunk and Earl had crashed in the bedroom with the single beds. Joe opted for the couch out here in the main room. He was stretched out over one end of what could be turned into a sleeper bed. Galvin hunkered down on the other. As he had done since he left his house, Galvin pushed away what happened with his daughter and the bee stings. It was Joe's night, after all. The horrifying thoughts of what happened by that alley dumpster two days ago never moved far from him though, and this quiet didn't help.

Joe knew what was pressing on Galvin's mind. He prayed before he said, "You have a lot on your mind."

"I wonder what would have happened..." Galvin paused. Where Kristen could open up and talk, he was the quiet one.

Joe turned and opened his arm across the couch. He held Galvin with his eyes.

From that warm, tender, embracing look—something Galvin thought only Kristen could give to him—Galvin experienced something odd. Maybe it was the night itself that made this sensation possible, or the fact that he was here in his family's cabin which held both love and good memories. Maybe it was the comfort from the fire a few feet away. Maybe it was that he had not slept for more than two consecutive hours since his daughter had been hospitalized because he would always check on her, but he knew without question something wonderful: Joe understood what he had been thinking.

Joe tilted his head. "Just say it."

Galvin paused for a moment, and then spilled. "I wonder what would have happened had we just gone ahead and brought home that kitten we saw last week from the SPCA. Would my little girl still have gone after the stray one she saw through that bathroom window?"

Joe raised his shoulder. "She's very caring, Galvin. She might have still left the shop on her own search and rescue mission."

"You know, someone actually found that stray kitten."

Joe nodded. He pictured the little guy in front of a blue bowl filled with milk.

Galvin rubbed his tired eyes. He felt twenty years older than he actually was. "Joe, there's a lot of things I've been wondering about lately."

Rather than speak again, Joe simply waited.

"I still don't get how you knew where the medicine kit was. How could that even be possible? You'd never been in that store before. And, even if you had, a medicine kit? Under the cash register? And it just so happened to have an EpiPen in it?"

Joe remained quiet, enabling Galvin to unpack more of this.

"We owe you our lives, Joe. You know this, and you shouldn't be surprised by what I'm about to share. Kristen told me she let you in on all the miscarriages. We don't make that too public, but you know this. Had we lost our little girl? We would have been lost ourselves. Truly lost. Our lives would have been ruined. You need to hear that. You're our savior. We owe you our everything."

Joe ignored one of the words Galvin used. He just slid around it. "I just did what I heard."

"You heard?"

Joe stared into the glowing embers after one popped and hissed. "I heard where that medicine kit was. The message came from inside."

"From inside *you?*"

"I mean, it came from God. I heard from God."

Religion and faith practices to Galvin had always been bland and soft, never shattering. As a young student he barely paid attention to his Sunday school teachers because he always thought they were just as dull as the Episcopal Priests he endured growing up. He didn't know what to think, let alone say.

"That might sound a little crazy, Galvin. "But it's true."

Galvin stared at the fire but saw nothing. "God, He talked with you. He told you what to do."

"Yes."

"For my little girl, for my Iris, He...He talked to you." He rose from his end of the couch and gestured to the back of the cabin and the one full-sized bed in the remaining bedroom. "I...I should get...I should get going to bed here, Joe." He stopped at the door to the bathroom. "Sure about not turning that couch into a bed? It's really no trouble."

Joe stood and reached for a nearby comforter. "Sure. I'm fine."

Galvin set his hand on the nearby wall near a clock his grandfather made. He considered what he just heard. "God, He talked to you?"

"He did."

"Is He talking all the time?"

"Yes."

Galvin turned back and took several steps into the living area. "From the time Kristen and I learned about her, I knew our daughter was special, Joe. I could never explain it. I just knew it though. Something about that baby, that pregnancy. The others we lost."

"They are special, too."

Galvin nodded. It was this night, this cabin, this sleeplessness, and this closeness with a guy he'd only seen before at a distance that made this possible. Not even with Kristen could he share what he was going to share with his couch mate.

Joe brought his knee up to his chest. He wrapped his arms around his shin and gave Galvin a look of great care. "Just say it."

"I miss them, you know? I miss them. And I talk to them, too. I think how old they'd be. Each of them. I'm the father of four."

"I know."

"What is God saying?"

"He's saying that you're a good dad."

"Can you be sure?"

From his dad's backyard, Joe thought of all the times he watched from a distance this man in front of him explore, share and play with Iris. "Oh, yeah, I'm sure. You, Galvin, are a good dad."

CHAPTER SIXTY

It was nothing short of a fairytale room. Elegant, softly patterned curtains reminiscent of cotillion dresses in the Old South swayed over large bay windows. In addition to this romantic flair, a four-poster bed fit for a queen made her feel important and pampered, if only for a day. A Depression era baby carriage holding a hundred-year-old porcelain doll greeted her in the soft morning light.

Betsy stretched out over the soft bedding that enabled her and her baby to sleep so well last night. She nestled her head back into a pillow that must have been made just for her. She closed her eyes again, and feeling content, sighed a deep, happy sigh.

It was Vanessa who came to her condo last night and informed her that Joe would be off with the boys on a men's night out. Taking her by the hand, she officially welcomed her to her bridal and baby shower. Vanessa had thrown Betsy a sweet, thoughtful baby shower two months ago, so Betsy didn't quite understand what this shower was all about.

"Sure," Vanessa said under her umbrella as they made their way to her car after Betsy had packed just enough things for an overnight. "That was a baby shower. This is a bridal and baby shower. There's a difference."

From the bed, Betsy opened her eyes to the ten-foot ceilings over her. She thought back on how this all came about as a surprise to her. Just yesterday, she learned the idea for this bridal and baby shower actually came from Jolie who booked three rooms at a nearby Bed and Breakfast weeks ago. Along with Vanessa and Jolie, whose room was next door, Earl's daughters, Jenna and Jackie, were here at the end of the hall. Last night at a dinner for five, Jolie shared very quietly and privately that Betsy's mom was not able to make this night. Betsy nodded gracefully, but knew the truth. Marrying a convict without a degree or a full-time professional career did not sit well with either her mom or her dad. Add to that the fact that she was carrying a beach ball in her belly and it was fair to say that neither parent would change their mind within the next five days. They would not be attending this small circus of a wedding. Saved from thinking more about that, she heard a gentle knock on her door. Jolie swept in carrying a delightful tray of breakfast treats and goodies.

"Look at me, just making myself at home here," Jolie announced near the door after knocking only once. "Did you even invite me?"

Betsy smiled. "I'm not sure, but you're definitely welcome."

Jolie stood beside the tall bed. Setting a full tray of breakfast food down in front of the woman of honor, the child in her clearly could be seen. "You'll have to taste everything. I already did downstairs. You're eating for two so you can eat everything, and then more."

Betsy slid her hand across the rich covers to hold Jolie's forearm. "This, this is wonderful. All of this."

Jolie suddenly remembered Dunk's wedding, and how happy she was for her best friend that day. Through Dunk, she had known little Joey since he was in diapers. In seeing this woman with the soft skin and inviting eyes, the very one who will marry the boy she has watched grow into a man, a realization overcame her. Weddings were not a time of loss; they were all about the gain. For Jolie, it was this girl with breakfast here. She'd be family soon. Jolie might never marry, and that was okay. She had this.

Betsy sat up. "What are you thinking?"

Jolie's eyes watered but she batted the drops away without a thought. "You said this is wonderful. You should know something. You are wonderful. We all want you to know how loved you are, and how special this time is for all of us." She lifted a lid off a plate of eggs

Benedict and ham slices. "God, for this food and the blessings of last night and today, we give you thanks. Amen."

"Thank you."

"Now eat!"

——————————

Along with Kristen, Betsy's old college roommate joined the party just after ten that morning. This was Betsy's third wedding gown shopping attempt. Those with her thought she had just been to one boutique, but she had actually been to two. Nothing was going well. Wearing a dress she hated, the third in thirty minutes, she stared at her belly and then at the train of the gown that, at a glance, looked like a three dozen rolls of bathroom tissue meet a Vegas showgirl costume. *This isn't how I imagined feeling on my wedding day. Nothing about this massive white thing is me. I'm lost in this overwhelming vanilla fluff and I don't know how to get out.*

The compliments were kind and generous. Of the three she had worn this morning, this one was the best in places—yet the worst overall. In the mirror, Betsy looked into her own eyes and all was revealed. "No, no. I can't do this." She started to break down. "I can't shop for this. I can't do this. I know Kristen has a bathrobe I can wear. It's white, which by the old rule books is not the color I am supposed to wear. And we'll get some volleyball net for a veil. I know you're trying—you're all trying—but I can't! I can't! This..." She didn't want to make a scene. By no means did she want to be a drama mama in a dress that cost as much as one very nice honeymoon.

Vanessa came to the rescue. "We just need to stop for now. All of this." She stood near the sales associate who had pushed a little too much. "We're going to say goodbye to this for now. We'll think about some ideas and options later. Isn't that right, Betsy?"

How can one person understand me so well?

Kristen remembered her place in front of mirrors similar to these, on a day much like this. Her wedding gown shopping went much worse, and she did not have the obstacle of a baby bump. In the end, Kristen realized, it was just a dress. Her mother and sister, charged with being super shoppers, had blown the selection event over the top. The stress was a nightmare.

"Yes," Kristen continued. "Let's get this off of her. Of course this is not Betsy. This is a good try, but it's not who this beautiful woman is."

No one panicked that in five days a woman eight months pregnant had to wear something to her own wedding.

CHAPTER SIXTY ONE

Earl held over the open car door a charming umbrella that Jenna and Jackie, true to their talents, had tastefully adapted and adorned about an hour ago, when it was certain the wedding in the park would be a wet one. Guests who had not seen the bride would be amazed how the umbrella actually highlighted most of the elements of her dress. Earl knew how Janet, who was not so far away today, would be so proud of her daughters' talents.

Holding the hand Earl extended, Betsy slowly began to exit a car that originally had not been intended to carry the bride. In fact, Ben thought the RR stood for Rolls Royce. No one told him they were actually Roland Rolls' initials. What mattered most was that the teen had come through on Betsy and Joe's invitation, and stood with the other guests under the tent.

Dunk, the best man, leaned into his son's ear. "Here comes the great unveiling of the dress, Joe. She's an absolute beauty."

As Betsy finally emerged from the car, Joe could not believe what he saw. His bride was amazing, beautiful, and stunning. She was perfect. In an elegant, golden gown with ivory trim and a high, intricate collar, Betsy stood still in the soft light of the moment. The bride's maid of honor, Betsy's college roommate, arranged the flowing veil behind a dress that was one third Elizabethan, one third fitted modern bride, and one third completely, utterly Betsy.

The name of Kristen's college theater professor came to her when she helped Betsy out of that last bridal monstrosity a few days ago. Two

phone calls and two hours later, a theater costume designer met the
bride-to-be in her home, and three days and three fittings later created
a dream dress, splendidly personal and utterly, magically, breathtaking.
On this gentle, rainy afternoon where the mist itself came to cover the
quiet, romantic location, this stunningly gorgeous bride arrived like
the sun. After being speechless for a full forty seconds, Joe's only word
was, "Wow."

With Earl at her side, Betsy floated up the short aisle laden with
flower petals Iris scattered a moment earlier. Jolie had found a way to
be licensed to marry couples. Holding a Bible, Jolie shared words she
never fully scripted in order to let the ceremony flow poetically without
pause. At the right time, Dunk handed Betsy's ring to Joe, and, with
Jolie's nod, Joe shared the vows he created himself.

He met his love squarely in the eye. "Today I say to God and to
the world that I promise my love forever to this woman I love, Betsy."

His voice changed. After he looked at those closest to him—
Vanessa, Earl, and Iris—it softened. His eyes again settled on his bride,
as he spoke to her alone.

"From the very day we met here, right here in this state park, I have
known a world through you that has always held hope. In ways I could
not name or explain, you have been a light to me in my dark times. You
fill my soul. You complete me. Even when we are not together, you are
never far away. Today, with this ring, I promise to support you for the
rest of my life. I promise to be there when you rise and when you fall,
when you need help and when you need to go alone. I will hear you. I
will hold you. I will never forsake you in sickness and in health, in our
good times and in our bad."

Joe slid the ring onto Betsy's finger. "Yes, this ring, blessed by God
and those here, stands as an unending circle and my unending love to
you, my friend, my love, and my life. With this ring, I marry you."

Betsy turned to Jolie who nodded to her maid of honor. Holding
Joe's ring, she said, "I have never told you this before. But no guy
measures up, except, of course, Mike, who is with us both as I share
these words to you. Somehow, by the grace and goodness of God, you

knew how, and where, to reach me with the place you chose to ask me to marry you, the treehouse. You found the place where I was the safest. You made sure, in your direct way, to hold me not just in the present, but in the past. This will make our future secure.

"I have learned so much with you, and beside you. You're my hero. I know—inside—you're shaking your head at that, but I also know that you have the tenacity of no one I have ever met. When I look at you today, Joseph, I see only you: tender, soulful, capable, unique, individual and wonderful. With this ring in my hand, a ring that I will never hold again, I promise that I will love you all the days of my life and somehow beyond this life. I will listen to you, run with you, support you, and dream dreams that are both yours and ours. I will grow with you in stature and wisdom. I will speak the words we need to hear openly and honestly."

Betsy slid the ring onto Joe's finger. "So wear this always, my husband, and know, without any doubt, that this unites us. Two souls are now one, even when death parts us."

Jolie said, "Joe, you may kiss the bride."

———————

The photographer, a former high school student of both Dunk and Jolie, didn't know who Roland Rolls was. This somewhat odd guy was not one the couple mentioned having their picture taken with, but brides and grooms couldn't think of everything, could they?

With Joe busy with his groomsmen, Roland held Betsy's hand when the two met for the first time. "You are beautiful. There has never been a more stunning woman on her wedding day."

"Thank you."

"You know who I am."

Betsy's words were measured. "Yes, I do. Mr. Rolls. And we are glad you could be here with us today. This is a day of beginnings. This marks a new chapter, one I call healing and hope."

Roland tilted his head and tried to ignore all his social interaction phobias. Today, he was determined to conquer them. To do so, he kept looking into Betsy's eyes. "When I said that you were beautiful, I did mean what I said. I also mean what I feel, and what I feel is your warmth from within."

Joe shook Roland's hand. "I am glad you are here."

The groom's words were so authentic they rendered Roland speechless.

Joe looked at his bride. "My wife is right when she said that this is a new chapter, one of healing and hope."

Roland could not stay in the moment. It was too much. He had work to do. Reaching into the pocket inside his jacket, he said, "Here is an address." He handed Joe a heavy card. It was a house number on a well-established street, several blocks from Betsy's condo. "It's new construction as well, and—of all things—I found that it has rocks for the long, sloping front lawn." He looked to Betsy and then Joe. "Big rocks."

Neither Betsy nor Joe knew what to say.

"This is your address. Your house."

"Mr. Rolls?"

"Joe, it's Roland." Before Joe could speak, Roland continued. "I didn't plug in any calculations as to whether you'd accept this wedding gift, or even *if* you'd accept this wedding gift. Imagine that. There is one stipulation to this heartfelt gift, however." Roland could hear his heart beating so fast in chest. "From time to time, I would like to see you. Visit you."

Joe couldn't speak.

Roland held the side of Joe's arm. "This is all new on one of the biggest days of your life. Do nothing more than just think about it for now."

Joe nodded.

Roland never predicted what he was about to say. Seeing these two newlyweds, he realized an error. "Wait, there is no stipulation here from me."

"Roland?" Joe asked.

"I actually misspoke. The house is yours regardless. It's time for your happiness, on your terms."

"But you'd like to see us?"

"Yes, I'd like to see you."

Aware of the schedule, the photographer moved the three of them into position. "Alright, on three, let's see a smile. One. Two. Three."

———•———

Near the site where the vows were exchanged, Dunk found Roland alone. He knew the scientist was counting the minutes until he could successfully, politely leave. Even small crowds were too much for him. Dunk knew he didn't have much time.

"It means a lot that you're here, Roland. I'm proud of you."

Roland asked something Dunk never would have guessed. "Have I done alright here? I haven't embarrassed him, have I? I haven't caused hardship or heartache?"

"No."

Roland's shoulders visibly relaxed.

Dunk would like to offer Roland a drink, but didn't dare. There were lines, boundaries, he knew he could not cross for the sake of Roland's ease and comfort. In slowly walking side by side, the two men found themselves at the opening to a path that led away from the other guests. Without too much thought, Roland followed half a step behind Dunk who, after a moment, slightly turned and asked, "Can I ask you something? Something personal?"

Roland's eyes flickered with a flash of anxiety.

"It's just a question. And you don't have to answer it now. You don't even have to answer it in front of me, but somewhere, sometime, I'd like to hear how you'd respond to this."

"Alright."

"Through Joe, what have you learned about yourself?"

Roland's eyes were completely still until he swallowed. "Had you asked me, 'Through Joe, what have I learned?' and left your question at that, I could supply you with enough material to keep you reading the rest of your life."

"But I didn't ask that."

"No, you didn't."

Dunk eyed Vanessa talking with Iris. He smiled at the woman he married not so long ago. From this new vantage point, he took in the sights of Jolie setting her arm on Earl's, and Jenna and Jackie buzzing about like servers. Turning just a bit, he saw Galvin and Kristen sharing a piece of wedding cake on one plate with two forks. "So, if you can, or when you can, please share. I would like to know what have you learned about yourself through all of this?"

Roland looked to his shoes which were much too wet. Nine broken or fragmented grass blades covered the tops and sides of both of them. The smell of six foods was too great, it was far too noisy, and the wafting scent of perfume from not one but both of Earl's daughters was unmistakably too much.

He tried to break through all of these distractions.

"Roland?"

"The truth?"

"The truth."

Keeping his eyes low, Roland answered, "I've learned, however scary it is, and how unpredictable, that I can love." With what he said, he knew he had to go. Now. Enough was enough. He couldn't handle more, and Dunk understood this.

"I'll walk you to your car."

"It's that obvious?"

"No, I just know you."

Under umbrellas, they walked together to the parking area. As soon as Roland's driver spotted the two, the car silently moved toward them.

Dunk faced Roland. "I will tell him that you love him."

"No, friend. Save those words for me."

CHAPTER SIXTY TWO

"Whoa! Has anyone ever said that you look *a lot* like Jesus Christ?" The hotel clerk stared at Joe. "If he had no beard like you, that is. Not that anyone really knows what JC looks like or anything. I mean like some earlier German artists or like Arians or someone like that would say he's all blond-haired and blue-eyed, and that's totally not your look at all, man."

"Yeah." Joe glanced over the counter. Thinking how his wife may want to get off her feet, he wondered how much longer this check-in would take. He'd just wanted to spend quiet time with the one he just married.

"I should look up Christ images online. I bet I'd find photos of you."

Joe nodded before turning back to his wife who had found a seat and ottoman that showcased her long, beautiful legs sliding out from a short blue dress that matched the color of her eyes perfectly. Not lifting her arm, she sent from her hand a little, happy "I'm good where I am and I love you" wave. He smiled.

The clerk clicked fast on the keyboard in front of him. "Hey, isn't written somewhere that Jesus had a twin?"

"I invite you to look up Christ not just online, but in scripture. Your question is a good one. Let it be a road to travel."

"You like even sound like him! Awesome!"

Joe nodded and smiled at the clerk's energy, good intentions, and interest. "Finding out about Jesus—and actually hearing Jesus guiding your soul—man, that can lead to a lot of freedom."

"How so?"

Joe turned to his wife. He was glad Betsy was comfortable. This could take a minute.

The clerk felt his face warming from within. He was not sure what he was experiencing in this moment with this customer standing in front of him, but it was good and true. He shook his head and marveled. "You *are* like Christ."

"If being like Christ means moving in a radical, unearthly direction," Joe remembered his drinking, the fight with co-worker Reggie, and the stealing, "then I am."

"Are you like a priest or something?"

"I sounded like one just then, huh?"

"So, you're not a priest?" The clerk spotted Joe's wedding band. "Oh, married."

Joe looked at his left hand. The new ring really did shine.

"How long have you and your wife been hitched?"

Looking at the clock over the clerk's head, Joe answered, "Five hours and fourteen minutes."

"Seriously?"

Joe smiled and nodded. "Seriously."

"Your room is number 401. Just take these elevators here to your left. Your room will be to your left."

Joe remembered the last time he was on the fourth floor of a hotel. "Thank you."

"Seriously? You got married today?"

Joe shoved his hand into the front pocket of his shorts as he walked away from the counter. "Seriously. Today."

"She's really—"

"Yes, she is. She really is."

The clerk sent his computer into suspend mode. "I heard you about the Bible. Thanks, bro."

"It's a good read."

The clerk eyes lit up. "Innkeeper! That's totally me! And there's room in this inn."

"You know that's Joseph and Mary's story, right?"

He nodded, blushed, and smiled. "Got it."

Joe gave off such a warm, inviting, easy expression. "Then get more. Okay? Read on. There's Simeon and Anna."

"They owned the inn?"

Joe's laughter spilled light everywhere. "They were two at the Temple where Joseph and Mary brought eight-day-old Jesus to be circumcised. You find their story in the Gospel of Luke. The two saw the newborn for who he was—God among us."

The clerk looked down at his own chest, and then back to Joe. "My name is Luke. I don't know where my tag is."

"Luke, God is among us, you and me."

The clerk raised his chin and returned to what Joe had said a moment earlier. "Those two, Anna and Simeon?"

"Yeah?"

"They saw something in the newborn?" Luke suddenly couldn't say more. For a reason that baffled him, he couldn't say what—exactly—he saw something in this newly married guy.

"They did."

"I see—" Luke tried to speak. He tried to tell Joe what he felt, what he instantly knew, but just as it had been there a second ago, it wasn't quite there now.

"You're good man." Joe started walking toward his wife.

"You too."

Joe turned. In the elevator, Betsy stared ahead, thinking. Her husband, the one to reach out and touch lives. Not taking her eyes off the shiny metal door in front of her, she reached for and held his hand.

Saw that coming.

———————◆———————

Her feet were not that swollen, yet Joe insisted she elevate them on a pillow at the foot of their king-size bed. Unable to stay still on the mattress, he was like a kid. "Look, honey, we can sleep one way on this thing, or the other. I mean, truly, there's the conventional way, or we can sleep on this monstrosity sideways."

"It's so big, Joe, it's like sleeping on one of the Hawaiian Islands."

Just as his lips moved to say a word, she stopped him. "No! Don't even say it! This is all the honeymoon I will ever need. Flying first to the West Coast, and then taking *another* flight over the Pacific? Even when I'm no longer pregnant, that is not happening."

Knowing he couldn't win that one because even in her first trimester Joe unsuccessfully introduced her to half a dozen exotic location travel brochures that she immediately declined, he visibly changed what he was about to say. "But this bed is like literal climate control. I mean, if you're hot—and you are hot, baby—" Joe puckered his lips to kiss, "then you could like sleep over here with just a sheet." He motioned to one side of the bed. "And if I'm cold, I could sleep over there under a small mountain of blankets."

"It's like the north and south."

"I bet, if we look closely, we'll find the Mason Dixon line on this thing."

She rolled her eyes. "You're crazy. Come here and kiss me, you cute young thing."

He did.

"You are not cold, Joe."

They kissed again, deeper this time, longer.

Suddenly, he remembered something and jumped off the bed. The radio he turned on in the room earlier went into a set of commercials as he fished and fumbled for what he had packed in his suitcase especially for his wife.

"Joe, what is it?"

"Hold on."

She stared at the ceiling which was not especially visually stimulating. "Joe?"

"Wait!"

She lifted herself by her elbows and appreciated the full view of her husband's back side.

"Got it!"

To her surprise, Joe presented a white business envelope with a white bow and ribbon over it. "It's your wedding present."

"Joe! I didn't think! I mean, there wasn't time. The dress, the cake, the flowers."

"You are my present." He nodded. "Open it."

"But I didn't get you a—"

Joe knew Betsy couldn't have had time to shop for even something simple. "Ssh. Open it."

She looked down at the envelope that contained only a paper or two inside, and then back into his eyes which revealed only that he wanted her to see what it was.

"Go on."

"What is this?"

"Hmmm, since I'm not telling you, I guess really the only way to find out what it is to…"

"Fine." She slipped off the ribbon and the bow. Deftly he handed her a pen from the polished nightstand because he knew she couldn't just tear an envelope with her fingers. A mechanical engineer would never do such a thing.

Using the pen as a letter opener, she pulled out his university college acceptance letter. She read only a few lines, but the letter from Illinois State congratulated him on being accepted into their second year philosophy program this fall. All his Bible College credits transferred.

Quickly she sat up. "Oh, my! Yes!"

He kissed her.

"Wow, I'm proud of you, husband of mine. This, this is wonderful."

They had talked this through weeks ago, after Joe had applied. The money would be tight but workable. "Now I'll work my way through school and the loans will be—"

She spoke matter-of-factually. "The loans will be something we pay off."

"We?"

"We."

He set his hands on her smooth, strong, lean legs, that still were all alluring curves and angles in spite of her advanced pregnancy. "You'll remain the chief breadwinner for a while. You're okay with that?"

"Joe, I love my job. You know this. I couldn't stand not doing what I do."

After the long set of commercials ended, a song came on the radio. Joe didn't hear it at first. When he recognized the tune, she asked for a victory dance.

He squinted. "A victory dance?"

She nodded.

"Now?"

"Now."

It was a fun, fast summer song with a good, strong beat. Joe scooched off the bed and thought of how he longed to make love with this gorgeous woman who looked so incredibly good pregnant. He started his dance slowly and methodically. He rolled his shoulders, rode an invisible mechanical bull during the chorus of the song, and when the second verse kicked in he moved his hips here and there. He laughed and then stopped.

"Oh no," she said, enjoying the private show. "You just keep on going."

Before the song ended, he climbed over her and extended his arms in a push-up, so as not to squish her or the baby. She reached up to kiss him. The scent of his muscles, the trace of the masculine crème he used when he shaved his face...*wow*. She never tired of that. Carefully, she found his lips and set hers under them.

"Victory dance," she said as she slid her fingers around his waist against his skin.

"Victory dance."

"I love you, Joe."

"I love you, Betsy."

CHAPTER SIXTY THREE

He hung the tuxedo up on its hanger on a strong wooden peg outside his closet door. Rather than put it in his closet, Earl decided to leave it out so he could remember the day. Sitting at the edge of his bed—their bed—he stared at it and did the math. One summer. Two weddings. Two tuxedos.

Oh, how Janet loved weddings. It didn't matter if she was close to the bride and groom or not, she just loved the whole event. Even though she never met Betsy, and would remember Joey only as a small boy, she would have been all aglow today. Happy himself, he imagined his wife walking through their bedroom door, earrings in hand, her dress as pretty as the moment she put it on all those hours ago.

I saw you dance with the bride.

Of course I was with her, Janet. You know me.

And you showed her the Duke of Earl moves.

He smiled. *I showed her the Duke of Earl moves.*

Did she laugh?

I'm old now, love. Of course she laughed.

And you ate a lot of cake.

He ignored how full his belly felt.

Did you have fun, Earl? Did you show the world how incredible you are?

Janet, you are the one who is incredible.

I love you.

A tear rolled down his face. *I love you, too. Always.*

As he continued to look at the tux hanging in front of him, he thought of the fiftieth anniversary party they would have had this December. She would have made him dress up for the event. That was certain. Undoubtedly there would be a third rented tux. His seventeen-year-old suit just wouldn't do.

Janet?

He couldn't see her.

Janet?

She was gone.

I love you always, I do.

•————————•

Galvin entered their bedroom quietly. "Iris is sound asleep. She's as still as she can be." Kristen set her hairbrush down. From the flicker in her eyes, he knew she had been thinking of their little girl. Tonight, with the wedding still so fresh between them, he had given her space and time to think back on the day.

She turned to him. "Our daughter was so lovely today, so beautiful."

"We're so lucky, Kristen. We are."

She began to think of what could have happened had the scene with the bee stings in the alley ended differently. "I just can't even begin to—"

He kissed her neck. "Me, either."

The dress she wore to the wedding suddenly slumped from the chair she had set it on to the floor. She reached to pick it back up. "Joe says he heard God. God told him where that medicine kit was."

In his over-sized t-shirt and pajama bottoms, Galvin moved to their bed, turned down her side of the covers, and fluffed her pillow. "He told you that too?"

"He told you?"

"At his bachelor party. That night. It was just the two of us. We were there side by side in the living room for a while, watching the fire get lower and lower. But yes, he told me."

Rubbing the collar of her lightweight, full-length nightgown,

Kristen moved to sit on her side of the bed. She couldn't face her husband as she thought about what she was going to say. "I think Joe is special. Really special."

"What are you saying?"

She looked out into the empty space before her. "I have no idea what I'm saying. I just know what I feel when I'm with him. It's just…"

Galvin remembered that night in the cabin with him. "Different."

"Yeah."

She took a good, long, deep breath. "He is special, Galvin."

He sat beside his wife and set his arms around her. "He saved her, Kristen. He saved our daughter's life."

She lowered her head, thought of God, and said, "You know, I read an article on what Jesus most likely looked like. He was a common looking man. He likely had dark skin because of his ethnicity and all the years he spent traveling under the sun. Likely he kept the Leviticus laws of the day and did not trim his beard."

"Joe doesn't even have a beard."

"I know. But I still see him. I see Jesus."

"Me too."

"Have you ever thought that maybe Jesus doesn't just have one look? Or maybe he has one look but, through the sovereignty of God, he appears differently to different people. He was born in Bethlehem and almost everyone in the overcrowded city didn't know it. The two on the road to Emmaus didn't know Jesus was the stranger among them."

"Maybe there isn't a set look."

Galvin held her closely. "But when you look into his eyes—"

"You know he's there."

⬥────────────⬥

Dunk had gone off to bed about an hour ago and left both his wife and his best friend out on the back deck to drink. The bottle was Jolie's idea. She raised her second glass. "To the honeymoon."

Vanessa clinked her glass against her partner's. "To the honeymoon."

"Where is it? Where did Joe and Betsy go?" Jolie asked. "They're spending a quiet night or two away, right?"

Running her bare feet over the boards of the deck, Vanessa answered. "Yes, they just snuck away for some quiet time."

Jolie considered this. "She probably can't travel very far. I imagine her doctor will soon have her on house arrest, if he doesn't already have her somewhat corralled."

Vanessa laughed. "Corralled. Makes me think of a horse."

"She probably feels sometimes that she weighs as much as one."

Vanessa met her friend in the eye. "She did look so beautiful today, didn't she?"

Jolie stared at the sky over them. "This is the ninth time you've asked me this today. Did you know that?"

Frowning, Vanessa looked into her glass. "Only nine? Good thing the night is young."

<hr />

Ben never should have tried to ask Wanda, the newest waitress, to go with him. He never should have even *considered* taking her. Betsy had given him false hope when she said two days ago that he could bring someone to the wedding if he liked. He should never have hope. He should have never tried. Of course Wanda rejected him. She wasted no time. As soon as he fumbled the question out, she shot him down. Ben may have been able to handle that rejection. He did make it through the wedding, after all. What she said of him tonight over the internet, however, crushed him. He had just asked her out. It was just one question, one simple invitation.

No one should be that cruel.

What Wanda started not only spread, but also it was added to by at least twenty-five classmates. The words were so cutting, so cruel. He had thought he was just never seen, now he knew he was ignored. With what he read, he also knew why he was ignored. The stabs about his mom and grandmom he would have expected, even though they were sharp, over-exaggerated, or just plain wrong. He was no wimp; he has heard many things over the years. But what they said of his burns...no one should be that mean, that vicious. And then twenty-five people, some of whom he barely knew or were all out strangers, went even further. Went even deeper. They crushed him. They truly crushed him. He had no tomorrow. He had no future.

Ben stared into nothingness before he swallowed this fact: he was not loved. Sure, today's bride and groom seemed happy he was there, but the truth of the matter was that the two would have been just as happy had no one been there. When he thought to himself that he was an extra, that he was not important, no emotion surrounded him this time. No aching feelings came to him as they had in the past. Certainly there were no tears. He had cried those all away. And this attack on his burns? It was all the more clear.

He swallowed. He could never look at himself in a mirror or at a photo himself again.

With no energy, he glanced down to his lap, and then at his normal looking hands. He was thankful the decision he had just made was not an emotional deal. This was just something that needed to happen. When Andy's Gun Store opened Monday morning, he'd buy a Smith & Wesson .357, which he read online will get the job done. He had the money he needed. Two months of tips from the ice cream shop will actually do some good.

As the morning sun peeked through the window blinds he couldn't close any tighter, Ben stared at the ceiling over his twin bed. *What do you do on the last day of your life?*

The gun was in. He checked. The seven day waiting period was over today. The store opened at nine. His alarm clock read 8:11 AM. He had not slept well because he had overheard on a talk show that those who take their own life spend eternity in hell. The two bottles of wine he 'borrowed' from his cousin's college graduation this past summer calmed his thoughts through the night. He felt like that was a good thing.

The note was set. It sat on his desk. He typed and printed it the night he bought the handgun. Two pages. It wasn't that hard to write. The trip to the bank was not difficult either. He just withdrew his whole account. Simple. Ben was surprised he didn't have much feeling about this. He had no regret, sorrow, or fear. His death wasn't making a statement to get back at anyone from school because there wasn't anyone that mattered that much, or, more specifically, he didn't matter much to anyone at school, except he was an easy target to so many. His mom and his grandmother didn't really matter that much either because, truth be told, he didn't really matter. He just didn't. They had checked out on him, now he checking out on them. Simple. This was not a big deal, not a big loss. This was just simply going to happen.

His clothes were set for today. He will put on old work clothes he had painted in and worn when mowing the lawn. Why ruin good stuff? The jeans and old shirt were nothing anyone would want. Everything good would go to the Salvation Army, including underwear and shoes. He did laundry yesterday. His closet was completely empty now, as was his dresser. He packed or pitched the stuff in his bedroom. Taking care of it was easy. He'd even vacuumed yesterday. His mom didn't need to clean up after him. He kept just enough of his belongings out on his bookshelf so his mom wouldn't suspect anything, not that she'd been in his room. Now that she was gone to work, he would pack those things too.

The note he'll leave sticking out of his jeans will instruct the people who find him to call her at work. He left her number for someone to easily see. Everything was set. The clock showed the time, 8:14. He rolled out of bed. It was time to get the gun.

While he never thought about it, this was exactly the weather he imagined he would have today. Sunny. Mild. It was a little chilly, but it would warm up by noon or so. The car started easily. No strange sounds came out from under the hood, and the radio came in clearly, which it often didn't do.

The woman at the Salvation Army drop-off came across as nice as could be. He didn't know Mondays were sorting days.

"Four big boxes? Wow."

"They're just clothes, ma'am."

She wore the smile of a woman spread a little too thin in the caring department. "Well, thank you."

After pleasantries he rehearsed one more time in the car, he came to the tough part: to look like absolutely none of this mattered. "The gun?"

"Sure," a big-bellied man said. A sales associate Ben had not seen before started to walk into the back of the store. Maybe he was an angel. Maybe he was the one to talk him out of it. But of course this grump with arthritis in his knees and an early lunch already on his mind didn't know anything about what this weapon, or this day, was about.

Standing alone for far too long, Ben wished the sales associate he ordered the gun from was here because conversation between them seemed less likely than with this stranger. He really couldn't afford to talk a lot. From behind, he heard the doorbell ring. He didn't turn. When the one who just entered came to stand near him, Ben sighed. It was a sign. The man he'd ordered the gun from last Monday ambled around the counter. With the original salesperson here, this should go much easier.

"Monday already?" The man set his jumbo hands on the counter. "Wasn't much of weekend now, was it?"

Ben just nodded. Less was more.

The man pulled out a folder out. "Here are some things you'll need to sign, son. Is your John Hancock ready?"

"My, my what?"

The man laughed. "Your signature."

Act calm. "Yeah. Sure."

With thick, big fingers, the man opened the paperwork.

Not reading all that he was signing—or simply not able to understand it now—Ben put his name here, here, and there. His fingers shook, but he hoped the man didn't notice. The first salesperson returned. He set the gun on the glass counter. It was in a clear, heavy plastic bag. *That's what's going to kill me. Okay.* Ben heard himself answer a question that had not been asked. In the quiet between the three of them, he added, "This is just for protection. Today, you just can't be too safe these days, you know?"

Like dairy cows in a stall, both men nodded.

⸻

With the keychain off and in the glove compartment, he set the car key under the floor mats. Purposefully, he didn't look at the clock on the dashboard. He didn't need to know that anymore. It was just simply time. Stepping out of the car, he checked his front pockets. Yes, the house key wasn't there. He did remember to put it where it could easily be found, and that was with the spare key they kept on the back porch if either of them locked themselves out. He checked his front pocket. The card that has his mother's work number on it stuck out just a bit.

Now he called 9-1-1. These were the last words he will say out loud. "Yes, I'd like to report a shooting. It's a suicide. I'm here in the Westbury Park off Elm. I mean the Elm Street entrance. It's a single Caucasian male, nineteen-years-old. He shot himself with the gun he's holding."

He set the phone on the driver's seat, grabbed the handgun in its bag, shut the car door, and walked away. Since the call had been made, there wasn't much time. His stomach knotted. He just didn't want to chicken out. He couldn't afford to fail.

⸻

Ben heard someone running.
"Wait!"
Joe?

He couldn't easily close the loaded gun. *Why?* It should just snap shut with the bullet inside. That was what it did at the store when the guy showed it to him.

Why?

It was Joe. He was close. Getting closer.

"Ben, hey."

I cannot fail. This cannot fail.

"I just wanted to talk with you. Just talk. Is that alright?

Close!

"I...I haven't seen you since the wedding. The ladies at the Dairy Barn said you called off sick. And I've missed you. You matter to me, Ben. You really do."

The gun closed.

Joe swallowed. He wished he'd been here five minutes earlier, but there was a reason he didn't yet understand about his timing. Minutes before he arrived, he knew exactly what Ben was trying to do. Moving slowly, Joe could talk him through this. "Just set the handgun down. Just set it down. For a minute. I just need a minute with you, buddy."

Ben looked scared.

"It is scary, buddy. But I'm here. I'm here. I found you, didn't I? And I'm not going to let you down, or let you go. I promise that."

For a second, Ben's eyes warmed, and then rolled away.

"I promise that, Ben."

No.

Joe stepped closer. From his short run, his chest rose and fell. "You might be feeling a little lonely now. Maybe you think no one listens to you, but that's not completely true. I'm here, Ben. I'm here to listen."

There was no response.

"I get that something happened. Something cruel. Words were said. Things were written about you."

Wanda wouldn't have told him a thing. Good 'ol Joe was just guessing.

"Ben, I know. I know you are hurting. Wondering if anyone cares." With authority that faded to warmth in his voice, Joe moved even closer. He stood four feet away. "I care. I care, buddy. I care about what you've heard, what you're thinking. I want to hear from you. I want to know what brought you here."

Joe nodded. "My ears, they work. Let's use them."

Lowering his hands, Joe continued. "Remember when we were on that back porch area of the Dairy Barn? It was raining hard, and it was just the two of us. I told you something. I told you something big, something true. I told you I needed you."

Joe took another step. "We are going to talk. You and me. Just the two of us. We are just going to talk and I'm going to listen to every word you say."

Ben could not speak.

"Now the gun. Just set it down."

"No." Ben would not hear any of this. He was set. He was done. No ceremony, no show. He raised the gun to his mouth and swallowed its tip.

Seeing Ben pull the trigger, Joe lunged forward. The sound of the bang—this enormous, terrible bang—shook even the ground. The sound hurt so much, so terribly. Ben's jaw, his cheekbones, and his teeth rattled in pain.

The pelting of blood was like spears. Joe spun away and landed face first. Ben fell too. Crashing down on his back, Ben stared at the sky. He blinked.

He wasn't dead.

⋆

Two ambulances parked at the scene. Easily the paramedics determined the one male shot through the jaw had a pulse. He didn't look good though; the single bullet exited the crown of the skull. The other young male at the scene may have a sprained wrist. Disoriented, he was in shock. No other symptoms presented themselves. The ambulance carrying the critical patient screamed away. The other lingered, since the cops were here. An officer climbed on board the ambulance. She studied the face of the one with his hand and forearm braced.

"The gun was in this hand," one of the two paramedics said in a low voice, pointing to the injury. "And there's a note in the pocket of his jeans."

"Mind if I take a look at that?" the officer asked Ben.

Ben nodded consent.

With a rubber glove on, the officer removed the note and read it. She moved the paper away as if the paper itself were dead. "You were going to kill yourself."

Ben didn't know how to talk.

The officer continued. "You tried to kill yourself and something else happened."

Waiting a moment often helped at times like this. The officer had seen this before, unfortunately. She repeated herself. "You tried to kill yourself, but something else happened, didn't it?"

Ben heard what could not be true. He panicked, grimaced. Hearing the gunshot in his memory for the first time, he convulsed so uncontrollably that the officer knew there was no sense continuing now. "Take him," the officer said to the paramedic. "While we haven't checked either car, the one running or the one parked beside it, there isn't much at the scene itself that hasn't already been analyzed."

"Failed suicide attempt?"

"Probably."

CHAPTER SIXTY FOUR

The two met at the nurse's station like bad storms about to collide. Both men had been crying, one more than the other. The redness in Roland's eyes appeared far less than in Dunk's, but Dunk could not believe the visible pain his friend showed. Roland's voice, level and measured, did not falter. "Update me."

No energy propelled Dunk's response. The words hung disconnected in space. "He's out of surgery. The swelling is the main concern now. The bullet passed right between both lobes, but the damage is significant. The next hours are crucial." Jolie joined her best friend as he said, "It doesn't look good."

Roland asked two questions. "Where is Joe? Where are his doctors?"

Dunk shook and quivered. He found he suddenly could not answer Roland, let alone move. Earl came to Dunk's side as Jolie walked Roland around the nurse's station to find Joe's surgeons, who had just spoken to all of them two minutes ago. Looking at a clock he did not need to see, Roland could not be a doctor now. He could not click his mind clear because he was the one who had been the one crying more than Dunk. The team treating the clone wouldn't let him in now, anyway.

The clone.

The tears filled Roland's eyes again. Joe was not a clone. Suddenly, like Dunk, he could not move. His thoughts jammed.

"He's coding!" he heard a medical team member say from what must be Joe's room. A rush of people raced up from behind and passed him. Powerless, the great scientist—who himself was a medical doctor—had no options. There was no other way to be present to Joe other than to bow his head. Roland, without reserve, prayed for the first time in his life. The first sentences were not trapped. "Mass Creator, he is not mine. He has not been mine." Wrestling with his next word, he set his top teeth into his lower lip. "Miracle. I need Your miracle, please. I need him here. Healthy and well. Hear me. This I ask in Your child's holy name."

Two tears flowed.

"Amen."

Nothing happened when Kristen heard the news. Nothing could happen, nothing at all. Through the glass door off the kitchen, she watched Iris who was outside in the driveway with several plastic drinking glasses. Since Joe and Betsy's wedding, the inventive one had decided she would be a florist. With her leaf and recent rock collecting experiences, she carefully arranged oak, maple, and elm leaves in each glass that will become centerpieces for her next coloring party with her new friends Daisy and Maxine, twins who lived three blocks away. *This was her life, and Joe will be fine.* The savior on earth who saved her daughter will be fine. She didn't feel herself shaking or crying when she thought this. *Joe will be fine. He will be fine.*

Vanessa learned who shot Joe. The sheriff, who was a no-nonsense woman she had dealt with many times before as a social worker, blurred protocol by sharing with her the name of the teen involved in the shooting. Still holding her phone in the lobby of the hospital, she couldn't believe she had the guts to call in this favor. This boy named Ben hadn't even been officially charged yet. The name didn't register at first. How could she possibly know the one who shot Joe? That she would know the perpetrator was something she never would have imagined.

When it hit her, it sunk quickly. In less than a second, the old Vanessa was back, the one in charge before she met, dated, and married Dunk. The kindness and love that took so many months to build disappeared in a flash. She was so angry she boiled. Burned. Melted. First her volcanic mess spewed at that aimless, spineless kid—that worthless little imp—then it splashed where it belonged, onto her. The truth slapped her in the face. She failed. She failed Joe. She knew Ben was in trouble. She knew the boy needed help, and what did she do? Nothing. She did not know how she was standing. She should be beneath the floor because everything ever said about being a social worker was true. She was a single tissue out to mop up a flood. She did too little, missed too much. Why didn't she step in further? She could have at least tried and then, as she'd done in the past, justified her actions—or lack of actions—with blame for the system.

God gave her the abilities to be both insightful *and* helpful, and what did she do? She patted the situation on the back. Telling Ben he was loved in a restaurant while he was working? Sharing something that should be private and profound when he barely had enough time to clear dishes from a nearby table? Leaving him a big tip? *Really?* That did nothing. She was quiet, and then her thought crushed her. *I did nothing.* Joe was upstairs. He may never be the same. *He may die.*

Oh, yes, she did hate her profession and her complete inability to see one lost and lonely soul screaming so silently for help. But that hate wasn't enough. No, white hot, there was only one thing that was enough—and that was her hatred for herself.

⊙—————⊙

He left his wife in the kitchen. Outside, he wished the air could feel fresh or somehow different—better—Galvin sat on a step and watched his daughter play in their driveway. He couldn't quite figure out what she was doing with all the leaves in the plastic drinking glasses Kristen never let out of the kitchen, but it didn't matter.

"Daddy," Iris called, "do you want to see what I'm doing?"

"Not now, honey. Not now."

"How 'bout later than, okay?"

Galvin didn't answer. Instead, he looked next door. Joe was there in the blink of his eyes. Sleeveless t-shirt. Muscles shiny with sweat. Happy, humming some tune Galvin couldn't quite hear from that Christian radio station Kristen played now. Like so many times before, that landscaping truck his boss let him use was parked nearby. Everything was just the same. Nothing had changed. No bullet had been shot. No significant, life-threatening injury had happened to Joe, right?

He knew who Joe was now, of course. He knew exactly who Joe was. Like so many two-thousand-years ago, he finally saw who Joe actually was. The landscaping truck wasn't here, of course, though he looked left and then right in the absolutely stupid hope of finding it nearby. Joe wasn't here, either. Unlike his wife who sat numb at the table inside, he wept. He needed Joe back. He needed Joe back.

⸻

"Stay pregnant," she said to herself. She breathed, just breathed.

"Yes," Earl said. "Stay pregnant. And you're doing just fine, honey. Just fine."

Walking into the low-lit room here on the third floor, Jolie had just rejoined the two of them. She'd come up from the ICU with no new news. The three didn't talk. They simply held hands. Earl prayed silently. Jolie worked hard not to cry.

The nurse Betsy had seen twice since being admitted came back to check on the IV. She told her patient that the sedative was working. Betsy wouldn't look at her forearm. The ulmintin injections. She was carrying Joe's baby. Of course she was. It was Joe's. And Mr. Rolls wasn't here yet. She asked, "Why isn't he here in his own lab?"

Jolie looked at Earl. They knew exactly what she was talking about.

⸻

Over the next three hours, Joe flat-lined three times. In a private room several doors down from the ICU, Dunk could not understand all the doctors were saying. Earl had joined them for this meeting, and holding Earl's hand, Dunk just watched Roland who nodded repeatedly to what the doctors said. When Dunk looked at Roland, he knew. It was time.

———

"I unplug him," Dunk said a few minutes later when the four of them stood out in the hallway. "It's me. I'm entitled. I get to unplug him."

Roland stepped in behind him. "You can't, Dunk. That's not how it is done."

"I...get...to...unplug...him. No one else. Me. My love. My love does this. No more experiments. No more machines. It's just us. My boy and me. I send him home."

Roland looked to the nearby doctor. She shook her head no. "Turning off the life support systems cannot be done by family."

"Then you're going to have to sue us," Roland said.

"Sir, that's not—"

"With the influence I have, this hospital could be closed in weeks."

"This isn't—"

Roland was quick. He looked to Dunk, Vanessa, and Earl before he said to the doctor, "This is how it will be done, Miss. His fingers touch the equipment. Your fingers touch his. I'll guide him."

As the doctor continued to protest, Roland silenced her with a stare that said Joe may not be the only one here who dies tonight.

———

Top to bottom, Vanessa tore herself in two. The Vanessa she uncovered in the hospital lobby was the one she stepped away from now. She had to. The dutiful Vanessa was back. She could fake it, at least for now. There was no other option. She said what was partially true. "I am here for you, Dunk."

Standing beside Joe's bed, Dunk sobbed. He wailed and wailed and wailed. He cried the fear and the frustration out first, and then the anger. And then the loss. *Love will do this,* he told himself. *Love will do this.* When his sea of sorrow receded enough to let love do what it is supposed to do, Dunk said, "Alright."

Roland moved to stand behind him. "You're going to—"

Dunk ignored him. His voice was gravel, but it was everything the man of faith had. "To Your great world above, heavenly Father, we send You the one we cherish and love. With Your angels of death and mercy here, guide his passage to Your Kingdom which has no end. Amen."

Through bloodshot eyes, Dunk looked at Roland. "You and me, Roland. Tell me what I need to do."

The doctor did hold Dunk's hand as he unfastened this, and switched off that.

Shuddering, Dunk stood up against the deepest, sharpest, most gut-wrenchingly profound ache only a father could know. There was a moment when life and death mixed in the air, and then Joe died slowly. He just simply stopped. Before a new and vast ache broke his chest, Roland whispered to himself, "It is finished."

Jesus' last words on the cross. It is finished.

•————————————•

A half hour later, Earl brought in a basin of warm water and set it on a nearby tray. Jolie gave Dunk the clean face cloth she had carried in her hand. She didn't tell him that the visiting pastor of his church left her with the message that he could come back at any moment. If Pastor Smith couldn't do this as ordained clergy, and they had heard he was at a conference four hours south, then she knew only Dunk could do it. The hospital chaplain stood nearby but was respectfully silent. Dunk wet the cloth and slowly, tenderly, washed Joe's face from the hospital sterilizations and antiseptics. So very carefully, he washed the sutures where the bullet entered. As best he could, he washed the bangs of Joe's hair, and then kissed his son's forehead.

"I will see you there, Joe. *I will see you there.* Until then, I will love you every day that I am here."

———————

Betsy asked Jolie to wait with the others by her wheelchair in the hall outside.

Joe's room was void of all machines, and the lights were low. She asked to be alone. Not since her last night of spring break during her junior year at college had she been this loopy. Because she couldn't quite feel her feet, she took it slowly.

"They let me out for good behavior," she said to her husband, who, despite the soft lighting and the clean face, was far, far gone. She knew he was already there. She would not touch his cool hand. Respectfully, she'll remember only its warmth. He'd want it that way. "I'll be good, Joe." She gently touched her side. "Right through the delivery. I promise."

She spoke to where Joe was now. "And I understand. I do. I've known about you since we met, since you first sprang up out of the water. I just didn't see it, or didn't want to see it at first." She stopped for a second. "You're hardwired. Christ died for the whole world. You died for one soul." She studied the fingers that caressed her so many times. He was still wearing his wedding ring. "It was supposed to be."

She dropped her head. "Just guide me here, okay? I'll take care of Ben. I'll continue with him, whatever you started, what God has planned."

Holding her eyes closed with fingers, she thought of Michael. "And you tell Mike up there that I love him."

This goodbye will be good, she told herself. This goodbye will be perfect because that was what she had here, a perfect love. She would remember his warm hands, yes, but she leaned over and kissed Joe's forehead once. She paused. *This is it. This is the last time.* She kissed his soft lips, not once, not twice, but three times. With a clear, strong voice, she said, "Joseph Messiah—Joe O'Dell—I will always, always do what I have done since God has given you to me, and that is love you."

Now her softness came through with a wave of tears. "Yes, dear soul—my husband, my best friend, and my life—I will always love you."

CHAPTER SIXTY FIVE

Viola Munson was learning something about love. No one was more surprised at this than she was—after all, she had seen and experienced so much in life—but yes, here and now she was learning about love. Had this happened a year or two ago, she would have wiggled her way into the private graveside service not because she cared about the convict who never did add up to much—after all, the college dropout probably would never get his lazy self back into a college of reputable standing—but, just like getting into Dunk and Vanessa's wedding as a scripture reader, she would have wanted to be at the graveside service to do what she did best: gossip to others about the event itself.

She wasn't that person now. Since she found out about the tragedy, she had returned time and time again to the memory of Joe and Betsy at the backyard dinner party the night before Dunk and Vanessa's wedding. When sitting with the couple who were not yet engaged, she had wanted the dirt. But love, she was learning, doesn't do that. She remembered the 1 Corinthians scripture Joe read at his dad's wedding. Love was patient. Love was kind. It was not jealous, boastful or proud. It was not touchy, or rude. It does not insist on its way, and Viola realized here in the cemetery that she had been living far too much of her life her own way.

She played judge and jury with Joe. When he was on the straight and narrow, all was fine. When they sold pies together at their church event, he was charming, funny, and able to connect with her. He saw the best in her, like few others ever had. When he didn't measure up however, he was doomed not by God, but by her. Her heart ached. Why didn't she see it? Why didn't she see him? How could she like him one day and then dismiss him the next?

She was thankful when the graveside service started because she could take her mind off her thoughts. As Pastor Smith's words brought assurance and comfort, she looked at Betsy's placid face. Rumor had it that Betsy O'Dell will crash sometime soon. She'll just fall apart, either before or, most likely, after she gives birth. That was a rumor though, and Viola wouldn't be a part of that. Specifically, she wouldn't be a part of that anymore. As Pastor Smith continued with the service, Viola knew that she had been one of the few spreading that rumor not only because she enjoyed rumors, but also she had thought it would be true. After all, what woman can lose her husband while she was eight months pregnant and not just completely fall apart?

Today, she knew the answer to that question. Looking at her now, Viola knew that young mother-to-be was going to do it. The round-bellied woman wearing the simple black top and loose dark pants will absolutely, positively make it through this. That was love. Yes, Viola realized, that was love she'd never seen, and love she'd never known. It wasn't just love between a husband and wife; it was God's love for Betsy, and Betsy's love for God.

Viola looked to the sky and asked herself if she loved God that way. She knew her answer. She didn't. She had been a member of the United Church of Christ since it formed in 1957, and in all those years, she was a Martha, not a Mary. She bustled about doing church business in the right, upstanding way it needed to be done. It was a business, after all, an organization. Someone had to see that countless potlucks and charity drives were organized, and that cards and gifts to active service men and women were sent on time. She saw to it that the lilies were ordered and would open in their full regalia Easter morning, that the Christmas poinsettias were not wilted, and that each and every worship service was planned well and went off without a hitch.

She looked down from the sky and into herself. She was not Mary

in that she never spent time with Jesus. As one heavy tear rolled down
her face, she realized today that would change.

———————

Humbled, she thought she could slip away, just retreat. This was
time for family.

"Viola." It was Betsy's voice she heard over her shoulder. She
couldn't keep walking away from the gravesite, could she?

"Viola."

The senior stopped, turned.

Flanked by two women, one being her mother, Betsy left her escorts
and waddled toward her. "I just wanted to thank you for coming."

"For intruding."

"Intruding? No."

Viola had never talked this way. She had never been this honest, this
real. "I was being nosey. You know that. My place was with the others
at the church, not here. I heard the funeral directors clearly. This was
to be a committal for close family only."

"But you are here."

For the first time in her adult life, Viola Munson did not know what
to say.

"And I see," Betsy continued, "that you're different now. I see a
change."

"Oh, Betsy. How? How are you doing this?"

From Viola eyes, Betsy knew the question the senior was asking. "I
don't understand everything that happened, and I never will. Not here,
anyway. I don't know how Joe knew about Ben that day. I don't know
how he even knew to go to the park at that time. But I'm not going to
malign God's character, or question His reason. I'm not going to be
angry."

"But how? That young man took Joe's life. It was an accident, yes,
but Joe is gone."

"In a way Joe is gone, yes."

"You know a lot about grief."

Betsy thought of Michael. "What I know is that God is the only one who will heal my wound. I'm pregnant. My mood will likely swing fifteen minutes from now. I will be hurting. I will be crying. Yes. But I have a free will, and with that free will—now more than ever—I choose to be with God."

She reached down and took Viola's hand. Together they continued walking toward the narrow cemetery road where cars were parked. Silence slipped between them. Looking into the future, Betsy said, "Ben didn't choose to be with God at the time of the accident. He acted on his own, and in darkness. As God is patient and merciful with him now, God is equally patient and merciful with me."

Viola realized again that any faith she had in all her years had been little or nothing. Now she saw. Now she understood.

"Viola, I know only a God of mercy."

"How are you doing this?"

The ground was uneven. Their shoulders came close. "I could be a blubbery mess, Viola, or I could still be hooked up to some sedative. But I know I love my husband, and he taught me more than I would ever learn alone. Joe was just *that wonderful*. And Ben? He needs us. He needs me. I can heal or I can hurt. I'm not going to sink. No, I'll sail. I'll sail with a God who loves me."

Betsy stopped. She saw the whole line of cars now from her vantage point. At the end of them stood someone all by himself. The tall football player from college, the father of her baby, just watched.

Leaving Viola to Vanessa and Dunk, she made her way down the row of cars. Tad respectfully stayed still until Betsy came closer.

"Hello," she said.

"Hello."

She knew what Tad was going to say. She could see it in his eyes. He didn't have to bring forth a word though. His tears told her how sincerely sorry he was for her loss.

◆———————◆

Alone in the kitchen the following morning, Vanessa kept her hair in its loose ponytail, and secured it using a rubber band from a nearby drawer. She didn't think about what she was going to do. Instead, she took the meat shears in one hand and chopped off her hair just above the tie near her head. She didn't need to measure her hair before cutting, but did so after the cut with a yardstick on the table. Yes, the length was fourteen inches. There was definitely enough hair here to donate to a company who made wigs for cancer patients. When she left her hair in the salon about an hour later, her very short style was back to her original color. Enough. Enough of who she was. No more fake, no more sweet. She had work to do, and little time to do it.

⚬━━━━━━━━━⚬

"Do you think you should have asked Dunk first?" It was Jolie who asked the question.

"What?"

"It's a pretty radical cut, Vanessa. It's a whole new look. You never thought to run it by your husband?"

Vanessa could not believe she was having this conversation. She turned from the very spot where she cut off that ponytail. "He owns my hair?"

Jolie sat at the table. "No, but he cares about how you're dealing with this."

"I can stay in the angry phase as long as I need to."

"I can see that."

"It gets my work done. It propels me. No, this isn't guilt. No, this isn't my weird thinking that Joe will come back or that I somehow have to punish myself."

"Sure?"

"Like Joe, I have work to do. That hair got in the way."

"You're not the Vanessa you were?"

Vanessa sat beside her friend. "I was so fiery mad, Jolie. So fiery mad. I am still mad. Mad at myself, yes. This is my processing. This is my realignment. And I've learned…I've learned I've been a fake with this Christian business. Sugary sweet. Accepting. And hollow. And I didn't realize it until this quake, this awakening." Vanessa leaned forward and shared the truth. "I became a deacon long ago to meet Dunk, not work for God."

"You're working for God now?"

"Yes."

"And?"

Vanessa met Jolie in the eyes. "And it's the best thing I can do. It's the best thing I have done. I know you're concerned, and it's kind."

"Vanessa."

"But this is a refiner's fire. It's really time for me to get serious with God." Vanessa sensed Jolie looking at her hair. "And yes, to answer your question, the color from the bottle can come back again."

"Good." Jolie unfolded her fingers. "Where's their number?"

Vanessa knew Jolie was referring to the hair salon. "What? Now? It's that bad?"

Jolie's expression did all the talking.

Vanessa set her palms down on the table. "Really?"

"Really."

◈┄┄┄┄┄┄┄┄◈

It was Janet. She came to stand behind and then alongside her husband. *The cemetery association would have done this. They would have finished the final grade here.* With the rake still in his dirty hands, Earl looked down at the work he had just completed. Topsoil. Grass seed. Fertilizer. Soft ground covering. A watering can now empty.

It's beautiful.

Earl had not been feeling well all day. Maybe a flu was on its way. He wiped his brow with his forearm. "I know."

And you had to do it.

"I did."

This one is so hard for you.

Earl teared up. "Losing you was one thing. But there was time, you know? We had time. We had a goodbye."

But losing a boy.

Earl shook his head. "I don't know that I can get over this one, honey. I just don't know."

You love him.

"He was my grandson."

I know.

When she slipped her hand in his, she disappeared, but he could still feel her. It seemed as though she was taking a leisurely stroll as she wanted for him to finish. She was close, just over the side of the hill. There was warmth between his fingers, a tingle. It was something he had never experienced before. He wouldn't call it pain racing up his arm, and it wasn't tightness in his chest. It was something else. For the first time in the sixteen years Janet's been dead, he heard her not beside him, but inside him.

Look.

Turning to a grassy area some distance from where he was standing, all Earl could see, opening before him, were rays and rays of sunlight. Then he heard the song, the fast, silly melody he danced to with his wife right there at their wedding reception. With lemonade and cookies, Joe, as an adult, was singing the tune right there at his kitchen table with Eddie Shafaun and the Satellites.

CHAPTER SIXTY SIX

Two funerals in two weeks was something Dunk O'Dell never thought could happen in his lifetime, yet it had. First his son, and now he was out on his favorite trail after attending Earl's funeral earlier today. To lose his teaching job could be next, right? Secularists said things come in threes.

Unable to go any further, Dunk stopped on the loop that always brought him comfort or solace. His feet were still sore from the dress shoes he wore to Earl's funeral. Looking down at the comfortable, well-worn boots now on his feet, he frowned. Those two shiny black shoes, otherwise known as torture chambers, should be broken in by now. They were fine for Joe's service. Or were they? He didn't remember. There was a lot he didn't remember about Joe's service, including how his feet felt after that long day.

Sometimes, when he held his breath, Dunk felt he could almost will his son's funeral away. He knew he was just being way too foolish about this, or more than likely, he was just way too sleep deprived. However, when he was alone like he was now, and intentionally silenced his breathing, it was as if he could erase the horror, stop the enormous pain. Yes, when air neither entered nor exited his lungs, he could put a stop on all his brokenness. That park scene with Joe and Ben never happened. There was no gun. There was no struggle. There was no single, fatal shot fired.

His son was with his expecting wife, of course. They'd drop over for a simple barbeque meal that Vanessa would make extra special with a salad, dessert, or, more than likely, both. All Dunk had to do was finish his hike out here and get to the house ahead of the newlyweds. The grill would be fired up, and a table cloth would cover the picnic table. It would be perfect, but it wasn't perfect. It wasn't going to happen. Joe and Betsy would never be over as a twosome again. There would be no salad. There was no dessert. There was barely a woman named Vanessa who lived with him.

She had changed so much since Joe died. It was not just her hair, which he did honestly miss; her whole persona darkened. The sweetness disappeared. Bitterness rested just underneath the anger she boiled onto herself. If the universe did somehow contain balance, he thought he could at least have her back. The old Vanessa, the one who talked with him, touched him, loved him, and held him under their bed covers—yes—she would be back. She would ask him to be close again, just like before.

He ached. He pictured the Vanessa that was. Her long hair curled over her shoulders. She didn't hate or blame herself.

A knot tightened in his stomach. With Joe gone, how long will it be before Betsy disappeared? It may not be soon, but she'll want to move on at some point. She'll have to. At first, she won't know how to say it, but the words or actions will come in time. Along with Vanessa, he'll become baggage Betsy should drop so that she can live her life happy in the present and future tense, not the past.

He stared into the future. He was going to lose his granddaughter. That pain rattled his core. And Earl, dear Earl. He couldn't even *think* about losing him. The old guy just wanted Joe's grave to look well cared for. He would have been here for Dunk through this, just as he had been when Joe was away. No, he couldn't lose Earl. Experiencing a type of adult ADD he never had before, his attention moved to two songbirds fluttering nearby. Busy chattering, they left as quickly as they arrived.

Silence. His world would be a lot lonelier now. Two funerals. Two weeks.

As soon as she heard the engine cut off, Iris knew she could race toward Dunk's parked car. Mommy made this rule clear: she could only run toward his car after a 1-2-3. One, his car had to be completely stopped; two, the motor wasn't making a single sound; and three, it was in their driveway. She knew when a car had stopped running, of course. After all, she was five-years-old now, and *all* five-year-olds know when to approach a car, and when not to.

It was not really *that* hard! He had pulled his car right where he kept it in his drive and it was silent when she started racing. Racing. She couldn't wait to tell him what she saw!

"Dunk! Dunk!"

Still in the mourning place where he was on his hike, he completely missed her sprint. Suddenly, her face was right there as he opened his car door.

"Dunk! Dunk!"

Iris knew how to read her neighbor's now familiar sad face. With her little fingers barely touching the base of the car window, she settled for a moment. Dunk O'Dell knew exactly what she was doing and this was a sight he would never forget.

God has this, he said as he swallowed. *God hears me and He knows my needs.* Reaching for the latch to open his car door, Dunk realized he may or may not have a granddaughter down the road, but he did have a neighbor, and she—absolutely, positively, and completely—was one of the most adorable gifts he had. He would enjoy her every moment he could.

"Dunk! Dunk! Come! I want to show you something."

He set one old hiking boot on his driveway and then the other. He stood. She found his hand and started pulling.

"You don't want to miss this!"

Anxiously, Iris led her friend to Earl's backyard.

Dunk felt clumsy. "You know, little lady, you probably shouldn't—"

"I know. I shouldn't play in his yard anymore. Not until the new people come." She stopped pulling on his hand. "When are the new people coming?"

He shook his head. *The house isn't even empty yet.* "It may take a while, Iris."

"Oh." She continued tugging.

She led Dunk to a small bush, about a third of her height. From nowhere, she said, "I didn't know Joe had a twin brother."

Joe's twin brother?

"When I was there, at the Dumpster. When my neck was all really big from the bee sting. I saw them both. There was Joe. There was his twin brother. They were identified."

Dunk couldn't believe he was hearing this. "You mean identical?"

Iris shrugged. "Yeah. Identical. There was Jesus. And there was Joe. They sorta kinda looked the very same. Joe was shooting the big pen into my leg. Jesus was watching."

"You saw Jesus and Joe?"

"Uh-huh." Grownups could be awfully pokey, for sure. She needed to get to the reason why she called Dunk over here, and this wasn't it. She pointed to the ground beside the bush. "There."

Dunk backed the conversation up. "Wait, you saw Jesus with Joe?"

"I can't see Joe anymore. He died. But he's still around sometimes. I can feel him."

"You miss him, too."

"He was my best, *best* friend. Now Maxine is my best friend. You're my next best friend."

"Oh. I see."

She anxiously pointed to the ground again.

Dunk looked. All he saw was the mulch Earl had so perfectly laid under the bush. Still thinking about what she had just shared, he took a longer look.

"Dunk, do you see it?"

He kept looking. There was nothing. Nothing unusual or interesting appeared to him. "Iris, I don't see..."

"There!"

"Iris..."

"There!"

She bent down and lifted a dirty white ribbon about seven inches long and a quarter inch wide. "Do you know what this is?"

Dunk carefully considered the find. He wasn't following her. "A dirty white ribbon?"

"Dunk! Do you know what it did?"

He turned back to his house suddenly. Tired and raw, he couldn't do this. He needed quiet time. He needed to be alone.

"Dunk!"

Three steps from Iris, he stopped. He felt Jesus, too. The Son of God was touching his shoulder. *Turn back,* he heard a voice say. It was Jesus. *Turn back.*

Dunk felt his heart close with heartbreak even more, but did as he was told. He pivoted.

Iris asked him again. "Do you know what it did?"

"It's...let me think about this. It's the rope a leprechaun used this past Saint Patrick's Day?"

"Leprechauns only use green rope, you silly. You should know that. I do."

"Oh. You're right. Only green rope."

"Guess!"

"Is it a part of a bracelet you once had?"

"Nope."

"One of those hair ribbon things you wear sometimes?"

"Dunk! No." She sighed indignantly, though he knew she was only acting. "It's from your wedding party."

"My wedding party?"

"Yeah. Your wedding party."

"You mean the party after the wedding? There in the church?"

"Right. Days before you and Vanessa got married me and mom helped Earl's daughters with these very ribbons. They were happy then."

Thinking of Jenna and Jackie, Dunk nodded. "They were happy then."

"We put little candies in thin white nets, and we tied the nets with these ribbons."

"You did, huh?"

Iris realized yet again that so many men have no sentimentality. "We did."

"Iris?"

Knowing what he was going to ask, she laughed. "No, I didn't eat *that much* candy, Dunk."

"Okay."

She started walking him back to his house. As she did so, Dunk thought of the little treasures that amazed little children. He took a good, long deep breath and smiled. At his driveway, she stopped.

He faced her. "What?"

"You don't get it, do you?"

Dunk shook his head.

"Even though it's dirty, you are still married."

Too tired to pretend, Dunk frowned. He did not understand what she meant.

Iris tried again. "Vanessa will be okay, Dunk. She is different now." The little girl frowned a bit, just as Joe would do when he was her age and had something big to share. "The ribbon probably isn't happy that it's dirty, but you know what?"

"What?"

"It's still a ribbon. It still does the same job. It ties things together."

Dunk thought of his wife. He remembered all the sharp words he had said to her after the dinner party where they had learned that Joe and Betsy were engaged. Vanessa had told him that he wanted so many things to be perfect.

Iris looked up at him. "She will be okay."

"Oh, Iris."

"She will be okay."

He couldn't take another step. "Little girl, you don't know what you've just said."

"Let's go find some more netting. Mom probably has some. Let's see what we can put together now."

Dunk looked beyond Iris' eyes and knew something his own eyes could not see, and that was that Joe was not far away. "Yes, Iris. Let's get started. Let's put things together."

EPILOGUE

I burned the ancient wrappings exactly one year after Joe died. As there was only one Jesus, there will only be one Joe. Jesus died for the sins of the whole world. Joseph died for the sorrow of one soul.

Joe was human. While as a youngster he showed great compassion for a boy his age with physical limits there in that fast food restaurant with Dunk, I couldn't consider a Savior who, as an elementary school boy, would intentionally shove a mentally-challenged classmate against a wall. Equally, I couldn't imagine a Savior who would rob two young women at knifepoint. But somehow, yes, in measurable and immeasurable ways, Joseph was also divine, at least in part. Somehow God was in him. Saving Earl's dog, knowing the lyrics to the Eddie Shafaun and the Satellites song over a plate of spaghetti in Earl's kitchen, saving Iris and then Ben, yes, God was in him as God is in all of us.

I could appear theological now, but this would not be accurate. While I know now that cloning ancient DNA was all a part of God's plan for me and that somehow—still today—Grand has her old, wobbly hand in this, Jesus can still be a struggle for me some days. When I shared this with Dunk a month ago, he said I'd come a long, long way. It is true. I do not understand Jesus just yet, but I've been trying.

Joseph, on the other hand, now there was someone I did understand. By that, I mean to say that I understand love—or I understand more about what it is to love and to lose. Each day that passes is not easier; it is only more familiar. I've talked to him. Somehow I know he hears me. He forgives me, too.

Dunk nodded when I shared this. He came to visit last week, to let me know that he and Vanessa will soon introduce me to the nine, twelve, and thirteen-year-old brothers they are in the process of adopting from foster care. While here, he also showed me a new baby picture of Betsy and Tad's daughter. Betsy and the little one still live in the house I bought for her and Joe. Tad rents an apartment about fifteen minutes away. Whatever they have, Vanessa tells me, is moving very slowly.

Unlike me, Betsy and Tad, Ben is not moving slowly. No charges were pressed the afternoon of the shooting. There couldn't have been. Joe's death was simply, purely an accident.

Or was that also God's plan?

Ben is alive now, truly alive. Weeks ago, I heard him preach. Betsy had everything to do with it. I wouldn't say Ben was good behind a pulpit. More accurately, I'd say Ben isn't good *yet*. But he will be. He has a fire, a depth, and a soul that once broken and now whole draws us—yes, even me—to hearing about the Living message available to all.

I have to go. Jolie is here. We have to go live the Word. Side by side, we'll be firing up our motorcycles.

It's time to ride.

PART I

QUESTIONS TO CONSIDER

1. In thinking of the prologue, if you are honest with yourself, it's clear that—*even for a moment*—we play God or we want to play God. What do you want to control? What has that desire for control brought you—a closeness to God, a distance from God, or something else entirely?

2. One by one, we are introduced to the characters of Dunk, Viola, and Vanessa. All three attend Presswater United Church of Christ, and serve on its deacon board. Though each displays admirable qualities, each is far from being a perfect representative of Christ or the church. Consider Viola's tendency to gossip, Vanessa's less than honest motivation for joining the church leadership, or Dunk's fearful response to seeing Roland Rolls' car. Can a faithful follower of Christ reconcile these kinds of inconsistencies?

3. Joe is full of mystery. He has a seemingly supernatural knowledge even from childhood, and displays many of the "divine" qualities we associate with Jesus Christ, yet he also appears to have very human qualities, like boyish silliness and even cruelty and a bad temper. Roland Rolls believes certain events prove that Joe is not the full manifestation of Jesus Christ. What defines Christ-likeness to you?

4. Chapter one introduces us to Joe through the eyes of Betsy and Mike. Each sees him differently, based on their own vantage point and life experience. Later, as more characters are brought into the story, each sees and describes Joe in their own way. Joe's people are messy and often conflicted. Is it settling or unsettling to consider that the life of Jesus Christ was not unlike Joe's in this respect?

5. At one point, Roland says to Larry [Dunk], "You are a peasant offering meager gifts to the king." On one level, he's right. On another level, he isn't. What is Dunk offering Roland? How does Dunk go about it? Christians encounter skeptics. If you are a Christian, imagine what you would say to Roland. Would scripture help you, and, if so, what scripture? Would you use real life experiences, why or why not?

6. Do you think Roland always planned to let Dunk and Joe go from the lab without tracking them, or in the seven days Joe and Dunk were in the lab, was there something the mastermind heard or saw that changed his plan?

7. In the final chapter of Book One, Joe disappears. Up until this point he is a very "solid" character. Though he clearly does not have all the answers, he has a deep commitment to those close to him. He also has a deep confidence in God. What sort of event can trigger even a person as solid in his faith and character as Joe to flee? Are we all vulnerable in similar ways? How can we safeguard against such a response?

PART II

1. Book Two begins with an account of Mike's funeral. From the impersonal delivery of a generic service to the light attendance of an uncomfortable crowd, the whole event is awkward and tense. Earl decides to speak without invitation. Are there times this is appropriate? Necessary? Do you think Earl's action required bravery? Would you want to do the same? Are there times you have declined to speak, and did you regret your choice?

2. Consider the relationship between Dunk and Vanessa. In the first section of this novel, Vanessa's agenda causes her to be less than truthful in beginning and pursuing a relationship with Dunk. Her agenda and methods seem shallow and rooted in getting what she wants and needs. In the second section of the book, their relationship actually develops and deepens despite the fact that they face unexpected hardship and disappointment. What are some of the challenges they face, and in what ways do these challenges change both of them and their ability to grow together? Why is this couple able to plot a positive course for their future, when similar challenges cause other relationships to dissolve?

3. Before Vanessa appeared on the scene, Dunk and Joe shared an extremely close father/son relationship. Although single or adoptive parenting is not unique, each has its own set of challenges. In addition, Joe and Dunk share very unique beginnings in Roland Rolls' lab. How did the circumstances of that relationship influence each of the men? What might have made it difficult for Joe to call Dunk dad? For Dunk to share with Joe his unique origins? For Dunk to let go of his parenting role and make room for Vanessa, or any woman, in his world?

4. After Joe flees the hotel at the end of Book One, he begins a spiral into addiction and hopelessness. He engages in a string of behaviors which are harmful to both himself and others. Think of all the ugly choices Joe makes, and the places he finds himself. These are the places so many people find themselves and identify as "the bottom." At the bottom, what did it require for Joe to begin to heal and find hope? What advantage might Joe have had over his workmate Reggie, the prostitute, or even his cellmate in the jail?

5. This is a story about praying people. In Chapter 23, Betsy encounters prayer and Jesus in a memorable way. At first she does not even understand she is praying, but instead thinks she is having an internal conversation with herself on her run in the rain, and then with Joe who is still missing. Have you ever been surprised, like Betsy, in prayer? Every character in the novel prays in their own way. Which one can you relate to most, and why?

6. Betsy tried to share her experience of praying to God with Tad. It did not go well. Have you ever struggled to share what God has revealed to you, only to have it poorly received? How did you feel in that moment? Did it cast doubt in your mind? Did it discourage you? Is there a "right" way to share moments like this with people who lack similar experiences and belief?

7. Though this novel deals with several characters that are struggling against feelings of hopelessness, Ben seems to epitomize this mindset. As a troubled teen, his self talk is full of the lies he has been encouraged to believe by the life he has lived thus far. What are the lies he is buying into, and how are they further eroding his hope for a future? In what practical ways can the church reach out to troubled young people like Ben with a message of God's love?

PART III

1. Book Three addresses the theme of fear, and the power we have to face our worst fears with God's help through the support of the people God gives us. Three couples present us with common scenarios about fear.

   - Consider Betsy and Joe. What fears might arise when a couple faces challenges related to addiction? Choosing a partner for life? Previous relationships that may have produced children?
   - Think of Galvin and Kristen. What fears must a couple face when they confront infertility, or the loss of a child?
   - Dunk and Vanessa are next. What fears are there for couples in middle age, as they watch their young adult children fly the nest and sometimes fall and fail?
   - Do each of these couples face fear in realistic ways, both individually and as couples? With which character or couple do you most identify, and why?

2. If Vanessa weren't so secure in her relationship to Jesus at the time of her wedding, clashing candelabras may have pushed her over the edge (instead of that antique vase). Can you share a time in your life when an event didn't have to be "perfect" because you knew of Jesus' perfect love for you?

3. Viola Munson stirs things up at the rehearsal dinner for Dunk and Vanessa. As she works the crowd, she expresses unkind opinions both externally and internally. She asks invasive questions, and is insensitive to the feelings of others. Though Viola is a stereotype of an old biddy, can you think of a time that you behaved similarly? Do you excuse uncharitable thoughts if you only express them internally? How might a strict policy of minding one's own business

and speaking only that which is true and encouraging save both you and others from harm?

4. Book three shows us how people who care for others speak up for truth. Sometimes that's confrontational, like when Earl helps Joe sober up, and asks Betsy if she's in for the long haul. Other times it's a word of encouragement to do the right thing, like Vanessa chasing Betsy down at her own wedding reception. It can be a word of encouragement to simply think a different way, like when Joe takes time to talk to Ben after work. Can you think of other times in the story when a character spoke up for the truth and helped lead another in a better direction? Can you think of similar instances in your own life? Was this an easy thing to do? Did it go the way you expected to? Was it helpful?

5. At least three different times, God speaks to reveal specific, necessary information. God tells Earl to send Betsy to the bus terminal to find Joe. God tells Joe to go find the Epipen used to save Iris, and even guides him in using it correctly. Finally, Joe is told to go to the park to find Ben as he prepares to shoot himself. Do you believe God speaks to us in our real lives today? If so, how? Have you ever experienced anything like this in your own life?

6. Joe feels God is instructing him to go find Ben, though he does not understand why. The call is clearly supernatural and Joe is obedient, yet he still wishes he could have gotten to Ben five minutes earlier. What do you think this wish reveals about Joe?

7. Joe loses his life in the attempt to save Ben from shooting himself, despite being obedient to God's instruction to go find the young man. As Joe's loved ones begin to understand this sequence of events, how do they react? What does this reveal about their understanding of Joe? Of God? Do you think their reactions may have had bearing on the new course Ben embraces for his life?

8. In the final chapters, Roland is present to Dunk and to Joe. How does Roland genuinely evolve as a result of these relationships? Are the changes a result of human or divine interventions? What do you imagine the future holds for the scientist?

9. What does Iris teach you?

10. The entire story of *JC* is a story of human connectedness. It unfolds many key relationships we share in all their sloppy, dangerous beauty. There are the obvious connections of lovers, family, and close friends. There are less obvious connections between neighbors, coworkers, church members, students and their teachers. Finally, there are the connections we share with near strangers we meet everywhere we go. Do you feel this story encourages us to see an obligation in those connections, or an opportunity? What risks might we take by engaging them fully?

11. What is a one sentence 'take home' you could share about this story?